ROMEO & JULIET.
SARAH & STEVE...

"What are you thinking about?" Steve asked.

"Well...how—how different you are from... well—" I hesitated, not wanting to say something dumb.

"It's all right. It's true. And you're not like any girl I've ever known." He picked up my hand and kissed it on the palm, and everything I was thinking went out of my head. I put my hands on either side of his face and bent toward him and kissed him. Then I was out of breath and I could hear him breathing. He stood up suddenly and pulled my face up toward his.

"How tall are you?" I whispered.

"Six one," he whispered back.

Then he let go of my face and put his arms around me and I put mine around him. His body was hard with muscle and it felt wonderful against mine. He kissed me gently. Then again, not so gently....

SUMMER
of
MY FIRST LOVE

A Novel by

Isabelle Holland

FAWCETT  JUNIPER
NEW YORK

SUMMER OF MY FIRST LOVE

Published by Fawcett Juniper Books, a unit of CBS Publications, the Consumer Publishing Division of CBS Inc.

ISBN: 0-449-70007-0

Printed in the United States of America

First Fawcett Juniper Printing: July 1981

10 9 8 7 6 5 4 3 2 1

SUMMER
of
MY FIRST LOVE

Chapter

1

Mother was furious when I told her about my summer job.

"You don't need a job, Sam. You know what the doctor said. Rest, relaxation, fun and games. After all those months in the hospital and all the extra studying, anybody'd think you'd be starved for a whole summer when you could just hang out on the beach."

Mother, who wrote books, used expressions like "hang out" very much the way she used foreign sayings such as *pied-à-terre* or *andiamo*. As a matter of fact, the foreign ones sounded, in her, more natural after all the years she and Father spent in Europe teaching at various universities. But every now and then she'd incorporate an Americanism usually brought home by my bother Peter, twenty-three and a graduate student at Harvard, or Mushroom, who was a senior at Radcliffe. Mushroom's real name is Margaret. My real name is Sarah, but only Father calls me that. That summer—the summer of Headlands, the summer of learning who I really was, the summer I fell in love—that summer I was seventeen.

It was the second year our family had taken a house at Cove Harbor. But the previous summer I had only been there for two weeks. The rest of the time I had spent at a rehabilitation place learning how to walk again. The spring I was sixteen I had been in a bad car accident. When I woke up sometime later my right leg was slung from a pulley above the bed and my head was bandaged. A year and three operations later I still couldn't run, but I could, if I had to, walk quite quickly, although if I did, I limped. As Mushroom said, my gate was like an oompa-pa beat: *BOM* di *BOM* di *BOM*, the *BOM* being when I came down on my right leg, which had somehow ended up a hair shorter than the other. The doctors said one more operation might even things up. But they weren't quite sure as yet whether or not it would be a good idea. Which left me pulled two ways.

I wanted desperately for my leg to be right. But just as desperately I did not want to have to go back into the hospital. People were full of advice:

"Face facts," Father said. "The fact is, you'll probably have to go. Probably in the fall. So what's the use of making a big thing about it?"

"You're going to have such a wonderful summer on the beach," Mother said, "Meeting new . . . friends, that you won't mind at all." It was the hesitation before "friends" that did it. As clear as though I were watching subtitles in a foreign movie I knew that Mother had started to say "boyfriends" and decided not to.

"Boys don't find me attractive," I said, as calmly as I could. "Even before the accident they didn't. So why should they now when I 've got all those scars on my leg?"

"You can swim early. Before anybody except the townies are out." The townies were residents of the industrial town that lay inland a few miles. Between the summer residents and the townies there was, we soon discovered, a more or less ongoing state of what Mushroom called "undeclared dislike", which, from time to time, broke into bursts of being declared. "You get up early, anyway," Mother said, carrying on her thought. "The rest of the time on the beach you can wear jeans."

"Mother," I said, trying to not give into the sense of despair that these conversations always brought on. "We've talked about this before." And I walked out of the room. That was when I started thinking about a job.

The following week, early in June, we went up to the Cove. School wasn't quite out, but because of the accident and operations I had missed half the school year, anyway.

8

"Not," my father said, "that at Miss Hall's that makes much difference."

Miss Hall's, in Manhattan's upper East Eighties, was filled with girls who weren't bright enough, or didn't work hard enough, to get into the better private schools such as Peter and Mushroom had gone to. Even before the accident, my academic record was a family sore subject, particularly with my father. Hence, his sarcasm. Peter and Mushroom were always brains. I wasn't. Every now and then Mother would make a vague attempt at explanations such as, "Well, Sam had such a mixed-up schooling with our being abroad in those years..." and let her voice trail off. But since people were inclined to point out that good European schools were usually as good as, or even better than, our best, that excuse didn't get very far. Father finally accepted my non-brain status and concentrated his attention on Peter and Mushroom. To him, with his Summa Cum Laude from Harvard and his First from Oxford, brains came before anything else. That had always hurt a little, but after a while I got used to it, and experience had shown that on the whole it was better for me when he didn't notice me than when he did.

The job Mother objected to my having was looking after two children, Jennie and Jamie King, whose mother, a Mrs. Brewster, had taken Headlands for the summer.

I had learned about it from a card Scotch-taped to the post office-cum-all-purpose-store window in Cove Harbor village. I had gone there to collect our mail. "And see if you can find Steve Novak," Mother had called from the upper balcony. "He's supposed to be building that extension onto my studio. To say nothing about the roof to your father's workroom."

I stopped on the path leading to the road on the other side of the trees and turned around. "Have you tried calling him?"

"He has one of those miserable tape things. I refuse to talk into them. They intimidate me."

I bet, I thought to myself, turning back. Since Mother spent a great deal of time taping long interviews for the "as told to" books she wrote, and taking huge chunks of material off the tapes her celebrities sent her, I found it hard to believe she felt intimidated by a telephone-answering machine. What it really meant, I thought, as I plodded back to the road, was that she wanted me to run this Steve Novak down and tell him that Mrs. Lacey would like him to stop everything and come and see her. Neither of my parents suffered from crippling modesty. My father was a professor of political science and wrote learned and scholarly articles for learned and scholarly journals. My mother, who had gained a wide reputation as a magazine journalist, had written one biography and two "as told to" memoirs which not only climbed up the best-seller list, but made her a lot of money and enabled the family to renovate the old frame house at Cove Harbor, and convert two previous sheds on the former farm property into his and hers studios, each with its own phone. But a bad storm during the winter had brought a tree down against one of the walls of her studio, and she was going to take advantage of having it fixed to have a small extension built to house her bulging library.

"It's nice to know that we have the best of both worlds," Peter once said, "with Father supplying the kudos and Mother providing the money to support it in style."

Actually, I liked the house better before it was renovated. Before the accident we had all come to see what Mother was going to buy. Sitting by itself above the water, it had a sort of wind-swept empty look. The house and the shutters, which were banging to and fro, both needed painting. Inside, the rooms were square and airy, and opened off a wide hall. It was cold the day we went up there, and the old paper was peeling off the walls, but there was a quality of light that I loved. "Of course," Mother said, "we're going to have to do something about bathrooms, to say nothing of closets. These rooms must have been built in the days of huge wardrobes."

"Don't change it," I said.

"And how would you like to be low man on the totem pole when it comes to lining up for your turn at the one bathroom, Miss?" Mother said rather sharply. "After all, you're the youngest. You'd be last."

"Which might make you first in the Kingdom of Heaven," Mushroom said, "but could be a drag when you're waiting to pee." Which was sort of a joke, because our family has been firmly rationalist and agnostic for generations. When I next saw the house, hobbling in on crutches two weeks before school opened the previous fall, I hardly recognized it. I'd temporarily been given one of the downstairs rooms so I wouldn't have to cope with the stairs. But one day, when everybody was out, I hauled myself up the staircase to see what had been done.

I realized that everyone would think it was a vast improvement. And there was no question, a private bath for every room made life a lot easier, especially when bathing with a leg in a cast was such a problem. The new walk-in closets were big enough to hold even Peter's and Mushroom's clothes and gadgets. But something had gone and I felt sad about it. The house was more comfortable, but different. A New York firm had designed a lot of the changes, but some of the smaller stuff had been done locally by this Steve Novak that Mother now wanted me to find when I went to collect the mail in the village.

I saw the card as I walked up to the post office and stopped and read it. WANTED: Baby-sitter for seven-year-old twins, boy and girl. Daily, Mon.-Sat., 9 A.M. till 3 P.M. Good pay. Call 682-7208.

"Who's wanting the baby-sitter?" I asked Mrs. Hobbes, as she handed me the letters and magazines.

"Mrs. Brewster. Mrs. King that was. The twins are Jennie and Jamie King. She's taken Headlands for the summer. More fool she. Well, we'll see!"

"Why, what's wrong with Headlands?" I knew the house. Everybody did, although actually all you could see of it were the chimneys above the huge trees around it. It sat by itself on top of the highest cliff in the area, which was also the point farthest east, jutting out into the Atlantic.

"We'll see," Mrs. Hobbes repeated cryptically. "Yes? Can I help you?" This was to another customer ambling towards the dry-goods section.

I went outside and stared at the card, memorizing the number. I knew suddenly that I wanted that job very much indeed. To anybody else it might just be a job or money or both. And of course it was both to me, too. It would be wonderful to earn something of my own. But most of all it would be a way out—a way out of having to sit on the beach and pretend that I didn't mind the fact that boys found me uninteresting. Since the accident not only were my legs fish-white as a result of being in the hospital all that time, there were big red scars all down my right thigh. And something had happened to the muscles, or maybe it was just having to be in bed so long, or having it in a cast; but while both my legs were skinny, my right one looked like something out of a deportation camp.

Besides, I thought, going in the opposite direction from our house, looking after little kids was something I was sure I could do. There were children in the hospital, and after I was in a wheelchair, I used sometimes to go to the pediatrics lounge and talk to them or read to them. One day in the hospital, when one of the residents caught me having an attack of self-pity he suggested I might like to help out with the kids. I felt like telling him to take his stethoscope and put it somewhere uncomfortable. But I was too abashed and beaten down at having been discovered mopping up my tears with tissue to do that, and to my surprise I found I really liked working with some of the younger children. That, along with needlepoint and drawing and other unintellectual things, were pursuits I was good at.

After a few minutes I reached the telephone booth that stood by itself on a cliff path. There was a pay phone in the store, but I wasn't sure I could conduct business with Mrs. Hobbes's ears quivering in my direction. Mother once said she was better than the Associated Press.

I dialed the number.

"Hello?" a little voice said.

"Jennie?" I guessed.

"How'd you know? Everybody says Jamie 'n' me sound the same."

"A good guess. Is your mother there?"

"Yes."

I heard the receiver being dropped, then little feet scampering. In a few seconds there were older feet coming towards the phone. "Yes?"

There was something about that voice that made me almost wish I hadn't called, but I thought about the beach with all those tanned beautiful bodies running around and took a breath. "My name is Sarah Lacey. My family has taken the white frame house on the other side of the cove. I saw your card in the post-office window. I'd like to apply for the job."

There was a short silence. "How old are you?" There was an odd note to her voice. I couldn't quite figure it out.

"Seventeen. But I'm very reliable." I rushed on. "I looked after kids in the hospital when I was there." And then wanted to kick myself when she said sharply, "What hospital?"

I named the big New York hospital where I'd been for so long, and then said, "I had to have an operation on my leg." That left out the other two operations. But I thought one was enough to mention.

"Oh, I see. Well, that's all right. I thought for a moment—but I hope your leg is better. Did you say your family has taken the old Baldwin house?"

Vaguely I remembered somebody saying something about

12

a family named Baldwin having been the original owners.
"Yes."

There was a pause. I could hear two children's voices,
sounding as if they were having a fight. Then a man's voice.
I thought Mrs. Brewster would say something, want to ask
some questions. I really didn't know what else to say, except
"Do you want me to come?" So I finally said, "Do you want
me to come?"

"Oh yes. Of course. Nine to three. Every day except Sunday, when I'll be home. Can you start tomorrow?"

My spirits soared. "Yes."

"Yes, all right, then I'll see you tomorrow morning.
Good—"

"How much are you paying?" I shouted suddenly. I wanted
the job, no matter what she was paying, but I thought I'd
better ask.

"Three dollars an hour. Is that all right?"

It was a dollar more than I would have had the nerve to
ask. "Fine," I said.

"Tomorrow," she said, and hung up. Just before the receiver went click I heard the man's voice, much nearer, saying
something. But beyond "Did you tell her—" I couldn't hear
the rest.

Wondering what it was she hadn't told me, I turned and
started back towards our house. As I walked I glanced
through the mail. To my dismay, there was a letter addressed
to Mother and Father from Miss Hall's. Letters from school
to my parents have never boded well—at least not if they had
anything to do with me. Letters about Peter or Mushroom
nearly always bore the glad tidings of scholarships, awards,
grants and honors. About me they were usually about too
many Ds or Fs or not living up to my potentialities (a phrase
much in favor among those who simply wanted to say that
my grades were lousy, and there was always somebody to
take my place if they didn't improve).

Forgetting not to limp, I walked back along the road that
led to the houses at our end of the cove. As I did, I turned the
letter from school over to see if by any chance the glue on
the flap had dried out, making the flap easy to pull open. I
was out of luck. The flap looked as though it had been sealed
for the ages. Gently, with a tip of my finger, I pushed along
the top to see if their licking machine had failed to wet any
area. Probably, I thought gloomily, the school had invented
pry-poof methods of sticking the flap down. The pyramids

13

were sealed no more firmly. Well, it would have to be a steam kettle. I had too much at stake to risk anyone's deciding I'd have to be tutored or take special lessons. That had happened to me once before and ruined my summer. While it was true that having to study might put a dent in Mother's plans for my social life, it was much more likely that it would give her the excuse she needed to forbid me taking the baby-sitting job. I could hear her now, "You can do your studying in the morning, Sam, and then be out on the beach with the other kids." What brains and academic achievement were to Father, a successful social life was to Mother. Mother never worried about Peter's social life. "A boy can always make out," she said often, forgetting for the moment what a sexist statement that was, "but a girl needs to develop confidence in all areas at the right time of her life, every step of the way." There were times when I wished she hadn't written that highly successful magazine piece, "Today's Adolescent: Sexual Consciousness at an Early Age." Like all her pieces it was brilliantly written and extremely well documented. Even so, it probably wouldn't have become so famous if so many groups hadn't made such a protest. Copies were snatched off newsstands and pulled off school library shelves in some of the more conservative parts of the country. As a result of all that free publicity, Mother was on talk shows from coast to coast, and when asked about whether her own children showed maturity and balance in their teens, she always talked about Peter's popularity and how Margaret had been at ease with the opposite sex since she was thirteen. She never mentioned me, and when one interviewer, looking at the biographical sketch in his hand, asked about me, she just said, "Oh, she's young still." And didn't mention that "young" in my case meant fifteen and sixteen.

"I realize that because you were overseas with us you've been isolated from your peers and I want to remedy that this summer," Mother had said as we were driving up to the Cove.

"My leg," I started to say.

"As I said before, you can do your sunbathing before anyone gets on the beach or from the top of the garage roof. And you don't have to be Venus in a bikini to be popular. If you just put a little effort out, Sam, everybody would love you."

"But I don't love everybody," I said. It was a dumb comment but was the only thing I could think of.

"Then you should try. People are not going to like you if you don't like them. And boys respond to a little encouragement. Unless you were a raving beauty, the twentieth century's Helen of Troy, you wouldn't get any attention sitting in a corner saying nothing." She glanced at me. "Would you, darling," and she reached over her hand and thumped my knee.

Various conversations along that line wafted through my head as I thought about the implications of the letter from school. I was determined to take that job. There was something else I was determined about, although I had told no one; it was still my secret: I was not going back to school, at least not the school I'd been going to, or any other form of high school. Nor did I want to go to college. I wanted to go to art school in the fall. I was going to be an illustrator of children's books, preferably fairy stories. I still liked them better than any other kind of reading, and still carried some of my old fairy tale collections with me wherever I went. Cloud-cuckoo land Mother called it. So I read them in bed at night. I was also writing a long fantasy, which nobody knew. Next to reading stories I liked writing them. But I knew my parents didn't approve of fairy stories or fantasies. Father thought they were childish things I should have put away by the time I was eight. Mother thought they did nothing to prepare me either for my social or my professional life. So I read them at night, sometimes under the covers with a flashlight. The funny thing was, if it had been porn, my parents, particularly my mother, would have understood.

Anyway, all of that was one of the reasons the letter from school struck me as ominous. I was still looking at the back of the envelope, running my finger over the flap to see if I'd missed a loose spot, when I crashed into something...

"You'd better look where you're going," a male voice said.

I looked up. He was tall and muscular and looked somewhere in his twenties. There was a tin hat on his head, the kind construction people wear, and underneath were very blue eyes set wide and a little aslant above high cheekbones. It was Steve Novak, the all-purpose builder and handyman from the town.

"Oh, sorry," I said automatically. And added, "And the same to you. You weren't looking either. Or you wouldn't have bumped into me."

"True." He stepped past me and went to his van, which I noticed now was parked on the left under some trees.

Suddenly I remembered that Mother had wanted me to

locate him. What with the arrival of the letter from school, and finding out about the new job, I had forgotten all about it.

"Mr. Novak," I said.

He turned, his hand on the van door. "Yes?"

"Mother wants to see you about building an annex to her studio."

He paused. "Your mother is—?"

"Mrs. Lacey."

"I see. Well, Mrs. Lacey should call me. Then we can make an appointment."

"She did. But you weren't there."

He frowned. "Wasn't the message tape working?"

"Mother hates tapes."

"That's too bad," he said, and got into the van.

I was absolutely astonished, so much so I had forgotten about the letter.

"Hey!" I yelled.

He stuck his head out the window. "Yes?"

I walked towards the van, forgetting to make myself not limp. "What about our shed?"

"As I told you, Miss Lacey, your mother should call and, as the tape suggests, leave her name and telephone number."

"But I just *told* you. She doesn't like message tapes."

"Then I'm afraid that leaves us at a standstill, doesn't it?"

Part of me wanted to giggle. People didn't often send Mother messages of that kind. But another part of me thought, who does this jerk think he is? I was still trying to sort the two out when he said, "What did you do to your leg?"

That put all of me on the side of deciding he was a jerk. I hate it when people ask me that question.

"I sprained my ankle kicking somebody," I said, and walked off, remembering this time not to limp, which meant I had to walk slowly.

"Try the other leg next time," he said, sounding cheerful, "and keep your ankle stiff." Then he drove off, while I ignored him.

Idiot, I said to myself. And then, what did I expect? He was one of the townies. My former opponents, Mother often called them. That was because most of them were Polish or Czech or some other kind of ethnic Catholic who used to picket her meetings when she started up a local chapter of the Family Planning Group she was active in. One of them once threw a ripe tomato at her and it went splat! on her new blue suit, leaving a huge blotch that never came out. Mother had a harder time forgiving that than all the hate letters she got. True, the head of the local women's group sent her a letter of apology for the ripe tomato, and also said they disassociated themselves from any hate mail. But Mother didn't really believe her.

I was halfway back to the house before I remembered the letter. I turned it over again and looked at the flap. There was a tiny tear up in one corner where I had pushed my finger. As of yet nobody would think anything about it. If I tore it open, could I seal it back up so that it wouldn't show?

"No," I said aloud to myself. "Mother'd know in a minute." I'd have to steam it open, which shouldn't be too difficult to arrange. I stuck the letter from Miss Hall's in my jacket pocket and took the rest of the mail to the house.

When I got there I handed Mother her letters.

"Thanks, Sam," Mother said absently, taking them. Then, as I was leaving, said, "Were you able to find Steve Novak?"

"Oh. Yes. I ran into him."

"So when did he say he could come?"

"He said you were to call and leave a message."

"Didn't you tell him I don't like talking to machines?"

"Yes."

"So?"

"He said that was too bad."

Mother lowered the letters she'd been looking at. "You mean to say that's all he said?"

"Yes." As much as I didn't like Steve, it gave me a little throb of pleasure. There was one person who wasn't going to conform to Mother's plan for better living.

"Of all the nerve! Well, he can just take his tool kit and shove it! There has to be another handyman around who's just as good!"

Grinning to myself, I went upstairs where I knew I could find a plug-in steam kettle.

Two hours later I sat out on the farthest rock of the little point north of our house, wearing my parka, and underneath that, a sweater. The sun was out and the sea and sky were both blue, the green of the trees was very green, and the rocks were a shiny gray. But out on that rock it was about ten degrees colder than it had been on the path going to the village.

The letter, which I had in my hand, was all that I had feared. In several paragraphs, with a lot of long words, it said that I would have to sit for an exam at the beginning of

17

the school year, and unless I did unusually well, would have to repeat the junior year. Or else. They were very polite at Miss Hall's, but the "or else" really meant that even a second-rate school like that had its limits, and I showed every evidence of moving beyond them. "As we are all aware, Sarah is not technically backward, but her scholarship aptitude is unusually low," etcetera, etcetera, etcetera.

Well, I thought, determined to look on the bright side, that could make it easier for my parents to accept the fact that I wasn't going back to school at all. But I knew I would have a fight on my hands, and the more I thought about it, the colder I felt. Perhaps, just perhaps, if I destroyed the letter, they wouldn't find out about the whole thing until the summer was over. And then it would be too late for them to talk about my taking exams or extra courses or more studying. Even better, I might not have to fight until just before we went home. And in the meantime there was this job. I would have enough of a problem about that; I didn't need the letter to make it worse.

Without any further thought, I took the letter out, tore it into small pieces and scattered it into the sea.

Chapter

2

The conversation between Mother and me about the job took place at eight o'clock the following morning. I had been hoping for enough luck to get me out of the house and on my way before she got up. Fighting with her after I had been employed for one day, rather than before, would, I figured, give me an advantage. But I hadn't counted on the fact that she was about to start on a new book, so when she walked into the kitchen at a few minutes to eight, I almost choked on my English muffin.

"Where are you off to?" she said, putting the kettle on for some more coffee.

For a second I thought about lying. But then I decided that would only make things worse, so I told her about baby-sitting for the King twins. She stood there, holding the kettle under the tap until it flowed over the top, her mouth slightly open. Then she turned off the faucet and slapped the kettle on the stove.

"The whole point of this summer," she said, "was for you to rest and make new . . . new—"

"Boyfriends," I said, and realized I was shouting. "That's all you think about. Me having boyfriends. Well I'm not interested! And if you stop me having this job with Mrs. Brewster, I'll never go to the beach. Never! I'll sit the whole summer out in my room. See if I don't!" I was near tears, but I didn't want her to know it. In my better moments I knew she didn't mean to be unkind. But she seemed to think I didn't have boyfriends out of sheer perversity. It didn't do anything for my ego to have to explain that no matter what I did they found me boring and unattractive. And anyway, she didn't believe me. She was a passionate upholder of the belief that looks had nothing to do with it and that with a little effort you could conquer the world. She was always cutting out articles or pieces alluding to the fact that Cleopatra was fat and certain famous beauties cross-eyed. "They just rose above it," she said. "Anyway, it's a meeting of minds and spirits that counts." Which I think made it possible for her to have this ambition for me to be the conquest of Cove Harbor and go on being a militant feminist at the same time. As Peter once said about her, "Mother has a talent for combining irreconcilables...."

But suddenly she was rather quiet. Then, "Who did you say? Mrs. Who?"

"Brewster," I muttered, determined not to give in to the huge lump in my throat.

"I thought you said her name was King."

"I guess she was Mrs. King once. That's the name of her twins, Jennie and Jamie. But Mrs. Hobbes said her name was Mrs. Brewster."

A thoughtful look came over Mother's face. "Mrs. Stoddard Brewster?"

"How should I know?" I picked up my parka and marched out. The tears were coming down my cheeks by the time I hit the path, but I had tissues in the pockets of my parka, so I kept wiping my face off as I climbed to the upper path beyond the village.

As it happened, I'd been to Headlands once before, during the two weeks I'd been in Cove Harbor the previous year. Mushroom had driven the car up the cliff and then along the path until we passed through the wide belt of trees and faced the back of the house. The front faced the ocean. Built of frame, like ours, it was about twice as big, with a great porch going around the first floor, and a second above. On the roof was a widow's walk. Painted gray, the house was in poor repair, at least it was when I had seen it the year before. The gray paint was peeling and some of the huge wooden shutters hung from one hinge and banged to and fro in the fresh wind that always blew around that point. It was a desolate-looking place. Mushroom had driven up as close as she could, using the overgrown path that led from the trees, and parking on what used to be some kind of gravel apron before the back of the house.

Getting in had been easy. We simply went up the porch steps and opened the door. The house was bare. Dust lay thick on the wide floorboards, paper drooped from the walls, the crystal chandeliers hung like dust-covered skeletons, the huge mirrors on top of the mantels in the downstairs rooms were clouded and opaque.

"Ugh!" Mushroom said, as we walked silently in our sneakers, not even the rubber at the end of my crutches making any sound. "It's creepy. Those cobwebs are too much, too Edgar Allan Poe!"

The webs, mostly in niched corners, were like gray lace, the spiders hung from one or two of them like demon weavers. Mushroom was right. The house had a strange atmosphere.

"C'mon, Sam, we'd better get back. Let's go!"

But I didn't want to. "I'm going to look upstairs."

"You can't go upstairs with those crutches. For one thing, we don't know how safe the stairs are. For all we know they might collapse the first time anybody puts a foot on them. Everybody says this place hasn't been inhabited for decades! I'm not going to let you go up there!" Which was a piece of bravado on her part, for all her years and size.

"I'm going," I said, and started up. It turned out to be surprisingly easy, much easier than getting up the stairs in our house far on the other side of the point. Why, I wasn't quite sure, but I was swinging myself up as readily as though I had been Tarzan. "Come on up!" I yelled. "It's easy."

But all the time I said that, I knew I didn't want her to come up. I wanted to be there by myself. I didn't stop to wonder at why I felt so strongly. I just knew I did. And the farther up I mounted, the stronger it got.

Finally I was on the second floor. For some reason, the sense of being on top of the ocean was far more powerful up here. The feeling of light, even on the gray day we visited, was overpowering. Without thinking, I directed my crutches down the hall to the front of the house, and rested my knee on the window seat below the huge windows above. The cliff was below, and below that, the rocks. I could see them, steel gray, pushing out into the sea far beneath me. I had had no idea the house was as close to the edge of the point as it was, so that the Atlantic Ocean seemed to serve almost as a moat. Why the sea should look different there from the way it looked at other points along the coast I didn't know. But it did, as though it had a relationship to the house that it had with nothing and no one else.

"Sarah, where are you?"

Mushroom's voice seemed to come from far away. "Coming!" I yelled back, not moving.

Then reluctantly I turned and started back down the hall. What made me go into the front room on my right, I don't know. It was a huge empty room with a bay thrusting out to the cliff's edge. There were no cobwebs here, and the paper was not peeling. A strange, but happy, feeling filled me as I stood there, my crutches braced against the floor. It was as though the room were friendly towards me.

And then I heard Mushroom's voice right behind me. "What on earth are you doing in this creepy room, Sam? It's freezing in here! I want you to leave right now!"

The funny part was, when we drove home, I not only didn't have the feeling, I almost didn't remember it. . . . And I hadn't thought about it when I saw the card taped to the window. Which was even more strange. Perhaps it was because it had all been so many months before.

But now, as I walked towards the trees that enfolded the house like a battlement, I remembered the feeling as clearly as though it had taken place the hour before. And it made me feel happy that I was going, quite apart from the fact that I would be earning money and doing something I wanted to do instead of making myself miserable on the beach.

Somebody had spruced up the house, at least on the outside. It had a fresh coat of paint, and the shutters were all properly attached. I walked up the steps of the porch and rang the bell.

It was opened by a middle-aged woman in a white uniform. "Yes?" There was something in the way the little brown eyes looked at me that made me aware of my stained, torn jeans and the fact that one of my legs was shorter than the other. I pushed it out of my mind.

"I'm Sarah Lacey. I've come to baby-sit."

She stared at me for another second. Her uniform was too tight, I thought. There were strain lines under her breasts and across her hips. Maybe that was what was making her cross. Then she stepped back. "Come in. You can finish giving them breakfast."

22

I stepped into the wide hall and looked straight down to the front door with its beautiful fanlight facing the sea. It didn't look much different from when Mushroom and I had been there. The hall was bare. The walls had been papered with a pattern that was white with a tiny, barely visible gray line, so that the effect was near-white. The chandelier above had been cleaned but looked dull. The wide floorboards were dusty and also dull. Even the glass in the front door ahead, through which you could see the sea, was dull, so that the effect of seeing the ocean that near was blunted. If it were my door, I thought, I'd polish it until you didn't even know it was there.

"This way." The woman spoke with impatience. She was standing at the doorway of one of the rooms.

"Sorry," I muttered.

As I came up she turned into a room that faced the front and the sea. Obviously, with the table in the middle, it was a dining room. But the table was small, so it looked over-shadowed and the room huge. A door beyond showed the beginnings of a kitchen. I stopped.

"Shouldn't I see Mrs. Brewster first?"

"You can see her when she gets up. She said you'd be here. I have to leave soon so I want to show you everything."

"Aren't you going to be here?"

"My time off is when you're here. I'm free from nine until three. So let's get on with it." She marched across the room and into the kitchen.

What a sourpuss, I thought. A real downer! Well, she wouldn't be here so I wouldn't have to cope with her. And anyway, I thought, following her across the dining room to the kitchen door, anything was better than having to sit on the beach. Then, as I entered the kitchen, I stopped.

Everything was different there, and much more cheerful. The paper was a soft pale yellow with little blue and green leaves and tiny red flowers. It was a large room with lots and lots of counter space and a big range on one side as well as what looked like an ordinary gas stove. Seated at a white table in the middle were two children dressed in identical jeans and T-shirts, with dark brown straight hair and brown eyes. They looked exactly alike and both had Dutch-boy haircuts.

"This is Miss Lacey," the woman said. "You're going to have to mind her. Now,—" she waved a hand towards one of the wall counters. "The coffee pot for Mrs. Brewster's coffee

23

is usually over there. It's all set up. When she rings, all you have to do is plug it in. Canned food, cereals in that cupboard up there, bread in the bread bin, vegetables in the other bin, and the first-aid box, which with these two you'll probably need, in the second drawer there. The twins get lunch at twelve." She went over to another door and took a coat off a hook. "I'll be going now." The twins were staring at me, wide-eyed over bowls of cereal.

"What do they eat, Miss . . . Mrs. . . . ?"

"Bowers. Mrs. Bowers." She seemed to say the "Mrs." with some emphasis. She opened the door. "They can have sandwiches. There're cans of tuna in the cupboard up there, and peanut butter and jelly—"

"I wanna peanut butter sandwich *now*," said one of the twins.

"Well you can't have it." She looked at me. "Mrs. Brewster gets up later. She'll want coffee. You'll know because, as I told you, she'll ring for it. And then you plug in the pot. If she wants you to take it up to her she'll ring twice, and you put the pot on the tray over there, take the sugar and cream from the refrigerator and carry it to her bedroom."

"But—"

"I'm off now."

She opened the door. A smell of wood rushed in. I saw a room half built of plain wood panelling. Through the spaces where the wood hadn't yet been placed I glimpsed trees and grass. In the middle was a wooden sawhorse with pieces of lumber beside it.

"What's that?" I asked.

"It's a garage, or will be, when Novak gets around to finishing it."

"Steve Novak?"

"Yes. Goodbye now." Stepping down into the half-built garage, she pulled the door after her.

The twin who wanted the peanut butter sandwich stared at me with big dark eyes. His—her—bowl of cereal was almost full.

"Which is Jamie and which is Jennie?" I asked, and realized instantly I'd made a mistake.

"I'm Jamie," both said, and giggled.

"Come on!" I said. More giggling.

"I can take your pants off and find out in a hurry."

"That wouldn't be nice," one of them said primly.

"We'd tell Mrs. Bowers," the other said. The bowl in front of that one was almost empty.

"All right." I decided I'd better not let them put one over on me at the beginning. Strolling, I went and looked out the window. Here, from this angle, the cliff curved back, so it was easy to see the rocks below, and nestled in the center, a tiny strip of sand, a little beach.

"You have a beach below," I said.

"Yes. But Mrs. Bowers won't let us swim."

"Why not?"

"She says it's dangerous." That was one twin.

The other twin said, "But other kids swim up the beach. We can see them from here."

I glanced back through the window, and saw, much farther up, beyond an island that sat offshore, a long strip of yellow sand.

"The townies go there," one twin said.

"They're common," the other filled in.

"Who says?" I asked.

"Mummy," the twins chorused, sounding very much like English children I had known abroad.

"*And* Mrs. Bowers."

"Isn't Mrs. Bowers a townie?" I asked, before I realized it wasn't a tactful question.

"No. She lives in the Cove. Anyway, she's from Scotland, really."

"Steve's a townie," one twin said.

"But I like him anyway," the other replied.

"He lets us carve wood and help him build the garage."

I stared hard at one twin, searching for any visible distinguishing mark. "Jamie," I suddenly said, risking a guess.

"I'm Jennie," that one said.

"So'm I."

They looked at me with infinite satisfaction. Well, I thought, I'd have to settle this one way or another. The window was not far from the chair of one of the little imps. Over a short space I could move rapidly.

I had the twin around the waist before he or she knew what was happening. There was a shriek. Clamping the twin around the waist with one hand, I attacked the jeans zipper with the other.

"No," the twin shrieked. "Stop her!" This was directed at the other twin, who was assaulting my back. I paid no attention but tugged at the zipper.

25

"What's going on?" a man's voice said from the door.

I paused long enough to look up. Steve Novak, in his yellow helmet, was standing in the door to the garage, a big saw in his hand.

"I'm trying to find out which twin is which," I said, trying not to feel embarrassed.

He grinned. "Well, that's one way to go about it."

I had relaxed my hold, and the twin under my arm wiggled out and fled through the door, followed by the other.

"Thanks a lot," I said.

"There should be other methods." He shrugged and went back to the sawhorse standing in the middle of the debris of the half-built garage.

"Can you tell the difference?" I yelled after him.

"Sure."

"Well, how?"

One knee up on the sawhorse, he stared at me, then took off his helmet and wiped his forehead on his sleeve. His hair was chestnut brown and curly. Under a high square forehead, his cheekbones and narrow, tilted, blue-green eyes made him look more Slavic than ever.

"What are you doing here?" Something about the way he said it, ignoring my question, put my back up.

"I'm the baby-sitter."

The good humor that had been in his face when he grinned vanished.

"I bet you need the job, too. That card only went up on the post office yesterday, but there were already a couple of kids from the town who were interested."

"Townies?" The word slipped out before I realized it.

"That's right. Townies. Polacks. The kind they tell Polish jokes about."

"Well nobody was stopping them from calling and applying."

"Since the card was on the post office at the Cove they didn't know about it until I told them, after I got home last night. My sister was one."

"Well I'm sorry if I did your sister out of a job, but I need it too."

"If you need money why don't you ask your father?"

"Why doesn't your sister ask hers?"

He put his helmet on and stared at me, coldly, his eyes going up and down. "Taking one thing with another that was a pretty cheap shot—even for a member of the rich summer colony."

"I don't see why it's any cheaper than your shot about asking *my* father."

"I bet you don't!"

"Well I don't."

He lifted up his saw again. "If you're supposed to be looking after the kids hadn't you better get on with your job? They're probably down in the water now. And the water around the point there is dangerous."

I had forgotten all about them. It was easier simply to cut through two of the open posts of the garage than go back into the hall and through the front door. I tore past Steve Novak and out onto the short lawn which sloped down to the steps that led to the little beach. But when I got to the edge and looked down I couldn't see them. What I could see was a little pile of jeans and T-shirts. My heart seemed to drop like a lump of cold iron to below my stomach. Going down the pebbly steps as fast as I could, I called, "Jamie, Jennie," with every other step. There was no reply.

When I got to the bottom, the water looked as calm and gentle as it ever did anywhere on this part of the coast, lapping onto the soft yellow sand. Not being experienced in such things, I didn't know whether the tide was going in or out.

"Jamie! Jennie!" I called. "I know you're here. Now come out!" But even to me, the words sounded like a joke. I didn't know where they were. I knew it. I couldn't believe they didn't know it.

Filled with guilt and scared, I stared hard at the blue water, squinting into the early-morning sun to see if—horror on horror—there were any small heads dotted out there in the deep. The trouble was, the sun was reflected on the water, so I couldn't see too well. Putting my hand over my eyes I strained to see if there was anything unusual on the water's surface. Then I thought I saw a dot, perhaps two....

"Jamie! Jennie!" I screamed.

My eyes were watering, and I had forgotten to bring any sunglasses. Well, I thought, I couldn't stand there wondering if the twins were out there. Swimming was the only exercise I had had since the accident. Almost from the time the bandages came off I had been encouraged to swim as much as I could. I was a strong swimmer, and it was just as well, I thought, pulling off my parka, because I was going to have to go out and see if those dots were the twins. There wasn't time to go to the house to phone the boat rescue team or the police or anybody.

I was busy unbuttoning the top of my jeans when a voice said above me, "Try the cave on your right."

At that moment I heard a quickly stifled giggle.

Quickly rebuttoning my jeans, I turned around and saw an opening behind me. There, sticking out of the shadows, were four short legs.

"Jamie, Jennie!" I said, and darted towards the shadows. Two small figures in swimming trunks burst out towards me. But this time I was prepared. They ran into my outstretched arms, which I then closed around each.

Months of being on crutches and hours of building the power of my arms in swimming paid off. The twins wiggled and squirmed and yelled and squealed, but they couldn't get loose.

"I'm not going to let you go," I said calmly, "until I find out how to tell you apart. Now either you're going to tell me or you're going to stand here."

"Steve!" one of them shouted. "She's hurting us!"

"No I'm not. And you know it."

What I didn't know was whether he'd believe me or not. And I didn't dare look up to see if he was still there. One moment's inattention and I'd be back to square one.

"Tell her how to tell you apart, Jamie," I heard his voice say.

"No!" the twin under my left arm yelled.

"Yes! Now do as I say!"

The left twin said sulkily, "I have a mole on my neck."

Steve's command was like magic, which did nothing to restore my self-confidence.

I let the right twin go and turned the left twin around. Sure enough, there, low on the back of the neck, was a small flat mole. "So you're Jamie," I said.

"You must be awful dumb to have to have Steve tell you," Jamie said.

I had not got off to a good start. And I had learned with great speed that there was a huge difference between two seven-year-olds in good health and filled with energy, running around on their own territory, and children I had helped entertain in the hospital who were sick, frightened, and isolated from their homes and families.

"All right, Jamie," I said, trying to remember that he had no way of knowing that being dumb was an accusation I

28

had—too often—heard before. "So that means I'm going to need your help."

He turned and gave me an unreadable look out of his dark eyes, snatched up his jeans and shirt and followed his sister scampering up to the top. I picked up my parka and followed, experiencing once more a feeling I was used to: being stupid and incompetent. "Thanks a lot," I muttered under my breath as I walked up the steps, directing my words, mentally, towards the unhelpful Steve Novak.

When I got to the top, I realized from the sound of their voices that the twins were inside the skeleton of the garage, chasing each other around the sawdust-covered ground. But even as I went towards them I heard him yell, "Shoo! Out! This is off limits!"

"Show us how to carve, Steve!"

"No. I'm busy!"

"Please!"

"No. And if you don't leave now I won't show you at all."

"Will you show us later?"

"Yes. But only if you get out now." He sounded so authoritarian, I thought. Yet he got instant obedience.

The twins ran out towards me. "Let's go down to the other beach and swim!" They yelled together.

"Are you allowed to swim now?" I asked.

A few hardy souls were going in, but the water was still fairly cold.

"Oh yes, sure, we swim lots, don't we, Jamie?"

"All the time!"

I hesitated for a second, then said, "I'm sorry, I don't believe you. I'll ask your mother."

"Mother isn't up!" said Jamie.

"She never gets up until nearly lunchtime," Jennie added.

"We'll ask her then," I said firmly. "Now go and get your sand toys. We're going to go to the beach farther down."

"Let's go to the townies' beach."

"No!" I said, much more emphatically than I had intended. I didn't mean to catch Steve Novak's eye at that moment, but I did. There was a cynical look on his face.

"It's not tainted," he said.

I ignored him.

I got them down to the beach nearer to our house and was able to invent enough games to keep them busy until noon. At that point, even their energies were beginning to flag, so they made no resistance to going home, which was a relief,

29

because their immediate reaction to almost anything was to argue.

When we got to the house Steve Novak was packing up his tools. Some more wooden frames had been put in place.

"Show us how to carve, Steve!" Jennie yelled, running towards him. Even in that brief time I had learned that she was more vocal and more assertive than her twin. But Jamie, once aroused, could be a lot more obstreperous.

"All right. But only for about ten minutes. I have another job to go to."

Putting down his tool kit, he picked up a piece of wood that had been vaguely shaped into two joined lumps, one big and one little. "Now take this sandpaper and rub it along this curve here, Jennie. And Jamie, you do the same to this piece."

I stared at them for a minute, torn between a desire to get them away from Steve Novak, whose control over them I resented, and admiration for the quiet and concentration in them he seemed to evoke.

"What's the wood?" I said finally.

"Balsam."

"You don't build with that, do you?"

"No."

He didn't explain further, and I was certainly not going to ask him more questions.

"Have you talked to my mother?" I finally said. "She wants you to do something about her study."

"I'll see if she's called as soon as I get back to the phone in my van."

"Steve has a phone in his van," Jamie said importantly.

"Kids, that's enough for today. I have another job I have to go to."

He took the two pieces of wood out of their hands, and placed them in a bag he put over his shoulder. "See you tomorrow."

To bring the matter of Mother's study up again would merely give him the opportunity of being even more surly. I took the twins by their hands before they had time to protest and got them into the house.

"Lunch," I said.

"I wanna peanut butter and jelly sandwich," a twin said.

I glanced quickly to see which one. But made the unwelcome discovery that their crew-necked T-shirts covered the helpful mole.

30

"All right." There was no reason they shouldn't have their peanut butter and jelly, and I was too unsure of myself to argue further. I knew I had always liked children, but I was beginning to discover that there was more to successful baby-sitting than liking babies. And having to cope with that pig-headed Steve Novak didn't help much, either. He could have made it easier for me if he'd wanted. Instead, he'd gone out of his way not to be helpful.

Of course, I thought, opening the kitchen cabinets to find the jar of peanut butter, he did stop me going into the water, but then he would have got into trouble if I'd drowned, so there was no point in giving him more credit than he deserved.

I made three sandwiches and poured three glasses of milk and set the kitchen table with plates and spoons. We were sitting there just about to begin when the door leading from the dining room opened and a woman came in.

My first impression was that this was one of the most beautiful women I had ever seen in my life. Tall and fair, with sea-gray eyes, she was in a long blue robe zipped from a high collar down to the floor. She made me think of my imagined picture of Isolde, the Cornish queen, the one who was loved by Tristan, but who was married to King Mark. Somehow I expected the twins to get up and run towards her, but they didn't. They just stopped eating and looked at her.

"Hello, kids," she said. Her voice, which was both sharp and hoarse, came as a surprise. It didn't match the way she looked.

"Hello, Mummy," they chorused, once again giving their imitation of well-brought-up English children.

Something pulled me to my feet. Mrs. Brewster stopped and looked at me a little vaguely. Then she seemed to focus in on me. "You must be...the baby-sitter." It was obvious she didn't remember my name.

"Yes. I'm Sarah Lacey."

"Nice of you to come," she said. "And you'll be here un-til—" She opened the refrigerator door and was gazing inside.

"Until three." Anxiety gnawed at me. Maybe she'd changed her mind. "Wasn't that the time you said?"

She pulled out a quart container of orange juice and closed the refrigerator door. "Ah, yes. That's the time Mrs. Bowers will be back." Going to the cabinet, she got out a tall glass, and poured it full of orange juice. Then she moved a little down the counter and picked up a large coffee pot.

Suddenly I remembered Mrs. Bowers telling me that Mrs. Brewster would ring, at which point I was to plug in the coffee pot. I hadn't heard her, of course, being outside. So the pot hadn't been plugged in, and I'd forgotten all about it. My insides gave a jump, which they were inclined to do when I felt nervous. I realized how much I wanted this job—and the money.

"I'm sorry," I stammered. "I was outside with the twins. I didn't hear you ring." I moved across the kitchen floor as fast as I could and plugged in the pot. "It'll be ready in a minute."

"You mean to say you didn't plug it in when I rang?" She didn't sound angry. Just dismayed.

"No. I'm sorry."

"She thought we were in the water and was going to go in after us," a twin said.

"How long will the coffee take?" Suddenly she sounded annoyed.

"N-not long."

She gave me a long look out of those sea-gray eyes. "That's the only thing I expect you to do for me, so please don't forget it again. Bring me a cup, black, no sugar, as soon as it is ready." And still holding the orange juice, she swept out, her blue robe trailing after her exactly as though she were indeed Isolde of Tintagel Castle.

"I thought Mrs. Bowers said she took cream and sugar," I heard myself say, rather stupidly fixing on this minor point.

"Sometimes she does," one twin said. "And sometimes she doesn't," the other one chimed in. "But she always wants her coffee *first* thing." The dark eyes, above a mouth well smeared with jelly, gazed at me.

"She'll fire you," the other one said. I still couldn't tell them apart, I thought unhappily.

"But she was in a good mood this morning," the first twin said.

"Maybe her hangover wasn't so bad," the other one explained.

"Hangover?" I said.

"Headache," the first twin explained. "Silly!"

"All grownups have them," the second added.

I'd been hungry for my peanut butter sandwich, but forgot all about it as I watched the pot.

"Mrs. Bowers says a watched pot never boils," one of the twins said.

32

I looked at him/her. "All right, Jennie," I said. It was a guess, but it sounded certain. There was a momentary look of dismay on the round face and I knew I'd been right. I grinned. I knew just how she felt. The more the grown-up world could be kept in suspense the better. "I'd have to find out sooner or later," I said. "But I won't tell anyone."

Jamie, who had been watching this, putting large pieces of his sandwich in his mouth said, "How could you tell?" A spray of crumbs and milk blew out with the questions.

"That's my secret." But I felt good for the first time that morning. Jennie's face was a trifle rounder than Jamie's, and her eyes a shade lighter—a little more hazel. I felt almost triumphant. Then I looked at the pot and was relieved to see the coffee was done.

Carrying a cup, and the pot on a tray, I left the kitchen, crossed the dining room and came into the front hall. Carrying the tray on level ground hadn't been too difficult. To carry it evenly upstairs was more of a problem but I made it.

"Mrs. Brewster?" I called out tentatively. "I have your coffee."

"In here."

It was the big front room facing the sea, the one that had given me such a comfortable, positive feeling. The deep bay window was still there, with the light pouring in.

"It's a beautiful room," I said, without thinking.

"I hate it."

I turned. She was sitting in a huge bed, the kind that has no head or footboard. Somehow the light that looked golden in the rest of the room seemed to glare on her face. She appeared much older than she had looked downstairs. And the hair that in the kitchen had seemed so fair showed plainly here that it had been streaked and colored.

"It certainly took long enough," she said. "You can put it down here."

I went over and put the tray down on the night table beside her.

"I can plug the pot in," I said. "I took the grounds out of it downstairs."

"All right. You can pour me a cup and then get back to the twins. Heaven knows what they'll do if left long enough by themselves. What time is it?"

I poured out a cup and handed it to her, then glanced at my watch. "A quarter to one."

"I'm going out shortly. You wait until Mrs. Bowers gets back before three. Then you're free, of course. If you can get the twins to take naps before going out again, it would be wonderful. You can go now."

The coffee was still sitting on the night table when I left.

The twins weren't at all interested in taking naps, so I settled for reading them a story from one of the books in their room, which was on the ground floor. Since it was the kind of tale I was trying to write, a sort of fantasy saga, I was glad to read it to them. The illustrations, I noted (with some satisfaction) were not as good as ones I could do already, let alone what I'd be able to do after studying in art school for a year or so.

Half an hour after starting to read I glanced up. Jamie was sound asleep on his bed. Jennie was sitting on her bed, trying to keep her eyes open, chewing on a pencil.

Pretending that I hadn't noticed how sleepy she was, I went on about the Fairy Princess and her best friend, the magic frog. "And then she met Prince Stefan," I read.

Jennie, her head almost down on the pillow, mumbled something.

"What was that?" I asked.

One more word came out, then she, too, was fast asleep. The word sounded oddly like "Steve."

When I knew they were both asleep, I went on reading, periodically glancing at my watch. At about two-thirty there was the sound of a car coming up the long path through the trees. In a moment it appeared, a black Mercedes. Then it stopped. A man got out. He was tall and extremely handsome, with curly black hair and an open collar with lots of black hair showing on his chest. Slowly he walked towards the house. When he was a few feet from the back door I was afraid he'd ring the doorbell, which would wake the twins.

Limping hastily into the hall, I opened the door before he could get to it.

"Hello," he said, stopping a few feet from me on the porch.

"The twins are asleep so I didn't want you to ring the bell."

"Oh, I wouldn't do that," he said. "I just come straight in. The door's always open." He pushed past me without a word and came into the hall. "Is Mrs. Brewster in?"

"Yes. She's upstairs."

"Well—run up and tell her I'm here."

He talked to me as though he thought I was a maid, and
34

I found myself bristling. But I didn't know how to tell him I wasn't. Finally I said, "I'm the baby-sitter."

"So—go and tell Mrs. Brewster I'm here."

The words "Go tell her yourself" were almost falling off my tongue, but I kept thinking of those three dollars an hour that could (maybe) add up to a couple of hundred before the end of the summer. I didn't know how much art school cost, but I could take at least one course with that, even if Mother and Father absolutely refused to send me. I turned slowly, my leg felt like 'ead.

"What's the matter with your leg?"

"An accident," I said, remembering suddenly the answer I'd given Steve Novak.

He lit a cigarette. "Too bad." He wandered into the room opposite the dining room.

I went upstairs, not hurrying. When I got to the top, I went towards the front of the house and knocked on the half-open door of Mrs. Brewster's room. "Mr. Brewster's here. He said to tell you."

"What!" She came to the door, screwing one earring on. She had on white pants and a blue blazer over a pale blue shirt. "When? When did he arrive?" Incredibly, she looked frightened.

"Just now. He said to tell you he'd come." I paused. "Mrs. Bowers isn't here, so I had to come and tell you." I was still trying to get across to her that I wasn't the maid.

But Mrs. Brewster swept past me and went downstairs at full speed. Swinging around the bottom of the staircase, she went into the living room and then stopped.

As I came down the stairs I could see her and behind her, with his back to the mantelpiece, Mr. Brewster.

Suddenly she swung around. "What on earth did you mean, telling me it was Mr. Brewster?"

I stood, one foot half down on the step below me. "Well, isn't it?"

"Were you trying some kind of a joke?"

"Hey! Wait a minute, Nancy. It's probably my fault." The man with curly black hair came forward. "I didn't tell her who I was." He started to laugh. "I guess she just assumed I was Stoddard."

I stared at him. It had never occurred to me he wasn't Mrs. Brewster's husband.

"Well next time, if you don't know, ask." The man was laughing, but she sounded furious.

35

"I'm not the maid," I said, angry myself. Money or no money, I didn't have to put up with that. "I'm the baby-sitter." I glanced at my watch. "And it's three o'clock."

I'd been going towards the twins' room, but as soon as I realized the time, I swung around and headed towards the kitchen, where I'd put my parka.

"Look, I'm sorry," Mrs. Brewster said. "It's just that—well, it's impossible to explain. I jumped the gun too fast. I know you're not the maid."

All this time I kept on walking towards the kitchen. It took me a minute to find my parka, which Mrs. Bowers had hung in one of the closets.

"Please stay until Mrs. Bowers gets here." Mrs. Brewster's voice came from behind me. "She'll be back any minute. I have to go out with Har—Mr. Schreiber. I completely understand now."

I paused in putting on my parka. "I charge for overtime."

"That's all right," she said quickly.

"Time and a half," I said, digging that out of some memory about union negotiations I'd read about somewhere.

"That's fine."

I took off my parka. "Okay."

"Thank you. It won't be long."

I followed her back through the dining room and down the hall and heard her say to Mr. Schreiber, "Sarah has very kindly said she'll stay until Bowers gets here, so there's nothing to hold us."

"That's good, because we're late. I'm not sure how long they'll wait for us."

Neither looked at me, or even into the twins' room, when they left.

Twenty minutes later, Mrs. Bowers turned up. I saw her coming up the long path from the trees and looked at my watch. Three-thirty.

I glanced at the twins. Both were still asleep, but were beginning to show signs of being about to wake up. I crept out and went to the kitchen.

"Thought you were supposed to be gone." Mrs. Bowers said. She was getting vegetables out of a big bin.

"Mrs. Brewster went out with Mr. Schreiber, so I had to stay here until you came," I said.

"Him!" she said. "All right. Run along." And then when I was leaving, she said, "Would you like a wee biscuit before you leave?"

"Biscuit?"

"Cookie."

"Thanks."

She gave me two chocolate-chip cookies, and I ate them as I walked down the path. Until I left the house, I didn't realize how tired I was. I had been in the house six and a half hours, but it felt like twenty-four.

Chapter

3

That afternoon I put a bathing suit on under my jeans and shirt and took a big towel out to the beach where I could try to do something about the puritan white of my legs and arms. There was no one at our end and only a couple of mothers with kids far around the other side of the bay. I also took my notebook, some pencils and an eraser, plus a book to read. I figured it would be at least a few days before any more of the kids my age came, because not all schools let out as early as ours, and I'd have a short while to get some color before the onslaught.

I took off my jeans and shirt and smeared my arms, legs and shoulders with some kind of oil. Then I lay back to get some sun on my front.

I must have been more tired than I realized, because the next thing I knew I heard some voices.

"Is she okay?" a girl's voice said.

I opened my eyes. Ringed above me were faces, six of them. I sat up in a hurry.

"Well at least you're alive." The speaker was a dark, handsome boy with blue eyes and a terrific build.

"You oughtn't to go to sleep like that on a beach," a girl said. I looked at her, too confused to be able to say anything myself. She was dark too, and very pretty, only with dark eyes.

"I'm sorry...I didn't..." Why was I apologizing, I wondered. I had as much right to be there as they had. It was the beach used by all the houses curved around the bay.

"I was tired," I said finally.

"Yeah, but you ought to be careful, as pale as you are. You could get a bad burn."

"Boy, you were in a really bad accident, weren't you?" That was a blond boy. He was also tan and well built and good looking. "What happened?"

I glanced down quickly. I'd forgotten about my scars for a moment, so without thinking had turned so that that side of my bad leg was uppermost.

"I had new bones put in," I said coolly. "It's a new kind of operation; they were using me as a guinea pig and are watching to see if it's a success."

There I went again, I thought, scrambling to my feet. Ms. Smart Ass. Why couldn't I just give them a friendly answer? Why couldn't they just not comment?

"No kidding?" That was the dark boy. "I've never heard of that, and my dad's an orthopedic surgeon, and I'm going to medical school when I've finished college."

"Don't worry, she made the whole thing up!"

I'd been just about to say I was kidding, but as I looked at the girl who spoke, I found my mouth opening and more insane words coming out. "I can give you the article about it in the medical journal if you're interested."

"Okay, I'd like to see it. So would Bruce here."

She stood there, one slender hip in a bikini string stuck out, a cigarette in her hand, her head surrounded by a curly blonde afro. She, too, was as tan as a piece of toast. Bruce, I reflected gloomily, must be the future doctor.

By this time I was standing and collecting the beach towel and book and looking around for the notebook. Where was it? Panic hit my midriff.

"What's this?" It was the blonde girl. The hand with the cigarette was holding the open notebook, the other hand was turning the pages.

"'"I've always wanted to know someone like you," he said, looking into the princess's shining eyes,'" she read aloud. "My, my, how womantic."

"Hey, that's pretty hot," the blond boy said, looking over her shoulder.

"Give me that!" I made a lunge at the book.

The blonde girl lifted it neatly above my head. "Don't snatch, now. That's not nice." She read some more: "'*The princess smoothed her dark beautiful hair...*' Why do princesses always have to be dark and beautiful? How about, 'The princess smoothed her ratty afro and shifted her two hundred pounds...'" The girl giggled, still dodging me. When I almost got the book she threw it to the dark boy. "Why don't you read some?"

I knew I was behaving stupidly, that I was just playing into their teasing, but my smart-ass attitude and tongue— my usual defense—had deserted me. No one had ever seen my notebooks. Rage gave me energy. I made on final lunge after her and tripped over a small stone, falling heavily. For a minute the pain was so great I thought I'd be sick. I caught my breath and held it, and swallowed. There seemed to be a blinding light around me. Dimly I heard one of the boys say, "For Chrissake, Linda—don't be such a sadist."

"Well, she shouldn't be such a smart ass. A civil question deserves a civil answer. Here, take it to her."

Something was thrown on the ground beside me. "Are you okay?" a boy's voice asked.

I wanted to be dead, to die at that moment and disappear and never be seen—at least by them—as long as I lived.

"Just go away," I said.

"But—"

"Go away. Leave me alone."

As the pain finally abated I became aware that I was alone. It was funny. Since we were all on sand, there was no sound to their footsteps, and my eyes were squeezed shut. But I knew that one minute they were there and the next they were gone.

After I felt steadier I got to my feet, furious with them and furious with myself. My legs were shaking, and I still felt a little sick. I saw them all down at the other side of the bay, where the mothers with the children had been. There were six of them, three boys and three girls. In addition to the two girls I had noticed, there was another one, quite small, with brown hair, and another boy with sort of reddish coloring. I wondered who they were. They all looked about my age. I glanced at my watch. It was nearly five. I'd been asleep in the sun for more than an hour.

Mother took one look at me at dinner. "Good heavens, Sarah! You're red as a lobster. How long were you out?"

"About an hour," I said as easily as I could. I was already sore, and experience told me I'd be even sorer before the evening was done.

"I said tan, not burn," Mother said.

"I fell asleep."

Mother opened her mouth, then saw my face and closed it again. "Never mind, baby. I have some stuff to put on it. We'll do it after dinner. How do you feel?"

"Okay." Truthfully, I didn't feel too well. But I was afraid that Mother would use that as an excuse not to let me go to Headlands the next day.

"How was the baby-sitting?" Mother asked.

"Fine. The twins are nice."

"Anybody else there?"

"Mrs. Bowers. She seemed like a sort of housekeeper type. Anyway she wore a white uniform."

"I mean of the family."

"No." I remembered my mistake about Mr. Schreiber and started to giggle.

"Tell!" Mother said.

So I told her about my mistake.

"Well you're certainly *not* a maid there," Mother said, even more indignant than I was. "Of all the nerve! I suppose the Brewsters think that because they're descended from about six signers of the Declaration of Independence they can order anybody around and look down on people." I could see that I had hit one of Mother's pet theories—snobbism versus egalitarianism. "I don't mean to arouse your fury again, but if it means your going there, I'm sorrier than ever you feel you have to have a job."

"I thought you didn't mind too much. When I said it was Mrs. Brewster you didn't seem so set against it."

"Yes, well..." She looked at me quickly. I braced myself, because I knew there was a motive floating around there. But all she said was, "I'll go now and get that goo for you to put on. I'm afraid it looks as though you might have quite a burn."

She was right. I did. By nine that night she was feeding me aspirin and fluids and trying to find out where she could get tannic-acid jelly. "The village store is closed, of course. Why does everything always happen when stores are closed and all the doctors are on vacation?"

I then heard Mother talking to the operator about a drugstore in the town and after that heard her dial. What I could hear of the conversation that followed sounded like her usual message to Steve Novak.

"I've just told you, this is an emergency. If your delivery boy isn't interested in earning a couple of dollars extra tip for bicycling out here, then perhaps you need another delivery boy.... No, I'm not going to leave my daughter alone here to drive into town.... All right. Five dollars. My daughter is in great pain...." I heard her slam the phone down.

"Patience," Mother said, coming back into the room, "has never been my leading characteristic."

"You sounded like the snob of all time," I said, remembering Steve Novak.

"Considering it's your face that's going to be one big blister, I should think you'd be grateful."

I was. I felt terrible. "Okay. Thanks," I muttered. I didn't really believe that bit about her not wanting to leave me alone. Ever since her run-in with the anti-family-planning townies, she'd been ready to fight with the townies over anything. "Primitive reactionaries" was only one of her favorite expressions for them.

Mother kept feeding me iced tea while we were waiting. "It just shows how blue-white your skin is," she said, piling the sugar into my tea. "You must be a throwback to some Celtic ancestor."

"Why Celtic?" I asked, sipping the cold sweet tea through swollen lips.

"Because they seem to have very thin skin with a pinkish undertone. That's why they have so many redheads. Anyway, it's very hard for them to tan. Whereas northern blonds like the Scandinavians get lovely gold tans."

"Lucky me," I said.

"By the way. Did you say the name of that man at the Brewsters' was Schreiber?"

"Yes. Why?"

"Because I think I've heard that name before—somewhere. I have a feeling he's something to do with real estate up here."

Forty-five minutes later the doorbell rang. Mother's lips closed in a firm line. Picking up her handbag, she disappeared. I heard her voice, then I heard a man's, which sounded vaguely familiar. Curious, I wobbled off the sofa where I'd been lying and went to the door. There stood a man I thought was Steve Novak until I got closer. Then I realized it was somebody younger who resembled him.

"Look," Mother was saying, "I said I'd give you five dollars and I will. I just don't have anything smaller than a ten-dollar bill. I'll give you a check."

"Thanks. I'd prefer the cash."

"Then you'll have to get me change for the ten."

"I have change," I said, fishing in my jeans pocket. I'd emptied my piggy bank before coming up here, and hadn't found a place to put the bills yet. "Here," I said, handing Mother five dollars.

"Boy, you sure got a burn, didn't you?" the boy said.

He had the same tilted blue eyes and high cheekbones as Steve, but his hair was lighter. It suddenly occurred to me that Steve Novak was very good-looking.

"Are you related to Steve Novak?" I asked, as Mother handed over the five dollars. I could tell she was furious by the way she was holding it out.

"Cousin," the boy said, taking the money. He looked about my age.

"I wish you'd ask your cousin to call me," Mother said. "I'm tired of working in a study with half the wall caved in."

"Have you left a—"

I knew what Mother was going to say and I just didn't want to hear it again. "Mom," I interrupted, "let's get this crud on me before I get any worse."

"Thanks," the boy said, and ran down the steps towards the bicycle.

"It's no use your fighting with Steve Novak about using his message tape," I commented as Mother was smoothing the jelly over my shoulders. "He's as stubborn about it as you are. Why don't you try calling him some time when he's in?"

"Like when?"

"Like now, or early in the morning. He probably works out of his home."

"Since when did you become Ms. Olive Branch for Peace?"

"Where's your way getting you?"

There was a long silence as Mother smeared some more jelly over my arms. "It's a pity with all that insight and common sense you can't apply it to your academic work."

"You can have common sense and still be stupid."

"You're not stupid."

"Father thinks so."

"No he doesn't." But I knew from the way she said it that she thought he did. "You know how your father is. The academy's been his whole life."

"He thinks I'm stupid and you think I'm unattractive to men."

"I don't think anything of the sort. It's you who—"

"And I don't want to talk about it."

"Then why did you bring it up?"

Silence reigned as she went to work on my legs. Then she said, "I don't think you're unattractive. You know I don't. You have lovely hair and eyes and being thin is the height of fashion. What's lacking...I didn't mean that..."

"Yes you did. And you're right. I don't have any confidence. Like this afternoon..."

I hadn't planned to tell her about the episode but it was out before I had stopped to consider.

"What do you mean?" she said. "What happened?"

So, rather grudgingly, I told her.

"Do you have any idea who they were?"

"They didn't stop for introductions. One of the boys was called Bruce and he called that female with the blonde fuzzy hair Linda."

More silence. "You know, Sarah, you do have a sharp tongue. And since I have one, too, I'm not throwing stones. I realize it's a defense mechanism—you hit them before they have a chance to hit you. Still, it does alienate people."

"I don't care."

"That is so palpably untrue I wonder you have the crust to say it."

I hunted around the sofa for the box of tissues Mother had put there and then blew my nose.

"Oh, baby, I didn't mean to make you cry. Come along now," and she gave me a slight hug.

I let out a screech.

"Sorry," she said. "I forgot about your burn. You're going to be a thing of beauty tomorrow. Are you sure you want to go to that job?"

"Yes," I said. I thought about telling her of my plans for going to art school instead of back to Miss Hall's, but decided not to. She was in an unusually sympathetic mood this evening, but I didn't want to press my luck.

"You're *red!*" the twins yelled when I walked in the next morning.

Bowers looked up. "Ach!" she said. "What've you gone and done to yourself?"

"Sunburn," I said briefly.

45

"You're going to have a fine set of freckles before you're done," she said.

"No I'm not." I was terrified she might be right. I had had freckles when I was about twelve and hated them. Slowly over the years they'd faded and I didn't want them back.

"What's wrong with freckles? Lots of people in Scotland have them."

"Sarah's gonna have freckles," Jamie and Jennie sang.

"You'll be sorry when I won't show you my newly invented game," I said, pouring myself some coffee.

"What is it?"

"I'm not going to tell you."

"C'mon, Sarah. Tell us!"

"Maybe," I said, sitting down and sipping my coffee.

There was a sound of hammering outside.

"That's Steve," yelled the twins, and flung themselves out of their chairs and through the kitchen door.

"I guess they like him," I said grudgingly.

"They'll get their fingernails smashed if he lets them play with his tools," she said, sounding cross. "You'd better go and have an eye to them."

"Don't you like him?" I asked, taking my empty cup to the sink. I found I was anxious for her answer.

"I didn't say I didn't like him."

"But you sound like you don't."

"You ask a lot of questions."

"What's wrong with that?"

"Ask me no questions, I'll tell you no lies."

"You're full of maxims," I said, and went out, still wondering what she had against Steve Novak.

Either they had found or he had given them some putty. Chattering to themselves like two sparrows, they were sitting on the concrete floor working on a purplish lump in front of them.

Steve was busy fitting a prefabricated piece of siding into one of the openings. "Putty?" I asked.

"It'll keep them away from the knives and the hammers." His helmet was off and his thick brown hair was ruffled and curly. It wasn't as long as the hair I was used to on Peter and his friends, or on most of the boys I'd come across in New York. But it had a gloss to it, as though he'd just washed it. I was right, he was attractive. While he was lean, he looked strong and his arms beneath his rolled-up sleeves were muscular.

46

I glanced up at his face and saw he was looking at me over a kind of makeshift table on which was a design of some kind. His face was broad across the cheeks but thin, and had a quality there was a word for, but I couldn't think of the word.

"You've been out in the sun," he said. "You ought to be careful. Your skin is so fair you'd probably burn very easily."

I could feel myself blushing at having been caught looking at him. I was sure he knew I thought he was attractive, so it was doubly mortifying when he pointed out how fair I was.

"Thanks a lot," I muttered.

"There's nothing wrong in being fair-skinned."

I suddenly thought of the six tanned kids the day before. "I was trying to get a tan yesterday when I feel asleep. That's how I got the burn." I hesitated. "Your cousin delivered some tannic jelly last night."

"Yes. Mark told me. He said you came to the door and had a fairly bad sunburn. He said if...Mrs. Lacey hadn't been...hadn't appeared so annoyed he would have suggested you order another product they have in the drugstore there. It's even better for burns."

"Oh." I remembered Mother's hassle with the drugstore over the phone and later over the five-dollar tip. "She doesn't mean to sound annoyed." I stopped, because I knew it was a lie. She had somehow never forgiven the townies for that rotten tomato that had been thrown at her. "Well, you know how it is. She had a bad time in the town last year when she was trying to get family planning started."

He grinned. "I remember. She got a ripe tomato on her nice suit."

"Well it wasn't a very friendly thing to do. Were you there?"

"No. But lots of my family were. It was another one of my cousins that threw the tomato."

"Oh." I decided that was a piece of information I'd keep to myself as far as my family were concerned. "Well, I don't think I'll tell Mother—not if she still wants her study fixed."

He grinned again and took a pencil from behind his ear. "That's probably a good idea."

"You must have a lot of cousins. They seem to be all over the place."

"Well you know us Polacks—big Catholic families. We're more on having babies than on so-called family planning."

"You don't mind being called a Polack?"

He made a mark on his design, then said, "Not if I say it—or another Polack does. But somebody outside? That's different!" He glanced up. His eyes were like two bits of blue steel. Then he laughed.

I remembered something my father had written in an article: something about only ignorant and stupid people using derogatory ethnic names. And once when a friend of Mushroom's whom she had brought home to dinner, said something about "spades" in a joke, Father said, in his most academic manner, that terms like that were not used in his household.

"I don't mind being called a WASP," I said now.

"Why should you, since WASPs run everything?"

I thought this one over. The phrase "the ruling elite" was one that both Peter and Father often used. It had never before occurred to me it meant us. "I don't feel like a ruling elite," I said.

He straightened. "And I don't feel like a Polish joke—just a guy."

"Then why use it?"

He turned and drew a metal tape measure across one of his panels. "Oh—to spit in their eye—to show people what they can do with their nicknames."

"But I didn't use it?"

"True. Maybe I was testing you."

Instead of feeling annoyed I felt pleased, as though he were saying in a sort of roundabout way that he wanted us to be friends. And then I remembered that I hadn't liked him—that I had mentally called him a jerk. Somewhere between then and now something had changed.

I strolled to the edge of the concrete floor and pulled up a grass blade and then tried to blow on it through my fingers to make a whistling sound, a trick Peter had taught me. What I was really doing was trying to decide whether or not I wanted to go on with the subject of big Catholic families, which lay like a challenge in the middle of what he had said. The trouble was, it was bound to end in a fight. Without consciously making a decision, I finally said,

"Aren't you afraid of overpopulation?"

"Obviously not. If everything—the distribution of food— were planned properly there'd be enough for everybody."

"But..." I'd helped Mother collate and sort her material, and I knew all her arguments. Heaven knows, I'd heard them often enough. Yet I decided I wouldn't go on with it.

48

He had been leaning over the desk making marks on his chart. Then he looked up. "But?"

"I suppose it's all in what you believe's important."

"That puts it into a nutshell."

I waited. "Are you married?" I asked.

He grinned. "Not yet."

"But you're engaged?"

"No." Pause. "Are you?"

"No." I was startled and must have showed it.

"Why do you sound so surprised? Why shouldn't you be engaged?"

"I'm only seventeen."

"One of the my sisters is seventeen and she's—well, not formally engaged, she doesn't have a ring or anything, but she's going with somebody and they plan to be married when he finishes school."

I found myself wondering intensely how old Steve was. It was hard to guess. Sometimes he looked no older than the kids I'd seen the day before, but he seemed and sounded lots older. "How old are you?" I asked, and felt myself blushing again. Maybe, I thought, with the burn, it wouldn't show.

"Twenty-three."

Six years older than me, I thought. The same age as Peter. Peter and his friends could talk philosophy and political science with Father, yet Peter seemed much younger than Steve. I wondered if Steve had gone to college, but didn't exactly like to ask. I threw away the grass blade. "I'd better take the kids out to the beach."

"You'd better cover up your arms if you do. And wear a hat."

"A hat? I've never had one."

"Maybe your mother has one."

I was about to say she didn't either, when I remembered that she did—a wide straw hat that she sometimes wore when she worked around the yard. "Yes. I'll take the kids over there and get it."

I glanced at him. "Have you and she managed to meet on the phone yet?"

"Not yet. The moment she leaves a message I'll call her."

"Why are you so stubborn about it? You know what she wants."

"Why is she? The tape's not going to bite her." The look I had noticed on his face before was back, and now I knew the word I'd been looking for: austere. He'd been smiling and his eyes had been crinkling at the corners. Suddenly he looked older and colder and further away. So he wouldn't know how I felt, I shrugged. "Well, you're losing business."

"There's only one other outfit within miles that'd do the job she wants done, and they cost a lot more. I can afford to wait. I have plenty of work as it is." He turned away. "Okay, kids, I'm going to have to use that corner. Out!"

My face stayed the color of beets for another four days and then started to peel. All that time I wore Mother's large Leghorn straw, and when I sat on the beach with the twins, wore long-sleeved shirts over my jeans. Determined not to encounter the six tanned bodies again, I got into the habit of taking the twins north of Headlands Point to the townies' beach. It was still early in the season and the place was almost deserted during the morning and most weekdays. But the first Saturday I walked to the edge of the cliff and started down on the townies' side, I stopped. The sand was fairly thick with bodies, many of them no more tanned than I.

Oh well, I thought. So what! And went on down anyway. A beach is a beach, I thought, and anything was better than meeting that horrible Linda again.

The twins, who'd brought buckets and spades, announced that they were going to try to find Australia and started digging. I got out a notebook—a much smaller one that slipped into my pocket—and started writing. I was still working on my saga, but knew that I could become so engrossed I could forget the twins until they'd finally reached Australia or decided to swim there, so I made myself look up and check on them at the bottom of every short page.

It was a good idea, especially if it had worked. What I forgot to remember was how easily I could forget to remember, so when a man's voice said above me, "Where're the kids?" I didn't, for a second, know what he was talking about. Then I did. Wildly I looked around. There was no sign of either Jamie or Jennie.

"Oh my God!" I jumped to my feet too fast and promptly overbalanced. "Damn!" I said, as my leg folded under me.

"You should stop kicking people," the voice said calmly. I looked up. There was Steve Novak in swimming shorts. His body was so terrific it depressed me. Everything was right. Shoulders wide, no fat, plenty of muscle and a nice tan. He wasn't as dark as the kids on the other beach, except on his lower arms, below where his sleeves were usually rolled up, but a sort of golden all over.

He was holding his hand out. Rather sullenly I took it and he pulled me up to my feet. "What was that crack about, the one about me kicking people?" I asked.

"Wasn't that what you told me, when I asked you what happened to your leg? You said you sprained your ankle kicking somebody." His face was absolutely deadpan.

I couldn't help it. I started to laugh. Then he grinned. "I suppose I deserved the answer."

"I had an accident—a car accident. My leg was smashed and I've had about four operations on it. It's a lot better, and after one more operation the doctors say it should be absolutely okay. I won't even limp. That ought to be some improvement!"

He stood looking down at me a minute. "You know—" he started and then stopped.

"What?"

"You seem to have an idea you're Ms. Ugly. You're not, you know. Not by a long shot."

There was something in his eyes when he said that. My heart started a queer uneven beat. I'd never felt this way before, except maybe when I had terrific fantasies about what it would be like to fall in love.

"Tha—thanks," I said. I didn't know what to say then. I stood there, feeling like a fool. Suddenly a girl's voice from behind Steve said, "Hey, are you coming? They're waiting for us."

I looked past him. The girl was about my age, very pretty, with blonde curly hair and a wonderful figure. My depression came back. He was just being kind, after all. If that was his girl she was dynamite, and I couldn't compete with that.

"Coming," Steve said. Then, "The twins, by the way, are behind that big rock feeling frustrated because you haven't yet discovered they're lost."

"Thanks." I produced my best smile, not wanting him to know how I felt.

I wish, I thought as he turned away, that I had told him I had a boyfriend. Maybe, I considered, as I shepherded the twins back up to the house, I could make one up. I was pretty good at making up stories on paper. Why not make up one for real life?

*　　*　　*

Father, Peter and Mushroom turned up the following week, and the house was full. Then one day it rained, and the water dripped into Mother's study, ruining some of her notes.

"Didn't you tell me you see that worthless Steve Novak every day?" she said, storming into the house with the sodden paper in her hands.

"He's not worthless," I said. "He does fabulous work. He's almost got their new garage done."

"Worthless or not, I want him to fix my wall pronto."

"Then you're going to have to leave a message on his tape."

"I will not talk to those wretched tapes. I won't do it in New York, I don't see why I should here. You'd think he didn't care whether he had business or not."

"Well, he has more than enough," I said, taking some pleasure in frustrating Mother. "He's as busy as a bird dog."

"Win, do something about all this, would you?" Mother said to Father, who was reading the paper. "Go after him with your best academic command."

"He wouldn't care," I said. "Why should he? He's not one of your students."

Father lowered his paper. "No one ever said he would. Since your mother seems to have a tape phobia, why don't you leave a message on this workman's tape for her?"

"Yes, Sarah, why don't you?" Mother said. "How stupid of me not to think of that sooner."

But I didn't want to. I wasn't quite sure why I felt so strongly that I didn't want to, and with Father looking at me out of his dark eyes I couldn't take the time to find out. It had something to do with fairness to Steve. "I don't like tapes either," I said. "Why don't you leave it, Father?"

Father stared at me for a minute. Then he got up and went to the telephone. A few seconds later I heard him dictate into the phone. "This is Winthrop Lacey. Please call either me or Mrs. Lacey at this number concerning the rebuilding of Mrs. Lacey's study." And he gave our number. Then he came back and sat down and started to read his paper again.

That night the phone rang. Mushroom went to the phone and then said, "I'll get her. Who's calling?"

She came back to the dinner table where we were sitting finishing our dinner. "Somebody named Steve Novak wants to speak to either Mr. or Mrs. Lacey," she said and then sat down. "Who's Steve Novak?" she asked, when Mother disappeared towards the phone.

"The local handyman," Father said.

"He's a builder," I said. "He's building the garage up at Headlands."

"Oh, is that house taken?" Mushroom said. "Who's there?"

"Mrs. Brewster and her twins, Jennie and Jamie King."

"Brewster, Brewster," Mushroom said, pouring herself some more coffee. "Why do I know the name?"

"What name?" Mother asked, coming back in.

"Brewster. Sam said somebody named Brewster has taken Headlands. I'm trying to figure out why the name seems to have some significance."

"Mother said they descended from six signers of the Declaration of Independence," I said.

"Not Mrs. Brewster, Mr.," Mother said. "Sam, I don't know why you seem to like Steve Novak. I find him extremely difficult. I wanted him to start work tomorrow and he says he can't until Monday, even though he knows perfectly well I've been trying to reach him since we've been here."

"Is he the only one who can do anything around here?" Peter asked.

"No. There's Williams & Son. But they're more expensive."

"Well, let's get them anyway," Father said. "This Steve sounds like a pain in the rump."

"What do you expect?" Peter said. "That town is real Archie Bunker territory."

I jumped on him.

"What d'you mean by that?"

"I mean these hard hats—"

"That's a slur," I said, thinking of Steve's yellow helmet.

"Well in this case it's deserved."

"Why?"

"Because I do a lot of legal work for minorities, and every time it's a question of affirmative action or busing for integration, you can absolutely depend on solid opposition from the ethnic communities."

"I thought it was the ruling elite you didn't like?" I said.

"When you're talking about corporations," Father put in, "he doesn't. Neither do I."

"Why are you suddenly getting so defensive about this Steve Novak?" Mushroom said. "Do you like him that much?"

I shrugged. "He's okay."

"Oh God!" Peter said.

"What do you mean, 'Oh God!'" All of a sudden I was furious.

53

"With all the kids on the beach, you have to go and pick a townie, and at a time when we're about to take a bunch of them to court. Probably including your buddy, Steve."

"Why're you taking them to court?"

"Because whoever owns that stretch of marshy dune north of the village is threatening to sell it to a developer who's going to put up some monster resort."

"You mean that wildlife sanctuary?" Mushroom said.

"Exactly. It's been a nesting place for wild birds from the time anybody's been here. Apparently the people who own it need the money and the town's going to give this Schreiber a contract to put up some tacky resort hotel or motel there. A conference center, they call it."

"Schreiber," I said. An image of the man who came to Headlands appeared in my mind. "Black curly hair?"

"How should I know? I've never seen him."

"Who's suing?"

"A local conservation group, along with Cove Village."

"Well, " Mother said, obviously cheered at the thought of a worthy cause, "I can always go and lick envelopes. So can Mushroom and Sam."

Chapter

4

The following Monday, Mrs. Brewster didn't ring her bell until nearly ten o'clock, which meant that I had to hang around the house trying to keep the twins entertained. I'd been reading to them from a big fairy tale book and trying to draw pictures to show them what the story was about. They wanted then to draw pictures themselves, so I found some paper in their room plus an old, mostly dried-up box of water paints, and we were all sitting around happily slopping colors when the buzzer sounded. Getting up, I plugged in the pot.

"If Mom comes down soon can we go out?" Jamie asked, staring towards the ocean.

"All right. What do you want to do?"

"Swim!" the twins said.

"I'll have to ask your mother. The water's still pretty cool."

"Other people swim. Steve and his girl swim. We saw them on Sunday when we were on the cliff."

"He was kissing her," Jennie said. And she made a loud kissing noise with her mouth.

Jamie tried to imitate her, but since he was lacking his front teeth he wasn't quite as successful.

I fought a sense of depression that seemed to be settling over me. "The blonde girl who was with him that Saturday?"

"No. That's Lisa. This's Maria. She's dark."

"He's got lots of girls," Jamie said with satisfaction. "They all like him." He looked at me from under his astonishingly long lashes. "Like you like him."

I achieved a shrug. "He's okay. Of course, he's a townie."

"Sarah likes a townie, Sarah likes a townie," Jennie sang.

"Yeahhhhh!" Jamie yelled.

Mrs. Brewster walked in. She certainly looked different without makeup, I thought. Instead of being large and surrounded by shadows, her gray eyes seemed lost in pink puff, and her face looked full. "Coffee finished?" she said.

I glanced over. The perk was giving one last blurp. "I think so."

Mrs. Brewster sat down. "Bring me a cup, would you, and some orange juice."

Irritated at myself for doing it, I went to the refrigerator and got out the juice container. Then I poured her a glass and managed to spill some of it on her lap as I handed it to her.

"Watch out!" she said. "This was just washed yesterday." She drank thirstily. If I told her she could pour her own coffee I thought she might fire me, and that not only meant I wouldn't have the money at the end of the summer, it also might mean I wouldn't see any more of Steve Novak, who still had her garage to finish. Except, of course, when he came to work on Mother's study, but seeing him around our house would be...different. Inhibiting. I got a cup out of the cupboard and poured coffee into it. Then I poured some for myself and brought the two cups to the table. Mrs. Brewster eyed my cup. "I trust Bowers made enough."

I put my cup down after a swallow. "Do you mind me drinking your coffee, Mrs. Brewster?"

She lowered her cup half finished. "Of course not. I'm sorry!" She put her hand to her head. "I don't know what's the matter with me. I guess it's safest not to say anything around me until I've had my coffee. I apologize. I have an awful—"

"Hangover," Jamie finished.

"How *dare* you!" Mrs. Brewster said.

It was frightening, the rage that appeared on her face. She raised her hand. Jamie got out of his chair so fast it turned over. Mrs. Brewster burst into tears, got up and left the room.

56

Jamie stuck his tongue out at her departing back.

"Jamie!" I said. I was rather sympathetic to the idea of defying parents, but there was something about his small face that shocked me. And it wasn't just the protruding tongue. Curiously, at that moment, and for the first time, I remembered Mushroom's reaction to the house when she and I had stolen in here the previous autumn. "Creepy," she had described it. And she had shivered. I remembered so much better my own sun-filled feeling in the upstairs room, Mrs. Brewster's room, that I had blotted out Mushroom's response.

"What made you do that, Jamie?" I said sharply, picking up his chair. "It wasn't very kind."

"I don't care." But he looked unhappy as he sat down again, as though he didn't know either why he had stuck out his tongue.

"She stinks," Jennie said thoughtfully.

"Jennie! That's not kind either. Why do you say it?"

"It's true," Jennie said. "She smells. Her breath smells."

I opened my mouth to argue when I suddenly realized Jennie was right. On one or two of the occasions when I had seen Mrs. Brewster, her breath did smell of alcohol. And this morning a curious alcoholic odor seemed generally to emanate from her. I didn't know what to say. Finally, out of curiosity, I asked, "Don't you love her? She's your mother."

I looked at Jamie. Slow tears were coming down his cheeks. "She doesn't love us," he said, and burst into tears.

"Oh, Jamie," I said. For the first time an affection for the little boy stirred in me. I'd thought of them as superprvileged spoiled children, but I remembered a psychology text I'd once read—actually it was one of Mushroom's college books that she'd left lying around—stating that there was more than one way of being deprived. Going over, I leaned over his chair and put my arms around him. I was unprepared for the violent hug he gave me, arms in a stranglehold around my neck. I gave him a kiss and a hug and then loosed him. I glanced then at the more reserved Jennie to see how she was taking this. Her big dark eyes were open and she was staring at us.

"I love you too," I said, giving her the same treatment.

She shrugged. "Everybody likes Jamie best."

"No. Not everybody. I like you exactly the same." I didn't know whether I did or not. But it seemed a good thing to say.

"Let's go swim," Jamie said.

"All right. Go put your bathing suits on under your jeans,

57

and bring some dry underpants that you can put on after you come out. Where'll I find the towels?"

"In that cupboard there," Jennie said, as they ran off.

For no particular reason—except that I liked the idea of red-and-blue towels for the beach—I took them from the bottom of the pile of towels in the linen closet. As I pulled them out something at the back went "klunk." When I put my arm back to see what I had knocked over, my hand returned with a vodka bottle. Well, well, I thought, wondering what to do with it. After a minute I put it back where I'd found it.

After a swim and brisk runs up and down the beach I brought the twins home more than ready for lunch. We walked through the two remaining open panels of the garage.

"Hi!" the twins yelled, throwing themselves on Steve.

"Watch the saw," Steve said. "Here—here's putty. Why don't you make a couple of ashtrays."

"Smoking's bad for you."

"Who says?"

"Uncle Harry."

"Well, not everybody agrees with Uncle Harry. Here's the putty. Go do your thing. No, not here, over at that table there. And whoever makes the best ashtray will get a present."

"What's the present, what's the present?" yelled the twins, jumping up and down.

"Wait and see!"

The twins ran off.

"I suppose," Steve said, putting a piece of board down on a long trestle and planing it, "that that would be called bribery and corruption."

"Justifiable," I said, and giggled a little. He glanced up from the heavy tool and smiled. My heart gave a funny jump. Yet a few seconds later I was sad, because I knew he couldn't feel about me the way I felt about him. From what the twins said, he had a lot of girls. And kissed them all. Of course. Yet he said that nice thing about me thinking I was ugly when I wasn't. Maybe that was how he had so many girls— making them feel good.

"What's the matter?"

I had been staring at my sneakers. "Nothing," I said hurriedly, and then looked up. "Who's Uncle Harry?"

He was still looking at me in a puzzled way. But he answered, "Harry Schreiber. The real estate man."

I remembered what Peter had said, and my heart plunged again.

58

"Is it true he's going to build some awful resort?"

"Why awful? Have you seen pictures of what it's going to be like?" He wasn't smiling any more.

"No. But Peter says that that part of the dunes has always been a bird sanctuary."

"Peter who?"

I toyed for a moment with telling him—or allowing him to think—that Peter was a boyfriend. But I knew it wouldn't work.

"Peter Lacey, my brother."

Steve looked sharply. "He's with that conservation outfit, isn't he? The one that's trying to get an injunction against Schreiber."

"Yes."

"Well," Steve said, removing the plane to a nearby table and picking up the panelling, "he's going to have a big fight on his hands. We intend to win. And we're going to."

The "we" made it certain that Steve was in this with Schreiber. "Couldn't he build it somewhere else? I mean, those birds have always used that part of the coast."

"Jobs for people are more important than birds. This is a depressed area. We have high unemployment. Building a resort will not only employ a lot of local people in the actual construction—Schreiber's promised that—but it'll supply a lot of jobs once it's finished. The birds will find some other place."

I stood there while he fitted the panel into the space, trying to think of something to say. I wanted to be on his side, yet all I could think of was the birds, trying to build nests and being driven out by noise and machines and bulldozers, and grass and shrubs and trees being knocked down and plowed under.

"I've finished, I've finished." Jamie ran up, his gap-toothed mouth open, his sturdy arm thrusting before Steve an object that could, with a lot of imagination, be called an ashtray.

"Mine's better." Jennie pushed Jamie out of the way and held up an object that more nearly approached a conventional ashtray.

"They're about equal," Steve said. "I guess I'll have to give each of you a present." And he pulled out of his shirt pocket two sticks of bubble gum. "Okay now. Sculpting time over. Goodbye." And he started picking up his tools and putting them into a bag.

"I'm hungry," Jamie yelled.

59

"Lunchtime," Jennie said, and trotted into the kitchen, chewing her gum.

I hesitated a moment. But I couldn't think of anything to say. Finally, after a minute, in which all I saw was Steve's back, I followed the twins into the kitchen.

That night at dinner I said, "Maybe the resort that Schreiber wants to build will create jobs."

"Who've you been talking to, Steve Novak?" Peter said. "That sounds like his line of argument."

"Yes," I said reluctantly. "He's working on the Brewsters' garage. Is it true?"

"Look, if they want this resort for jobs, all they have to do is agree to build it a couple of miles inland. That sanctuary is only a strip along the coast, and a lot of the birds are coastal birds."

"Maybe if they were a couple of miles in people wouldn't come. Especially if they can't see the ocean."

"Who's side are you on?" Peter asked. And then, "I guess that's a stupid question. You're on the townies' side."

"Come on, Peter. Don't be so holier than thou," Mushroom said. "I'm for the birds, too, but it's not all good and bad. The townies have their point, too. They do need jobs."

Silence. I gave Mushroom a grateful look. "Thanks," I said to her later, as we were going to bed.

"It's okay. But I'm bound to admit, though I stuck up for you, that Peter has a point. The townies are being as stubborn as mules. They could have put the hotel a couple of other places. Farther up the coast, for example. It's just as good for their purposes. But they picked that particular strip to be ornery."

"Why?" I said.

"Ask your buddy, Steve Novak."

I let that go by. "By the way," I said. "Did he and Mother connect over her study?"

"No. She called Williams & Son, and they're coming out to make an estimate."

On the whole I was relieved. I didn't want Steve and my family to get together.

The next morning, Mother astonished me by supporting my having a job with Mrs. Brewster.

It started with Mushroom saying, "Why do you want a job, Sam? Why not put in some R&R time? If you're going to have more surgery in the fall you can use it. And you could also get a little tan."

"Don't mention the word," Mother said. "Can't you see where she's peeling? Last week she went out to get some tan and fell asleep. Boiled lobster was the effect when she came in."

"And now you have freckles," Mushroom said, peering at my face.

"I think they're cute," Mother said. "But it wouldn't hurt to have a modicum of tan as background," she went on. "Just don't fall asleep."

"Take the day off," Mushroom said.

"I can't. I mean if I did, she might get somebody else."

"If you have a job then you have to take it seriously," Mother said.

"Granted," Mushroom said, "but why do you have to have a job, Sam? We're not exactly poverty-stricken."

"I want to save some money." I spoke before I had thought.

"What for?" Both Mother and Mushroom spoke.

"A secret project," I finally answered.

"What kind of a project?" Mother asked. I could see she had suspicions of any secret project I might have.

"If I told you," I finally said, "it wouldn't be a secret. Besides, a person's entitled to have her own secrets." Which was pretty clever of me, because it was a quote from one of Mother's own books.

Mother looked at me intently. "Secret, but not subversive."

I shrugged, refusing to commit myself. I knew perfectly well she would think my idea of leaving school and going to art school would be about the most subversive thing I could think of.

"By the way," Mushroom said. "Isn't there a Brewster son somewhere?"

"Sam's charges are called King," Mother said quickly, so quickly that my attention that had been alerted by Mushroom's question was even more alert after Mother rushed in with her comment about the twins.

"What son?" I asked.

"Oh, Stoddard Brewster had a son by a previous marriage, I believe," Mother said carelessly. "Or so somebody told me."

"How old a son?" Mushroom asked.

"How's Piper?" I asked. Piper was at Harvard and had been Mushroom's boyfriend for about two years.

"We've broken up," Mushroom said.

61

"About nineteen," Mother said.

"Oh." Mushroom sighed. "Well, lotsa luck, Sam. The old man's supposed to have millions. Mom, stop kicking me. What are you trying to tell me?"

"That the Brewster heir is too young for you, but not to mention it too obviously around me." I said. "Mother knows I am allergic to that kind of propaganda."

"Oh. Well, if he's cute and cool who'd need propaganda?"

"Sam would," Mother said. "There are already some cute and cool boys on the beach, but do you think Sam'd go near them?"

"What's the matter, kid?" Mushroom said. "Don't you believe in the opposite sex?"

"I think it's all very boring."

Mushroom stared at me out of her large dark eyes. "If I really believed you meant that, I'd immediately recommend a good psychiatrist."

"I keep telling her," Mother said, "that beauty is in the eye of the beholder, particularly if you're looking in a mirror. She seems convinced that she's Cinderella's older and uglier sister."

"I thought her inferiority complex was about grades."

They were talking about me as though I had left the room. "Why don't you wait a minute?" I said nastily. "I'll leave so you can say whatever you want."

Mother sighed. "Come *on,* darling. We're teasing you. We didn't mean it that way."

"All you need," Mushroom chimed in, "is a little tan and a lot of confidence. I'll tell you what, why don't you sit on our roof this afternoon? I'll supervise the exposure of your fair white body. You may not end up looking like the Scandinavian bombshell, but you'll look a little healthier."

After three more afternoons of Mushroom's saying to me every fifteen minutes, "Okay, now turn over and let me put some stuff on your back (or front)," I did indeed have a mild bronze that showed promise of turning into a modest tan.

I hadn't talked to Steve in all that time. Or, to put it more accurately, he hadn't talked to me. The twins would rush up to him as usual, and he'd hand out bits of putty or wood for them to play with, and I'd stand around for a few minutes to see if he'd say something. But he didn't. And although each time I saw him we were either going into the house or leaving it for the beach, I'd swear to myself that this time

I'd say something—about the weather, the sand, the water, anything—when I actually got to within a couple of feet—it never failed—my tongue would freeze. I didn't even know why myself. I was sure he was terribly angry at my whole family because of Peter and the conservationists (this summer), and because of Mother and her family-planning project (last summer).

The town paper was full of the conservationists' injunction against Schreiber Realty, with articles and editorials on what the building of the resort could mean to the townsfolk and interviews with men who'd been out of jobs for months. There were also periodic jibes about summer people who would close up their luxury townhouses or cooperatives and come here to cool off for a few weeks, which, one editorial went on, seemed to the visitors to entitle them to tell the year-round residents how they should live.

"These yokels aren't to be believed," Peter said one night, rattling the paper. "It isn't as though they didn't have six other places to put their damn hotel. Every ornithologist in the country has told them that this small strip of dune and marsh is about the only place for some of the wildlife in the whole area. If that went, some of the species might well become extinct."

I thought about this one morning, sitting on the beach below Headlands while the twins dug a ditch in which they were burying small pieces of rock. The birds were flying overhead, squawking and swooping around, diving for fish and running over the sand. Was the sanctuary where they nested? I tried to imagine the beach without them, and felt sad. I must have dozed off, because the next thing I remembered was a voice behind me.

"Hi! I'm Charles Brewster."

I turned, half expecting Phoebus Apollo. What I saw was a tall, skinny boy with red hair, a big nose and outsized horn-rim glasses.

"Nancy—my stepmother—said you'd be here," he said.

"I'm Sarah Lacey," I muttered, sitting up. He really was homely, all ears, nose and large hands like paws. And then I felt better because, beside him, I looked as brown as an Indian.

"You're gonna burn," I said. "The way I did about ten days ago."

"I've brought protection." And he shook out a long-sleeved shirt and thrust his arms into it. "And I have this." And he

63

unfolded a battered cloth hat. All of this made him look funnier than ever. Thinking about Mushroom's interest, I wanted to crack up. Piper, her boyfriend, was terrifically good-looking, and for all her brains, Mushroom had once said that although she was aware that intelligence would last longer for a serious relationship, muscles were what turned her on.

"Yeah," Charles said now. "I know I look like a freak. Go ahead and laugh." The funny part was, he didn't sound as though he cared.

"That's not what I was smiling about. I was thinking about...well about something my sister said...." Which didn't make anything any better. Why should I be thinking about something my sister said if it didn't have to do with Charles one way or another? "She was talking about how I didn't tan," I added, and saw that wasn't an improvement, either.

"As you can see, I don't get a tan. But I've learned to live with it." He took a book out of a bag. "You don't mind if I read, do you?" He peered at me out of his thick glasses.

"No, of course not." I still couldn't believe that this was the Brewster heir.

"Do I have a smut on my nose or something?"

"No. Sorry. I didn't mean to stare." I turned my head away. I felt uncomfortable at first, with him sitting there, long pointy nose buried in a book, his stork legs crossed under him, tacky hat lowered over his face. But after a while I had the curious feeling that he had...I fumbled mentally over the words and finally decided the only way to put it was that he had withdrawn his presence—as though all of him that counted was absorbed in his book.

Turning my own back, I stretched out, head towards the water, my chin on my hands. Then I turned my cheek sideways, and drifted off to sleep again. A while later I woke up, glanced at my watch, saw I'd taken a ten-minute snooze, then discovered that the twins were missing. They didn't miss a trick, I thought, scrambling to my feet. But by this time I was up to their games. Walking carelessly, staring out to sea, I made a sudden turn into the big cave to the right, where the water flowed in and out. Then I pounced behind a huge rock, and saw two little figures scuttling out as fast as they could, giggling.

"Okay, kids," I said, and gave chase down the beach. A

few minutes later they let me catch them, mostly, I decided, because it was their lunchtime.

I thought that Charles wasn't aware of any of this, until, as we picked up our towels and buckets and spades, he said, without raising his head, "Bye."

"Bye, Charles," the twins chorused.

He looked up then and smiled. His smile was the one attractive thing about him, I thought. "Keep cool, kids," he said.

Just before we left I glanced over his shoulder to see what he was reading. The title made no sense. *Unseen Spaces*. As I walked up the beach behind the twins I tried to figure out what it meant, but couldn't. Then, as we started to climb up the cut-out steps of the cliff, I became completely absorbed with the thought of Steve, who would be in the garage above.

As usual, the twins rushed at him, and he doled out more putty. Once again I had sworn that I would say something to him and rehearsed it on the way up the cliff. This time I burst out with it before my tongue had time to freeze. "How's the garage going?" I exploded the words as though they were corks from a bottle.

"How does it look?"

I hadn't really noticed how it looked for some days. Now I saw that the side facing the back, away from the beach, was almost finished. Panelling reached to shoulder height. Above that was some kind of opaque glass or plastic.

"It looks fine," I said. The words seemed flat. The silence between us remained. Just to keep going I said, "Most garages don't have windows, do they? I mean, you can't even see light through them."

He bent down and put another strip of wood on his trestle table. "No. So you have to use electric light all the time, day or night. This way you don't. It's expensive, more expensive than plain panelling, but it saves energy, which should appeal to you." There was an ironic note in his voice which rubbed me the wrong way. I felt as though he were making fun of me.

"I'm surprised you care," I said.

He looked at me then. "You mean Archie Bunker types like me don't care about things like the environment or energy." Which was indeed what I had been thinking.

"I didn't call you Archie Bunker."

"True. Your brother was the one who did that."

That was exactly what Peter had said, of course. But I

65

wondered how he knew. Steve's long, narrow blue eyes were watching me. "And in print, too." Going over to where his parka was, he took a piece of newspaper out of one of its pockets and brought it to me.

I looked down. There, circled, was a letter in the Letters column of the newspaper, a letter signed Peter Lacey. It said:

> I never knew that Archie Bunker was a secret writer of editorials for the *Leominster Bugle*. But I should have known. His style is on a par with his politics, which are on a par with—but I must restrain myself. This is, I am told, a family newspaper, dedicated to promoting what these and other destroyers of the natural world call "The American Way of Life." Whoever wrote that editorial probably fought in Vietnam and took great pleasure in defoliating that country along with massacring its women and children.
>
> Peter Lacey

It was Peter's style, all right. I always thought he was privately sorry that he was about ten or twelve years too young for the Vietnam War, because he would have revelled in the anti-war movement. He had been fourteen years old at the time of the Kent State shootings and ever since his world had been divided into good guys and bad guys on that model.

"He didn't say anything about you," I said finally, knowing it was a cop-out.

"He didn't name me, if that's what you mean. But it's pretty obvious what he thinks. It's also pretty snobbish ... and patronizing. But you probably feel the same way."

"Since you haven't bothered to ask me, you have no right to say that. But, just for the record, yes, I do think the same way. I like to watch the birds on the beach. And if you and your friends have your way, there won't be any more." I was near tears, which made me madder than ever. "Why can't you put the hotel two miles inland?"

"As your brother suggested at the last public meeting."

"Well, why can't you?"

"And how many people do you think would stay there if they can't even see the ocean? A resort like that is either on

66

the ocean or right away from it near some other advantage—
like a lake. Or in the mountains. But two miles from the sea,
and blocked from seeing it by the ridge that lines the marsh!
Come on...."

"You really don't care about the birds...and things."

"Do you?"

"Of course I do."

"Okay—name me four kinds of birds that nest in that
particular place."

I stared at him. The truth was, I hardly knew a sparrow
from an eagle. "That's not the point," I said. "You don't have
to be an...an ornithologist to want to keep a bird sanctuary.
It's the principle. People like you—"

"Principle! People like me?" He threw down the piece of
wood he was holding, which clattered on the trestle table and
then seemed to bounce off. Steve walked towards me. It was
weird, but it took all my determination not to back away.
There was something in his face that was frightening.

"Let me tell you about people like me, Miss Lacey. Your
father teaches political science, doesn't he? So you should
know ordinary history. Do you know why they had the draft
riots in New York back in the 1860s?"

I'd heard of them, of course. But I hadn't a clue as to what
had caused them. Of course, even I knew the Civil War was
to stop slavery, so that like World War II it was a good war.
"That was different," I said. "That war was—"

"The riots, Miss Lacey, happened because people like you,
young men like your brother, were fine when it came to
principle—the slaves must be freed and all that stuff—but
when it came to the actual fighting, all those principled and
rich aristocrats paid poor Irishmen to go and get maimed and
killed on the battlefields in their place. That's why the Irish
rioted. The draft was about as equal then as it was during
the Vietnam War. Only this time the draft board did the
dirty work for them. The college students got deferred. People
like my brother fought the war."

"And killed Vietnamese women."

For a minute I thought he'd murder me.

"My brother got killed, Miss Lacey. Dragging a soldier
back to safety. He'd brought two back already. But a Cong
got him on the third. He got a Medal of Honor, which we
have at home instead of him. And later, because he wasn't
around to help out as we planned, I had to leave college early
to support the family. So you want to know why that resort

is going up where it is? Because all the people who didn't fight the goddam war, who marched safely behind banners saying "Hell no, we won't go," supported by all their teachers and parents, these are the same people who come here and tell us how to run the town and take our beaches and act as though they belong to some superbreed. That's why we're going to build that hotel where we want to build it, where it will give us jobs and security. This is one war we're going to win. And you can tell that to your brother." And he picked up his parka and stalked off.

That evening at dinner Peter was excited at the progress of Operation Wildlife, as the conservation group called itself. "We'll just lie down in front of the bulldozers," he said.

"I thought the court has put a temporary stop on the whole thing, anyway," Father said. "To be followed by a hearing."

"Yeah, but there's a rumor that a bunch of toughs from the town are going to go ahead."

"You sound as though somebody had just given you a thousand bucks," Mushroom said.

"And I thought you were going to visit Bob Barrett at Southampton," Mother put in.

"Slight change of plan. Bob's coming here."

"Thanks for telling me," Mother said drily. "When can we expect the honor?"

"Next week. But he'll be staying with Bruce."

"That's good. I don't mean to be inhospitable, but I'm starting a new book, so it's going to be every man—and woman—for himself, kitchenwise, except for dinner, and we can all take turns for that." She glanced at me. "By the way, Sam, your father and I are going to a cocktail party tomorrow night at the Thornes'. Why don't you come along? There'll be some young people there."

"And what about me?" Mushroom said indignantly.

"You can come, too, if you want," Mother said. "It's just that ... well, I want Sam to have a better chance at meeting people."

"It isn't as though there weren't several thousand on the beach every day," Peter said.

"Try not to be so dense," Mother said sharply.

"What about?" Peter looked at me, frowning.

"For a fairly bright lad ..." Father started.

"Mother thinks I have trouble with the opposite sex," I

said in a loud voice. I was furious. I hated everybody talking about me as though I were some kind of lab beetle in a bottle.

"Oh," Peter said. "I see. Well, why don't you come and help us out at conservation headquarters, Sam? Lots of kids are going to be in on that."

"Your friend Steve might not like that," Mushroom said.

"So what!" Peter commented.

"Don't be ridiculous," Mother said. "And stop teasing her. Sam, you and Mushroom are almost the same size. I bet she might let you wear that dark pink dress if you asked her nicely."

"I have plenty of dresses of my own," I said, knowing it was a lie. What with one thing and another I hadn't had time to do much shopping.

"Well do me no favors," Mushroom said. "I might want to wear it myself, anyway."

But when the following evening came and I put on a blue dress that was left over from the previous summer, it was both too short and too big around the middle. I was staring at myself glumly in the glass on top of the bureau in my room when Mother walked in. She had on white pants and a blazer and looked terrific. "My God!" she said. "You can't wear that. I hadn't realized you'd grown, Sam. Although," she said, sighing, "I did know you'd lost weight. With the whole world trying to get thinner, you must be in a minority of about point-oh-oh-five that needs to gain. I don't know whether I envy you or hate you for it. But that settles one thing, you're going to try Mushroom's dress."

"Look, Mom, I don't really want to go. I'd sooner stay here. If it will make you any happier I'll go out on the beach." What I really wanted to do was to take a beach towel, my notebook and pen, and sit in a particular angle of rock I'd marked for myself. Another rock beside it shielded my hiding place from the house, and the rock jutted in a way that supported my back and also hid me from the main part of the beach. But until the rest of the family disappeared out of sight, I'd sit there in the middle of the open beach in my jeans and shirt and look as though I'd stopped being afraid of being there—which was Mother's ambition.

"No, I want you to go. And I've made up my mind about that pink dress."

"I don't think Mushroom wants me to wear it," I said. "You heard her. She might want to wear it herself."

"In that case, I can't imagine why she's in her new lavender one waiting downstairs for the rest of us to get started. Take that off. I'll be back right away."

I thought about digging in my heels. I hated parties. But Mother seemed set on my going, and since I wanted to keep working, I might as well oblige her in this. In a few seconds she was back with Mushroom's dusty-pink dress over her arm.

I had to admit once I had it on that Mother's eye for what would look good on whom had, once more, proved infallible. It was exactly the right shade of pink, neither too light nor too deep. When I had it on, my skin looked tan, my hair seemed a richer chestnut and my eyes looked a smoky green. "The fact that it's big around the middle is all to the good," Mother said. "Because this belt goes around and it will show off your tiny waist." Mother was right about that, too.

I stared at myself in the mirror.

"Come to my room," Mother said. "There's a long mirror there and you can see yourself better."

When I stood in front of the mirror I felt a curious little thrust of surprise and pleasure. At school I'd worn the school uniform of navy-blue skirt and white blouse. At home I'd mostly worn jeans, especially since I'd hurt my leg, and before that I'd barely been a teenager. I didn't know I could look . . . well . . . almost pretty.

"You see?" Mother said.

"You're right. Thanks."

When I went downstairs Mushroom turned around.

"Look at Sam," Mother said.

Mushroom whistled. Then said, "I see what you mean. Sam, that really looks smashing. Better on you than on me."

"Thanks. Are you sure you don't mind me wearing it?"

"Considering the way you look, absolutely not. Go out and slay 'em, kid."

Father and Peter came into the living room from the front porch. "Isn't that Mushroom's dress?" Father said. He looked as he always did, handsome and distinguished in his dark pants and seersucker jacket. Peter was in jeans and shirt.

"Yes," Mushroom said. "But Sam is borrowing it for tonight."

Father looked at me out of his light blue eyes and didn't say anything. There was a slight silence.

"Doesn't she look terrific?" Mother said.

"Very nice," Father said. "Are you ready? Okay. Let's go. Can we drop you?" he asked Peter.

"No, I'm going to catch a lift," Peter said. "See you later."

The Thornes lived between Cove Harbor Village and Leominster, the town. Mr. Thorne was a former colleague of Father's who had retired and who wrote books on American history. They lived in their house all year round, but kept an apartment in New York which they used during the winter for going to plays and concerts.

"Why do you think there're going to be young people there?" I asked Mother. Somehow Father's coolness towards my wearing Mushroom's dress had dimmed my enthusiasm a little. I wondered if it really looked as well as I thought it did, or as Mother and Mushroom told me it did, or whether they were just giving me some propaganda to build me up.

"Because Laura said her niece and nephew are staying with them, her younger brother's children. Apparently the Hodges' parents—that's the name of the niece and nephew—are in Africa or India or somewhere else inaccessible. Anyway, they decided not to take their children, who've come to spend part of the summer with the Thornes."

"I wonder if I've seen them on the beach," I said nervously.

"Now don't get a complex about them before you even get there," Mushroom said. "Just remember, you look terrific."

The trouble with that statement, although I knew she meant to be kind, was that I felt as though she were feeding me a line, rather than telling me the truth. Father, who was driving, looked at me in the rear-view mirror. "You do look pretty, Sarah. I meant to say that before."

"Thanks," I said, and smiled at him in the little mirror, but he was looking out the window to see if there was a car coming before he crossed the intersection. I tried hard to feel pretty.

The niece and nephew turned out to be the blond boy and girl whom I'd seen that day I fell asleep on the beach. The girl was the one called Linda who'd read aloud from my book. Like Mother, she had on pants and a blazer.

"I don't think you've met, have you?" Mrs. Thorne said. She was a vague, pretty woman, a lot older than Mother.

"Sure," Linda said. "That day on the beach. What did you say your name was?"

"Sarah Lacey." I wished there were some pill I could swallow that would make me disappear.

"Hello, Sarah. My name's Linda Hodge." She grinned. "Written any good books lately?"

The blond boy who was like her gave a snort. "Don't pay any attention to her," he said. "She likes to tease."

"Yes, Linda's a great tease." Mrs. Thorne sounded even more vague. "Well, Linda, I leave the young people in your charge." And she went off, trailing voile print.

"Do you want to go outside and have a drink, or do you want to come upstairs and have a joint?" Linda said cheerfully.

I'd never had any pot and was dying to try. But I didn't want to do it with Linda. "I think I'll have a drink." I said, as casually as I could.

"Suits me. I think I'll join the small pot party upstairs. Go straight through the front room to the porch. The bar's outside."

"I'll take you out," her brother said. "By the way, my name's Jim."

"Hi." I said.

"Look," Jim said, as we were about to cross the porch, "I see somebody I have to talk to for a minute. The bar's straight ahead. You can't miss it. I'll be with you in a minute."

I waited to see where he'd go when he jumped off the porch onto the grass and went off to the right. Somehow I knew even before I saw that it was the dark girl and the boy named Bruce who had come from around the house. The girl had a long wraparound flowered skirt and a turquoise tank top. She looked chic, cool and devastatingly attractive. Both Jim and Bruce, like my father, had on dark pants and seersucker jackets.

I hesitated. I didn't want to go down the porch steps and onto the lawn by myself, let alone walk up to the bar and ask for a glass of wine or a Coke. What I wanted to do was go home. The pink dress might look terrific, but it felt like exactly the wrong thing to wear. I couldn't figure out whether I was over- or underdressed. Either way, it added up to being wrong.

Moving back into the shadow of the porch, I saw Mother, who was talking to three or four people near the bar, looking around, and I knew she was trying to see where I was. In a minute her eyes lit on Jim and the other two, both of whom had drinks in their hands. As I watched, I saw Jim lift the girl's drink out of her hand and take a swallow. She gave him a mock tap on the cheek, and he bent over and kissed her. I moved farther back into the shadow of the porch where it went around the side of the house. From where I was standing, I could see the sea, far away and shining under the twilight sky. The house was up on a slight hill, which was the reason the sea was visible from where I stood. Far to my right, behind the three still standing, was a grove of trees, whispering and shushing in the breeze that had blown up since we had arrived. I knew that to my left, along the coast and out of sight, was the disputed strip of land that the town wanted for its resort and that Peter, my brother, was preparing to protect with protest marches. I wondered how many miles it was away, and how the Thornes felt about it. And as I wondered I also knew that I was deliberately keeping my mind off the unpleasant fact that I wanted desperately not to be at this party.

A sense of isolation that was all too familiar settled down on me. I had felt it abroad, where I had always been a foreigner. I had felt it in New York, where, in a curious way, I was still a foreigner. I was used to it. I didn't even mind it, as long as I could be by myself and do what I wanted to do. But to be trapped in a party where there was nobody I wanted to talk to, and where nobody wanted to talk to me, had all the makings of a nightmare.

"Hello," a man's voice—a voice I knew well—said behind me.

I whirled around and stepped onto the side porch. There, half sitting on the porch rail, was Steve Novak. On the floor beside him was a drink.

"Steve!" I said. And as I did so knew that here was one person who, for all our fights, never made me feel like a foreigner. "Oh, Steve," I said again. "I'm so glad to see you."

Without thinking, I stepped forward. I was dimly aware that he had moved away from the porch rail. Then his arms were around me and mine were around his neck and he was kissing me the way I had secretly imagined he would.

Chapter

5

It was the most wonderful feeling I had ever had in my life and I wanted it never to stop. In a minute he took his mouth away and pulled my head onto his chest. Through his chest I could feel and hear his heart going *pock*eta *pock*eta *pock*eta, *thump*ity *thump*ity *thump*ity, and I knew my heart was doing the same.

"I didn't mean that to happen," he said after a minute. He sounded out of breath.

I looked up at him. "Are you sorry?"

"No. My God, no! Maybe I ought to be, but I'm not." He put his hands behind my head and bent his own. Then his mouth was on mine again. His lips were warm and gentle. He slid his face over and kissed me somewhere in front of my ear and folded his arms even tighter around me.

We stood there for a while like that, then I said, "Why didn't you mean this to happen?"

"Maybe because we're not the best possible combination going around. And besides, as you told me, you're only seventeen."

"But you said your sister, the one who is planning to be married, is only seventeen." I could feel myself blushing in the dark. Would he think that was somehow some kind of a

75

hint that he should propose? Why did I say such stupid things? "I didn't mean—"

"That's all right." His hand came up to my cheek. "I know what you meant." Then he stepped back. We both turned and leaned over the railing. It was getting dark. Mr. Thorne was going around turning on little lights that were hung from branches of the trees. We stood there for a minute, not looking at each other. Then Steve reached across and took my hand. And we held hands, standing there, not saying anything.

But then we heard voices coming around the side of the house. Steve's hand closed over mine, and we stepped back across the porch into the shadows of the house.

"Look, Jim," I heard Linda's voice. "Nobody said you were responsible for her."

"No." I recognized the voice of the boy who had said he'd be back in a minute. "But I have a feeling that she doesn't know anybody. And we're the only young people here."

"Well, there're plenty of middle-aged types who like sweet young things in pink dresses, and since I can't see her around, one of them is probably chucking her under the chin somewhere. Relax. We have plans, and I don't think she'd fit in with them."

Steve must have heard me catch my breath when I realized they were talking about me. He squeezed my hand harder, but by mutual consent we stayed right where we were. Then their voices got fainter. I saw a match flare, and in its light the tight curls in a halo around Linda's head. There were four of them, so the other two would be the dark boy Bruce, from the beach, and the dark girl in the long flowered skirt.

When they had gone Steve said in an even voice, "I'd have enjoyed knocking a few teeth down some throats, but it would have been a dead giveaway about how I felt about you, and I'm not sure how you feel about that."

I wasn't sure, either. In one way I'd have liked to climb onto the roof and make a public announcement about how I felt about Steve. But Steve was a townie, and the more I thought about that, the more I could imagine some of the feedback—especially from my family.

"Yes," I said doubtfully. Then, "That sounds funny, doesn't it? Worrying about that."

Now that the others had gone, we moved out of the shadow back to the half-light of the porch rail. Steve sat on it and took my hand again. The light there was dim, but having come from the dark, I could see more clearly than I had before.

76

Unlike the other men, Steve had on a dark suit and tie. Also, of course, he didn't have on his helmet, and his light brown hair was curly and much shorter than the others'. It was funny, I thought, he was near my brother's age; they were both tall, both well built, although Steve had slightly broader shoulders, and both had light hair. Yet the difference between them was overwhelming. So overwhelming, in fact, that I wondered what Steve was doing here at this party, among people like the Thornes and their friends.

"Do you know the Thornes?" I said.

"Sure. Why? Did you think I was party crashing?"

"No. Of course not. It's just..." It was another of my stupid statements that popped out before I had thought how it would sound.

"Just that I'm not like the other guests—a townie," Steve said drily. "All right." He squeezed my hand. "I shouldn't tease you. I did some work for Mr. Thorne and he invited me."

I was quiet, thinking that however tactless I'd been to say so, Steve was as different from the others as though he'd come from another planet.

"What are you thinking about?" Steve asked. He still had my hand in his and was looking at the palm as though he were a gypsy about to read it.

I hesitated, not wanting to sound tactless again.

"Don't be afraid."

"Well...how—how different you are from...well, Peter, my brother, or...or the other kids on the beach." Even though he told me not to be afraid, to myself I sounded as though I were trying to put him down. "I didn't mean it that way...at least, I did, but it didn't sound the way I meant it to."

"It's all right. It's true. And you're not like any girl I've known. The others—well, if I haven't known them most of my life, they've come from the town or know people I know, or some of my cousins, or something like that." He picked up my hand and kissed it on the palm, and everything I was thinking about what other people thought or were like went out of my head. I put my hands on either side of his face and bent down towards him and kissed him. Then I was out of breath and I could hear him breathing. He stood up suddenly and pulled my face up towards his.

"Sam!" I heard Mother's voice float out. "Sam, where are you?"

Steve took his mouth away and held my head against his

77

chest as he had before. I'm not short, but I hadn't realized how tall he was.

"How tall are you?" I whispered.

"Six-one," he whispered back.

"Sam!" Mother said, her voice a little nearer.

"That's Mrs. Lacey, isn't it?" Steve said, in a low voice.

"Yes," I whispered back. "And that's me she's calling."

"Is that what they call you? Sam?"

"Yes. My brother Peter called me that when I was a baby, and it stuck."

After a minute's silence Steve said, "I like Sarah better. It suits you. Very New England." We stood there for a minute, our arms around each other. It was funny, I thought. I'd always hated the name Sarah, and the reason I'd hated it was because it sounded very New England, as in "New England spinster." But when Steve said that that was the reason he liked it, everything about the name felt and sounded different.

"Sam!" This time Mother sounded much nearer—in fact, just around the bench in the porch.

Steve whispered, "I'll go around the other side of the porch. If...when you've finished talking to your mother, and if you want, come there. I'll wait about fifteen minutes. If you can't make it—I'll see you tomorrow." And he was gone.

I stood there, feeling disoriented and let down. The question occurred to me, What if Mother had seen us together? All I had to do was to let myself think about that a minute, and I could hear voices in my mind—Father's, Peter's, Mushroom's, even Mother's. Maybe especially Mother's. My insides seemed to sink a little. In some way they'd ruin it. Whatever Steve and I had, they'd spoil. I knew that with a kind of overwhelming conviction. "I'm here, Mom," I called out.

"Why on earth didn't you answer me?" She sounded irritated.

"I just came out here. I was inside."

"What were you doing in there?"

"Going to the bathroom."

"Oh." Mother came around the porch and up the steps. "You ought to be with the other young people, Sam. That's why I insisted on your coming."

"They're...well, they're all old friends, Mom. They don't know me. You know how it is." Always before when Mother had brought up this topic—how I ought to be with the young people—feelings of inferiority had washed right over me. I knew people—young people—wouldn't notice me because there wasn't anything about me worth noticing. At least not to them. But now I didn't care. It didn't matter. Steve liked me. He hadn't said so, but I knew it, just as I knew he preferred me to any of the other summer girls on the beach. It was a golden secret, like a great bubble of sun inside me. "I don't mind," I said, and wanted to laugh. Mother had no idea how much I didn't mind.

"Well, I do mind," Mother said, exasperated. "If you go around expecting everybody to reject you—they'll reject you. Then you'll feel even more rejected and the whole cycle will begin again. It's the self-fulfilling prophecy," she added gloomily.

"I don't feel rejected," I said, and knew that for the first time in my life it was true.

"I'm extremely glad to hear that," Mother said, sounding as though she didn't believe a word of it.

My problem at the moment was how to get Mother away from the porch and to leave me alone so that I could go and be with Steve.

"Where's Dad?" I asked.

"Talking to Matthew Thorne and a couple of the other men about the injunction. Which reminds me. Sam, I want you to go into the village headquarters and volunteer to help—lick stamps, fold papers, anything."

Of course I knew why. Most of the summer young people would be there doing the same thing. "I have my job, Mother," I said hoping she would remember Charles Brewster.

"I've been thinking about that. And I really believe Mushroom is right. You ought to be getting all the rest and relaxation you can before the fall. Thanks to Mushroom you have the beginnings of a tan, and you're certainly slender." She sighed. "As someone once said, you can't be too thin or too rich—certainly not too thin anyway. Anyway, I think working on your social life is more important than making pocket money."

"I met Charles Brewster the other day," I said carelessly.

"Oh? What's he like? Attractive?"

I thought about Charles's ginger hair, long nose and stork legs. "In an...an intellectual sort of way."

"He doesn't seem to be at the party here," Mother said. "I somehow thought there'd be more young people here, but the Hodge kids only invited Bruce Thompkin and Mary Larson."

79

"Where's Mushroom?"

"Politicking for the injunction with that young Congressman over there."

I followed where Mother seemed to indicate. Sure enough, there was Mushroom, her lavender dress looking almost gray in the lanternlight, talking to a tall dark man of about forty.

At that moment, the four young people came through some trees at the side and made for a car parked in the driveway. While Mother and I watched, they got in, the car started and they drove off.

"Well," Mother said. "There goes your excuse for being here. I might as well collect your father and we can go home and have some dinner."

"Oh, there's no need to go yet," I said, desperate to get rid of Mother so that I could go and find Steve. He'd said fifteen minutes, but I was afraid it was much more. "Why don't you go and have another drink or something? I have to go in the house a minute, but I'll come out and go and talk to Mushroom."

"What do you have to go in the house for? Everyone's out here. I don't want you to do your old trick of getting some book and going off into a corner."

"Anybody would think you weren't a writer." I tried to laugh. "That's terrible advice for an author to give."

"You know very well what I mean, Sam."

I was silent for a minute, trying to will Mother to go. "I'll just go in the house for a minute," I said. "Then I'll come out and go home with you and Father."

"What—"

"I have to go to the bathroom," I almost shouted, and then could have killed myself, remembering that I'd just finished using that excuse.

"Are you sick or something, Sam? You've just been."

"You know how it is when you drink a lot."

"What have you been drinking?"

"I hadn't been drinking anything, but I said, "Wine."

"Well, don't overdo it. All right, go into the house, but if you're not out in ten minutes I'm coming to get you. You've just got to stop hiding yourself."

"Sometimes you sound like you think being a social success is the only thing in the world that matters. For somebody as liberated as you, always writing books about psychological health, I think that sounds pretty funny." I was quite sure that Steve would have gone by now, and that infuriated me.

"I don't think being—as you call it—a social success is the

only thing in the world, Sam. But I've worked with women—middle aged women—who've spent their entire lives thinking they were unattractive to the opposite sex, and because they believed they were, they were. When they finally saw that it was all in their own heads they'd wasted about twenty years. I don't want that to happen to you. And healthy relationships are extremely important."

"See you later," I said, opening the screen door to the hall and going into the house. I knew this was an argument that could go on all night, and I wanted to see Steve before he'd gone.

I thought at first he had. After waiting long enough to hear Mother's footsteps going down the porch steps into the back garden, I pulled open the screen door to the back of the porch and slipped out. There was nobody there. Tiptoeing, I went to the edge of the porch. "Steve!" I whispered.

"I'm down here."

I saw him then, standing on the back lawn in the shade of one of the big spruces. Running down the porch steps, I ran straight into his arms.

After a minute he pulled away and said, "I heard you talking to your mother. You're going to have to go home with her and your father in a minute. I'll talk to you tomorrow morning. I have a lot of paperwork to do and have to get back to my office."

"I didn't know you had an office."

"Sure. I'm in business for myself. I have to keep accounts."

"Tonight?" I said. "You have to do them tonight?"

"I don't have to," Steve said slowly. "I only came to the party because I thought it would be good for my business. I didn't know you and your family were coming."

"If you'd known, you wouldn't have come?"

He didn't say anything for a minute. He had his hands cupped around mine and was holding them against his chest. "We have to do some thinking," he said. "This could get out of hand."

I didn't want to hear that. "It'll be all right," I said.

He kissed me gently, then not so gently. Then he let go of my hands and put his arms around me and I put mine around him. His body was hard with muscle and it felt wonderful against mine.

I lay awake nearly all night, deliberately reliving every kiss, every feel of Steve's arms around me, every touch of his

81

mouth. I felt so different I was afraid that once we got into the house and turned on the lights Mother and Father would know immediately I had changed in some powerful way, that something terrific had happened. But all Mother said was, "You must have got more burn today, Sam. Your cheeks are red."

It wasn't burn. It wasn't even excitement, or at least not all excitement. Some of it was the scratching of Steve's beard. I'd never slid my cheek against a man's before, and I found it thrilling. That night, as I lay in the dark, going over everything, kiss by kiss, I suddenly knew why people slept together.

I'd always known about the facts of life. Mother had given me my first book on sex education when I was about ten and was furious when she discovered I hadn't finished it. Nobody'd ever stopped me from seeing any movies I'd wanted to see or reading books I wanted to read. It was just that I could never imagine what sex *felt* like. Maybe it was because I'd lived abroad so long and never really known many American kids who'd had experience and talked about things like that. Once Mushroom said, only half kidding, that I was retarded about such matters, and I'd always been pretty sure that she and Mother both thought my whole sex life was terribly backward. To be truthful, I'd always thought it was a huge fuss about not very much and that the only reason people made such a thing about it was because it had once been like forbidden fruit.

But now I knew different. As I thought about how Steve looked and felt I could feel my heart getting more and more rapid. I'll see him in the morning, I thought, and a wonderful, quivery feeling went down the backs of my legs.

Of course, as luck would have it, Mrs. Brewster was up early that morning, ringing for me to plug in her coffee, so the twins and I got to the beach before Steve arrived. The time on the beach crawled by, but finally lunchtime arrived and we scampered up the side of the cliff on our way to peanut butter and jelly sandwiches. I knew Steve was there before we even got to the almost-finished garage, because I could hear him hammering. I imagined the moment when we would look at each other, and my heart started to beat rapidly again.

But it didn't go like that at all. He didn't look at me. When the twins flung themselves on him, he gave them pieces of putty and then, after showing them how to model it into

82

something that looked more or less like a bear, starting gathering up his tools.

"I'm hungry," Jennie screamed, flinging herself up the stairs into the kitchen.

"Me, too," her brother shouted, pushing in front of her.

I stood, waiting for Steve to turn around. But he didn't. After putting the putty in a box, he leaned over the trestle table and started checking some plan pinned on it.

"Come on, Sarah!" the twins yelled.

With the twins yelling my name, he had to know I was there. Was he mad at me? Had I done something?

I was still standing at the foot of the short steps that let up to the kitchen.

"Sarah, what's the matter? Why don't you come and fix lunch? I'm hungry." The usually more placid Jamie had come down the stairs and was tugging at my T-shirt.

"All right, Jamie," I said. "In just a minute."

It was weird. I would never have believed it possible after the previous evening. But my tongue was having its old trouble—not functioning. I had to do something, say something. But I stood like a stump, paralyzed in tongue and everything else. Finally I got my mouth open and was about to say Steve's name when a man walked through the half-open front door of the garage, the one facing away from the sea.

"Steve?" he said. He was standing with the light at his back, so all I saw at first was a round aureole of curls. Then he came farther into the garage and noticed me for the first time. "Oh, hello!" And there was a flash of teeth.

Steve turned. "Oh, hi, Harry."

"Ready to inspect the site?"

"Sure." Steve unpinned the chart on the table and started rolling it up. He still didn't look at me.

Once, years before, when I had been a new girl at a school, I had said or done something that had run up against a school taboo or violated a local code of some kind. No one spoke to me for about a week. All the girls (it was a girls' school) looked around me or over me or through me. After a few hours of this I felt as though I weren't there: that I was really just a lump of air that everybody could see through. At the end of a week I got sick and managed to stay out for a month. Something must have happened while I had been away, or perhaps they'd forgotten about whatever it was that made them mad. Anyway, when I got back, everybody was quite ordinary, and treated me the way they'd treat any new girl.

I hadn't thought about that in a long time, but I thought about it now, because bad as it had been before, it was far worse now. Steve had held me and kissed me, yet he was acting as though I were a piece of air.

"Steve!" I finally blurted out.

"Yes?" He said. He still didn't look at me.

And then Mrs. Brewster came down the kitchen steps into the garage.

"The twins are yelling for lunch, Sarah. Hadn't you better go and fix it?" Without waiting for my answer she looked over at Harry Schreiber. "Hello, Harry. Are we ready?"

"Ready and waiting."

Mrs. Brewster whipped around to where I was standing. "I thought I told you—"

That was as far as she got. I ran up the steps into the kitchen and slammed the door.

"We've been waiting and waiting," Jennie said.

"We're hungry. Mom said you ought to be in here feeding us," Jamie chimed in.

"What's the matter, Sarah?" Jennifer asked in a gentle voice. It undid me. I drew in a breath, and felt the tears start out of my eyes. "Nothing," I said, and, with the tears coming down my face, went over to the counter and began getting out bread, peanut butter and jelly.

"Please don't cry, Sarah," Jennie said, coming over and taking my hand. "We love you, don't we, Jamie?"

"Yeth," Jamie said, and took the other hand.

"Thank you," I said, sniffed, and leaned down and hugged them. "I love you, too." Then I stood up, blew my nose and finished making the sandwiches. "Next week we're going to branch into tuna fish," I said. "Enough is enough with this peanut butter and jelly."

That afternoon I managed to get myself, my notebook and my pen out to my hidey hole behind the big rock. I achieved this while Mother and Mushroom were upstairs, and Father and Peter in the garage. I also took my journal out, and starting my writing with that. I've been keeping a journal most of my life, and it's one of the reasons why I think I'm going to be a writer as well as illustrator. Many of the pages are drawings of places I've been or faces I remember. But there's a lot of writing in it, too—how I feel about things as well as what's happened. Nobody knows about the journal because I've always kept it a secret.

I wrote for a while in the journal and then went on to my book—or tried to. But writing for the book just wouldn't come. I couldn't squeeze a word out, and as I sat there it seemed crazy that I ever thought I could get into art school or write and draw anything that would sell. Which left me...which left me nowhere, with nothing.

I suddenly decided I didn't want to sit out there by myself any longer. A lot of people must have come out on the beach, because although I couldn't see them from where I sat (and they couldn't see me, which was the real idea for my being there), I could hear them. But if I went inside Mother might not have gone back to her studio for the afternoon and she'd be sure to have an idea of something for me to do. Or worse, she'd take one look at me and know that something was horribly the matter. I'd been afraid that she'd notice at lunch. But I got there late, and she and Father were in the midst of some argument, which was also involving Mushroom and Peter, so other than passing me some chicken and potato salad, nobody noticed me.

I drew my knees up to my chin and thought about an item I'd read once in *The New York Times*: that the suicide rate for teenagers was higher than for any other age category. That was something else that suddenly seemed more understandable.

"Mind if I sit here?"

I only heard the question when I realized, dimly, that this was the second time somebody had asked it. I looked up. There, grungy hat and all, was Charles Brewster.

I moved my feet a little. "Help yourself."

Actually, there wasn't a lot of room. I was sitting on a small kidney-shaped segment of sand between the tall rocks behind that protected me from being seen, and the flatter rocks in front, which ran straight on to the sea. Unless somebody swam in from the sea at a certain angle, no one would know anyone was sitting in this narrow strip.

"How did you know I was here?" I asked, making more room. I was a little annoyed at having my personal hideaway discovered. On the other hand, Charles's being there was taking my mind off suicide.

"I didn't." He folded his long skinny legs and sat down. Except where it was burned an angry red, his skin was pink, and there was almost no hair on his chest. "I thought I'd found the perfect retreat yesterday morning when I came

85

across this. So finding you came as a shock—no insult intended."

"Same here," I said. "I didn't know anybody else knew about this place."

Charles, who was in the process of opening a large book, paused. "Do you want me to go away? On the principle of first come first served, you've staked out your claim to this this afternoon."

It occurred to me that I couldn't imagine Peter or Mushroom asking that. "No, it's okay. You can stay."

"Thanks." He opened his book, pointed his long nose into it, and in a minute or two might as well not have been there. It was a trick I knew, because I could—sometimes—do it myself. But not as well, I thought, drawing lines in the sand. If people were around, no matter how hard I tried to concentrate, I'd know they were there.

"You can really forget people are around you when you read, can't you?" I asked, breaking my own rule about not interrupting somebody who was trying to read.

"Ummm," he said.

I sighed. I knew he didn't want to talk. I opened the notebook with the story again and stared at it. I had reached the point of my fantasy where my hero, Tristram, was entering the cave of the giant who knew where the princess was. The giant always ate everyone and everything that came into his cave. So Tristram was being extremely brave to go in at all. But his love for the princess was so great that there was no obstacle he would not try to overcome, no danger he would not take...

It was only when a drop splashed onto the page that I realized that (a) I was crying, and (b) I was crying because I was thinking about Steve. Not only would he not go in and tackle the giant on my behalf, he wouldn't even speak to me, not even enough to tell me what was wrong. I started searching around my jeans pockets for a handkerchief or tissue.

"You might as well have this."

I looked up. Charles was holding out a crumpled tissue.

"It's clean," he said. "It just looks like that because it's been in my pocket for a while."

"Thanks." I blew my nose and wiped my cheeks.

"Is there anything I can do?"

I shook my head.

"Is it anything you want to talk about?"

I shook my head.

"Okay."

I could feel him withdraw into his book.

"Thanks, anyway," I said.

"De nada."

"What does that mean?"

"It means it's okay. Forget it."

I stared at my book for a while, not really seeing the words I'd written, listening to the sea slapping gently against the rocks, and the seagulls screaming as they wheeled above. After a while I looked up at them. Some were white and some were gray and white and some were almost black. Of all birds I was probably more familiar with them than I was with any others—except, of course, for the ever-present droves of New York pigeons. But gulls were all over the Hudson River and Riverside Park, and bobbed, with folded wings, on the surface of the reservoir in Central Park, looking like cork models of themselves. Staring now out to sea, I could see them on the ruffled surface, swaying and dipping with the waves. But the gulls weren't the only birds riding the water. There were smaller, darker birds, and darker, larger ones, as well as larger colored ones. Then there were the birds running along the wet sand where the tide had just pulled away. Sitting where I was, I could barely see them, but if I strained up and looked beyond the lump of rock, I could catch a glimpse of the tiny legs, running like black needles. I'd never paid much attention to birds before, and I knew I was doing so now for a reason. The reason was the two-mile strip of marshy dune where Steve and his friends wanted to build their resort, and which Peter and the conservationists wanted to keep for the birds. "Name me four kinds of birds that nest there," he'd said. And I hadn't been able to think of any....

Why wouldn't he speak to me? One answer that kept coming back was that he was sorry the previous night had happened and he probably thought I was running after him, making a fool of myself.... I wished I could curl up in a small ball like a wood louse and disappear forever. Then suddenly, out of nowhere, rage, like a hugh mushroom-shaped cloud soared out of me. How *dare* he not speak to me, that son of a sea cook (a favorite expression of my grandmother's, who would not use the usual swear words). He might think he was not speaking to me, but he'd learn sooner or later that I was not speaking to him...that I would never speak to him, no matter how much he wanted me to speak to him, how much he *yearned* for me to speak to him....

A fantasy formed inside my head: There was Steve, his face strained and worried, his tin hat in his hand, waiting at the kitchen door of Headlands for me to notice him. He could see me through the glass panel of the door (which in my imagination would have recently replaced the solid wood), but I had closed and locked the door, and even though he knocked and knocked I would pay no attention, and went right on, making the twins' peanut butter and jelly sandwiches and talking to them as though he weren't outside. . . . But obviously I did not have complete charge of my imagination, because all of a sudden, Steve put on his tin hat, punched a hole in the glass with his fist, opened the door, charged in and took me in his arms, covering my face with kisses and begging to be forgiven. . . .

"I said, it's raining," a voice said beside me.

"What?" I looked up and promptly got splattered in the face with drops that were also pouring all over my book and making the ink run.

"Oh!" I said, and got up.

Charles, looking more storklike than ever, was busy unfolding a thin slicker and putting his head through the hole in the center. It wasn't a jacket but a kind of a long poncho. Tucking his book under his arm he set out at a trot over the rocks in the opposite direction to our houses. Since he seemed to be headed towards the shell of an old boat house, I followed him.

"It's just a shower," Charles said, sitting on a cracked bench in the boat house and putting his feet on the opposite side.

I sat down beside him, since there was no other place to sit. The shack was just barely big enough for a dinghy, and was open at both ends. It had long ago been abandoned, and the sea slopped around beneath the cracked floorboards, but it at least kept off the rain.

"Charles," I said after a minute. "You know that marshy strip of sand there's such a furor about?"

"You mean the one where the town wants to build a resort?"

"Yes. That's the one."

"Sure. Why?"

"Well . . . my brother, Peter, is working with the conservationists to get an injunction passed so the town can't build the hotel there. He says that some ornithologists claim that if that's built there are a lot of birds that will become extinct. Do you think that's true?"

"I don't know. Probably. Why?"

"Well . . . Steve, Steve Novak—do you know him?"

"He's building our garage."

"Well, when I was telling him that, about the birds, I mean, he said to me that the hotel would mean jobs for the people in the town, where there was a lot of unemployment, and anyway, could I name four kinds of birds that nested there, and I couldn't."

"He's got a point. A lot of people who're carrying 'Save Our Wildlife' posters probably don't know a sparrow from a vulture and don't care. They're just out to demonstrate their moral superiority over the hardhats."

"You mean you think Steve's right?" I said. And just mentioning his name made my heart start beating faster.

"Not necessarily. Steve and his gang are showing their share of pigheadedness, too. They don't like the summer colony, and this is their way of showing it."

I remembered what Steve had said about his brother and the Vietnam War. After a sort of silence Charles said, "What's all this got to do with you?"

"Nothing," I said quickly. "I'm just interested. Can't a person be interested?"

"Yes. But you've certainly been behaving in a funny way. First you cry, then you look grim, then you go off into some kind of never-never land, staring straight ahead and not even hearing me when I speak to you. And every time you mention Steve's name you get red—even your nose. Are you in love with him or something?"

"Of course not," I said. My throat ached and I wanted to burst into tears.

"You don't have to jump down my throat. I don't care whether you are or not. It was just a friendly scientific inquiry."

"It's stopped raining," I said. "I'm going back to the house."

"Mom said you were going to come to the Wildlife headquarters to volunteer," Peter said the next morning at breakfast.

"I'd love to." I was thinking of Steve. "As soon as I've finished baby-sitting."

"I think I should warn you it's not that glamorous. I mean, it's mostly scut work."

"I don't care what kind of work it is. I'll be *glad* to do it."

"I'm only saying that because a few of the beach kids turned up expecting to march or demonstrate in front of TV cameras, and it's nothing like that."

"I'm not doing it for that reason," I said, knowing that Peter had no idea just how true that was.

"Yeah, well, the other reason some of the kids have shown up for a while is to develop relationships."

"If that's Sam's reason, I can see Mother's fine hand in it," Mushroom said.

"It's not that either." I was beginning to feel annoyed. "Maybe you don't want any volunteers."

"Now hold on, I didn't say that. We can use all the help we can get. But it's the licking envelopes, typing address labels and writing letters kind of help that none of the boys are capable of doing and most of the girls look on as sexist."

"You sound bitter," Mushroom said mildly.

"I want people who're committed, not just a bunch of elitist dilettantes."

"My, my," Mushroom said. "On with the revolution."

"By the way," I put in, mostly because I couldn't stop myself, "can you name four kinds of birds that nest in the marshy dune area?"

Peter looked up at me, his light blue eyes boring into me. "Sure. About six types of ducks, a couple of kinds of geese, sandpipers, dowitchers, the great black-backed gull, the eider duck, teals. Why?"

"Just curious," I said.

"Well, we have a pamphlet on the birds there, which I would be happy to have you read. In fact, you ought to read it."

"Okay."

Peter was giving me another of his piercing looks. "I thought you were buddies with Steve Novak and his bulldozer boys?"

The rage was still warming my blood and giving me support. But it couldn't protect me altogether from the pang that squeezed my heart when Peter said Steve's name.

"Well you thought wrong," I said emphatically.

"Okay. You don't have to yell about it."

Mushroom was looking at me now. "You've only eaten half your muffin. Aren't you hungry?"

"Starved," I said, picking up the other half, which managed to look both dried-out and oily. Somehow I got it down.

90

I was determined to get the twins out on the beach before Steve arrived so he wouldn't have any chance of not speaking to me, but luck was against me this time. Mrs. Brewster didn't ring her bell until nearly ten, and I could hear Steve using his hammer and saw and other tools long before that.

"Your mother didn't ring before I got here?" I asked around twenty to ten.

"No." Jamie, who liked cutting out things, was moving a huge pair of scissors around an ad in the local paper.

"Where's Mrs. Bowers, by the way? I haven't seen her in days."

"She got mad and quit," Jennie said. "I wish Mom'd hurry up. I wanna get to the beach." She was sitting, chin cupped in both hands, swinging her legs violently.

"You know we'll have to wait," I said. "As soon as your mother has had her first cup of coffee, we can go."

"Let me cut some," Jennie said, plunging her arm across the table. I knew disaster would occur very rapidly unless I intervened. Jennie's patience was short-spanned, and the scissors were as big as her forearm.

"I'll show you how to make a battleship," I said, trying frantically to remember the folding technique that had been taught me by some English nanny.

"Okay, show me."

It was strange, I thought, how much trouble I'd had telling the twins apart and how little I had now. Half a dozen differences that I couldn't see before had become obvious: Jennie's face was broader, Jamie's thinner; Jennie's eyes were a lighter hazel than Jamie's; Jamie's new front teeth were beginning to grow in, but were still much shorter than Jennie's, and so on.

"Still, you're very alike," I mused aloud.

"Exactly," Jennie said with such passion that I looked up. "We're *exactly* alike."

"No we're not," Jamie murmured very quietly.

Interesting, I thought. But it was not a subject that would contribute, at the moment at least, to peace and harmony. "Why did Mrs. Bowers quit?" I asked.

"She and Mom had a fight," Jamie said, looking at his cutout with great admiration. For some reason a canning company had elected to use a leopard as an advertising symbol, and the big cat was stretched in a leap across the entire page.

*　　*　　*

"That's a beautiful leopard, Jamie," I said, trying not to think about the hammering going on in the garage. At every sound I could see Steve's tanned arm, with its muscle bulging below the rolled-up khaki shirt.

"It's not a leopard. It's a jaguar."

"Sorry."

"It's all right. Not everybody can tell the difference. Steve told me about it."

I decided not to say anything. At that moment the bell rang.

"Let me plug it in," Jennie yelled, and ran towards the pot.

"You know how to do it?"

"Of course I know. It's *easy*. *Anybody* knows that."

"Just making sure." I watched her push the plug into a double socket, which in turn was affixed to an outlet on the wall above the counter. "Now come back and finish your battleship." The paper ship was finished just as Mrs. Brewster's steps sounded from the hall. "See?" I said to Jennie, getting up, placing the ship on the table. "These are the funnels." I got a tall mug out of the china cupboard and the pitcher of milk from the refrigerator. The sugar was already out, but I made certain the spoon was there. As I had discovered, sometimes Mrs. Brewster took everything in her coffee and sometimes she took nothing.

"That doesn't look like a battleship." Jennie said indignantly, after a moment of staring at our creation. Jamie was pushing his jaguar across the table, making ferocious noises.

"Of course it does," I said automatically. My old nanny had told me it was a battleship, so it was a battleship.

"Good morning," Mrs. Brewster said, sweeping in and turning towards the coffee pot. I had only a glimpse of her face before she turned, and I decided that the sooner I got the twins out the better.

"Come on, Jennie and Jamie. We're going to the beach."

Mrs. Brewster's voice split the air. "It's the *only* thing I ask you to do for me in return for the considerable money I pay you. You might at least put the plug in right. Now I'm going to have to wait until it's perked, and all because you don't do your job properly!"

Mrs. Brewster still had the mug in her hand as she whipped around and stared at me out of her poached-egg eyes. For a beautiful woman she was a mess. As a matter of fact, she didn't look beautiful. She wasn't even pretty. Her face was puffy, her skin was blotched and her hair looked like straw.

I registered this as I wondered what on earth had happened to the plug Jennie had put into the socket.

"What happened?" I said finally. "Why didn't it start perking?"

"Because you didn't put the plug into the socket. One prong went into the socket and the other slid above it. As you would have noticed if you'd bothered to look. Why you can't—"

"Don't talk to me that way," I said. "I'm not your maid."

A little hand crept up into mine. I looked down and saw Jennie's eyes fixed on mine, and squeezed her hand. "I'm sorry about the plug. I guess I wasn't noticing."

At that moment the coffee pot, as though offering some kind of apology, produced a timid "plop-plop." Obviously Mrs. Brewster had remedied the mistake.

"All I ask you to do," Mrs. Brewster started, her voice higher and louder than before, "is to plug in the coffee pot. Surely that one thing..." It was like a stuck record. Perhaps my anger was already there, waiting to find some excuse to fizz out. The hammering outside stopped. I heard a wooden panel being scraped along the trestle table, and had no trouble imagining Steve going over his careful workman's job, his long, rather flat-ended fingers running gently along the surface, to see if it had been planed correctly. The image, which I had seen in reality several times, was so vivid that in the midst of all the hullabaloo over the coffee, it occurred to me that Steve had both love and respect for the wood he was working on. Which was odd in somebody who wanted to put up a resort on a bird sanctuary....

"And furthermore..." Mrs. Brewster was saying, her face screwed up in irritation.

"My job was to take care of the twins, Mrs. Brewster," I said, my anger coming to my help. If there was anything I didn't need, I thought, it was one more person in the world telling me how incompetent, unsuccessful and/or unattractive I was.

"I've asked you—"

"Is your hangover bothering you?" I said, and wondered where the words had come from.

"How dare you!" She moved suddenly towards me. "How dare you accuse me—"

But I had had enough. On some level I knew all her noise and bluster was just bluff. But it didn't prevent me from resenting it. I was fond of the twins, but enough was enough. Mother was right. There was no reason I had to put up with it.

I let go of Jennie's hand and picked my parka off the chair. "Goodbye," I said. "Maybe you should hire somebody who knows more about coffee pots."

I didn't bother with the kitchen door. Steve was obviously sorry that he and I had had that evening of the Thorne party, which meant that he wouldn't even look up, let alone speak to me. He and Mrs. Brewster were a fitting pair, and I wanted nothing more to do with either of them. Marching down the hall, I opened the main door facing the back and slammed it behind me. I was halfway home before I thought about the money I now would not have.

Chapter

6

As that thought struck me I slowed, and as I slowed, another enemy pounced: as vivid as a movie in my head was the memory of Steve kissing me—his tenderness, the way his mouth felt against mine, the hard surface of his body. He liked me, I thought, I know he liked me....

But if I let myself think that, I knew, I'd go back...I'd go back and ask him what was the matter. Which would be like pleading, which I couldn't, mustn't do....There had to be other jobs. I decided the moment had come for me to apply for that volunteer work Mother was talking about, or maybe even find another job posted in the village. Changing directions, I took the path to the village.

The village of Cove Harbor is really just a street and a little pier that runs out into a bay, with the coast curving gently out on each side. It was never a big harbor, and even at the height of its activity had only a small fishing fleet. Now there were not too many fishing boats, but a few still used the pier, and it was also used by the summer people who had boats.

I glanced at the post-office window as I passed, hoping to see some more cards advertising jobs taped to the glass. There weren't any, so, after pausing, I went in and asked Mrs. Hobbes if she knew of any other job openings.

"No. There aren't any." She eyed me. "What happened to baby-sitting for the King twins?"

"I quit," I said briefly.

She looked at me, her glasses glinting. "I thought you might."

"Why? Why did you think I might?"

"Never mind. I just thought you might." And she folded her mouth down in a way that indicated she wasn't going to discuss it any more. I knew, because I'd seen her do it before, so I didn't intend to lower myself to ask her. Shrugging, I left the store and wandered along the path that led to the village street, passing the phone booth I had used when I first called Mrs. Brewster. Which made me think of the twins. How would they manage? Who would look after them? "It's not my business," I said aloud, and turned into the village street. A good place to ask would be the office of the local newspaper.

Mr. Haggerty was the editor of the *Cove Harbor Herald,* a weekly that consisted mostly of ads and gossip and long articles about gulls, other birds, fish, bird watching and sailing. I'd met Mr. Haggerty a couple of times, simply because it was impossible not to meet people if you were at the Harbor for longer than a week.

"Hi, Sarah. I hear you're looking after the King twins. How's it going?"

"I quit," I said. "Do you know of any other jobs? I really want one."

He looked at me from under his shaggy brows. "Saving up for something?"

"Yes."

"Umm. You're already the fifth young person who's asked me. You planning to be a journalism major like the others?"

"No, I—" But I hadn't discussed my plans with anybody, and I was afraid that if I breathed a word to anyone at all, somehow it would get back to Mother. "It's for a private project."

"Okay. Can you type?"

"Yes. I took it in school."

"How much money do you want?"

"I was getting three dollars an hour for a six-hour day."

"How many days?"

"Six."

"That's more than a hundred, a hundred and eight dollars a week. I can't pay you that. Maybe seventy-five."

"You mean for a job here?"

"Sure. Isn't that why you came here?"

"No. I was just looking for a job and I thought you might know if there was one."

"Well, Marty down at the pier wants somebody to clean fish. Interested?"

I shivered a little. "No."

"Joe McWhirter wants somebody to work on his boat, but it means going out for a week at a time, and if you ask me, he won't take a girl, no matter what any feminists say."

I shook my head. "No. I don't want that either. How come there's a job here? Did somebody quit on you, or did you fire them?"

"Neither. My former assistant got a job he'd been angling for on the town daily, so I couldn't blame him for preferring that. You didn't tell me whether or not you wanted it."

"Why aren't you giving it to the five journalism majors?" I asked suspiciously.

"Because they all want to write the lead articles, the front pages and the editorials, which I write myself, and I'm not about to give it up for anybody. So far, all you've said is you want a job. And that tilts me in your favor. I'd let you do a little reporting. But there's room for only one writer on this here paper, and it's me."

Mr. Haggerty, who had taken over the *Cove Harbor Herald* after an early retirement due to ill health, had once been managing editor of one of the nation's great newspapers, so his imitation of a crusty New England editor was a local joke—one in which he shared.

"That's not the kind of writing I want to do," I said, and then nearly bit my tongue with irritation.

"Oh, ho! So you are interested in writing. What kind?"

"Sort of fantasy science fiction. But nobody knows about it, Mr. Haggerty. I mean no one. Not even Mother. Especially—" I stopped, because it sounded peculiar.

"Especially not Mother, eh? All right. I can keep a confidence. I can only use you a few hours a day, say three. So when do you want to start?"

"I could start now." I wouldn't be making anywhere near as much as Mrs. Brewster was paying me, I thought, and wondered suddenly if I'd been a little too sensitive. Then I remembered the strident voice and pinched, angry face. Unfortunately, I also remembered the twins, which produced, again, a twinge. Well, I rationalized, pushing the thought away, they were undoubtedly used to dealing with her. I also pushed away a sudden image of their faces, still and watchful, in their mother's presence.

"Okay," Mr. Haggerty said. "Over there is a collection of the last three months' editions—twelve or so papers. I want you to go through them and write down all the names of the people mentioned. Then look them up in that card-file drawer over there. If the name is already on a card, add the date of the new mention, and the page, and about three words saying what it is about. You'll see the style of thing if you look at the cards. If it's a new name, then make a new card."

I went over to the pile of papers stacked at the end of a table. It sounded pretty boring, but I told myself it was really no worse than thinking up games for the twins and trying to pretend that all those bodies on the beach weren't full of tan and beauty and glamour and all the good things of life. And at least I wouldn't be trying to ignore the fact that Steve Novak was ignoring me. Anything would be better than being around him and having him not talk to me, I thought, pulling a chair up to the table.

Actually, it wasn't so bad. After working my way through half of one paper I said, "Can I circle the names, so that when I want to check back for spelling or something I can find them more easily?"

"Sure. Go ahead. And when you've finished with a paper, put it on the pile on that shelf there." He pointed to a dusty collection of papers on a bottom shelf of the bookshelves lining most of the room.

After a while I got interested in reading the little paper. I hadn't paid much attention to it before, even though it came to the house—after all, I'd only seen it for the two weeks of the previous year I'd been there, and only two this year. But the articles about the birds were interesting.

"I guess you're against the resort being built, aren't you?" I said after a while.

Mr. Haggerty'd been pecking away on a typewriter, but he stopped.

"You mean my pieces sound biased?"

"No. You haven't even mentioned the resort, but you like birds, don't you? You sound like you do."

"Oh yes, you can certainly say I like birds. In fact, I like them better than almost anything, except working on a newspaper. But I've tried to be careful about not climbing onto some sort of moral high horse about the resort."

"You sound like Steve Novak," I muttered.

He looked at me, his gray-black eyebrows drawn together. "You know Steve well?"

"Not *well*," I said, emphasizing the last word. But my heart started its pocketa-pocketa beat. Thumpity thumpity. I stared down at the page, trying to concentrate on an account of Mr. Cunningham's new dinghy.

"Pretty good-looking fellow, isn't he?" Mr. Haggerty said.

I didn't say anything.

"I'm talking about Steve Novak."

"He's okay—if you like the type." I drawled out the words, trying to sound casual.

"Most of the girls hereabouts, not to mention the town, do like the type. I wouldn't say he suffers from lack of female attention."

"I bet." I wished I'd left the subject of birds alone. Everything seemed to lead to Steve.

"Well, I'll tell you about the resort." Mr. Haggerty sat back in his swivel chair and put his hands behind his head. "Taken on its face I'm against it—at least I'm against its being built on that strip of marsh and dune. But the brouhaha that's being cooked up about it is going to make everything worse. Like the Civil War. Did you ever make any particular study of the Civil War?"

"No. Not especially. But I thought it was a good war to stop slavery."

"In that sense, it was. But it was a war that needn't have happened at all if the self-righteous on both sides hadn't decided that the other side needed to be punished."

"Steve said—" I started before I remembered that I was trying not to think about him.

"Steve said what?" Mr. Haggerty asked after a moment.

I circled a name in black crayon. "Steve said that the townies feel that the summer people come up here, thinking they're superior, and try to tell the people in the town what to do with their lives. Like Mother, I guess, and her family-planning project." I couldn't help giggling a little. "When she got the ripe tomato on her blue suit."

"Yes, the townies do think that, and with some reason." He paused. "The guy who puts out the paper twenty miles up the coast is devoting his entire sheet to a crusade against the resort. The daily in the town is on the side of the builders.

I've decided—on a day-to-day basis—not to mention it. What I would really like to see happen is that Schreiber and Co. would choose another site, which they might do, if one were found, and if everybody would stop shouting. And the towns-people do desperately need another industry of some sort to supply jobs. It's no use snarling about jobs going to the sun belt, and then not doing everything possible to create them here."

"Where else could a resort like that be built?"

"There is one obvious place."

"Where?"

He looked at me for a minute, then unclasped his hands. "Well, like your project, I'm going to keep that private for the moment."

"Okay."

It took me about three and a half hours to finish that job, and by the time I was through I was hungry. I got up. "I'm going to get some lunch."

Mr. Haggerty, who was busy editing his own piece, nodded.

It suddenly occurred to me that one of the advantages of looking after the twins was that I got lunch. Never having bought lunch in the village I wondered how much it was.

As I passed his desk, Mr. Haggerty said, "Think you'll like the job?"

"Sure." I looked at him. "You're positive it pays at least seventy-five?"

"That's the guaranteed minimum. Why?"

"I'll try to find something to bring in some more, to make it up to what I was getting."

"Well, I'll tell you. You seemed to be doing a good job. I'll throw in lunch. Here's a couple of bucks." And he handed me two dollar bills.

I took them and put them in my pocket. "Thanks."

"And there's no rule that says you have to buy your lunch. You can always pocket the money and go home." He winked at me.

I grinned back. "That's true."

"Here's today's paper, hot off the press. You can read it while you eat."

"Thanks. When do you want me back?"

"Drop by tomorrow. I may have something for you then. But just don't get any ideas about taking over the paper for a crusade. I'm speaking from experience."

"You mean about the sanctuary. I thought papers were
100

supposed to take political stands. That's what my father says."

"That's his opinion, and he's entitled to it. But not every argument is the forces of light against the forces of dark—in other words, it's not all *Star Wars*."

I grinned. "Gotcha."

I walked home with the paper, determined to save the two dollars and add it to the art-school kitty. When I got to the house it was long after everybody's lunch hour, and the place was empty. But I could hear Mother's electric typewriter clacking away in her studio, and wondered if she'd had the wall mended yet. But the tree had fallen on the other side, so I couldn't see from the kitchen window.

I made myself a tuna-fish sandwich, then sat down with it and a soda and read the paper. Mr. Haggerty was right. Other than mentioning that the conservationists had opened a volunteer office, there was not a single mention of the big argument. Turning over to the back page, I examined the classified ads, on the off chance that somebody wanted something done for pay. There was nothing in the way of a job. My eyes kept going back to a single ad under the heading "Home Needed": "Stray dog, slightly lame from accident, needs home. Am leaving area and cannot keep. Will have to have destroyed if no home found. Call 289-6023."

It was the "slightly lame from accident" that reached out and pulled me. Besides, I'd always wanted a dog, but my father didn't like pets in the house, so we'd never had any. Don't make waves, I told myself. Life would be difficult enough in the fall, when I refused to go back to school and went instead to art school. I didn't need to make him mad now. I turned the paper over and decided I might as well go through and circle all the names for when I'd have to enter them on cards.

Then I nearly jumped out of my skin when a voice I knew only too well said from the kitchen door, "Where's Mrs. Lacey?"

Steve Novak was standing there, one arm braced against the opposite side of the door, his tin hat on aslant, his tool bag slung by a strap over his shoulder.

"I expect she's in her studio," I said, putting as much ice as possible into my voice.

"Then would you tell her I'm here?"

I looked down and slowly turned a page of the newspaper. Without looking up I said, "Is she expecting you?"

101

"Yes, she is. Furthermore, she asked me to come over here."

"My," I said, not making a move. "That must have been one of the few times she managed to catch you on the telephone."

"She left a message on the tape, which will give you an idea of how much she wanted to see me. So maybe you'd better go and tell her I'm here."

I still didn't look up. "You can go yourself. The studio is around the house to the right there. You can hardly miss it."

I heard him step down the two steps leading up to the kitchen door and wished there were something more I could do to punish him. So—according to Mr. Haggerty, he had plenty of female attention, did he? Well I certainly wasn't going to add to it. What galled me was that I'd fallen for his long meaningful looks and potent charm. If I'd been a raving sex bomb it might have been different, but it was pretty obvious now he was just seeing if he could collect a trophy from one of the summer colony. Maybe Barbara or Linda had turned him down.... The more I thought, the madder I got. It was like worrying a sore tooth. I finished the last of my soda and got up, deciding I might as well go and volunteer with the conservationists. It would show Steve Novak exactly what I thought of him and his opinions, and it might even help the birds. As I rinsed off my plate I wondered if Steve'd be working on Mother's studio. I'd barely turned off the faucet when I heard their voices approaching the kitchen door.

"...all right," Mother was saying, "so you'll work on it during the afternoons from two until five. How long do you think it'll take you to rebuild the old wall and make a new extension?"

"Three weeks to a month. It's not that complicated. That is, unless it pours rain. That'd slow it down."

"And I suppose I'll have to find somewhere else to work in the afternoons. Well, it can't be helped, although I wish you could do it full time and get it done twice as fast."

"I have other commitments."

"Well, if you'd just called me sooner—"

"This is the best I can do, Mrs. Lacey. Now if you want to try someone else..."

"As you know very well, Mr. Novak, I did try the Williams Company, but their prices are out of sight, so it's Hobson's choice. There really should be more competition up here, certainly from the consumer's point of view."

I could hear the beginnings of another crusade. If there was anything Mother hated it was being caught in a take-it-or-leave-it situation.

"If there was more industry up here, and more jobs, there would probably be more services to choose from. Unfortunately, for us, that's not the way it is."

I couldn't resist glancing over my shoulder. If there were cats or dogs, I thought, their fur would be standing upright. Steve's jaw was looking very square and his eyes glinty under the shadow of the tin hat. Mother had on her face what all of us in the family called her "forward march" expression. But I could almost see her weighing the pleasure of treating Steve Novak to a lecture on the importance of the environment and conservation as against the importance of getting on with her book in her studio.

"Tomorrow afternoon, then," she finally said, and stepped into the kitchen.

"At two," Steve said, getting in the last word.

I watched him walk across the grass and up the path to where his van was parked.

"Pigheaded hardhat," Mother muttered under her breath. "I'd give a lot to find somebody else to do the work."

Just before Steve got in the van he turned around and looked. I pretended I was staring past his shoulder at the sea.

"Sam, I'm going to ask you to let me use your room in the afternoons. I can put my portable on my lap and sit on the bed. I'd sit down here, except that this kitchen can become Grand Central Station and I need privacy. If you're going to be working up at Headlands and doing volunteer work in the afternoon, you won't need it."

For some reason I decided not to bring Mother up to date on my job situation. An idea slithered past my mind. "Okay," I said. Then I picked up the paper and walked back to the village, past the newspaper office, to the volunteer place. Outside the volunteer place was another phone booth.

It was odd, I thought, dialing, how a number you'd read only once would stay in your mind. When a woman's voice answered I said, "Are you the one who put the ad in the paper about the stray dog?"

"Yes." The woman sounded as though she were relieved. "I had that ad in last week's paper and got not one call. I'd just about given up and was going to take Jill to the pound this afternoon. It's really too bad, she's a sweet dog."

"Why can't you take her with you?" I asked in a panic. I hadn't planned on being faced with such a decision so soon.

"Because my husband and I are going for a year to England, and they won't let you in there with a pet. They take it away and put it in quarantine for six months. It's to keep out rabies, which seems to be sweeping the continent, so I suppose I can't blame them. But we don't want to do that with Jill. The trouble is her back leg isn't in too good shape and nobody seems to want her. When can you come by?"

I played for time. "Where are you?"

"Fourth house from the north side of the bay. The name Palmer is on the mailbox outside."

"You're part of the summer colony."

"Not exactly. We're not natives, but we've been living in the village. We came up early, which is how we found Jill. Somebody had run over her, and at the time we didn't know that John—my husband—was going to get this fellowship, we took her to the vet and then brought her home. But I wonder now if it wouldn't have been kinder just to let her die while she was still half-conscious."

I pushed away the thought of Jill's lameness and did some hasty reappraisal. There was really no use in getting Mother and Father mad at me. For a minute I'd thought I'd trade off having a dog against being cooperative about Mother using my room. But I could use that trade-off better in the Battle to Come, as I was beginning to think of the upcoming struggle. And I might have to go back to the hospital in the autumn anyway. Who would take care of the dog then?"

"I tell you," I said. "I think I'd better not get any more involved with this, since your time is so short. You'd better try and find somebody else—"

"So we'll see you in about half an hour," she said, cutting straight across me. "Bye." And she hung up.

Of all the high-handed things! I thought indignantly. She could just hold her breath until I showed up. I thought this all the way back up to the village and along the other side of the bay, furious at myself for letting her get away with such a ploy. But, just before she'd hung up, I'd heard what I thought sounded like a whimper, and I couldn't quite get it out of my mind.

Twenty-five minutes later I got to the house. It was, as they said, the fourth from the end along the village area of the bay. Many of the other houses looked empty. So did the fourth house. Sitting tied to a tree in front was the most depressed-looking mongrel I'd ever seen in my life, an expression on the small, pointed muzzle that made it plain the wretched animal had learned always to expect the worst.

"Jill?" I said, halfheartedly.

She stood up. The tail lifted and moved a bit from side to side. I went over. She backed. I stood and held out my hand. After a minute she came up and sniffed. She looked like a small, black border collie with white markings on her chest and paws. Then she got up on her hind legs, front paws on my stomach, and looked up at me. On her collar was a note: "If you really can't keep her, then you'd better take her to the pound. I can't. We've left for New York." There was no signature.

I was so angry at the woman's manipulating me into doing her dirty work I could hardly think. Just to make sure she'd gone, I went to the house and rang the bell. When no one answered, I rattled the doorknob and peered into the window.

"It's no use, she's gone," a voice said.

A large woman was coming out of the house next door, a basket full of clothes under her arm.

"She had no right to go off and leave me with having to do something about this dog."

"You can leave her there, if you want. I'll call the pound to come and pick her up."

"Don't you want her?"

"With four children and three cats? No. No more animals."

"What about any of the other neighbors?"

"They don't want her either. Mrs. Palmer even tried to bribe some of them." She spread a sheet out onto the line and then peered at me between that and the pillowcase next to it. "Don't worry about her. She's not your responsibility. And, anyway, she's an ugly dog. Who'd want her?"

I stared down at the ugly dog, and had the weird feeling that she'd understood what the woman had said. Her black head seemed to be bent toward the ground. I went over to the tree and untied the rope. "Come on, Jill. We're going home."

Jill and I looked at each other for a minute. I could feel the woman watching me, and turned back towards her. "I don't think she's at all ugly," I said.

Twenty minutes later I walked into the conservation volunteer office. Peter was sitting on a table, talking to a couple of boys I'd seen on the beach. Linda and Barbara were both there, at another table. Linda was on the phone and Barbara was stuffing envelopes.

"Hi," I said, when Peter looked up. "I've come to volunteer."

"Where'd you get the mutt?"

"Somebody's left her. She doesn't have a home."

"You know what Dad says about animals in the house. He has a thing about it."

"He's not going to make me get rid of Jill."

"That's not a dog's name."

"It is now. You told me you needed help. What do you want me to do?"

"Is the dog housebroken?"

"I don't know." I hadn't even thought about that.

"If he makes a mess, you can clean it up."

"She. She's a she. And I'll clean it up."

"Do you type?"

"Yes."

"Good. Nobody else seems to. Here're are some form letters with a list of names. I want you to start typing up the letters, addressing them to these names."

For anyone who'd learned touch-typing, which I had, it was easy to copy a form letter without thinking what the words meant. I'd typed for half an hour before I started taking in what the letter was saying, which was something about the needs of the environment as opposed to the materialistic greed of special interests. As the sense finally came to me my fingers slowed and I really read the letter.

> Dear——:
>
> We are writing to you as a member of the community who is known to be deeply concerned about the environment. A conglomerate of special interests, whose sole motive is profit, is trying to buy a wildlife sanctuary—one of the last of this area—in order to build a resort on the land, and is using every loophole and trick to prevent our attempt to stop them. The conglomerate has a squad of powerful lawyers. All we have is a small volunteer force, little money and a profound need for all the help we can get. . . .

The forces of light against the forces of dark, Mr. Haggerty had said. *Star Wars*.

"What's the matter? Why have you stopped?" Peter was looking over my shoulder.

"I thought the townies wanted the resort because they have high unemployment here and it would supply jobs."

"Whose side are you on?"

"On the side of the sanctuary, Peter. But it's not . . . it's not the forces of dark against the forces of light."

"That sounds like you're quoting somebody. Who is it? Steve Novak?"

Pocketa-pocketa, my heart went. Why was everything so complicated? "No, not Steve. But what if it was? He has a right to his point of view."

"If you think that way, then we can do without your help," Peter said. "We need people who're going to be one hundred percent on our side."

"Hey, come on, Peter," one of the boys from the table spoke up. "It's not all that black and white. I told you that letter came on awfully strong. And we wouldn't be in such a hot position if we had to back up some of those claims you've made in court. I mean, we don't know it's a conglomerate."

"It's a perfectly safe bet. You can be sure of that."

"We really don't need that much more help, Peter," Linda said. "Better that we have a few people who are really for the conservationists than half a dozen halfhearts."

"Yeah. You're right."

I shrugged and got to my feet. "Come on, Jill," I said, furious, but trying not to show it.

Mushroom suddenly walked in with the Congressman. "Where are you going, Sam?"

"I've just been told my services are not needed by Peter."

"Are you on your high horse again?" Mushroom looked at Peter.

"Excuse me," I said, and walked out.

Jill and I played on the beach before we got home. I found a stick and threw it, and Jill, lame leg and all, suddenly seemed to remember that she was born to herd sheep, because she tried to round up a bunch of sparrows. Then when she got the stick in her teeth, she hurled herself around in a big circle, came back and laid it at my feet. When I got home Mother was in the kitchen fixing dinner.

107

"Hi," she said, then stared at Jill, who still had the stick in her teeth and was looking really happy for the first time since I'd known her. Jill put the stick at my feet and waved her tail.

"What's that?" Mother said.

"That's my dog. Her name is Jill."

"You know your father—"

I stamped my foot and saw Jill go under the kitchen table. "It's my dog and I'm going to keep her. And I'm tired of being put down by everybody and never having what I want considered and being insulted in public by Peter and ignored by—" I stopped just in time, and then burst into tears. "Come on, Jill," I said. "I'm sorry I scared you." And I ran upstairs to my room, hearing Jill following cloppity-clop behind. Once she was inside I closed the door and sat on my bed. Jill jumped up beside me. I put my arms around her and gave myself up to feeling sorry for myself. As I looked around the room I felt even sorrier. Mother had moved her typing table, typewriter, paper, a stack of books and a portable file in my room, leaving about one square foot of space between the bed and all the rest.

In a minute there was a knock on the door.

"Who is it?"

"Me," Mother said.

"All right. You can come in."

Mother came in and sat down. "Who put you down?"

"Peter." And I told her about it.

Mother sighed. "He gets that from me, I'm afraid. I have a tendency to think in all black and white terms. It's very useful if you plan to go into politics. Seeing both sides of a problem may be just and fair, but it doesn't get things done."

"He's my brother and he put me down in front of other people. I wouldn't do that to him."

"Peter is not a people person. He sees issues, not people." She hesitated. "I'll talk to him."

"Don't bother. I don't want to work for his crummy outfit, anyway."

"About Jill," Mother said tentatively.

"Look, you can use my room and fill it up with your stuff while your study is being built, but only if you stick up for me and Jill to Father."

"Well after all, Sam, it *is* my house."

"And mine, too. Don't you remember? You said in that

108

book that put you on so many television shows that children's rooms should be as sacro...sacro..."

"Sacrosanct," Mother said gloomily. "So I did. All right. We'll have this *quid pro quo*. I'll use your room, and I'll try and help you with Jill. Although I must say," she started to say, getting to her feet, "if she had a pedigree a mile long it would help."

"I thought Father was all power to the people. Well, in the dog world she's people."

"Sam, if you go through life expecting people to be logical and consistent you're in for a lot of heartache."

I never knew what Mother said to Father, but by the time Jill and I went down to dinner, it was all fixed. Father looked at Jill and simply said, "A very democratic dog," and went back to his magazine.

We were finishing dinner when the phone rang. Mushroom went to answer it. "It's for you," she said to me, coming back. "He sounds very nice. I meant to ask his name, but forgot."

My heart gave a huge leap. Steve? I wondered.

But it was Charles. "Hi," he said. "Do you think we could talk somewhere?"

"When?"

"Now."

"Where?"

"How about the beach? It's not completely dark yet, and anyway, there's going to be a moon."

"All right." Somehow I knew it wasn't a date-type date he was inviting me for.

"Who was it?" Mother said, as I came back.

"Charles Brewster."

"Well, well." Mother looked just as pleased as I knew she would.

"And it's not that kind of date," I said. "He just wants to talk to me."

"Big oaks from acorns grow," Mushroom said.

"Oak schmoak," I said.

Jill and I ran down to the shore and I found another stick for her to retrieve. Charles, looking like a heron wearing spectacles, was skimming stones into the water.

"Your dog?" he said, when he came up.

"Yes."

"Let me throw that for you," he said. And then, "What's her name?"

109

"Jill."

"Okay, Jill, run," and he hurled the stick down the beach. Jill took off, found the stick, worried it around, and then flew back with it.

"She's going to be a terrific dog," he said. "How did you get her?"

I told him about the ad and finding her tied up in front of the house. As I did so, I remembered something. "The woman said she was lame from an accident, but she sure doesn't look it when she runs."

"She might have gotten over it. Or maybe it shows up when she walks. That sometimes happens. We had a Siamese cat once who walked as though she had arthritis or were a hundred years old. But she ran like a deer."

We both watched as Jill came walking towards us. Charles was right. When she walked her gait was uneven. But when she ran she showed no limp.

"What did you want to see me for?"

He picked up the stick and threw it again. "I wanted to ask you to come back and look after the twins."

"I can't. I've found another job."

"Oh. I'm sorry. At least I am for us."

"Can't you find somebody else?"

"You don't know the number of people we've tried—before you came. Looking after the twins six hours a day is not the world's most entertaining work, and an awful lot of the kids are tied up with this conservation thing. Anyway, the ones around here don't need the money, so there's no particular way to tempt them."

I remembered what Steve Novak had said about his sister. "Why don't you ask Steve Novak?" I said, putting every effort into making my voice sound normal.

"We did. Both Nancy and I. But his sister has got herself tied up with another job, and according to Steve, there's now some feeling among girls in the town that if one of them was hired, and a summer girl came along, the townie'd be let go and the summer resident hired in her place. For which you can't completely blame them, I suppose, because it's happened before. Anyway, whatever the reason, I spent most of the afternoon trying to find somebody and not succeeding."

"Who's Nancy?"

"My stepmother. Mrs. Brewster."

"Oh, yes. I forgot." I walked slowly along the beach, my

toes scuffing through the sand. "Why can't Mrs. Brewster look after them?"

"I think you know the answer to that. Because she's not capable at this point. She's often half crocked in the afternoon, and if not, then she's liable to take off with Harry Schreiber if he turns up. She's not exactly your steady, reliable, well-balanced mother. What's more—" He paused.

"What?"

"This probably sounds like flattering with intent to influence you, and it probably is. The twins like you better than they've liked anybody. And they've done better with you. At least they stay healthy and behave. They're nice kids, and the future for them isn't too rosy. I just wish they could have a decent summer."

"You're not related to them, are you?"

"No. They're my step-siblings. They're Nancy's by her previous husband, Joseph King. But he died, so they don't have him. My own father and she aren't getting along too well, and I can't see Harry Schreiber trying to be a second father to them."

"Do you like her? Your stepmother, I mean."

"Let's sit down," Charles said suddenly. Folding his legs under him, he sat down. In chinos and shirt he looked less like a stork than when in bathing trunks, but he still resembled Daddy Longlegs. I sat down beside him, and Jill trotted back and forth sniffing the sand and inspecting the small holes made by sand crabs.

"I don't dislike her," Charles said after a minute. "There's not a hell of a lot to like or dislike. And I do feel sorry for her."

"Why?"

"Because she's sort of out of her depth. She was some kind of a minor actress who married into the jet set—that was about three husbands ago, then Joseph King, then Dad. All she really had were her looks, and they're beginning to go. My father will probably divorce her, and then God knows what will happen to her."

I picked a pebble off the sand. "He doesn't sound too kind."

"He isn't. I don't mean he's a monster or anything like that. But she's not the kind of woman he thought he'd married, and tolerance of other people's failings is not his strong suit."

"He sounds like my father."

We sat there for a while. The sky in front of us, which had

been alternate pink and gray streaks, became almost entirely gray, then dark blue, and was now turning navy blue and charcoal. It was very quiet. Even the gulls weren't shrieking.

"Have you ever seen this marshy dune everybody's in such a state about?" I asked.

"Yes. Haven't you?"

"No."

"You ought to go and look at it. It's beautiful."

"How do you feel about this sanctuary thing?"

"I think it ought to be left alone."

"Do you work at the conservationists' volunteer office?"

"No." Silence. Then, "Harry Schreiber goes out with Nancy, you know."

"Yes. So?"

Charles sighed. "She's not the world's brightest person, and he's something of a wheeler-dealer. I think he'd sell out the townies as fast as he'd sell the sanctuary. But everybody knows that Nancy goes out with him, and if I showed up at the volunteer office it could make things even harder for her than they are now."

I was thinking about Charles and Steve. They weren't alike at all, except that in their different ways they seemed so unlike the other boys around. "Charles, how old are you?"

"Nineteen. Why?"

"You seem older."

"I know." Lots of kids would have been flattered at that, but he didn't seem as though he had been.

"Where do you go to school?"

"Princeton."

"Freshman?"

"Senior."

I absorbed that. "How old were you when you went?"

"Sixteen. I also went to some summer schools."

"Why? I mean, since you were ahead of the game anyway, why summer schools?"

There was another silence. Then, "I've never been very good at the nonwork things. I mean, I like studying, which is like admitting that you enjoy being a male chauvinist pig or a fascist bigot or something. It's considered socially undesirable."

I giggled a little. Then I said, "I know all about that. Being socially undesirable, I mean. Mother wants me to be a terrific social success and a smash with all the boys. Father wants me to be a tremendous brain, like you. I'm not either. Anyway, I've never been around other American kids much. And then, last summer, when it looked like I might be, I was in an accident and had to spend most of the summer in the hospital."

Charles still didn't say anything, and it suddenly occurred to me that he was the only person who'd never asked me what was wrong with my leg. "Everybody always asks me what's wrong with my leg. But you haven't." I was starting to think that maybe he hadn't noticed, when he said,

"Any time anybody has ever said anything about the way I looked it's always been uncomplimentary, so I took a vow a while back never to make any observation about anybody else's looks. What kind of an accident?"

"A car accident." And then I said something that I had never said before, although I had been asked about it. "Father was driving."

"That's too bad. Both that it happened and that your father was at the wheel. Has it affected your relationship?"

"We've never talked about it."

We sat there for a minute, then I felt something push against my head, followed by a slight whimper.

"I guess Jill wants to go home."

"Maybe she's hungry. Have you fed her?"

"Gad!" I forgot about feeding her."

"Well I bet she hasn't forgotten about being fed."

"I don't have any dog food in the house."

"Give her some scraps until tomorrow. Or the store is open until nine, you can still go there. It's only about eight."

I got up. I think I will. There's no use activating any more opposition than Jill already has."

"Don't your folks like her?"

"Father doesn't like animals in the house."

Charles was brushing the sand off his pants. "I'll walk you to the road. Then I'd better get back. What's the other job you've found?"

"It's with Mr. Haggerty at the *Herald*."

"Well, that's something of a coup. Bruce Thompkin wanted to do that this summer."

I felt a spurt of pleasure that he should have chosen me over the all-conquering Bruce. Then I remembered the reason. "Mr. Haggerty doesn't want anyone who wants to write for the paper. He says there's only room for one writer and that's him. He took me, he said, because all I said I wanted was a job."

"What do you do for him?"

"Scut work. Catalogue names, file, type, that kind of thing."

"It probably beats baby-sitting at that."

Guilt prodded at me. "I guess. Maybe."

"Does it pay well?"

"No. Only seventy-five. I was getting over a hundred a week from Mrs. Brewster."

"If more money would bring you back to Jennie and Jamie I'd be happy to up the ante."

For some reason I felt insulted. "Mother said you were rich."

"I am. Which doesn't mean I'm not a penny-pincher. But this would be worth it."

"I'm not for sale." I said angrily.

He stopped in the path. "I never said you were. But to offer somebody more money is a perfectly legitimate offer in the job world. And as far as your work is concerned, you've joined the great army of the employed."

"I don't want to work where I'm yelled at and put down."

"I can't blame you for that. Nancy doesn't know what she's saying half the time. What was the occasion? When I tried to get an explanation out of her, she said she'd no idea why you'd quit."

"She's got to be lying!"

"Not necessarily. If she had a raging hangover she probably doesn't remember anything but that."

"Well if she's so anxious to have me back, then why doesn't she call me and apologize?"

"Because I am. And the reason I am is that if you don't come and do some of the baby-sitting, then I'm stuck with it a large part of the time. If Harry shows up, off she goes and half the time I don't know it until I want to go out myself and find that the twins would be all alone. Or she's *non compos mentis*."

"Why didn't you say so the first time?" I muttered. "Instead of all that butter about my being better with them than anybody else, and they liking me more."

"It may have been butter, but it wasn't artificial butter. It was perfectly true."

"Well I told you, I have another job."

"Full-time?"

"Yes," I said, knowing it wasn't true.

"Because it doesn't seem to me that Haggerty has enough work for a full-time slavey. Maybe you could do them both."

"This is supposed to be a vacation," I said, as we came to the fork where I would go on to the village and he would go over to Headlands.

"True. Okay. I just thought I'd try. 'Night."

That night I dreamed about Steve. Jill, filled with the dog food I'd bought her at the store, slept stretched out beside me. In my dream I was standing in the middle of the marshy dune, which looked just like pictures of the Amazonian rain forest I'd seen in photographs. I was surrounded by babies of all species, including snakes and lizards. Jill was tied to a huge tree, and Steve, at the edge of a clearing, was about to shoot her.

"No!" I screamed, and woke up, my heart pounding.

Jill, waked by the noise I made, started licking my face. I put my arms around her and burst into tears. What I hadn't told Charles was that my real reason for refusing to go back to Headlands was that Steve would be there, and I felt that I couldn't bear to have him ignoring me every day.

It was at that point that I remembered that he was coming to work on Mother's studio in the afternoons. Well, I thought, turning over, and feeling Jill curl herself into the small of my back, I would just stay away from the house from lunch until dinner.

Chapter

7

Mrs. Brewster was on the telephone before I finished breakfast, so humble and apologetic that I wanted to squirm. And she offered me a dollar an hour more. I was pretty sure that came from Charles, so I refused. No matter what Charles said, taking it would make me feel as though I were trying to scrounge more money out of them. "You don't have to pay me any more, Mrs. Brewster. It's just that I've taken another job."

Perhaps I could have held out if I hadn't heard Jennie's voice in the background. "Is she coming, Mom? Did she say she'd come?" And the fact that I could tell it was Jennie, and was able to distinguish between the twins even over the phone, was the final straw. Besides, I remembered from the night before, I wanted to be away from the house in the afternoons. So I agreed to go from one to five. Four hours. And I'd work for Mr. Haggerty in the mornings. As Jill and I walked to the *Herald* office I figured out that four hours a day, six days a week, at three dollars an hour would be...seventy-two dollars. Seventy-two plus seventy-five equalled...one hundred and forty-seven. Feeling somewhat cheered, I whistled for Jill, who was taking a personal interest in every grass blade, and when she bounded up and flung herself at me, I gave her a hug. As I stroked her quivering black coat it occurred to me that she had a lot of love and trust for a dog that had undoubtedly been pushed around most of her life.

"Yes, it's okay," I said, as I avoided her joyous tongue on my face. "You have a permanent home. I promise."

Fate is a funny thing. If I hadn't stopped to hug Jill, Steve would have been gone by the time I got to the bend in that road, just short of the main road. But I had stopped, for perhaps two minutes, and when Jill and I finished our mutual hugging and kissing and in a burst of joy and energy ran around the blind bend in the road, Steve's van was barreling in the opposite direction coming towards us.

I had a vision of an oncoming truck and wheels, and Jill's plumy tail as she scampered ahead. Then—

"Jill!" I screamed, and flung myself at her. She gave a tremendous yelp, and I felt a hammer blow on my back that sent us both sprawling to the opposite bank.

"Jill, Jill," I cried, and realized that I was holding her. She gave a slight wuff. I put her down. Her leg seemed to give way.

"Are you all right?" Steve was standing beside me, his van on the other side of the road, its cab door open.

"You've hurt Jill," I said furiously. "It isn't as though she hasn't been beaten up and run over by everybody else. You had to race like a maniac in that killing machine and knock us down!"

"Well damn it, I didn't see you. Don't you know better than to run around a blind corner like that on a country road? What did you expect up here? Stoplights?"

"You were going too fast and ought to have your license taken away."

Jill barked. Steve and I were standing at the side of the road shouting at each other.

"It's people like you who are the menace," he yelled. "Anybody who lived up here would know better than to walk on the wrong side of the road around a blind corner with a mutt that doesn't know how to obey."

"She is not a mutt!"

"Well what would you call her? Of course she's a mutt. She's the stray that Palmer woman's been trying to get rid of."

"And I suppose your solution would be to take her to the pound and have her destroyed the way you want to destroy all the birds and other wildlife in the sanctuary. It's people like you who're ruining the environment. You probably hate all birds and other forms of animal life. The way you hate me," I heard myself saying, to my horror.

"I do not hate you. You ought to know that very well. I don't hate you. That's the problem. If you were different... older or out for a good time... then. But it won't work. And I'm not going to—"

I must have moved my shoulder at that point, because a pain shot up my back. I took in my breath. Even so I was thinking more about what he said. "What do you mean you don't hate me? After... after... after the other night you won't even look at me. Let alone speak to me. What do you think that makes me feel like? It makes me feel like... like..." Maybe it was my shoulder. Whatever... I could feel the hated tears coming down my cheeks. Jill jumped against my leg and licked my hand. Which was nice of her, considering the competition.

"Oh, baby, I didn't mean to make you feel like that."

And then the sun burst out and birds sang and the planets wheeled and Steve's arms were around me, and despite the fact that it was agony, my arms were around his neck and we were standing on the main road to the village kissing again and again.

Half an hour later we were sitting on the other side of the opposite bank, that is, when we weren't lying.

"I've never felt like this," Steve said.

"You sound almost angry about it." His curly hair, a light chestnut that shone in the sun, was above me, and I ran my finger along his hairline. "Do you think you'll ever be bald?"

"I hope not. Dad still has his hair. He doesn't have many of his teeth, but he's got his hair."

"Why do you sound angry that you've never felt this way before?"

"You know the answer to that, Sarah. We come from different places. I'm the town handyman. You're the daughter of one of the rich summer people."

"We're not rich. Professors don't make much money."

"Maybe not. But there's a class difference there, and don't let anybody tell you there isn't. I told you I'm what your people call a Polack. Your father would have a fit if anybody told an anti-Semitic joke or an anti-black joke. But I bet you he and his friends tell Polish jokes. We're the ethnics. The

119

hardhats. You mean to tell me you haven't heard all those good liberals take off on us?"

I didn't say anything, because I had. "It doesn't make any difference. You're not a handyman, anyway. You're a builder. You make things. That's creative."

"Yeah." He rolled over on his back. "And that's what I'm going to remain. A builder plus handyman. But I make good money and I'm the only support of my mother and four brothers and sisters."

"What about your father? He's not dead, is he?"

"No. He's fully occupied being the town drunk. When he's not in some state drying-out place, he's in our local taverns or on our local skid row."

"I'm sorry," I said. And then understood for the first time why Steve got angry when I suggested that his sister ask their father for money—why Steve thought that was a cheap shot. "I didn't know that about your father, Steve, before, when you thought I was making a dirty crack."

"No. I know you weren't. I realized it afterwards. I shouldn't have jumped you like that."

So that was why Steve had to support his family. What was it he'd said about his brother, the one killed in Vietnam? "You said something about because your brother was killed you couldn't stay in college. But you couldn't have been in college then. That was years ago."

"No. I'd just started high school. But Tony, my brother, was working, in construction. The plan he and I dreamed up when we were kids was that he was going to go into building and I was the son who was going to get an education and move into the professional class. I wanted to be an architect. So I'd go to college and when I had my degree, he'd be about ready to start his own building company and I'd join him as architect. It was all very neat. We'd clean up and make some beautiful houses into the bargain. Then he got drafted—no deferment for working boys like Tony. He was the kind that nobody wrote or made speeches about. He didn't get into drugs or frag his officers. He just did his job and made sergeant and got killed. Until then, he was making pretty good pay—at least for that time—and sent a lot of it home. When he went, that went. Mother was working, so I went on and got a scholarship and went to college for a year. Then she got sick and had to quit for a while. So I left college. Our family has always gone to parochial schools, and that costs money. Not a lot. But some."

120

"Couldn't they go to public school?"

"Our public schools are maybe one degree better than yours in New York, but that's not saying a lot. They have terrible discipline problems and a third of the kids are on some kind of drug. So, public school is out."

"Well I think all this class stuff is stupid. What's important is how we feel about each other."

He raised himself on one elbow and looked down at me. "Do you really think that, Sarah? Really?"

"Of course I do. Oh Steve—I was miserable when you wouldn't talk to me. I hated everything and everybody."

"I wasn't too happy myself," he muttered, and brought his face down on mine. He was on top of me, almost, and I could feel his heart, hammering away, and the heat of his leg against mine.

That strange, quivery feeling that I'd had before flickered along my legs. Absolutely nothing seemed to matter except being close to him. His hand slid down my back, his thumb in front against my breast. I slid my hand down his leg, feeling the tough jeans cloth. Was this what all those porn books were about? It didn't seem even distantly related to them. I put my hand up around his neck, felt his tongue touch my lip. His breath was coming in short jerks.

It was Jill who stopped us by barking. Steve raised his head, and I heard then the soft shushing of pine needles under somebody's shoe. He stood up and walked quickly to the top of the bank and I heard his voice.

"Oh hello, Mrs. Barrett." I wanted to giggle, because he still sounded breathless.

"I was coming to look for you, Steve. You must have left word on your tape that you would be working on our fence today, and there's a phone call for you. I thought you must have been delayed, but then I saw your van down the road and thought you might have decided to take a snooze in it."

"No...I was just...er...catching up on some paperwork. I'm sorry I was held up. I'll be along in a few minutes."

"Is that your dog?" I heard her say.

"No...yes. I just adopted her. Come here, Jill."

Mrs. Barrett's house was the one nearest to ours. I knew that he had been working for her because I, too, had seen his van outside the path leading to their cottage. I could also tell by the way he talked that he was trying to keep Mrs. Barrett from finding out that I was sitting a few feet away on the other side of the crest. Which gave me a funny feeling. If it had been somebody I knew, would I have done the same? Yes, I knew, I would. What Steve and I had was private. Other people knowing would spoil it. And yet...part of me still wanted to shout it from the roofs and have everybody in the world know that Steve Novak loved me. Steve loved me....

"Steve," I said, when he had managed to get rid of Mrs. Barrett and come back, "do you love me? I love you."

He was standing, looking down at me. "Do you have to ask? Yes, yes! I love you. I've been doing nothing but think about you since that night. And I'll think about nothing but you for the rest of the day, whatever I'm doing. I know that. Until I see you again."

My breath caught again. "When..." I asked.

He sat down beside me and put his arms around me again. After we'd kissed he said, "Can you meet me here tonight? I'll have the van and we can go somewhere."

I knew without his saying so that he didn't want us to be where people would see us. It hurt, but I also knew it was the way it had to be. If I had any doubts, all I had to do was to think about Peter. "What time?" I said.

"Eight?"

"Yes."

For some reason we were whispering.

That night after dinner as I was strolling to the screen door Mother said, "Where are you going, Sam?"

"For a walk," I tried to sound casual.

Mother looked at me hard. I continued to stroll to the door.

"With whom?" Mother asked.

The words "with Steve Novak" were in my mouth. Afterwards, I wondered how different things might have been if I had spoken them and laid everything out in the open. But I didn't. I was about to make up some acceptable lie when Mushroom, who was waiting for her Congressman to show up, gave me a kind of arch look and said, "Maybe his name would be Brewster, n'est-ce pas? Sam?"

I looked as mysterious as possible and then grinned.

Mother relaxed. "Have a good time."

Steve was waiting beside his van door. I rushed into his arms. We got into the front of the van and kissed some more. Every now and then cars drove past, but Steve had parked in the Barrett lane, so the headlights wouldn't pick us out. After a while Steve pulled away and said, "How about a movie?"

122

"Sure." I was a little surprised, because there was only one movie house near, and half the summer colony could be seen there any night. Then I said, "You mean in Leominster?"

"No, I was thinking about Barryton. They have a bunch of movie houses there." It was, I realized a good choice. Barryton was a medium-sized town just far enough away for us to be reasonably sure that there wouldn't be any people from Cove Harbor or from Leominster.

"Fine. What's showing?"

"Does it matter? Bound to be something. They've half a dozen houses."

We drove there, with Steve steering with one hand and holding my hand with his other. Every now and then we'd kiss some more. It was queer. I wouldn't have minded skipping the movie and spending the evening driving around in the van with long stops from time to time. And the strange thing about it was that the few times boys had made passes at me—the brother of a friend in Germany and a boy I'd met at a Miss Hall's dance—I'd hated it, and hated the fact that was all the boys seemed to want to do—to neck: make out. Yet that was what I wanted to do now, and was having to work a little to keep from feeling hurt that the movie was Steve's idea.

Still, it was a good movie, science fiction with a touch of horror. We sat near the back, eating popcorn, with Steve's arm around me. Every now and then he'd bring his lips near my temple, brushing it with his lips.

Afterwards Steve asked if I'd like to have a soda, so we went to an ice-cream parlor and had milkshakes. As I was eating mine I looked around. Most of the kids there were years younger than Steve—a sort of high school crowd.

"We should have gone to a bar or something," I said.

He looked up at me from his wide-set eyes. "Did you want a drink? You're pretty young for that, aren't you?"

"Good heavens, Steve, where've you been? The kids in high school have wine and beer."

"I know," he said in a strange voice. "That's one reason my brothers and sister go to parochial school."

"I bet they have stuff to drink there."

"Not with those nuns they don't."

"I thought nuns were liberated."

"These aren't. Their habits may be shorter, and their hair shows outside their veils, but I don't think they'd put up with any more nonsense than the old-fashioned kind did."

A strange thought occurred to me. "You're pretty old-fashioned yourself, aren't you?"

He seemed to tighten up for a minute. Then he grinned. "You sound like my young sister."

"Do you live at home?"

"More or less. I have a place with a phone, for business. It's really just a loft, but I've partitioned off a corner as living quarters. But I stay around the house two or three days a week, to keep an eye on the kids." He glanced at his watch. "It's time we were going back."

We drove back to the same turn in the road and borrowed a piece of the Barrett's driveway to park in.

"What would happen if the Barrett's suddenly decided to drive out?" I whispered after a few rather breathless minutes.

I could feel Steve's heart hammering against me. "Since they're both well over sixty I don't suppose they're cruising around the countryside at this hour." He sounded out of breath. He pulled away then. "I'll walk you back to your house."

"Do your folks know you're out with me?" he asked as we walked across the sand.

"No." I told him what Mushroom had said about Charles and giggled. "Anyway, Mother thinks it's Charles."

"She wouldn't mind that at all," Steve said drily.

We came up on the dark side of the house, away from the sea. There was a light on the porch, but we stood away from it in the shadows. "Do you have a key?" he whispered.

"No. It's not locked. What time is it?"

"About eleven-thirty. Do they go to bed early?"

"My father doesn't."

"Well, go ring the bell or whatever. I'll stay here and make sure you get in."

I hesitated a minute, wanting to say, "Come on up to the front door with me and meet Father," and hating myself for knowing I wouldn't. "Goodnight, Steve," I whispered.

He took my hand, then leaned over and kissed me, gently this time and my bones felt as though they were water.

"Steve," I whispered. "Steve, darling."

He kissed me again, the same way, and said something I didn't understand.

"What?" I whispered.

"It's Polish. It means beloved."

"Tell me again. Tell it to me softly."

So he said it again, and it was still ringing in my ears

124

when I went up and cautiously turned the front-door knob in case it was unlocked. It was. I opened the door, then turned and waved.

Father, who had been reading a copy of *The New York Times,* which he had sent up here daily, was standing up, holding the paper, plainly on the verge of coming to open the door. The low ceiling light shone on his head. It was odd, I thought, something I hadn't noticed, but his hair was chestnut and curly, rather like Steve's. Except, of course, that there were gray streaks in his.

Father sat down again. "Had a good time?"

"Yes, thanks."

"Who'd you go out with?"

"A boy I know."

"It's pretty late, isn't it?"

"We went to a movie."

"Oh." He was still looking at me, his paper in his hand, hanging down to one side. "You're growing up. I hadn't noticed."

"I'll be eighteen in the fall." Eighteen, a grown woman, legally. At eighteen I could marry whom I liked.

"How's your leg?"

"Fine." The thought of my leg dragged me back, back to being a little girl in the hospital, to being told exactly what to do every hour of the day. "It's really fine. It doesn't even feel shorter."

"Your limp is a lot better, but don't forget, you'll probably have to go back into surgery in the fall. So don't wear yourself out. Get plenty of rest."

"Goodnight," I said, and went up the stairs. Maybe he didn't mean it as a putdown, or pushback, I thought, going into my room, but it felt like one.

My room was a mess of Mother's papers, but Jill was in the middle of my bed, and her ecstasy at my return made up for the chaos.

The days were beginning to get longer. It was gradual, of course, but the dark seemed to arrive later and later. It was still broad afternoon daylight when, in my new schedule, I left the twins at six in the afternoon. They were so flatteringly pleased to have me back that their behavior was near-angelic.

"I'm afraid they'll sprout wings," I said to Steve one day when I had arrived a little early. He was doling out pieces of putty and suggesting various shapes they could be working on while he was fitting the garage doors.

"I wouldn't worry too much. And keep your eyes sharp. After so much saintliness, they're due for a major outbreak of bad behavior."

I smiled at him, and he smiled back. The twins had run out of the garage for a minute and he leaned forward and swiftly kissed me. "Hors d'oeuvres," he said, "before the main meal."

My knees still turned into water when he did that. A huge feeling of being loved poured over me. In my whole life I'd never had it before. And it was not until Steve gave it to me that I could understand that sense of something missing that I'd always experienced.

"Steve..." I said.

He smiled. "What?"

"Nothing. Just Steve." I watched him wipe off and polish a metal gadget of some kind. "How do you spell your name?" I asked. "Steven with a v or S-t-e-p-h-e-n?"

"Neither, as a matter of fact. It's S-t-e-f-a-n."

"Oh. Stefan. I like that."

He laughed. "We'll make a Pole out of you yet."

"Will you?" I heard the anxiety and eagerness in my voice. He had never said anything about our future. Neither had I. By some unspoken agreement we stayed away from it. Yet I wanted more than anything else to believe that he thought of us in terms of "always."

"Sarah—"

"Yes?"

"Nothing." He gave the gadget a last swipe and went over to measure it against something on the doorpost. The twins ran in and I couldn't pursue it. Maybe, I thought. Just maybe—and pushed the thought away before I'd really let it surface.

"Still Charles?" Mother said one night, as I strolled out of the kitchen after helping her load the dishwasher after dinner.

"Of course." I kept on walking, afraid that if she saw my face she'd know I was lying. I'd never liked telling lies. In fact, I hated it. But I was now used to it, and when my conscience prodded me, which it did from time to time, I'd tell myself that it was only because of stupid and artificial social divisions that I had to lie about Steve in the first place. Once or twice in the three nights out of five I would slip out to meet Steve in the Barretts' driveway, I was tempted, out of the blue, to say to Mother. "It's not Charles I'm meeting these nights. It's Steve Novak, the handyman who's repairing your study." But something always stopped me.

There were nights when Steve and I didn't go out, nights when he said he had to work or go to some meeting of his union in Leominster.

"You're your own boss, Steve. How come you belong to a union?"

"I'm a construction worker and builder and paid-up member of the union."

"What are you having meetings about?" It was an idle question, except I was interested in everything about him.

He hesitated, then said, "Union business." We were sitting in the front of his van just before he walked me to the house. Then he said, "That's dodging the question. What we talk about mostly is the injunction the conservationists are trying to get."

It was the first time in a while the subject had come up. And since my brother had invited me out of the volunteer job, I had managed not to think about it.

"Well," he went on when I didn't say anything, "you asked."

Suddenly I remembered something Mr. Haggerty had said. "Isn't there any other place that resort could be built?"

"That's not the point," Steve said, and his voice had the hard edge to it that I hadn't heard in a while.

"Mr. Haggerty says," I started, and then wondered if I should keep my mouth shut. The newspaper editor had been kind to me and was trying desperately to keep his paper out of the fight.

"Haggerty says what?"

"He said it was sort of like the Civil War. That the real trouble is that both sides are more interested in punishing each other than in the birds or the building. Do you think that's true?"

I expected Steve to deny it hotly. But he said nothing, his hand sliding back and forth along the steering wheel. Then, "There's no way you could know how strongly people in the town feel. It's not just this year. If your mother and her friends believe in family planning and all that, fine. But they don't have to come into the heart of the state's most Catholic area to open up their headquarters. My mother, other people, saw

127

it as the slap by Protestants, WASPs, against Catholics and ethnics."

"I wouldn't exactly call us Protestants."

"Well, you're sure not Catholic."

"No."

"Or Jewish."

"No. Father says we're humanists."

Steve made a funny noise. "Whatever that is."

"Well, Catholics send missionaries, don't they, to places where they want to convert people to what they think is right?"

"Yes."

"Well then why shouldn't humanists do the same?"

There was another silence. Finally Steve said. "It's late. I'll walk you to the door."

"Steve," I said. "Don't be angry."

"I'm not angry."

"Yes you are. I can hear it."

He'd started to open the van door, but he paused at this and rubbed his hand against the back of my head. "I'm not angry, darling. I just—we can't shut out the rest of the world forever."

"Yes, we can. What we feel is more important." I reached up and put my face against his, and touched my tongue against his cheek. It tasted salty. I heard him draw in his breath. Then he turned and pulled me close to him and started kissing me. I closed my arms around his neck. After a while his hand slid down my side and then it was on my breast, his fingers cupping it, his thumb moving back and forth across the nipple. I felt strange and wild and hot all over, as though nerves in my breasts went right down my legs.

"Come on," he said, his voice oddly thick. "Let's get in the back." And then, as I squeezed past the seat, "Can you make it?"

It was dark back there, but he pulled a blanket from somewhere and put it, double, on the floor of the cab. The interior smelled of machine oil and metal, but I was so excited I barely noticed.

"Sarah, Sarah," he muttered, a few minutes later. Then, "Take these off."

A while later neither of us had on anything.

"You haven't done this before," he whispered, as his hands, gentle and probing, moved over and in me, "have you?"

"No." I could hardly breathe. "Did you think I had?"

128

"No. I knew you hadn't. Which is why I tried..." Then we were both silent. I didn't dream that my body could feel like this.

"Oh, Steve, Steve," I whispered, my own hands reaching out.

Then he was lying on top of me.

"This...it may hurt," he said.

He thrust against me, his skin hot and moist on mine. There was a sharp pain. "Ouch!" I said. Our bodies started to move in some kind of rhythm that we both seemed to have known all our lives. Then, Steve gave a final convulsive thrust and everything exploded.

"Sometime," Steve whispered, lying beside me in the dark of the truck, "we'll go to my place where I can turn on the light and see you."

I was running my hand up and down his chest and stomach, feeling skin, hair and muscle. "I'm not very beautiful, and I have scars."

His arm was under me, and he closed it, drawing me to him. "You are to me. I fell for you the first time I saw you, with your pale hair and gray eyes and skinniness. You looked like a lost princess in a fairy tale, even though you were giving me smart backtalk. You also looked like a one hundred percent New Englander."

I put my head on his chest. "Do you like that?"

"I guess I must."

"I thought you hated it."

"That, too."

I decided not to pick up on the word "hate." We'd just get into the areas where we always seemed to fight.

"Tell me about the scars," he said.

When I'd finished he said, "I didn't know you might have to go back into the hospital. That's too bad. I'm sorry."

"I may not. It's just possible that I won't. The last doctor said the leg might right itself, and I *don't* limp that much." That wasn't exactly what the doctor had said; he'd said, "You may adjust to its present length so well that you won't notice it and your body won't be thrown out. It sometimes happens. Not often. But sometimes."

"Well, that won't be too bad. And then it'll be right."

A little chill went over me, why, I wasn't sure. But I knew I didn't want to go back to the hospital.

We didn't say anything then. I lay there, watching the

129

shape of the leaves and branches against the moon through what I could see of the windshield. Then slowly, gently at first, everything seemed to start again and build and build to another shattering explosion.

Later, we walked back across the sand, hand in hand, not talking.

I said, "I didn't have any idea sex could be like that."

"What did you think it would be like?"

"Kind of yucchy."

"I'm glad it wasn't yucchy."

I said, carefully, "Steve, have you had a lot of girlfriends?"

"A fair number."

There was another silence. Then, "But I told you, at the beginning, it's always been different with you."

"Charles," I said one day, when we were both on the beach watching the twins, "do you mind if I ask you something?"

"Go ahead."

I looked at him. He hadn't taken his nose out of his book. His skin was pink in blotches where I could see it, but he was mostly covered in a khaki shirt and chinos, and his beat-up hat covered his face.

I took a deep breath. I'd been trying to think how to ask this, and there was just no way except the direct way. "Has anybody said anything to you about our going out?"

"You mean like four nights a week?"

My heart sank. "Yes."

"Of course. You didn't think in a place this size if you said you were going out with me that sooner or later somebody wouldn't say something like, 'I see you and Sarah Lacey are really becoming an item, ha, ha'?"

"So what did you say?"

"I said, like out of the best nineteenth-century novel, 'I'm a lucky guy.'" He looked up then. "I've no objection to being useful, since it doesn't seem to take any effort on my part. But it would have been a good idea if you'd mentioned it to me. I could easily have said something unhelpful, like 'Who? Me?'"

I was busy drawing signs in the sand. "It's Steve Novak," I said.

"I knew that much."

"How? Nobody knows."

"I've seen the two of you talking around the house. Steve keeps a pretty impassive countenance, but your face is a dead

130

giveaway. So putting that together with the obvious fact that whoever it was you didn't want it known, I came up with the answer: Steve." Charles looked at me with an odd, ironic look on his face. "It's funny in a way that it finally turned out to be you that got Steve—that is, among the summer people."

"How do you mean?"

"He's a good-looking guy with plenty of whatever it takes to attract the female. But so far he's given them all the brush, even Nancy."

"Mrs. Brewster?" At first I couldn't believe it, then, as I started to think it might be true, I was horrified.

"Sure. Why not? The older-woman-younger-man thing is big right now, and my father's never around." Charles was looking at me with a strange expression, kind but impersonal. "But don't worry. Steve kept his distance. I've never discussed it with him, but I'd bet his reasons were more political and social than anything else. He'll work for the summer people, but he's not about to have truck with them—until you. But then you're sort of different, too."

I'd always known I was but never thought it was a particularly good thing. "How different?"

Charles shifted his legs. "Hard to say, exactly. You're not mad for a suntan or beach games. You sort of stand outside. Like an outsider." After another minute he said, "Like me, too, I guess."

I looked at him. "I've always felt like an outsider, different. But I never thought it was something I could do anything about." I held up my face to the sun. Funny, I thought, all my life I'd been convinced that to other people I was either unattractive or stupid or both. But because of Steve I felt beautiful and brilliant. One night we'd skinny-dipped and then made love on a deserted strip of sand several miles to the north of the townies' area. The moonlight was bright, and Steve said to me, wonderingly, "You're lovely, like a flower." In the moonlight my scars didn't show. Then, later, after we'd made love, he said, "Did you ever read 'The Little Mermaid'? The Hans Andersen tale?"

"Umm," I said. I was lying, tummy down, on the sand, and Steve was pouring a little trickle of sand up and down my back.

"I think she must have looked like you, after she lost her mermaid's tail."

". . . And Steve's something of an oddball himself," Charles went on.

I came back with a snap, my loyalty ready to fight. "What do you mean?"

"Have you ever met his family?"

"No."

"Well, when Father decided he wanted the garage rebuilt, he asked me to do the arranging, so I was the one to get in touch with Steve."

"I'm surprised your father didn't have that other expensive outfit, even though I'm sure Steve's work must be just as good."

"It's better. Steve is an artist in his way, a terrific craftsman. It's a pity he had to stop school. Anyway, I went over one day to look for him. He himself was born in Poland, you know. How they got out during that cold-war period I'm not sure. But they did. His people still talk Polish at home. His mother is good, hard-working Polish middle class. His father's people were a cut above, wiped out by the war. He was a teacher or professor of some kind. Anyway, getting over here must have used up his last burst of energy, because he hasn't done much since except sit around and drink. It's too bad. But Steve had a pretty good education at home, besides school. And of course like most immigrants, particularly those from the eastern bloc with families back there, they were all passionately anti-Russian and pro-American. As you probably know, his older brother, Anton—Tony—fought and was killed in the Vietnam War. When Steve got a scholarship to one of the Ivy League schools, they were terrifically proud. But when he got there, he found himself on the wrong side of almost all the campus politics. It would have been much better, in a way, if he'd gone to a state university, but he wanted the best and applied for it and got it. Then, when the money ran out at home, he had to leave. But I think it gave him a bad taste in his mouth for the gilded youth of the country."

What Charles said made so much sense I sat and thought about it. So Steve and I were both of us, in a way, outsiders. And so was Charles. "You're right," I said to him, "you're an outsider like me, like us. Only yours is because you're so brainy and years ahead of everybody."

Charles grinned. "It has its problems. I'm not trying to change the subject, but have you noticed that Jamie is about to try and eat a land crab?"

"What?" I shrieked. Then I whirled around. Charles was

right. Quietly and thoughtfully, as he did everything, Jamie was about to bite on a wiggling object.

"Drop that!" I yelled.

Jamie immediately took off. So did I, catching him just in time. Having disposed of the land crab, I brought him back and devoted myself to getting him and Jennie to build two sandcastles with a bridge adjoining—a feat involving bringing a certain amount of seawater up in their little buckets to get the right consistency of sand. While they were patting the bridge in shape I said to Charles, sitting nearby, "So you don't mind if I go on saying I'm going out with you? You'll support me if somebody asks?"

Charles pushed his hat back off his face for a minute. In about twenty years, I thought, he'll look pretty distinguished.

"No, I don't mind. As long as there're no complications. But I don't want to have to go to bat for a relationship that I can't even enjoy."

"Okay. I'll remember. Thanks. There won't be any complications." I wasn't sure why I added that. Maybe because I wanted it so much to be true.

It was a few days later that I saw the much-disputed wildlife sanctuary for the first time.

One afternoon at three o'clock, after I had got the twins up from their nap and given them their milk and cookies, Mrs. Brewster, looking very chic in a sort of paisley silk dress, sailed into the kitchen and said that she and Mr. Schreiber were taking the twins to a children's party up the coast and to get them dressed and ready. The twins weren't anxious to go. The sea was now warm enough for them to swim and they would miss their afternoon dunking. But with the promise of ice cream and presents, they allowed me to put them into their best clothes and then into Mr. Schreiber's black Mercedes. And I had the rest of the day off.

I was going up the path to the main road when I was overtaken by a dilapidated and rather ancient coupe.

"Wanna go for a ride?" Charles asked.

"Sure."

"Climb in."

"Where are we going?" I asked, as he put the car in gear and we took off.

"First through the village main street to lend credence to this hot affair you and I are supposed to be having."

I giggled. Then, as we waited for the village's one stoplight,

133

and saw Bruce, Linda, Peter and an assortment of others coming out of the volunteer's office, I giggled some more. "It'll be all over."

"Isn't that the idea?" Charles said, roaring up the coast road. "Throw them off the scent." He yelled above the acceleration.

But he slowed down after a while, and we ambled up the coast road, beyond the next village and the one after that, and then on to an area that seemed to have no building or habitation of any kind for miles. Charles didn't talk much, and I sat and thought about Steve.

Suddenly I was aware that we had come to a stop. To our right and a little below the road stretched mile after mile of sand and marsh, with numerous little inlets and streams running between banks of reeds. In between some of the banks were shallow pools, big puddles, really, reflecting the sky. There were clumps of reeds everywhere, some higher than others. And slowly, as we sat in silence, I heard a sort of twittering, a soft but powerful chorus of hundreds and hundreds of birds. Many of them were in the various pieces of water: the streams, inlets, pools, in the ocean itself, although it was far out to the right. White, black, brown and multicolored dots, wings folded, riding on the water. And swimming up a stream near us, single-file, were a mother duck followed by six ducklings.

"It's the wildlife sanctuary, isn't it?" I said in a half-whisper. But even though I spoke in a low voice, there was a flutter of wings from the bushes near us and some birds took off.

"Yes."

"It's *filled* with birds."

"You ought to see it at either sunset or early morning. The sky is almost literally black with birds of various shapes and sizes."

"What are they all?"

"Teals, terns, gulls—God knows how many kinds—geese, dowitchers, every sort of duck you ever heard of, countless waterfowl of various types, sandpipers...I don't even know half of them."

"There're so many."

"I guess they know they're safe—or have been."

It was awful, being torn like this, I thought, and terrible to think that Steve—my Steve, who seemed so sensitive and

134

compassionate—would bring in bulldozers and destroy all this.

"Isn't it too marshy for a resort?"

"Well—they'd have to drain it, of course."

After a while Charles turned the car around and drove south. I noticed then something I hadn't noticed before; a wire fence, stretching on either side of the road, marked off the sanctuary.

Long after we'd left it I said, "Why did you take me there?"

"I don't know. It wasn't a plot. I hadn't even thought about going there till I found myself in front of the fence. I wasn't trying to make life harder for you. I guess I wanted to see it again for myself."

"Mr. Haggerty—" I started, and then remembered that he had asked me not to repeat what I was about to burst out with.

"What about Mr. Haggerty?"

"He said not to tell anyone, so please, don't repeat what I'm going to say, but he said that he knew of another place they could put the resort instead."

"I know." Charles sounded rather grim. "Headlands."

"Your house?"

"That's right. Our house."

"But that'd be a perfect solution!"

"It might seem so to you, but it doesn't seem that way to my father, and it certainly doesn't seem so to the bulk of the summer colony, who envision it becoming another Atlantic City. That's partly the reason for all the rancor. That was the original site Schreiber had put his eye on. Our family hadn't been up here in years—we have another place in Bar Harbor. But some of the summer people wrote to Dad when he was contemplating selling Headlands, so he came up to look at the bay here and the house, which he hadn't really bothered to stay in for a couple of decades—he'd rented it out most of the time—and decided he liked it better than Bar Harbor. So, he refused to sell it to Schreiber.

"Unfortunately, the plans for tearing down the house and preparing the ground for a large hotel had already been drawn up. People were actually hired to begin the whole construction job. There was wholesale rejoicing in Leominster, from where the construction company came, and then whammo!—Dad called the thing off just before the papers were going to be signed. The townies were pretty mad. Then somebody somewhere discovered that the sanctuary was not state land, but was owned by a person or company who could be talked into selling it—I don't know all the details. Maybe it was a holding company who had thought to build there themselves but found it would be too expensive, so they leased it to a wildlife outfit and the lease was about to fall due. Anyway, Schreiber heard about it and put in a bid for it."

"Has the sale gone through?"

"No. Or at least I don't think so. Schreiber certainly doesn't want to repeat the other company's mistake and find himself with an enormous tract of marsh that he can do nothing with. So he's waiting to see if the conservationists succeed in getting a permanent injunction."

"If everybody knows about this, why was Mr. Haggerty being so cagy with me?"

"Maybe he knows a new wrinkle that I don't."

"He seems very fair-minded, not taking sides."

"He is. He could also lose his paper if he does choose sides and chooses wrong. If he's for the resort, he'll lose every last member of the summer community and all the villagers. If he comes out against the resort and it gets built anyway, they'd probably succeed in closing him out."

Charles sighed. "But now you can see why the townies are so furious and determined. The same people who ganged up on them before, by writing to my father, have ganged up on them again. It's become a sort of class war. Which puts you and your boyfriend in the middle...."

That night Steve and I had gone skinny-dipping again, and were lying under a sort of overhang of rock. We were holding hands and not talking much. Somehow, all evening I hadn't been able to get out of my mind those ducks paddling single-file behind their mother. For me the whole sanctuary thing was focused in those ducks.

"Steve," I said, "have you ever seen the sanctuary?"

It was incredible, the way I could feel his muscles go tight all the way down his body.

"Let's not talk about it," he said.

I held his hand hard and said, "I want to tell you about the ducks."

He sat up. "No. I said we weren't going to talk about it."

"You don't care about birds, do you?" All I felt when I said that was sad.

"That's the second time you've said that, the second time you've implied I don't give a damn about... about nature or

136

the environment or animals or birds." He sprang up and reached for his pants. "Get dressed."

"Steve—"

"I said to get dressed. There's somewhere I want to take you."

We didn't talk all the way back down the coast. I sat there feeling isolated from him and totally miserable. Finally I said, "Don't be angry with me."

He didn't say anything for a minute. Then, "I'm not angry with you. I'm just tired of being pushed into . . . into some kind of stereotype. Tell me something. Do you know any doctors in your particular social set in New York? Did any of your relatives go into medicine?"

I had no idea what he was talking about. "What—what are you talking about, Steve?"

"Just answer me."

I pulled my mind away from its overwhelming preoccupation with our relationship and said, "Yes. Uncle Peter, the one my brother was named for, is a doctor, why?"

"That's really terrific. Does your conservationist brother— or you—tackle your Uncle Peter when he comes to your house over the animals that are blinded and tortured in various ways so that your uncle and his friends can hand out prescriptions certified as safe? Or does your brother accuse him of being some kind of subhuman monster as he sits down at the dinner table?"

I couldn't think of anything to say, which sometimes happened when somebody I cared about or was close to became angry with me. A sort of paralysis gripped my mind.

"Well?" Steve demanded.

Finally my thinking processes unlocked themselves a little. "Medicine is supposed to help people."

"And jobs aren't? Two textile factories closed in the last three years, one permanently, the other just moved. Cheap clothes are coming in from the Far East. Families that had homes are on welfare. They can't help it. The young people who want jobs have to leave. This resort would create, altogether, about a thousand or more jobs, maybe two thousand, when you take in all the allied trades." He leaned forward and wiped the windshield, which was beginning to fog up a little. "In answer to your question, yes, I've been to the sanctuary. When I was a boy I used to go a lot. I like it. But I'm one of the few guys my age from my neighborhood who has a job. If you think I'm going to say to the others, "Guys, I'm sorry about your mortgage and families and schools, but from where I sit, which is pretty safe, I think you ought to be willing to sacrifice for the wildlife around here."

He was sitting hunched over the wheel, peering at the road, not because it wasn't clear, but because of the tension I could feel in him.

Then, instead of keeping to the coast road, he suddenly veered right onto the main road leading into the town.

"Where are we going?"

He didn't answer.

"Steve?"

"My place."

I was pleased, but also worried. Furtively, trying to see my watch by the dashboard light, I held up my wrist. But the dial was too small and it was too dark. "What time is it?" I asked.

"I don't know." He glanced at his own wrist. "Eleven."

"It's getting late. I want to see your place, Steve, but maybe we'd better do it another night. Mother's pretty relaxed, but even if we turned back now, it'd be nearly twelve before I got home. And she might say something to Charles."

"She still thinks it's him?"

"Sure."

"And of course that makes it all right."

I didn't say anything, because there was nothing I could say.

"Well, that's understandable, I guess. And whenever I get to feeling put down by all this, I remind myself that my family would be as horrified if I took you home as yours could ever be."

"Would they be?"

He looked over at me. "You'd better believe it. I can see my mother now while I tried to explain to her that you came from a long line of Protestant humanists. She's a daily communicant. There are two peoples who are going to remain Catholic if it kills them. One is the Irish and the other is the Polish, and for the same reason. For centuries their conquerors and invaders did their best to make them something else. Which is probably the reason we're still all so pigheaded about it."

"Yes, but you're...we're...over here now."

"And you think that's so different?"

"Isn't it?"

"From where you are I guess it looks that way."

138

We drove in silence for a while. Steve put his hand out and took mine. "It's not your fault."

I squeezed it back. "I thought the only people who felt this violently were blacks."

"There's a difference though. Social activists like your brother, and probably most of your friends, would be busting their gut to find work for the town if it was black unemployment. And maybe they'd even tone down some of their rhetoric if destroying the sanctuary and building the resort would help the black community." He leaned forward to peer into the dark where two roads converged. "But we do not figure as official targets for their social conscience."

"That's not very consistent."

"Who was it who said something about consistency being the hobgoblin of small minds?"

"I don't know. You tell me."

"Emerson, I think."

We drove for a while. "Who is it you want me to meet?"

"A friend of mine. A friend named Chico."

"Chico! That doesn't sound Polish."

"It isn't."

"Well, who is it?"

"You'll see," Steve said, and laughed.

The town of Leominster was like a lot of New England towns. There were old and pretty parts, particularly around the town square, but nearby, on the river, were factories and plants, many of them now empty, and during daylight the entire town looked grim and encrusted with industrial dirt.

Just off the square, running along the main road through the town, was a strip of bars, discos, porn movie houses and seedy-looking stores. We drove along this for about three blocks before turning off towards the river. As we waited for a stoplight, I stared at an open door from which blared disco music and a flashing pink light.

"Have you ever been to a disco?" I said to Steve.

"Sure. Haven't you?"

"No. Will you take me? I'm dying to go to one."

"Well, I dunno. They're pretty hairy around here. Maybe, some other place."

A crowd of young people came surging out of the disco. Just then, the light changed and Steve stamped on the pedal.

I craned my neck around. "That looked like some of the kids from the Harbor."

"Yeah. They sometimes turn up at the discos or theaters

139

in the town. But they'd be smart to go somewhere else about now."

"Because of the sanctuary fight?"

"I told you. You don't know how people feel—especially the younger town kids who're looking for jobs. All they need is for some of the summer people to come and try and take over one of the saloons or discos some night—not only here but a little farther out, where there are a couple of other discos!"

"Why don't we go there?" I asked, and knew the answer before he said anything.

"Because it wouldn't be just me taking out a girl. You know that, Sarah. Everybody would get into the act—your family, my family. I'm not ready to make that many waves, are you?"

By this time we were driving down one of the narrow streets between tall loft buildings. It must have rained, because the cobbles were wet and there were hazy rings around the streetlights. Nobody was about. Steve pulled up beside one of the buildings. "Well, are you?"

I stared down at my hands, thinking about our making love in the back of the van, beside the water under the overhanging rock, under the trees in a couple of places. All the kids at school talked a lot about sex and having relationships, but I couldn't think of what went on between Steve and me as just a relationship.

After a minute, Steve put his arm around me. "Sometimes I feel twenty years older than you, instead of just six. Sarah, for us to think about marriage, we'd have to be so sure—so damn sure. Nobody in my family's ever been divorced. It may be the national pastime now, but not with us. We believe in the family, the Church and children, and when we marry, it stays. That's why I've always known, or thought, I'd marry somebody I'd grown up with, who was the same."

"I've never known anyone that religious."

"It's not even being religious. It's just—a way of life."

"Do you mean you don't even believe whatever it is your church teaches? You just go along?"

"Of course I believe. It never occurred to me not to. And for God's sake—that doesn't mean I'm holy or good or a saint. I've done all the things any single guy does. My mother hoped I'd be a priest—but I knew from the time I was thirteen that wasn't for me. I like girls too much. But marriage— that's...that's serious. Anyway, I can't afford it right now.

140

My business is just on the edge of really getting into the black, and I've got two more years of parochial school fees to pay."

We sat there in the dark and the quiet. It was beginning to rain again, and I watched the water collect on one of the building ledges and drip into a puddle underneath.

"I've never asked you," Steve said, "but are you...you are taking precautions, aren't you?"

I was angry. "I thought you didn't believe in birth control."

"Let's not get into that. Are you?"

I hadn't been. I'd thought about it, of course, but I certainly didn't want to go to a doctor in the Cove, and to go to one anywhere else would have been complicated. Besides, my period had arrived on the dot after we'd made love several times, and somehow I had talked myself into believing that I wouldn't get pregnant immediately afterwards, anyway.

"No. And anyway, I had my period. You remember? I told you, and we didn't...we didn't make love that time or the next."

"I'll take you to a doctor and you'd better let him take care of it—give you the pill or something."

"What have your other girls done?" I asked, angry and hurt and hating myself for saying that.

"Don't be like that, Sarah. Any girls I've...I've been with were the kind I figured knew how to take care of themselves. You're different....I told you, I've never felt about anybody else this way. Please don't cry." He put his arms around me and held me. "I love you," he said. "I love you."

And I knew it was true. Even though it might not be enough, it was true. He cared about things like family and church and life-style, and all I thought about was being with him. After a minute I said that to him.

He sighed a little. "You may be right. I was really only outside my world—in your world—for two years, when I was in college. And then Mom got sick and I came back. Sometimes I wonder whether I came back because it seemed like I had to go to work right away or because I wanted to come back anyway."

I sat up and blew my nose on the handkerchief he handed me. "Do you find us that horrible?"

"Not horrible. Attractive. That's part of the problem."

"How do you mean?"

"Well, you...people like you...are good-looking, well educated, you have terrific freedoms....One of the priests I once

141

knew called it your cool Protestant New England world. But you don't seem to have the absolutes that I grew up with and that I guess I need, the gritty rocks that are there, under you, when things slam down on you. Relationships don't seem to matter to you so much. When one doesn't work, you try another. You live more in your heads...."

"I don't. You're making me into...into a type: genus WASP, female. And I'm me, Sarah Lacey."

"You might be surprised how much you'd feel like genus WASP female if I ever took you home to where you're the odd one. It's only when you're floating around alone in somebody else's world that you come to see how much you're a product of your own." He rubbed my head. "You know, darling, we don't have to decide this tonight. Come on up. I want you to meet Chico."

Steve locked the van after us, then opened the door to the loft with his key. The elevator doors opened horizontally, that is, one went up and the other down and we stepped over the lower one. Then the elevator went slowly up, the doors opened, we stepped out and Steve flicked a switch to the side. I gasped. We had stepped straight into a huge space, an enormous workroom filled with every kind of tool, tables with electrical devices at the end, stacks of lumber, a wall hung with all kinds of implements and pieces of furniture just begun, partly finished, and completed. A small table, with a shelf underneath it and graceful legs, was to my right. Farther along was a desk. A tall set of bookshelves, with odd carving on it, was against one wall. There was the frame for a sofa, with crosspieces forming the arms and backs. It was finished, but not varnished, and the natural wood looked almost as smooth as stone.

"Steve—these are beautiful. Did you make them?"

He was standing in the doorway. "Yeah."

"They're so simple and yet elegant."

"Have you ever seen Shaker furniture?"

"Some. That's beautiful, too. Sort of like this."

"For my taste, the Shakers made the most beautiful furniture ever. Oh, it wasn't highly elaborate or sophisticated like Sheraton or Hepplewhite. But when I started making it, that was what I used as a model."

"Do you sell these?"

"Some of them. I make it for friends, too. That bookcase is going to be for my sister." He came over and bent down. "And this is going to be a first-communion present for my

142

niece, Tony's kid." He took from behind a table a small rocking chair, exactly like a big one, except on a smaller scale. It was painted black with intricate gold ornamentation.

"She'll love it," I said. I looked at Steve's hands. They were rough and rather sinewy, and flattened and coarse at the fingers. But they were touching the wood, stroking it gently, almost the way he touched me.

I became aware that I had been hearing a strange noise, a sort of chirping. "What's that?"

"What?"

"That noise."

"Oh, that." He grinned. "Come along."

We crossed the wide space and came to what I thought was the wall at the far end, but that seemed to have a door in it. "This way." Steve opened the door.

I saw then that this was the part he spoke of as partitioned off. He'd obviously put in a ceiling, or the much smaller space would have felt like a well. As it was, it was a low-ceilinged, roomy studio apartment, opening into an L-shaped kitchen, and then from there into a big, rectangular room with what looked like a dressing room and bath off to one side. The walls were painted a beige, there were red curtains on the two big windows, a sofa, a carpet, a table, chairs, flowers and a couple of paintings on the wall. Hanging from the ceiling was a cage. Inside the cage, talking his head off with excitement, was a green parakeet.

Steve went over and opened the cage door and held out his finger. The bird, chattering something that sounded, oddly, like "Pretty Chico, pretty baby," stepped carefully out onto his finger, walked sideways and back along it and ruffled his feathers with excitement.

"Sarah, meet Chico. Chico, this is Sarah. She says I don't like birds."

Chapter

8

It was three o'clock by the time I crept into the house. Ten minutes later I was in bed with Jill beside me, still expressing hysterical enthusiasm after my absence. My last thought before I went to sleep was of Steve, fixing drinks for us at his kitchen sink, Chico perched on top of his head, bending forward, grooming his eyebrows.

"What's he doing?" I asked, seeing the green bird atop Steve's thick hair, bending over and running his beak over Steve's brows.

"Grooming my eyebrows. It's a mark of great affection. Birds do it to each other."

Steve was a little abashed at the little parrot's obvious regard for him. Yet it seemed strange and wonderful and rather touching that a hundred and seventy or so pounds of human being, and four to six ounces of bird, could have developed such a definite and affectionate relationship with one another.

"How did you come to get him?"

"My brother won him at some kind of fair and took him home, but Mom has a cat, and the poor bird nearly had a nervous breakdown, even safe in the cage, because Tom would stalk him along the top of the bookshelves. So, I brought him here."

"Do you let him loose a lot?"

"He's always loose when I'm here. He sits on the desk or work table."

"Doesn't he have droppings?" My mind was on the copious pigeon droppings adorning various statues in New York.

"Yes, but they're easy to wipe off. No worse than a litter pan or cleaning up after a dog." He seemed almost defensive.

"So you see," he said, driving me home later, "I'm not a hater of nature or birds."

I reached out my hand. He took his off the steering wheel and clasped it. "It's just that there are no jobs, Sarah. And a family-type hotel with swimming pool and golf club and horses and stuff would give a shot in the arm to the whole area." He loosed his hand and put his arm around me.

"Isn't there another place you could put the hotel? Really, Steve, any other place at all?" I was seeing those ducks again in my mind.

"Harry was going to buy Headlands till some of the summer people decided it would screw up their nice, quaint Harbor and wrote to Charles's father. He's got another place and was all ready to sell it, but after he came here he decided he wanted to keep it. So—there went that."

"I know, Charles told me."

"Do you like him?"

"Sure. He's nice. He's sort of a loner."

"Yeah. If they were all like him there wouldn't be such a problem."

I didn't want to talk about the problem. I felt peaceful and pleasant, just sitting there with Steve's arm around me, so we stayed like that, without saying anything, for the rest of the drive home.

I slept late the next morning, and wasn't expecting anyone to be around when I went down for breakfast. So I was surprised to see Mother sitting there reading a leaflet that I recognized as being put out by the conservationists. She looked up as I came into the kitchen. "Good morning, Bright Eyes."

"Hi."

"That was quite some hour you got in last night. Where had you been?"

I should have known, I thought, making a big to-do about

146

pouring coffee and adding cream and sugar, that thinking I had got away with it was too good to be true.

"We went into the town," I said. If Bruce and Linda could go to some of the discos, there was no reason why (theoretically) Charles and I shouldn't.

"What on earth did you want to do in that dreary place?"

"There are some discos there."

Mother stared at me. "I find it hard to imagine Charles Brewster, who looks more like a heron than a heron, gyrating around a disco."

"Oh, well, you know, everybody does it."

"Yes. Or, I suppose." Pause. "You and he certainly seem to be making a regular thing of it. But why doesn't he ever come for you here at the house? Certainly things are more easygoing here at the Cove, where we live in each other's pockets. And I realize that some of the old courtly customs have gone by the board, but picking a girl up before going out with her is still considered the norm, isn't it? It was when Mushroom was your age, and that's not so long ago."

I buttered some toast. Why hadn't I thought about that before? "Well, you know, we usually go up the coast somewhere, so it seems silly for him to come right around to the other side of the Harbor."

"No, it doesn't seem silly. It just seems good manners. I want you to tell him next time to drop by for a drink or something before you go out."

"Okay."

I concentrated on hoping that Mother would decide to go out and work on her book, and felt mildly indignant that she seemed less preoccupied with it than usual. Mushroom once said that when Mother really got launched on a book, she, Mushroom, could get nine months pregnant and Mother might just comment mildly that maybe she should try cutting out desserts.

"How's the book going?" I asked.

"Very well. But it would go even better if I could stop worrying about you."

I swallowed a piece of toast. "What are you worried about? I'm doing fine. And I've got a boyfriend. You've always wanted me to have a boyfriend."

"What I've wanted for you is to be happy and free and self-confident."

"I'm terrifically happy."

"You are at moments. Every now and then your face is

147

like a bursting sunrise. But other times you look older without looking happier. You look different, Sam, and whatever it is has happened in the last few weeks and I haven't been doing my job and paying attention."

"Yes you have. Your book—"

"Bother my book. You're my job."

"You've always said that a woman is more than just a mother, and I agree with you."

"Yes, well, she is. But there's something about you that's bothering me, and I'm not sure what it is. Are you sure you're okay, sweetie?" She put her hand across the table, grasping my arm. Part of me was terribly touched, because Mother's not usually that demonstrative. But most of me wanted to get away. "Look, Ma," I said, half joking, "you've always wanted me to grow up and be socially successful and bright and so on, and now I am and you're getting into a state about it. I'm just getting older."

"Yes. That's what I said. And I'm delighted you're being a social success. Charles seems like an awfully nice boy, and God knows you couldn't get more distinguished and well-to-do than his family...."

"So what's worrying you?"

"I don't know. That's partly why I'm worried. I wish Mrs. Brewster were something other than a moron with a drinking problem."

My stomach sank in dismay. If Mother was minded to do some research on Charles and me, I'd be in trouble even sooner than I thought. I knew the Great Awakening—that it was a townie, Steve Novak, with whom I was going out, and not Charles Brewster the Tenth or whatever—was bound to come. But I kept counting on being able to put it off...and off...until maybe Steve and I would have arrived at...something.

"I have to go to the village," I muttered.

"And that's another thing. You seem to have developed into some kind of workaholic. You never go on the beach with the other kids. Yes, I know, you're sensitive about your scars and all that, but for heaven's sake, Sam, once people have seen them they'll forget about them, and now that you're going out with Charles you don't have to feel like such a wallflower, and your father and I do wish you'd get some rest and relaxation."

"You make it sound like castor oil."

"Well it's not castor oil, it's what we pay a huge price to

148

rent this house for—so you children can have a decent place for the summer for fun and rest and swimming and all the other goodies children are supposed to have."

"And you and Father hate it?"

"You know we don't, Miss Smart Ass. Why are you being so contentious?"

I didn't know. "Sorry," I muttered. I got to the door. "I like working," I said as I stood there. "Maybe I'm going to be an investigative reporter," I said, "and work on the newspaper is good experience."

Mother had got up but was staring at me. "I keep having the feeling you just made that up."

Walking along the beach on my way to the village I ran into Mushroom.

"Mushroom," I said suddenly, "do you take the pill?"

She stopped and looked at me. Mushroom and I are the same height, but she has a terrific figure and was looking tanned and gorgeous in a one-piece white bathing suit.

She stopped. "Yes. Why?"

"Could I take your pills?"

"No, of course not. You have to see a doctor yourself." She looked at me frowning. "Everything okay?"

"Sure. Why not?"

"I don't know."

"You act like I shouldn't be...needing the pill. I bet you were taking it when you were my age."

"No. I didn't have the occasion to use it until I was twenty. But I realize things move faster now even than then." She hesitated. "I take it you and Charles..."

I didn't answer, but just looked in a sort of embarrassed way at my feet. I was tired of lying.

"I tell you what," Mushroom said, "I'm going with Gene into Boston tomorrow. Why don't you come with us? You can see a doctor there."

"Okay." I'd have to take the day off, but it couldn't be helped.

"You...do you think you're pregnant?"

"Oh no. I just thought I'd maybe better start."

Mushroom was looking very closely at me. "You've changed, just in the past couple of weeks, or that's since I've noticed. Sam, how long have you and Charles...have you been making out?"

"A few weeks," I muttered.

"And you haven't been using a diaphragm or anything?"

"No. I mean, how could I? You have to go to a doctor for that, too, don't you?"

"Yes, of course. Has Charles been using anything?"

By this time I could feel my cheeks burning. Why they were burning I wasn't sure, whether it was because Mushroom kept zeroing in on Charles, when it wasn't Charles, or because we were talking about sex, which I found embarrassing, I didn't know. "I don't think so," I muttered.

"Well surely you'd *know*."

And of course I would, or thought I would. I had this curious feeling that if it were Charles I was having a relationship with, I could answer the question better. Somehow things would be more talked about. But I couldn't even be sure of that. After all, Steve was the only man in my life with whom anything like this had ever happened—in fact, the only man I'd ever gone out with.

"No," I said rather loudly. "I mean, yes, I do know. He doesn't—er—use anything."

"You mean to say that you've been doing this unprotected? Sam, you've got to be crazy. Why didn't you ask me?"

I was getting mad, the way I always did when somebody pointed out that I was being my usual idiotic self. "Look, all I asked was a simple question. I don't need to be told how dumb I am—for the umpteenth time!"

"All right, all right. My God, you're sensitive! I didn't mean to sound like I thought you were stupid. But Sam—do you *want* to have to go through the whole abortion bit?"

It was like a word out of a dark closet. Not that it wasn't used around our house. Mother had been very active in the movement to have abortions legalized, and if there were any groups she hated more than the anti-family-planning groups, it was the anti-abortion societies. Those really raised her blood pressure. But I had never thought of it in connection with myself. Somehow it hit me like a stone in the face. "No, of course not," I muttered. And then, "I've gotta go." I tried to brush past Mushroom, but she barred the way.

"Don't look like that, Sam. It's all right. Honest. It's not that big a deal, I shouldn't have said it that way. Three of my friends have had abortions, and it's far from the end of the world. I just meant—listen, don't worry. Go with Gene and me to Boston and I'll take you to a doctor and he can put you on the pill. Okay?" Suddenly she leaned across and kissed me. "You're such a baby. I guess maybe it's because you've

150

been oddly isolated from other American kids. I always thought it was a great break for you being brought up abroad. Now I'm not so sure. We'll start tomorrow at about nine. If Mom asks why you're going, I'll tell her that I'm taking you to an early birthday lunch or something. You want me to ask Charles?"

"No," I said loudly and emphatically, panicky that she might, indeed, say something to him. "I'll ask him. But I think he has something he wants to do."

"I must say being in love doesn't seem to be having much of an effect on him. I passed him the other day and waved, and he just stared blankly at me."

"He gets terrifically involved in a book when he's reading," I said quickly. "Sometimes I have to yell to get his attention."

"Well it's not my idea of love's young dream. But then I'm not you. The studious type probably appeals to you."

If she only knew, I thought, what did appeal to me! "I guess so," I said.

"I've decided to devote an issue to the whole sanctuary hassle," Mr. Haggerty said that morning when I finally got in. "I prefer being twin brother to an ostrich, but even I can't ignore all the flying fur and feathers." He looked up at me from under his eyebrows. "Be interested to know what you think, in view of the fact that you're related by blood to the leader of one of the sides, and seem to be having a heavy romance with one of the leaders of the other."

I stared at him, feeling my stomach contract with fear. For a minute I thought about denying it. But there was something about Mr. Haggerty's expression that told me it would be useless. Also, I discovered I was tired of lying. Leading a double life had turned out to be more of a strain than I had figured. Though there was no question of how worthwhile it was. Steve was worth anything.

"How did you know?" I asked finally. "We didn't think anybody knew."

"Probably nobody does, except me. But you've passed my house sitting in Steve's van two or three times when you've been heading north, probably to some private portion of the beach up there. And since I've heard nothing about it from the usual bush telegraph, which in a small summer place like this is nearly always highly active, then I have to assume that it's something neither of you wants known. Am I right?"

I nodded.

"Just as well, probably. The way things are heating up, neither one of you would be in for much sympathy from either side." He seemed to glare at me from behind the thicket of gray-brown brows, but I had begun to realize that it was all show. He was a kind man. "Sure you know what you're doing?"

"Yes. Of course."

He didn't say anything.

"Why do you say that?" I asked.

"Because I wondered. People don't talk much today about class and background. It's unfashionable. Nevertheless, they're important, when it comes to anything permanent. Steve is very much a first-generation Polish-American, which makes him even more Polish than the second- or third-generation kids around the town. Also, he comes from a deeply religious family, and with the new Polish Pope, their sense of pride and religious identity has increased. And he's a proud and stubborn young man. Very able. Pity he didn't finish college. Might have loosened him up a little, helped him get rid of some of the chips on his shoulder. But he went at a bad time for him—and his experiences just reaffirmed his sense of isolation from the mainstream."

"You think religion is that important?" Steve seemed to think it was, but I had been holding onto the hope that he was exaggerating it.

"Depends. Sometimes yes and sometimes no. You get two kids growing up in New York—one, say, sort of vaguely WASP, and the other Jewish. If they go to the same private or prep schools and the same college, they'd have more in common with each other than either one would have with a Baptist from the South. But that's probably because actual religious practice doesn't matter that much with either one. Any more than it likely does with your family. But with people like the Novaks, you've got a different proposition entirely. They've probably been practicing their Catholicism in the face of the Communist government at home, and now they're doing it in the face of American secularity. So it means a lot to them. You'd both have to be awfully sure that's what you wanted for it to work. And if you lived here, then *you'd* have to make all the adjustments. Don't make any mistake about that. You'd have to go into their world, not the other way around. And the feminists could bleat their heads off till doomsday, but if you lived here, that's the way it would be. For it to be any different, you'd have to pick up and go some-

152

where else different and start from scratch. And Steve takes his family responsibilities seriously."

I was standing, staring at him as he talked. Every word was like the jab of a hammer. Then I got angry.

"I'd be happy and proud to be part of Steve's family," I said, and realized a minute later that I was, in effect, making a public announcement about it, for the first time. "But I'd rather you didn't mention it to anyone right now. Not because I wouldn't be glad to...to live here with Steve. But it's a secret for the time being."

"Okay. Just thought I'd mention it." He leaned forward and picked up a sheaf of papers. "Here's the rhetoric from both sides. Editorials from the town's paper, pamphlets from the conservationists' groups, letters to the editors on the subject. I'd like you to read it all and give me your opinion. It's not that I haven't read it," he said, "it's just that I'd like to know how a young person with a foot in both camps will feel."

"Okay." I held out my hand. I had been happy not to read any of the local papers or propaganda, working on the same ostrich principle that Mr. Haggerty seemed to favor. But I supposed that it was time I saw what was going on. "Oh, by the way," I said, "I won't be in tomorrmw. I'm going to Boston."

"What's in Boston?"

I grinned. "Baked beans."

"All right. Come back with an intelligent approach to our local hubbub and I'll call it square."

"I'm going to Boston tomorrow," I told Charles, when we were all on the beach that afternoon. Mrs. Brewster was either out or upstairs when I arrived, and I planned to leave a note for her, but I also felt it necessary to tell Charles in case Mushroom should have an impulse to say something to him. I was sorry now I'd told her. I should have let Steve take me to a doctor, as he'd said he would, instead of yielding to the impulse to ask Mushroom about her pills, but it was done now, and Mushroom, who is much more open than I am, could easily take it into her head to tackle Charles on the subject of her little sister.

I took a deep breath and glanced at Charles, who, as usual, was sitting under his floppy hat, reading a book.

"What are you reading?" I finally said, when he didn't comment on my statement about Boston.

He didn't even look up. "A book on international law."

153

"Are you planning to be a lawyer?"

"Yes. Is there something you wanted to ask me, Sarah? If so, ask. No reason to go futzing around asking me what I'm reading."

"How did you know there was something I wanted to ask?"

"You've been working up to something for the past half hour. It was all over your face."

"What? What was all over my face? Why do people always say they can tell what I'm thinking? I can't tell what other people are thinking—at least not most of the time. But everybody and his brother seems to be able to tell what I'm thinking. It's degrading."

Charles glanced up at me. His glasses had slid towards the end of his nose and he looked like a cartoon of the absentminded professor.

"Oh, I don't know. Actually it's rather appealing. That's why I like you. At least—one of the reasons I like you. You don't seem as lacquered, as finished off, as competent to make a fool of me, as most of the other girls around."

I smiled at him. "I like you too." Then my smile dimmed. Would he like me as much when I told him about why I was going to Boston and the role he was supposed to be playing?

"So? What fruits of the flesh am I supposed to be enjoying now?"

"Mushroom, my sister, is taking me to Boston tomorrow to help me find a doctor to give me the pill because I said we hadn't used anything."

"And how long are we supposed to have been letting passion run rampant?"

I giggled. "About six weeks."

"One of us has to be pretty dumb."

"I don't think so at all. I'm not...this is the first time...for me...and Steve said all his other girls were the kind that he thought could take care of themselves."

"I see. Well, okay. But I'm damned if I'll be able to keep a straight face if I'm supposed to tell your sister that the whole thing slipped my mind, or keep my composure if your brother or your father comes at me breathing smoke and fire and pointing a gun. I'm willing to help, but I draw the line at getting shot."

"Charles, you're wonderful, thank you." And I leaned over and kissed him. He gave me a strange look, then went back to his book.

* * *

154

That night, as I was slipping out to see Steve, Mother suddenly said to me, "I thought I asked you to invite Charles to pick you up here and have a drink with us."

"Well I will," I said. "But I haven't had a chance to talk to him yet." I was trying to slip out the kitchen door while Mother was busy filling the dishwasher. Mushroom was helping to clear the kitchen table. Peter hadn't come home from dinner. Father was in the living room.

"Well talk to him," Mother said sharply. "I really don't like this sneaking off night after night without his even bothering to come here. Nobody's ever accused me of being old-fashioned, but the old-fashioned idea that a boy has to take a little trouble to go out with the girl of his choice isn't such a bad one, and it isn't such a bad idea for him to know that her family considers it important, too. I'm surprised at Charles. His own mother was, if anything, on the stuffy side, and he lived with her a lot more than he lived with that playboy father of his."

"Was his father a playboy?" I asked, sneaking slowly towards the door—anything to get Mother off the subject of Charles picking me up. I was really worried, because if Mother got this bee in her bonnet and became serious about it, she could be as tenacious about that as anything else she put her mind to.

"His father was—is—an extremely able businessman who came from the strictest kind of high-principled, stodgy New England family and proceeded to rebel against every single tenet they ever held. If he hadn't been so smart and made so much money, they could have washed their hands of him with great virtue. Unfortunately, he rescued the declining family fortunes, so they couldn't afford to ignore him. Now remember what I said, Sam. I want that young man to pick you up."

"Okay, Mom, for heaven's sake. I'll tell him." And I escaped out the door.

"We haven't got too much time tonight," Steve said as we emerged from our first long kiss. "I have to go to a union meeting in about an hour."

Nothing, I thought, seemed to be going right tonight, but I swallowed my sense of grievance and asked, "What's the meeting about?"

Steve didn't say anything for a minute. Then, "About the conservationists' injunction. It looks like Schreiber may abandon the whole attempt and try farther down the coast,

155

which will be great for the people there but won't do anything for this town."

My spirts had soared for a few seconds. Schreiber's moving his plans to another area would solve a lot of my problems, but, as Steve pointed out, it was hardly a solution to people who wanted to have jobs.

"Maybe something else will come along," I said.

"Like what?"

I had no specific ideas. Finally I said, "I don't know." Then, "Is it very important to you, Steve? I mean, you work all the time." I knew the minute I'd said that that it was the wrong thing."

"If you mean will I be out anything, the answer is no. After all, even if Harry moves his operations somewhere else... well, anyway, as you say, I have work, regardless. But why do you think it's strange that I should care about guys I grew up with, so many of whom are looking for jobs, when your lot tie themselves in knots over the local wildlife?"

Suddenly, in my mind, I saw Chico perched on Steve's head, and bending down, grooming his eyebrows, while Steve mixed our drinks. Steve had introduced me to his little friend for a purpose: to let me know he wasn't indifferent to creatures of another species. Yet, there was something missing in the point he was making.

"If you're a person, you can pick up and go somewhere and find a job, Steve. If you're wildlife, then maybe you just die—or some of you do. And once an environment like that's gone, it's gone for good."

Steve sighed. It occurred to me that tonight he sounded more tired than he had recently. "That's not true either, Sarah. There are places that oil companies have used for drilling areas, and then when either they've found the exact location or decided there isn't oil there, they've restored it—grass, reeds, water, bushes, trees, everything, and the wildlife has come back. But of course they won't do that up the coast if they build on it. And anyway, I don't want to argue the matter with you. On that I guess we'll just have to settle for being on different sides."

A little sliver of alarm went through me. We had had arguments before. Yet somehow, throughout, there had been the feeling that the argument itself would lead to our agreeing, eventually. Now it seemed as though Steve had given up that thought.

"Steve," I said, and kissed him on the cheek. He put his

arm around me. I whispered, "You love me just as much, don't you?"

"Yes," he said, turning his face against mine. His lips were on mine, gentle and tender. "Just as much. If anything, more."

"You sound sad."

"Yes... well, my kid brother got into a fight and got his head split open and is in the hospital. He seems okay, but they're not sure yet if there's any concussion."

"How old is he?"

"Thirteen."

"That seems an awful lot to happen in a fight between two kids."

Steve was running his fingers up and down the back of my head. "The other guy punched him hard and he fell. That's how he got the crack in his head—if he did crack it."

Mr. Haggerty had said that Steve took his family responsibilities seriously. Perhaps that was why he seemed so down. I tried to imagine how Peter would feel if I cracked my head, but beyond the fact that he might come and see me or bring me some flowers, I couldn't see that it would depress him. On the other hand, I had two parents, and Steve's brother didn't. "What's his name?" I asked.

"Well, his Polish name is Kyril. Which really means Charles."

"You seem terribly worried. Is he really in danger?"

"No. I don't think so. He's a tough kid."

"Then what is it?"

"I guess I feel bad over what he fought about. Apparently some kid he goes to school with said that I seemed to be backing off from supporting the union. His father or older brother or somebody had said so. That's one reason why I have to go tonight. The guys are beginning to wonder if I'm a hundred percent for them."

"Well you are, so why should they doubt it?"

"Because I've been sitting here with you, or up at our beach, or even at the loft, when they've been meeting and planning strategy. And because I haven't been seen out at the usual discos and bowling alleys with the usual girls. They know something's going on. That's one of the disadvantages of living in a small community. There's a lot of help when you need it, but people are used to knowing what everybody's business is."

I sat there, snuggled against his chest, my head under his

157

chin. How long had we been going together? Six weeks? Two months? It seemed much shorter. But it was mid-June when we'd had our first date and it was now the second week in August. It had all seemed so easy and even fun, going out with somebody secret. But now Mother was riding me about Charles picking me up and Steve's friends were beginning to wonder if he was being loyal to his side.

"I wish we could go away, Steve. You could build anywhere. You're a terrific craftsman, Charles said so. And I could get a job and go to art school. And then it wouldn't matter about what our families and friends said."

"And what are my brothers and sisters supposed to do in the meantime?"

"You could send money back to them."

"And let them run wild without a man in the house to hold them in line? Maybe you don't know adolescents very well, but this is the time they get into trouble—drugs, booze, stealing cars for kicks. Don't think there aren't kids in town who don't do that, because there are. My mother is a strong woman, but she has to work too. I ought to be there for another few years."

"If you got work somewhere else—maybe down in the south where you say there're jobs—you could move them all there. And it might be better for them."

Steve was quiet for so long that I wondered if I'd said the wrong thing. "Steve?" I said. "Are you mad I said that?"

He laughed suddenly. "No. I've thought about it, too. There's a lot of building going up in the southwest. An old army buddy of Tony's wrote and said he was involved in construction there and did I want a job? Don't think I haven't thought of it."

"Well why don't we, that would be great."

"I am thinking of it. I just don't want to seem like some kind of fink to the guys up here. And my mother's friends are here.... It's not that cut and dried." He kissed me again, gently. Then turned me in his arms and kissed me not so gently. I pressed hard against him, hungry for him, for all of him. After a minute he said, in a thick voice, "Let's get in the back."

My heart was beating so rapidly I could hardly speak. "What about your union meeting?"

"I'll just have to be late."

I was in bed before I remembered that I had forgotten to tell him either about Charles or that I was going to Boston.

158

"And how long have you been having intercourse?" the doctor said the next day.

"About four or five weeks."

"And neither you nor the man has used any protection?"

"I don't think so. I mean, I haven't. And I don't think he has."

The doctor was a kind, youngish man, so I added, "I'd know, wouldn't I?"

He smiled. "Yes, I think so, although he could, theoretically, slip on a rubber and wear that without your knowing, unless, of course, you'd touched him with your hand, felt him. Have you always?"

As I nodded, I could feel the blood rush up again. It wasn't that I was embarrassed, and I certainly wasn't ashamed. I was proud of the love that Steve and I made together. It was just terribly private. Crazy as it seemed, even when thinking about it myself, it was as though Steve and I had invented it, that nothing, exactly like that, had ever happened before.

"And you say you got your period on time, and that it was normal in every way?"

I nodded again. "Yes."

"Well, let's examine you."

Afterwards, the doctor said, "Well you don't seem to me to have become pregnant, although it's technically possible for you to be, say, one week along. Let me get a few facts about your family's medical history." And he asked me questions about Mother and Father and my grandparents, some of which I could answer, and wrote the answers on a long yellow sheet. Then he looked these over and said, "Well, I don't see any contraindication to your taking the pill—no reason you shouldn't have it. I'll give you a prescription which you will start on the fifth day of your next menstrual cycle, using the day you start menstruating as day one."

"But what'll I do till then?"

"I can fit you with a diaphragm."

"All right."

When I left I went to the drugstore, waited for the pills, bought the jelly that the doctor suggested I use with the diaphragm, and then with paper bag went and sat in the Common to wait for Mushroom to pick me up. Going to the gynecologist, I decided, was a dismal experience. And I still didn't know what I was going to do about Charles picking me up on the nights I went out with Steve.

"Everything's okay?" Mushroom asked, when she and Gene walked up.

"Fine," I said, grateful that the Congressmen was with her, inhibiting her from asking any more questions.

That night I was figuring out how I could get out to join Steve without Mother's seeing me go, when, half an hour before I planned leaving, the front doorbell went.

"Answer it, Sam, will you?" Mother called out from the kitchen.

As soon as I opened the front door I could see Charles's long skinny body through the screen door.

"Hello, Charles," I said.

"Hi. I've come to pick you up." he said, looking bland.

"But—"

"Good evening, Mrs. Lacey," he said over my shoulder.

"Hello, Charles. Nice to see you. Why don't you come in for a drink before you and Sam go on?"

"Thanks, I'd like to."

I was standing there like a log, my mouth half open.

"Well, Sam," Mother said, "aren't you going to join us?"

"Sure," I managed to say.

"Good evening, Charles," Father said, reluctantly putting down his newspaper.

"Good evening, sir. Don't mind me. Go on with your paper if you'd like."

"Certainly not," Mother said. "He can act like a father and a host for once."

Father made a wry face. "The decision seems to have been made for me. However, I am delighted to see you. I was talking to one of your professors the other day and he tells me that you might be thinking of going into law. Is that true?"

"As of the moment, yes. I still have time to change my mind."

"It's good training," Father said, going over to the trolley table that served as a bar, and lifting the top off the ice bucket. "Scotch? Bourbon?"

"Thanks, maybe a very light gin and tonic."

I couldn't help glancing frantically at the grandfather clock in the corner. It was now a quarter to eight and I was to meet Steve at eight.

"We have plenty of time, Sarah," Charles said in a voice packed with meaning. "Absolutely no need to hurry."

I turned and looked at him. He was sipping his drink and

looking blander than ever. Finally I sat down and waited. Obviously I couldn't possibly leave the house with Charles, whom the entire family assumed to be my boyfriend, sitting there arguing points of law with my father, while Mother ignored the dishes and beamed with approval. For a while I felt guilty, then, as I considered how little Mother would beam approvingly if it were Steve sitting there I became angry. Why was Charles doing this? What could it mean?

I glanced up at the grandfather clock again. Three minutes to eight. I got up. "I think we ought to go, Charles."

"For heaven's sake, Sam. Charles said there was no hurry." Mother sounded really mad, as though I were about to deprive her of something to which she had long been entitled.

How could I have been so stupid, I wondered? Of course— Charles had some message for me from Steve. But that thought made me even more anxious to get him outside to where he could deliver it.

Charles put his drink down. "I guess we really do have to go, Mrs. Lacey. Come on, Sam." It was the first time he'd called me that.

There was a chorus of "Don't be back too late," and "Have a good time and next time stay for dinner," to all of which Charles responded politely.

"You saw Steve," I said to him, as soon as we were a safe distance from the house.

"Your unmaidenly impatience to be alone with me—at least as far as your family sees it—is flattering, but I think you're overdoing it."

I ignored that. "What message did he send?"

Charles stopped still in the middle of the path leading to the road. "He spoke to me before he left work this afternoon and asked if you were coming over to sit with the twins. You know you two should really set up some kind of communication system. He'd obviously hung around hoping to see you, and he must have been in a swivet of anxiety about how to reach you without arousing all kinds of suspicions."

"Well he works on Mother's study in the afternoons."

"And how is he supposed to use that? Send messages about how he can't meet you during the evening via her? If he doesn't feel free to speak to any member of your family, or to telephone and leave a message, then what good is it to work at your house in terms of leaving word? He could just as easy be employed at the other end of the Harbor."

161

"I hadn't thought of that," I said as we started walking again.

"It seems to me you haven't thought of a lot."

When I didn't say anything he went on. "Plainly you must have told him that your family thinks you go out with me, because finally, at around three, he came out to where I was sitting and asked stiffly if he could speak to me. Then he asked if I would take a message. When I said I would he told me to tell you that he can't meet you tonight. Something about the union meeting that he was supposed to be at last night but never got to."

"Oh," I said. "I see."

"I wonder. Using me as a courier has got to be pretty difficult for him. It's not as though I were one of his buddies. Do you realize all the admissions he has to make just in that simple act? That he can't telephone you, that he can't go by your house and leave you a note, that he can't ask a member of the family to tell you whatever. He had to act like some goddam spy, and for a guy with his pride that's got to be fairly horrendous. He's not a kid, Sam, he's a man."

I knew it was true. But I said, "He's the same age as Peter."

"Peter may be macho man on the campus and political circuit, but he hasn't grown up yet, Sam. Steve has."

"I don't like the name Sam."

"All right, Sarah. Although I like Sam better."

"Why?" I was thinking of Steve's statement that it suited me, that it was very New England. "Steve said he liked Sarah better. That it was very New England and that I was very New England."

"Poor guy," Charles said.

"What do you mean?"

"I mean that that's a very revealing statement. What he admires about you—besides, of course, your fair white body—is a sort of spare New England aristocracy, something that comes out of the New England nineteenth century. It's what most of the ethnics found when they came over here a hundred years ago, and they wanted and admired and hated it all at the same time, because it put them down and made them feel like immigrants."

"But Steve's family only came here after World War II."

"That doesn't make any difference. It probably struck him the same way."

"But you like Sam better. Why?"

"How the hell should I know? Maybe because I'm rebelling

162

against all that—after all, my own family's been stuck in that particular mold since the year one. Maybe because it makes you more approachable."

All the while we talked we were walking up the beach. The moon was high and big again and the moonlight was a broken shaft of gold across the water, broken where the waves peaked and then fell.

For a while we didn't say anything. It seemed to be strange walking on the beach with Charles when I had been out so much with Steve, and the diaphragm that I had, with great difficulty, inserted felt more uncomfortable with each step.

"Let's sit down," I said.

We ambled to some rocks right below the Headlands and sat on top of them.

For a while we didn't say anything. Charles's long legs were crossed and he stared, yogilike, at the ocean. I sat with my knees drawn up and my arms around them. After a while I said, "I wonder where everybody is. During the day it's packed with bodies around here. Now there's nobody."

"In cars, in movie houses, in some of the discos in the town, in the two bars in the village, in beds in each other's homes."

"But we aren't."

"No."

"What's the matter with us? I don't mean Steve. I mean you and me."

"I told you, we're outsiders, all three of us, including Steve. We're outsiders for different reasons, but the result is the same. We're not entirely comfortable with what's supposed to be our own kind, yet we're not comfortable altogether outside it, either. So we sit wedged on our various fences, wondering which side we should jump off on."

I thought about that for a while, staring at Headlands. There was light on downstairs in what I knew to be the kitchen, and another upstairs. The twins' room was dark.

"Why are we outsiders?"

"You'll have to answer that for yourself as far as you're concerned."

"Because of my legs?" No, I knew it wasn't that. "No. The accident only happened last year. I've always been one. It's because my whole family values terrific brains and terrific looks and I don't rate high with either."

"It's got to be more than that. Plenty of kids feel that about themselves. But you don't seem to hang out a lot with other kids."

163

"I guess it's because I've been abroad so much. And where I've been kids don't hang out together the way they do here. There, you're with your family more."

"Probably. It sounds reasonable."

"And you? Is it just because of your brains and because you like to work?"

"Immodest as it may sound, yes. I've always been at least a couple of years ahead in school at the same time that I wasn't developed physically as much even as the kids my own age. In some respects, for a long time, I was a kind of a joke—a cartoon of a quiz kid, all head and glasses. If I could have been a terrific athlete along with the I.Q. they'd have over-looked it. But I wasn't, and I did have a physical disability which I seem to have grown out of—at least for the time—which added its factor to the whole thing."

"What was your disability?"

"Kidney problems. I'm okay now, more or less. But I had to have treatment periodically, which meant that I couldn't go off to body-building camps, that kind of thing."

"Are you okay now?"

"So I'm told. I haven't felt any ill effects now for some time."

"Did you mind?"

"To tell you the truth—no. I take it you did. But I found a lot of the things that would have made life easier for me with the other kids fairly boring. I like to read. The only form of exercise I like is walking, and that's a solitary occupation. So don't go feeling sorry for me, the way you do for yourself."

"I don't feel sorry for myself."

"Yes you do. You're a pretty, bright girl, no matter what your inferiority complexes may say, and you go around acting like the wallflower of all time."

I was about to deny it hotly when it occurred to me that Steve had said more or less the same thing. "Steve sort of said that."

"Steve is a very bright guy."

"Coming from you—why do you think he's an outsider?"

"Oh, he's something of a practical idealist. If his father weren't a bum and he was third-generation instead of first, I think he'd just get out, finish his architectural degree and become one of the upwardly mobile immigrants in the tra-dition of all pioneers who came over here and made it on their own. He's got the guts and ability. But he happened along at the wrong time in our history to be able to just go off and

164

climb the ladder. He'd feel like a rat on several counts if he left home now, so he's stuck there. And nobody's going to let him be moderate, not his side and not ours. Have you been reading any of the stuff the volunteer office has been putting out?"

"No. Mr. Haggerty gave me a fistful of stuff to read. Not only the conservationist side, but editorials from the town papers."

"That should send your juices up before you go to bed."

"Is it really that bad?"

"You'll see when you read it."

I stared at the ocean for a while. "What do you think's going to happen?"

"I think there's going to be a public bust-up of some kind, with the fanatics of both sides egging everybody on. If the extremists would just shut up, the rest could get together and work something out. But they won't."

I was staring up at Headlands, which was on top of the cliff above us. A young woman seemed to be leaning out of the twins' window holding a light of some kind.

"Who's that girl you have there in your house?"

"What girl?"

There was such a sharp note to Charles's voice that I turned to look at him.

"What girl are you talking about?" he repeated.

"The one I just saw. She was standing in the twins' window with a light, it almost looked like a candle."

"I don't see any girl."

I looked back. The twins' window was dark. "Well, she's not there now. But she was."

"There's no girl in the house. Just Nancy and the twins."

Charles was looking at me intently. A queer feeling crawled up my back. I glanced back at the house. Something flared red, then dark, then red again. It was only a glow that grew bright and then dim by turns, but I knew beyond any doubt that something in the house was burning. "Charles— look, something's on fire."

Chapter

9

"Come on!" Charles said, scrambling to his feet. We started up the path to the cliff head, Charles's legs covering huge chunks of the steep hillside.

I had been happily oblivious of my gimpy leg for some weeks, but was powerfully reminded of its limitations as I struggled to keep up with him.

Finally we were at the top, and Charles lit out across the wide expanse of grass and scrub, with me hopping unevenly behind him. We could smell the smoke from the lawn, although the night breeze was blowing it in the opposite direction. Once we were inside the house, it was almost overpowering.

"Call the fire department," Charles yelled at me, as he tore upstairs.

I went to the downstairs phone and dialed the operator. "Send the fire truck," I said when she came on. "We have a fire at Headlands."

"Is it a big fire?"

"I don't know."

"There's a small fire truck for the village, but we also use the town's fire department."

"Send for both, quickly," I said. "There are children here."

Then I slammed down the phone and ran towards the staircase.

Charles suddenly appeared at the top of the stairs, coughing and spluttering, carrying a twin. "Here's Jennie. Take her. I've got to go back for Jamie and Nancy."

Charles put her down. "Go downstairs to Sarah."

"I wanna get Jamie," she yelled and started back into the smoke.

"You go downstairs to Sarah." Charles lifted her down to me a few steps below.

I reached up. "Come on, Jennie. Don't hold things up. The quicker Charles can get back, the quicker he can get Jamie. Now you stay here, or better still, go downstairs. I want to help him."

"No," Jennie whimpered.

"Don't leave her," Charles called back from above. I knew he was right.

"Let's sit here, Jennie," I said. "There isn't too much smoke, and when Charles gets Jamie, we can help him."

But Charles seemed a long time coming. I kept a firm grip on Jennie, who was yelling repetitively, "Jamie, Jamie, wake up, wake up!" I found myself praying, although if anybody had asked me, I would have said I was an atheist. "Please let Jamie be all right . . . please."

After a while I heard two sounds, one right after the other. The first was a child coughing, followed in the distance by the sound of a siren.

"Charles!" I called out, over the rapidly increasing noise of the siren.

"Here," Charles said above me. His voice sounded hoarse and muted. I looked up. He had wrapped something around his mouth and nose and was toting Jamie across his shoulder. I got up and ran upstairs and started coughing.

"Get back," he whispered. "It's getting worse. Get the twins downstairs. I have to go back for Nancy. Is that the fire engine?"

It was. I heard the truck roar across the lawn but did not have time to go to the back of the house to see. Then, "Go let them in," Charles croaked, "or they'll break down the door. I'll look after the twins. Hurry!"

I reached the door just as there was a loud banging on it and flung it open. The fireman who stood there in his helmet, holding an axe, looked about nine feet tall. "It's upstairs," I said, and stood back, as more firemen poured into the house trailing a hose. They moved fast.

"Get those kids out of the house," the fire chief roared at me from halfway up the stairs. Then, as I came to the bottom of the stairs, "Who else is up there?"

"A woman, the children's mother, and a young girl."

"What rooms?"

I tried to give directions to the main bedroom and then the twins' room where I had seen the girl. "And Charles," I yelled. "He's Mrs. Brewster's stepson. He brought out the twins, and he's gone up for Mrs. Brewster."

Holding the twins by either hand I watched two of the men disappear into the smoke upstairs.

"Okay, get them outside," another firemen told me. "Are they okay?"

Jamie was still coughing a little, but they seemed otherwise fine.

"Mom?" Jennie asked, a quaver in her voice.

"She'll be okay," the man said reassuringly. "Now go with the young lady here."

Snatching sweaters off the hat rack in the hall, I took the twins outside and held onto them as I watched the firemen stamp into the house, and heard them yelling.

"Will they get Charles?" Jamie asked.

I was worried about the same thing, but I said, "Yes," as firmly as I could, telling myself that I would prove to be right.

We were standing there when there was the sound of another fire truck, and a much bigger one swung off the cliff road and onto the path leading to the house. It pulled up a short way away from the smaller truck. Obviously it had come from the town. One of the first people to get down, huge in fire hat, was Steve.

"Steve!" I yelled, not thinking.

But with all the shouting and yelling and stamping he didn't hear me. This truck and its firemen made far more noise than the first.

"Steve!" I yelled, and this time the twins took up the chorus, "Steve! Steve!" They yelled.

He heard then and turned, saw us, hesitated, then came over.

"Hi," he said, standing a few feet away.

"Charles is in there," Jamie said. "Will he be all right or will he burn up?"

"And Mom," Jennie chimed in.

169

"I'm sure they'll be fine," Steve said soothingly. "Just wait here and let me go and see what's happening."

He had barely looked at me. "Steve?" I said.

He looked at me then. "Are you okay?"

"Yes. Did the operator send for you, too?"

"We were already on the way. Word came in on one of our guys' CB radio band that there was a fire in the village, so we came anyway. Most of us are volunteer firemen. I've got to go and see what's going on," he said, and stalked away.

The twins and I stood there for what seemed like a long time. Since that first glow in the window when the girl was leaning out I hadn't seen any actual flames. But puffs of smoke were still trailing from the windows. The town firemen that had driven up all seemed noisy and cheerful.

"Will they get Mom?" Jennie asked, her hand holding mine so hard it was almost pinching.

"And Charles?" Jamie said.

"Yes."

"And the girl?" Jennie said, looking up at me.

I looked down. "Of course. Who was she, Jennie?"

"I don't know."

I was puzzled. In the back of my mind I had somehow worked it out that the girl was an additional baby-sitter that Mrs. Brewster had hired for the evenings. Obviously, though, I was wrong. "Well, maybe I had her age wrong, seeing her from that distance. Perhaps she was a friend of your mother's."

"Mother was asleep," Jennie said.

"She went to sleep right after dinner," Jamie added.

"Passed out, really," Jennie finished off, with a sophistication that seemed both bizarre and pathetic.

I glanced down at her quickly to see if she was trying it on as an experiment to see if she could shock me. But Jennie's dark eyes were fixed on the house. She had produced the tarnished, hackneyed words as a simple statement of fact. Both twins were in pajamas, and over them, the sweaters I had brought out. The days were now hot but the evenings were still cool, and their feet were bare on the damp grass. But short of going in to find shoes or sneakers for them I didn't think there was anything I could do about it. My mind reverted to Steve. Was he all right? He was still inside with Charles. Was it safe? My question was answered in a minute. Steve reappeared out the back door, his arm supporting Charles.

"Charles," Jamie said, and ran over towards them.

Jennie and I followed.

"Is Charles going to be all right?" I asked, trying to get Steve to look at me.

"Fine. Just a little smoke problem. The fresh air will put him right." Steve was talking to me, but he was looking at Charles, who was half sitting on a plinth in front of the door.

"Whew!" Charles said. "That's one profession I can cross off my list."

"What?" Jamie said. He had run up to Charles and put his hand on Charles's knee.

"Fireman," Charles said. "Thanks, Steve. I was about ready to go down."

"You'll be okay. I have to go back and help with Mrs. Brewster. Where's that girl you told the other fireman about?" This time Steve looked at me.

"What girl?" Charles asked.

"The one Sarah told us about," Steve said.

"I didn't see any girl," Charles said, looking at me.

"I know you didn't. But that was how we discovered there was a fire. Don't you remember?"

Charles stared at me for a moment. "Yes, I remember now." He had a funny look on his face, but didn't say any more.

At that moment a fireman leaned out of one of the back windows and yelled, "Bring a stretcher!"

"Mom?" Jennie said.

"She's going to be all right, honey," one of the firemen said. "Just smoke and...her...just smoke." He glanced down at Jennie and then at me. "But she ought to go to the hospital for tonight just to have them check her out."

Two men carrying something disappeared into the house, and a few minutes later came out with Mrs. Brewster on the stretcher wrapped in a blanket. She seemed somewhat awake. "Where...what..."

Charles got up and went over to her. "You'll be okay, Nancy, but they're going to take you to the local hospital."

She blinked once or twice, then suddenly sat up with a cry. "The twins!"

"We're here, Mom. We're all right. Charles rescued us. We're here!" And they both ran over.

With a sob Mrs. Brewster clasped them to her. "My darlings," she said. I wondered how much was real and then decided I was a mean witch.

The fire chief came out and walked over to me. "We've

171

looked everywhere and there's no other person in the house. No girl—no one."

"That's all right, chief," Charles said. "I think she must have run out."

"If she ever was there." The fire chief was glaring at me.

"Of course she was," I said. "Why would I make up a thing like that?"

"Who was it?" Steve asked. He'd kept about ten or twelve feet away the whole time. By now I realized that he didn't want the others to have any idea of any relationship between us, and although I knew all the reasons, I felt ashamed, ashamed of him and ashamed of me. And very angry. I turned away from him and noticed suddenly that the lawn seemed full of people.

"Where did they come from?" I said.

One of the firemen answered, "From all over. In a small place everybody turns out if there's a fire. Hi, there, Mrs. Hobbes."

Belatedly I recognized the lady in charge of the post office and dry-goods store.

"Charles," I said, "why don't you and the twins come home and spend the night there? We have room. There are pull-out sofas in Father's and Mother's studios as well as downstairs. And there's an extra guest room anyway."

"Okay, thanks. I think we will."

"Will you be all right?" I heard Steve's voice. But I refused to turn around and look at him.

"Fine," Charles answered. "I feel much better and there's no problem breathing. But I think I'd better wait until the fire chief says everything is out. Why don't you take the twins home, Sarah?"

"We want to stay, we want to stay," yelled the twins together and alternately.

At that moment a third van, an ambulance this time, turned onto the lawn, and the two firemen picked up Mrs. Brewster's stretcher from where they had laid it on the path. In a minute or two a couple of medics sprang out of the ambulance and lifted her inside.

"Why don't you take these four and drop them off at the young lady's house?" one of the firemen said. "They're okay, but they could do with a lift."

"Okay," the ambulance driver said. "Wait until we've got the woman here settled, then you can come and crawl in."

While they were still getting Mrs. Brewster ensconced, the

172

fire chief appeared again. "Well, it's all out. There doesn't seem to be a lot of damage—that is, apart from the upstairs bedrooms. You're not going to be able to use those for a while until the smoke has cleared away, and you'll probably have to have the place painted before the smell will be gone. But you can see how you feel."

"How did it start?" Charles asked.

"We're not sure. I want to come back with an investigator tomorrow and examine the place in daylight. But it looks like it might have been a cigarette. Do you all have places you can stay until then?"

"Yes, thanks," Charles said. He stood up. "Considering everything, I don't feel too bad."

All the firemen except Steve walked away. I still wasn't looking at Steve but I knew he was there.

"Do you feel like walking?" I said to Charles.

"Since the alternative would be flying, I think the answer has to be yes."

"The ambulance could back up nearer," Steve said.

"No, I'm fine. Thanks again, Steve, for getting me out. I owe you one. A big one."

"Not that big. There were others around, and you would have made it on your own."

"I'm not sure. Not at all sure. I felt like I was going down for the count. So the debt remains." He smiled at Steve and held out his hand. Steve took it and smiled, too.

"Come along, let's go over to the ambulance," I said to the twins. I took each by the hand and started forward. I could feel Charles and Steve following. When we got to the ambulance the driver said, "If you both sit in the front with a child each on your laps I think it will be easier all around. You'll be squashed, but Mrs. Brewster shouldn't be too crowded in the back."

"Fine," I said.

"I'll get in the middle," Charles said, and stepped in. "Hand me a twin."

I handed him Jennie, then turned to Jamie. "If I hold out my hand you can get up inside and on my lap, can't you?"

"Sarah?" Steve said.

"Hey, Steve!" a fireman from the town truck called. "Let's move it. The bar won't be closed for another couple of hours. Let's get back."

"Okay, in a minute," Steve said. Then, again, "Sarah, look, turn around, I want to talk to you."

173

I pushed Jamie up on the seat. "I'll join you in a minute and you can get up on my lap then," I said to him. Then I turned.

"If you're so ashamed of...of our relationship that you have to put on an...an act in public, then I don't think we have anything real going for us."

"I'm not ashamed," Steve said. "Far from it. And the act you say I put on is as much for your sake as for mine. Just what do you think would happen if some of your friends here thought you and I...well you know what I mean."

"I do know what you mean, and as far as I'm concerned, I don't care. But you obviously do. And I'm sick of it. Goodnight, Steve." And I piled into the front of the ambulance and pulled Jamie on my lap.

"Are you ready?" the ambulance driver said. "If so, let's go."

I didn't even look at Steve as we drove off.

Charles was put in Father's study. The sofa pulled out into a bed and there was a bathroom attached. "And I'm not really doing very much there for the moment," Father said, "so feel free to use it as long as you like."

"Thanks. But I'd better try and put the place—our house, that is—back into some kind of livable state tomorrow. The firemen probably caused more damage with their boots and axes and water than the fire itself."

"Probably," Mother agreed. We were all sitting in the living room having hot drinks. The twins, with some of my socks on in place of their own sneakers, were sipping cups of cocoa.

"I'm going to put you two in the guest room," Mother said to the twins. "It's next to Sarah's room, so you won't feel lonely."

"By the way," Peter said. "Who was that girl that was supposed to have been there but the firemen could never find?"

"How did you hear about her?" I asked.

"Oh, some of the firemen were talking about it when we roared up. We were in the volunteer office when the fire engine went past, so we followed them."

"I don't know," I said, straightening Jamie's mug. His eyes were slowly closing and the mug he was holding was tipping gently toward the floor. "She must have got out. Who is she, Charles?"

"I don't know. I've never seen her," Charles said. He sounded uncharacteristically brusque.

"Do you know who she is?" I said to Jennie, who still seemed relatively awake.

"No. She never says anything. She's just there."

"She must say something," Mushroom said. "Is she another baby-sitter?"

"No. And she never talks."

Jennie's eyes were beginning to look heavy, too. But they opened when Peter asked, "Well, when does she turn up? Is she a friend of your Mother's?"

"Mother doesn't like her," Jennie said.

"Then what's she doing there?" Mushroom asked.

"She lives there," Jennie said. "Only she isn't there all the time."

"Why doesn't your mother like her?" Mother asked.

"I don't know. But every time she's there and Mother comes in the room she says it's cold and hadn't we better put on sweaters." Jennie gave a huge yawn.

"Watch out," Mother cried, and rescued Jamie's cocoa just in time.

For a minute there was silence. Once again I was experiencing that odd little shiver.

"You'd better get them upstairs, Sam," Mother said.

"Come along, twins." I got up, put both cups of cocoa on the coffee table, and rousted the twins from their place on the sofa. "Bedtime."

I woke up early the next morning. The birds were creating a terrific ruckus outside, the sun was sending long, slanting rays through the window. And Jill's tail was thumping against the bed. I looked at my clock. Five. Then I sat up and became aware that for the first time in many weeks, my leg was sore and stiff. It was probably all that running up the cliff path to the house. The only thing that would help my leg, I knew from long experience, was a long soak in a hot bath, so, after letting Jill out for a few minutes, I went to the bathroom farthest away from my parents' bedroom and sank into hot water, while Jill waited impatiently on the bathmat. While I was lying there I thought about the girl, about the fire, about the house, about what I would do with the twins today, about Mr. Haggerty's articles—about anything except what I'd been trying since the night before not to think about: Steve and me.

But it wasn't much good. I hadn't any success with not

175

brooding about Steve the night before after I'd gone to bed, so it was one o'clock before I went to sleep and I wasn't having any luck now. Just thinking about him made me angry, but the anger was better than the pain that lay below it, so I concentrated on how anxious he was to keep people from knowing about us, and how furious that made me.

After a while I got out of the tub, let the water drain out, turned on the cold shower, got back in under it and then dried off. By this time it was only a quarter to six, and though I wanted some coffee, what with one thing and another, I didn't feel hungry. I glanced in at the twins before I went downstairs, but they were sound asleep. So I collected Jill and all the articles that Mr. Haggerty had given me and went down to the kitchen. First I put down some food for Jill, who went at it with enthusiasm. Then, over a cup of instant coffee, I started to read.

Forty-five minutes later I knew why Charles said that the extremists on both sides were going to push everybody into a fight. One side was as bad as the other, and they were both virulent.

The editorials from the town paper referred to the conversationists as kooks, do-gooders, elitist liberals, whited sepulchres (something to do with a quotation from the Bible), and hypocrites. "How nice," one of the editorials finished, "that they can, at the end of the summer, all return to their rich suburban homes or urban condominiums with the gratifying feeling of having saved the marsh for the wildlife. After all, why not? It's not their jobs, their schools, their homes that are at stake."

The letters published in the same paper, many of them signed "Local Jobs for Local People," got down to harsh terms and suggestions as to what the conservationists could do with themselves, their good intentions and their families. They were childish, but there was an ugly note that underlay much of the writing. These people saw their homes and their livelihoods threatened, and were ready to pick up the nearest weapon in defense.

Peter's outfit was more sophisticated, wrote better prose and managed to be just as nasty with more finesse. "And somebody," one of the pamphlets said, "has to be making a buck or so out of this. Probably many of those who are anxious to turn this coast into another Atlantic City or Coney Island are genuine in their claim that jobs and only jobs provide the motive for their sordid politicking. But we have been given

176

reliable information that at least one leader of the "Local Jobs for Local People" outfit, as they call themselves, stands to make a pretty penny if this resort atrocity should go through...."

"Yuch," I said aloud, and went to fix myself another cup of coffee.

As I watched the kettle I fought a gathering sense of depression. By logic I should have been one hundred percent on the side of the conservationists, not only because my inclination lay in that direction, but because I was mad at Steve. But logic had never been my strong suit. And the vicious undertone to some of the expressions on either side made me feel a little sick.

"Hi," Peter said behind me.

I turned. "Oh, hi." I glanced at the table where the papers were spread out. "I'll clear that off."

"I can get it," Peter said, standing and reading some of the papers. "that's juicy early-morning reading you have there."

"Yes." I had an ardent desire not to get into a discussion with Peter. He was much brighter than I and could always paint me into a corner and then proceed to annihilate any argument I might come up with.

"Where did you get all this from?"

"Mr. Haggerty loaned them to me."

"Why?"

"Oh, he just wanted to know what I thought—strange as it may seem." I didn't mean for that last piece of bitterness to creep through.

"And what do you think?"

I debated saying "I really don't want to talk about it," because I didn't. But it would demonstrate to me (if no one else) what a total coward I was. "I think it's a pity that the fanatics on both sides seem to be the ones that get all the publicity."

"I don't think there's anything fanatic—in the perjorative sense that you seem to be using it—in wanting to preserve what's left of our wildlife."

I could see the swamp ahead of me as easily as though it were spread right there at my feet. I would never in a thousand years win an argument with Peter and I knew it. Nevertheless, I closed my eyes and stepped forward. "Peter, for heaven's sake, it's also natural for people who are out of work to be worried about getting jobs. You know that. You're always talking about more jobs for the ghettos—this is no different."

"Oh yes it is. Don't be kidded by all this Local Jobs For Local People crap. There's big money behind this—corporate money, and there are two or three of these so-called Local Jobs people who stand to clean up if they can put a resort in here. That's what we're fighting. Not the unemployed."

"That's not true, Peter—"

"And how the hell do you know it's not true? Have you been into town? Have you talked to some of these so-called out-of-work types? Because some of us have. One by one if they think their confidence is secure, they'll talk."

"Well if you're so sure, why don't you name names? Make these leaders who're out for a buck come out and defend themselves?"

"Don't worry," Peter said, taking the screaming kettle off the stove and pouring it over some instant coffee, "we're going to. We're beginning to get some evidence and we will."

"Hey, that's my boiling water you're helping yourself to."

"Boil some more. You've already had a cup, and I want something before I have to leave." He filled the kettle from the tap and put it back on the stove. "I don't understand you, Sam. You claim you're all for animals, like bringing home this mutt here, but instead of coming and helping us, you're working for that mealy-mouthed Haggerty, who's terrified he'll butter his bread on the wrong side. Move, dog!" He went to push Jill aside with his foot. Unluckily, his foot slipped. There was a yelp and Jill shot up. "Sorry, pooch!" Peter said, sitting down. "That was an accident." Then he started reading some of the letters in the newspaper.

"You're really something!" I said, furious, although I knew it had been an accident. "As long as you can be against something you come out as the great idealist. But you don't seem to mind kicking my dog."

"I did not kick your dog. I was simply trying to move her. And you don't seem to be able to distinguish between sentimentality and principle. You bring some untrained stray home from God knows where and force it on the household when you know Father doesn't care for dogs in the house—"

"And you'd step over a starving dead body to make a speech about the poor and hungry. Steve said—"

I stopped there, appalled. The silence was like silence during a play in the theatre, when you feel the audience holding its breath, waiting for it to be broken. With part of my consciousness I heard Jill get up and then sit down behind me, well away from Peter. I looked down at him, expecting him to jump up and point a finger at me. But he went right on reading. Finally he said, still without looking up, "Steve Novak, I take it."

"Yes."

Then he looked up. "What do you expect on my part? Surprise? I've seen the two of you riding in his van. He's a buddy of yours. I guess that's the reason why you take such a broad-minded view. He's been feeding you with his notions. Well let me tell you about your friend Steve Novak. He's in this for what he can make. If Harry Schreiber can put over this deal, he's going to hire Steve to form his own construction company to build the resort. He'll clean up, what with kickbacks from suppliers and so on. So Steve has nothing to get out of this but profit."

"That's a lie." I said.

Peter looked at me steadily. "Are you sure? Do you know that for a certainty?"

I didn't, of course. But I would have bet anything on it, so I said, "Yes. I'm sure. I'm positive. And why don't you ask him?"

"I fully intend to. In court. We'll see how far your hardhat boyfriend will go. Whether he'll be willing to perjure himself." Peter got up. "See you in court."

"Peter!" Automatically I started collecting the papers and putting them in a pile.

He turned. "Well?"

Every atom of common sense I had told me to leave it there. But I couldn't stop myself. "You're wrong. Wrong about Steve. He could have taken a job in the southwest with a friend of his brother's. But he didn't, because of his friends up here who don't have jobs. No matter what you say you can't deny that there's unemployment up here, that people are worried about their families. I feel about the marsh the way you do. But they feel that jobs are more important than...than birds, and although...I agree with you about the sanctuary, you've got to see how they would think that. I mean...it's only reasonable....You have to be able to see the other side."

"You remind me of all the people who justified what the Nazis did on the grounds that the Germans had been unfairly treated after World War I. There's right and there's wrong, Sam, and there are times when you have to take a stand. What's

179

a few birds to somebody like Steve Novak, or Harry Schreiber, when it comes to money?"

"No, you're wrong, Peter! I know Steve doesn't hate birds. Why, he's got one. Chico—"

And off I went, babbling about the little parakeet and his chirping and his sitting on top of Steve's head and the relationship between them that was so poignant and touching. Finally, my voice ran down. "So you see, he doesn't hate birds."

Peter was staring at me. "That's very interesting," he said. "I'm glad we had this chat. By the way, what were you doing in Steve Novak's apartment?"

It was like a crater at my feet that I hadn't seen in my rush to justify Steve. Finally I unglued my tongue. "I went with Charles when he had to go see Steve about their garage."

Peter shrugged and turned away.

Jill and I went for a long walk on the beach. I figured that if the twins woke up somebody would keep an eye on them, and I wanted to be alone. I was upset by what Peter had said; even knowing that he was lying it was as though he had defiled something. Yet, for all my words in defense of Steve, I was still angry at him, and nothing could change my basic feeling that if he was so anxious to pretend we didn't really know one another, then that, too, demeaned us both.

When I got back I discovered that Mrs. Brewster had already called and said that she would be picking up the twins at ten o'clock.

"She sounded surprisingly chipper," Mother said. "Considering."

"Considering what?" I asked.

"Considering that she probably had a hangover, not to mention the smoke she swallowed."

But although Mrs. Brewster looked pale and puffy under the eyes when she arrived, she seemed reasonably well put together. "I made them let me out of the hospital at eight this morning," she said. "God knows there's enough to do to get the place cleaned up. You'll be by this afternoon, won't you?" she asked me, eyeing her children, who were putting away Mother's scrambled eggs with much enthusiasm.

"Yes."

"By the way," Mother said. "Who was that girl that Sam—Sarah—saw?"

"What girl?"

180

"The one you don't like," Jennie piped up.

"There's no girl." Mrs. Brewster rose to her feet. "Come along, children."

"But Jennie saw her, too," I said.

"Utter rubbish and nonsense." Mrs. Brewster's face seemed to have gone an odd yellow. "Thank you very much for your help, Mrs. Lacey. I know my husband will be most grateful." And sounding like a good imitation of a grande dame she swept out the kitchen door, shepherding her twins in front of her.

I sat eyeing the pile of newspaper sheets that I had put on the sideboard and nibbling an English muffin.

"What's the matter, baby?" Mother said. "You look like you just lost your best friend."

"I'm tired," I said. "And I don't really know why." But of course, once I thought about it, I did. I hadn't slept. More to the point, I was upset about Steve.

Mother glanced at me. "You look a little peaked. You'd better take it easy today."

"Mother," I said, "why does Peter have to be such a holier-than-thou pain in the ass over this whole sanctuary business?"

"Because that's his nature, Sam. I told you that. That's his great blind spot. He revels in being against. If he'd just lived a hundred years ago, he'd probably have been some kind of ranting evangelist accusing people of being in the grip of the devil—much as I hate to say it. Because he is my son and he does have his very lovable side. What's bothering you in particular?"

I told her about what he'd said. "And I can believe what you say about his being some kind of a hellfire preacher if he'd lived earlier, because he'd go on about the devil just the way he goes on now about money and profit. And the men in the town do have reason on their side."

"Yes, well, they probably do, although you can't expect me to be too charitable towards that bunch. I still remember the ripe tomato on my nice blue suit. But added to everything else, did you know that the attorney who's suing for the injunction against Schreiber has asked Peter to help him with his brief? And Peter is nothing if not a passionate advocate. What interests me far more is why you care so much? What's your concern?"

For a moment I almost told her. I wanted to. The tiredness I felt seemed to be getting worse. But I'd spilled my beans for

181

the morning. Instead I got up. "I'd better be getting over to the paper, Mom. I just feel the way Mr. Haggerty does. The fanatics on both sides are spoiling for a fight, and it's a shame. That's all."

"Sometimes a good fight can be a lot of fun," Mother said thoughtfully. "But you have to have the right temperament for it."

"You mean, see everything as black or white."

"I suppose so. As you know I have an inclination towards that myself. Maybe Peter gets it from me."

"You're not like that, Mom."

"Being older and being a mother is inclined to mellow you—despite your best efforts." She smiled and then leaned over and hugged me.

I hugged her back.

"Well," Mr. Haggerty said. "What did you think?"

"I think you're right about the kooks at both ends wanting to get everybody into a fight."

"Would you like to do a piece on it?"

"I thought you said you didn't want anybody writing in the paper except you."

"I don't—most of the time. But by now everybody knows me and knows how I think. It might have more effect if a fresh eye—or rather a fresh pen—got into the act."

I thought about what Charles said, and couldn't help wondering if Mr. Haggerty was trying not to walk out on a limb himself and risk losing his paper.

"In case you think it's because I want to use you to get over my point of view I'd better tell you that I think there's a good chance this paper won't survive, no matter who wins."

"Why?"

"Because if the town loses, then that's the end of the advertising on the back page, which, if you'll notice, is heavily sponsored by town merchants. If the sanctuary loses, and the resort goes up, then they'll need a much larger paper here and will probably bring in their own."

"Won't they use you?"

"No. And I don't think I'd want to run a resort town paper, anyway. I'm too old and crotchety and too much of a hermit to put up with that. I like the paper the way it is. It really isn't much more than a personal newsletter, and it's exactly right for the amount of activity I should have."

"All right. I've never written anything..." I stopped, once

again remembering my fantasy. "I mean any…article or journalistic piece—"

"Except, of course, for that private project that you're so secretive about."

I grinned. Mr. Haggerty's face was absolutely straight, yet I knew he was smiling. "That's right."

"Well, Sarah, it's time to broaden your horizons." He pointed, "There's a typewriter, a better one than you've been using for those cards, and paper. Commence!"

I went and sat down at the typewriter, and just from practice, rolled a sheet into it. When I tried to strike one of the keys nothing happened.

"It's electric," Mr. Haggerty said. "On the right you'll find a little doohickey that you can switch on. That's right."

I jumped as a light went on above the keyboard. Then I struck the keys again. The action was so fast I thought for a minute that the machine was going to run across the room.

"You'll get used to it."

I stared at the sheet of paper. My mind had strayed off the vital subject of the sanctuary, and was wrestling with something else that had been temporarily driven under by Steve and the upcoming battle. "Mr. Haggerty," I said suddenly, "something very funny happened." And I told him about the girl I saw at the window and that Jennie also had seen from time to time, but that no one else had caught sight of. "And the weird thing is that Mrs. Brewster got very upset when we talked about her."

Mr. Haggerty didn't say anything for a minute, then, "Well, what's your theory?"

"I don't know," I said slowly. "The whole thing is terribly peculiar."

He didn't say anything for a while, but gazed out at the bay that stretched in front of the back window. Then, "There's a story that a Matilda Brewster, brought there as a bride in the 1880s, sometimes puts in an appearance. Her only child was drowned in the bay there when she was about three. Nobody seems to know how it happened, but the baby disappeared and then, in due course, the body was washed up on the beach above the bay. They say Matilda's ghost protects children and is friendly to them, but is hostile to anyone who isn't a child. Only children or young people have ever claimed to see her. According to the one account of it I could find, she was a little like a female Peter Pan—never really grew up and never overcame her distrust of the adult world." Mr.

Haggerty turned and smiled at me. "I think you must be the oldest child ever to see her."

I stared at him, remembering how Mushroom hated the house. "Last summer, the only time I was here, before, I guess, the Brewsters came back, my sister, who was then about twenty, and I went over to look at the house. My sister hated it, and couldn't wait to get out of it. But I had the strangest feeling there. It was a gray day, but I felt as though the upstairs room—the master bedroom—was full of sunlight."

"Maybe Matilda was trying to warn you of something."

"Of what, I wondered. "Has anybody else that you know ever seen her?"

"Yes. My daughter."

"Recently?"

"No. That was ten years ago, when I first moved here."

I waited to see if he would say anything else. When he didn't I said, half joking, "Was she trying to warn her of anything?"

"Afterwards I thought perhaps she might. Ann, my daughter, also drowned a week later."

Again there was that little shiver. "I'm sorry," I said after a minute.

"But I wouldn't worry about anything she might be trying to warn you of. She was probably trying to protect the twins, to attract attention to the fire so that they could be rescued."

I stared at him over the typewriter. "Do you really believe in ghosts?"

"Let's say I have an open mind. I'm writing up an account of the fire that I got from our local fire department. I knew that you summoned the fire department and was going to ask you about it. You'd better tell me how you knew about it."

"Because of Matilda. I saw her in the window." And I told him about Charles's and my share in the rescue, and how Mrs. Brewster reacted the next morning. "Jennie said that when she, herself, was seeing Matilda, her mother simply thought the room was cold."

"Well, that's supposed to be the standard reaction to the presence of the psychic." There was a pause. Then, "You'd better get that piece about our local controversy written. I'd like to run it before everybody shoots everybody else."

184   *   *   *

At one-thirty Mr. Haggerty said to me, "Don't you have another job at one that you're supposed to go to?"

"I'm going to be late today."

"Okay. Just so you know it's late. I don't want you to lose track of the time because you're doing something for me."

I looked up at him. "Why not?"

"Because if you lost that job, you might be inclined to hit me for more money and I'd have to refuse."

I smiled and went back to the typewriter. But I was not happy, and I couldn't keep my mind on the piece I was supposed to be writing. I had tried to keep thoughts of Steve at bay, but the nearer the time drew when I was supposed to go to Headlands, where he'd be finishing up work, the more I became convinced that my feelings would pop out all over and we'd be back to our old problem: Steve pretending we didn't know each other more than casually, and me with my wounded feelings all over my face. I had told him that if he was ashamed of our relationship in front of his family and friends, then maybe we should stop seeing each other. The thought of our not seeing each other was terrible, but I couldn't endure any more standing around waiting for a crumb. If my presence embarrassed him, then I'd remove the embarrassment. Technically, he was supposed to be starting work on Mother's studio shortly after two o'clock, so if I didn't leave the newspaper office till just before two I would certainly miss him. And I would be sure not to return home until he was finished there.

And what about later this evening when I was supposed to meet him at the usual place? I would cope with that when the time came.

My plan worked depressingly well. Mrs. Brewster was not pleased that I had turned up an hour and a quarter later than usual, but Steve had gone, so it was worth it. A fire inspector was in the house, looking over the upper floor to see if he could determine what caused the fire, and there were three young people from the cove, pulling out damaged furniture, washing walls and even beginning to paint.

"We're going to have to sleep downstairs," Mrs. Brewster said rather crossly. "At least there the smell is bearable. Upstairs it's overwhelming. Only two coats of paint will help."

I thought about trying to get Jennie to talk about the girl—Matilda, if it was indeed Matilda—but there were people around even on the beach. And the truth of the matter was that the nearer the evening came, the more anxious I became. The only thing that helped was to invent and organize vigorous games that kept us all busy and wore us out.

"No date this evening?" Mother said after dinner.

"I think Charles wants to get some sleep," I said, and felt as though I would choke on the words. Who ever said, "the more you lie the easier it gets"? Wrong, wrong, I thought. Every time I confirmed my family's belief that it was Charles I was going out with, I felt worse.

"I should think he might," Mother said. "Inhaling smoke can make you feel lousy."

It was awful. I had been home on evenings after Steve and I had started going out together. But those were times he had other things he had to do, so I was able to relax and work on my book or talk or watch television. This time I couldn't concentrate on my book, I couldn't concentrate on anybody else's book, and I couldn't think of anything to say. So I sat like a dummy in front of the tube watching some stupid game show of morons, by morons and for morons.

"Can't you think of anything better to watch than that?" Father asked.

"No," I said. "It's just about my level."

How long would Steve sit there in his van, waiting for me? Ten minues? Fifteen minutes? A fantasy formed in my mind: Steve sitting in the dark of his van, the light from the main road filtering through the trees of the Barretts' drive and then through the windshield. Steve would check his watch from time to time. His watch was a big steel one, with minutes and seconds and the date on it. Then in another five minutes he'd check his watch again, thinking it was at least ten minutes and discovering it wasn't. He'd turn on the radio to one of his two favorite stations—one played classical music, which he preferred most of the time, and one played what Peter calls perma-press music—mostly show tunes from the thirties and forties. Sometimes when we were driving and the classical music station would be on, Steve would suddenly change it. Once I asked him why. "It reminds me too much of my father," he said once. "He taught me about music."

This fantasy brought Steve so close to me that I found my eyes filling with tears. Quickly I started another fantasy. In this one Steve waited fifteen minutes, shrugged and drove away. The trouble was, this fantasy made me cry even harder.

"For Pete's sake," Mushroom said, coming back into the

living room, "why are you crying over that stupid game show?"

"I was thinking about something else," I said.

"You okay, Sam?" Father asked.

"Fine." It was hours later that it struck me Father had called me Sam for almost the first time in living memory.

At ten o'clock the telephone rang. "Sam," Mushroom yelled from the kitchen extension. "It's for you."

My feet almost didn't touch the floor on my way there. "What's happened?" Steve asked. He sounded terribly worried.

I couldn't answer. Suddenly the whole act of standing him up struck me as childish and petty, and I felt ashamed. "Oh, Steve," I finally managed to get out.

"Are you all right?"

By now I was crying. "Steve? Can you wait until I get there? I'll be there as soon as I can."

"I'll come and get you if there's something wrong."

Funny, I'd done the whole foolish thing because he wouldn't do anything as public as coming to get me, and here he was, offering to do so. "No. I'll be right there."

"Where are you going?" Mushroom yelled as I flew out the kitchen door.

"Be back soon," I yelled in return, but didn't stop. It was lucky that Mother had gone up to take a long hot bath.

I didn't stop running until I got to the truck. Steve was standing outside. "Steve!" I said, and flung myself in his arms.

"Are you all right, baby? Are you sure?" His voice was tender and filled with concern. How could I have doubted him? Self-loathing filled me. I was so glad to be in his arms I cried for another five minutes.

When I was finally finished mopping up with Steve's handkerchief he said, "What happened? I waited and waited. Then when I tried to call, the line was busy, busy."

"That was Mushroom talking to the Congressman. They're having some kind of thing."

"No wonder he doesn't get any work done for the district."

I gave a watery giggle.

"What was it, sweetheart? Your family giving you trouble?"

"No." Finally I told him. "I was angry because you were so secretive about our relationship. I thought you were ashamed of me. When you came up with the fire truck, you seemed to be afraid even to say hello to me. I guess my feelings
187

were hurt. Anyway, I was...well, I guess I was trying to say that if you felt that way, maybe...maybe we should call it off. But Steve," I raced on before he could comment, "I was *miserable.*"

"For Christ's sake!" He removed his arm. "I thought I told you that it was as much for your sake as for mine—if not more. Half the guys on our fire truck were high. We'd all gone to a bar after the union meeting, and the beer flowed. Then one guy who had this CB told us about the fire at Headlands and before anyone knew anything, we were half-way down the road on the way there. In the mood they were in all those guys needed was one hint at what was between us, and they'd have been ribbing me about you all the way home. And I don't want that. Because they'd be assuming that we were just having a roll in the hay, and I don't want them talking about us—especially about you—like that."

"Oh."

"And I'm sorry you don't like that, but you don't know them the way I do. Teasing a guy about a girl he's engaged to marry is one kind of teasing, and it's a hell of a lot different from the kind of horseplay they go in for when it involves some gal who's good for a roll in the hay but not for marriage."

I wanted so much to say, "But why can't we get married?" But I didn't. I knew how he felt and knew it wouldn't do any good. Finally I said, "I'm sorry."

He didn't say anything, but sat on his side of the cab, staring through the windshield, frowning. After a while I put my hand on his arm. "Are you angry with me, Steve? I wouldn't blame you, but are you?"

He turned his head so that he seemed almost to be staring at me in the dark.

"Steve?" I said.

"You know you're right in one way," he said finally. "We can't go on like this. I know you think I'm holding off com-mitting myself because I'm afraid of our differences. Well, I am. But running around like this in the dark, going where we won't see people, pretending we don't know each other when we're in public, is no kind of preparation for...for any other kind of life." He stopped.

"Well what are we going to do?" I asked finally.

"I'm going up into northern Maine next Monday. I want to look at some lumber a friend of mine has up there. If I can bring it back in the van I can get it a lot cheaper than if I had it sent. I'll be away a couple of nights." He stopped. I held my breath. Then he said, "Do you think you could get away to come with me?"

"I'll manage, somehow." My heart was singing. It would be wonderful, the two of us together, for two whole days. I didn't know how I was going to do it, but I would do it.

Chapter

10

In the end, getting away turned out not to be that complicated. I was still wondering what excuse I'd use when a letter arrived from Sandra James, one of the few close friends I'd made at school. Her family had taken a cabin on a lake in that part of Maine that bulges up into Canada. I read it on the way back from collecting the mail from the post office and almost gave a shout when I came to her sentence, "Why don't you come up and visit us here? It's beautifully cool and we have a boat."

I stopped and stared at her invitation. Then I checked the amount of change I had in my jeans pocket. After that, it was easy for me to telephone her from the phone booth near the post office and arrange for her to telephone me at home in about an hour after I reached there before I left the house for the newspaper office and invite me to stay.

"Sure I will," the loyal Sandra said. "I think that's terrific. Do you think you're gonna elope?"

"We want to be by ourselves so we can think about it. You know how it is with families."

"Don't I just! Particularly since you're not of consenting age."

"Of what?"

"You know, consenting age. If you wanted you could accuse him of statutory rape. Until you're eighteen it doesn't matter how willingly you go with him. If you're younger than eighteen you're jail bait. My father, who's a lawyer, explained it to me once."

"Oh." That had never occurred to me before.

"Anyway, I'll phone in an hour. But how are you going to manage about his picking you up?"

"I can catch the bus into Portland and say I'm going to take another bus from there."

"Well. Have fun. And tell me all about it next year."

"Okay." There was no point in telling her that I had no intention of being in school next year.

I was braced for trouble from Mother, but when Sandra called on schedule and I told Mother about the invitation, she said, "I'm just delighted. I think you've been doing far too much, and if Sandra can persuade you to lie in the sun on the lakeside or in a boat and do nothing, I'll consider myself in her debt. I'm just sorry she only asked you for two days."

"I think her parents have guests coming after that," I improvised.

It all went like clockwork. I didn't ask Mr. Haggerty and Mrs. Brewster about my two-day vacation. I told them. Somewhat to my surprise they seemed to accept it philosophically. Carrying a small bag, I took the bus into Portland, and Steve was waiting there in the bus station. After pausing long enough to make sure Mother or Mushroom or Peter hadn't decided to come with me at the last moment, he came up and said, "May I carry your bag, ma'am?" and took it from me as I giggled.

It was an incredibly wonderful two days. We sang as we drove, and stopped off and swam and bought hot dogs and took them down to the rocky edge of the water and made love in the woods. I hadn't realized until we'd been traveling some hours how much of a family burden each of us carried around back at the Cove. Half the time when we talked, we talked not only for ourselves, but for our kindred communities as though we were the heads of delegations trying to negotiate peace.

We cracked feeble jokes and laughed like maniacs. We checked into motels and Steve signed us in as Mr. and Mrs. Steve Novak.

192

"Hello, Mrs. Novak," Steve said, coming naked over to the bed.

I turned over on my side, watching him. "You know, you're absolutely gorgeous."

He grinned and put one knee on the bed. "Are you speaking as a connoisseur?"

"Of course. From my vast experience."

He leaned over and kissed me between my breasts. "And you're beautiful," he whispered. "More beautiful than anyone I've ever known."

"Even with my scars?"

"What scars? They hardly show. If you don't believe me, look for yourself."

It was weirdly true. They had become much paler. "Maybe it's because I'm in love."

"*Amor omnia vincit.*"

"Or something."

One of the nights they were having a dance in a small hotel and Steve and I crashed it. Steve, I discovered, was a terrific dancer, much better than I was, although he kept on insisting I was good and with practice and the right coaching—his—would be good. He even knew how to do a Viennese waltz, because, he said, they used to have them in dances given by the Polish-American Society, and after we'd had a few turns with Steve counting "*one* two three, *one* two three, *one* two three," I got the hang of it and we went twirling around the room with the other older small-towners. When my head started to swim he taught me how to reverse. We were so good that the MC at the dance came up and complimented us and asked us who we were, and Steve introduced us as Mr. and Mrs. Novak.

"My, you're young to be married," one of the older women said, looking at me. "And where's your ring?"

"That's my fault," Steve said, while I, with my typical lightning response, stood with my mouth open. "I thought it was bad luck to try it on before the wedding, and it turned out to be much too big. It'll be ready when we get back from our honeymoon."

"You're on your honeymoon? Wow!" that produced a lot of handshaking and kissing all around, plus congratulations and champagne. I'd never seen Steve so lively. His cheeks were flushed, making his cheekbones look higher than ever. His blue eyes above, narrowed with laughter, were long and tilted up. "You look like a portrait of a Slav," I said. "Smashing."

His eyes narrowed even more as he laughed. "I am a Slav—watch out for my Tartar ancestry!" And he made a kidding pass at me.

We made terrific love that night, waking up and starting all over again, in honor, Steve claimed, of his wild Tartar forebears.

The subject of my age came up the following night, and not so pleasantly. We'd stopped at a motel on a lake and Steve was signing in. I was watching him write Mr. and Mrs. Steve Novak in the register, and was trying it on in my mouth when I glanced up and saw the desk clerk looking at me. It was not a friendly look.

"How old are you?" he asked.

"Nineteen," I said.

"You don't look that old."

For once my wits were working. "That's very nice of you," I said, putting on a slight upper-crust accent. "Thank you."

Maybe it was the effect of the accent, maybe it was because he was in enough doubt to figure that anyone who really was younger wouldn't sound like someone who was older receiving it as a compliment. The man finally stopped looking at me. Steve picked up our bags and we walked to our room, which was outside and part of a cabin of four rooms.

When we were inside Steve looked at me, then walked around the room for a minute. It was seedy and smelled of dust. We had only stopped there because of the lake.

"I don't like this place," Steve said suddenly. "And I don't like that man."

"I don't either. But I thought he believed me."

"Maybe he did, maybe he didn't. But if he has any second thoughts, what he'd do is call the local cops and I'd find myself in the clink for consorting with a minor."

I remembered what Sandra had said. "What'll we do?"

"We'll just go."

"What about the money you paid for the room?"

"I think we'll forget about it."

I felt bad, knowing how hard Steve worked. "I'm sorry."

He came over, put his arms around me and kissed me. "Don't be, sweetheart. You're worth every penny of it, multiplied by pi R squared to the tenth strength." He held me and we kissed.

"And I'm sorry about being jail bait."

"Who gave you that expression?"

"Sandra. She mentioned it. And it's only just true. I'll be eighteen in September."

He kissed me again. "I don't want to wait until September. Let's find another motel."

We sneaked out, leaving the lights on. Luckily, the van was parked off to one side, so our departure wouldn't be immediately noticeable by the central desk.

"Now," said Steve, when we found another motel on the other side of the lake, "do you have any makeup with you?"

I had a compact and some lipstick. That was all. "Put on some lipstick," Steve said. "Can you put your hair on top of your head?"

I shoved it up and unearthed two bobby pins from the bottom of my bag. "Yes," he said. "That makes you look older. Maybe only about six months older, but older. Put on those high heels you have in your bag, and stay outside when I register."

The man at the desk didn't even bother to look at me. And it was a much nicer room anyway. But we were tired, and we only made love once before we both went to sleep and didn't wake up until the next morning.

The next day we drove back to Portland. We didn't talk much. Sometimes his arm was around me, and sometimes my hand was on his leg. But even though I didn't want to think so, it was as though everything that kept us apart was a shadow that got darker and darker the nearer we reached home.

"I'd drive you all the way to the road leading to your house, but somebody would see us sure as anything. That'd be the one moment they'd drive past."

What if they did? I thought. There must be something in ESP, I thought, because he glanced at me, then pulled off the road into a small clearing and parked the car, turning off the ignition.

For a moment we just sat there. It was a beautiful place, with tree branches sweeping down almost to the car and the sound of a brook tumbling down a tiny waterfall.

We stared at the waterfall for a moment, then almost as though there were a signal, turned and put our arms around one another and started kissing. "I'd like us to be married," he said. "But I have to think and I'd have to break it to my family. And I want you to think. Sarah—you're very young. You don't know...I just can't make myself completely con-

195

vinced you'd be happy. Do you think you would be? You don't know my family. But I know yours. You have no idea how different they are."

"I'd be happy with you," I said. "I'm absolutely positive."

He rested his face on the top of my head. "I hope," he said. "We'll talk again in a couple of days."

When I knew Steve and I were going to go away, I'd been worried that my period would arrive the day we left and spoil everything and was enormously relieved when it didn't. I was always pretty regular—every twenty-eight days, with one day's difference, more or less, at the most. When the thirty-first day and then the thirty-second arrived I started to wonder. I couldn't begin using the pill until day five of my period, so, of course, I hadn't been able to start it. But I'd worn the diaphragm faithfully, or almost faithfully, and was only without it once or twice, when, as Steve put it, we suddenly came over passionate. If I could have talked to somebody about it, I wouldn't have minded so much. Once or twice I almost said to Mushroom, casually, something like "I suppose having sex a lot can throw off your schedule." But however much I rehearsed it I couldn't get the words out. So it seemed easier to let the whole thing go for a day or two. It was at that point that everything in the community that had been bubbling under the surface suddenly boiled up.

It started when the court in the town announced that the conservationists' suit for an injunction against Schreiber & Company would be heard the following Thursday—three days ahead.

"Heard about the injunction?" Mr. Haggerty said, as I walked into his office.

"Yes. This morning, over the radio."

"I guess your brother will be pretty pleased."

"Pleased" hardly described Peter's wild yell of triumph which I had heard coming from his room, where he had his radio on. Jill, who'd just come in from her morning run, promptly went under the table.

"That'll fix their little red wagon," Peter said, clattering down the stairs. He didn't even wait for coffee, but shot out the door. I heard his car start up and rear off.

"That piece of yours ready?" Mr. Haggerty asked.

It had gone clean out of my head. "No. I've been away, and forgot about it."

"I must say you don't have the killer instincts necessary for an investigative reporter."

I grinned. "No. Do I have to do it?"

"You don't want to?"

I shook my head. My reason was a sort of fatigue that I couldn't seem to shake off. Nothing, except for Steve and me, seemed entirely real.

Mr. Haggerty stared out the window. "Do you think a piece like that would do any good?"

"No. People think what they want to think."

Mr. Haggerty looked at me then. "That's a very defeatist attitude in one so young."

"I suppose so." It was hard to explain my weird feeling that whatever was going to happen had already been decided, only we didn't know what the decision was going to be. "I think this morning I'd just rather type and file cards."

"All right." He paused. "There's some kind of lesson of irony in all this, I suppose. There's a whole bunch of youngsters from the summer group who'd salivate at the opportunity to do a think piece on the community war that's about to start—even if I swore them to as much objectivity as they could swallow. And probably an even greater number from the town. Here I offer it to you and all you want to do is file cards. Who knows, maybe that's why I offered it to you!"

I grinned at him and started typing the cards. The thing about typing and filing cards was that I could go on doing it, no matter how unreal everything seemed—everything, that is, except Steve and me and the time we'd had together. And then, as I went on automatically feeding the cards in the typewriter, typing names, issue dates and page numbers on them, I suddenly became aware of something that had been hovering in my mind just out of reach: The second night when Steve and I were away, the night we were so tired, I had had a strange dream. I had dreamed that I was asleep in the big master bedroom up at Headlands and then, in my dream, I felt something warm on my eyelids and opened them, and a stream of gold light was coming in the window. And sitting on my bed, sewing, was a young woman I instantly knew was Matilda Brewster. Why I knew it I wasn't sure, because she wasn't dressed in the clothes of a century before. As a matter of fact, she had on a perfectly ordinary modern white dress. But it was Matilda. In my dream I sat up and said, "Why are you here? What's going to happen?" She put down her sewing and started to answer, but there was a sudden noise so loud

197

that I couldn't hear what she was saying. "What?" (in my dream) I yelled. And then I woke up. The loud noise was coming from outside the motel. Throwing aside the covers, I went over to the window and peeped through two slats of the blind. A huge truck, parked in front of the motel, was revving its engine and preparing to move.

"Come back here," a drowsy voice said. I turned around. Steve was smiling sleepily at me from the bed, his tousled brown hair on the pillow, the morning light on his eyes making them look almost green. Then he held out an arm, long, tanned and muscular. I went over. My body against his brown arm as it went around me looked fish-colored.

"I look like a fish," I said.

"Snow white," he murmured. "Come and get warm." And he pulled me down beside him. In less than five seconds I forgot all about my dream and the noise and everything else.

Until now. What was it Matilda's ghost was supposed to do? Warn against danger to children? A little quiver went over me. Then I could feel a light perspiration break out over my face. I put my hand up and brought it away, wet.

"You all right?" Mr. Haggerty said.

"Yes. Why?"

"Because you look a little odd. Are you sure you feel well?"

"I'm absolutely fine, thank you."

Nevertheless, I was glad when noon came and I could leave. But after a tuna-fish sandwich and Coke at the Cove drugstore I felt restored and able to romp with the twins on the beach that afternoon.

Two days went by. Steve had told me that he would be working most nights on an extra job he was trying to finish. I caught glimpses of him in the now almost finished Brewster garage and occasionally in Mother's studio, but only if he happened to be visible walking across the grass. Every time I came home I'd pause at the porch, listening for sounds of hammering or other construction work, and if I heard it, fight the temptation to go and talk to him. The trouble was, if Mother was out there talking to him when I came looking for him and she saw my face and heard my voice she'd know in a minute how I felt about him, or if I went there and started talking to him and she showed up it would be as plain to her as though it were in foot-high letters.

And why do I care? I wondered. What would happen if she did know? What would happen would be that Steve would find himself with a full-blown situation, and I couldn't—or didn't dare—do that to him till he wanted it that way. With him marriage was for keeps. Mother and Father were among the few couples I knew where neither had been divorced or remarried. Among people halfway in age between Mushroom and my parents, there weren't any that hadn't been divorced at least once. I liked the way Steve looked at it. That was the way I wanted to look at it, too. So the least I could do was not crowd him. But it was hard not to linger in the Brewsters' garage, and not to run out to Mother's studio for a couple of minutes when I got home.

"How's Steve Novak doing in the studio?" I said once to Mother when we were setting the dining-room table. I hope my voice sounded as normal as I was trying to make it.

"He's doing a good job, unfortunately."

"What do you mean, unfortunately?" My question shot out as though from a gun.

"Why are you snapping my head off? Because it irritates me that such an arrogant young man should not do something wrong that I can complain about."

"He's not arrogant."

Mother turned and looked at me.

"I mean," I amended hastily, keeping my head down, "he's never seemed so to me."

"Oh he hasn't? Well what do you think all those messages he sent through you about leaving work on his miserable tape were, if they weren't arrogant?"

"He just said that because it sounded so high-handed of you not to want to use a tape." I could hear my own voice, hot and indignant, and knew that I was behaving like a brainless idiot and scuttling my own best interests. Yet I couldn't stop myself.

Mother put down the silver she was holding. "Sam, what's this young man to you?"

"Why should he be anything to me?" I muttered, making for the kitchen door. "I just don't think you're being just. Oh, hi, Mushroom!" I greeted my sister as though she had just reappeared after a decade or so in Siberia.

"Hi yourself. Didn't we see each other a minute ago?"

I clawed for an excuse. "I thought you were going out to dinner."

"I *am* going out to dinner. Why should that seem unusually dangerous? Gene hasn't, to my knowledge, turned into a man-eating tiger in the last hour."

"I have to go to the john." I slid past her and flew upstairs.

199

"What's happened to our Sam?" I heard her ask Mother.

"I don't know, but I intend to find out."

I lingered in the bathroom as long as I dared and was relieved to hear Peter stamp into the house, making his usual ruckus. Maybe in all the confusion Mother would forget about my strange behavior.

But she hadn't.

The moment I reappeared she said, "What's the matter with you, Sam?"

"I just had a slight bout with the runs," I said. It struck me that that was the kind of excuse that could account for almost anything. "I felt queer for a minute."

"What do you mean, queer?" Mushroom asked. She was looking at me intently.

"I think it must have been something I ate," I said.

"When's dinner?" Peter said, coming in. "I'm starved, and anyway, I have to go out afterwards."

"How's the injunction going?" Mushroom asked.

"The hearing's been postponed to next week. But I don't think there's any doubt that we'll get it. That Schreiber doesn't have a leg to stand on. He'll be violating a state wildlife law, or at least that's what we think we can prove."

"I thought it was private property," I said.

"Who told you that?"

"Charles Brewster."

"Oh." It was pretty obvious Peter was expecting a different answer. "Well of course he's got his own vested interest."

"What do you mean by that?" I was surprised at how indignant I felt.

"I mean his mother's going out with Harry Schreiber."

"Stepmother," I said.

"It's not the same thing by a long shot," Mushroom agreed.

"Well he seems to think he's got to show family solidarity."

"Is that so bad?" Mother asked.

Peter shrugged. "It depends where your priorities are."

"There are times," Mother said, looking hard at Peter, "when I'm not absolutely convinced I did a perfect job of bringing you up."

Peter grinned. "How can you say that? I'm just like you. On with the crusade!"

"That's what I mean."

His smile congealed a little. "Maybe your principles are getting middle-aged spread."

"That'll be enough out of you, Mr. Smart Ass. I hope I'm

200

around when you start to suffer your first self-doubt. It should be a historic moment."

Several mornings later I suddenly threw up. Luckily I was having breakfast alone when the nausea hit me. I knew I couldn't make it to the upstairs bathroom, so I raced to the kitchen sink. Then as I stood there, rinsing out the bowl, I thought about what it could mean.

It could mean I was pregnant.

The word carried its own shock. I stood there, watching the water swirling around the sink, feeling panic scald through me. Then giddiness seemed to explode in my head and my fingers gripped the side of the bowl. But slowly, as memories of what Steve had told me about Polish-American attitudes towards families and babies trickled through my mind, the dizziness and panic began to recede. A timid hope started to emerge: Maybe, just maybe, instead of being a disaster, this would make things between us stronger. Perhaps now we were going to be a family.

I took a deep, shaky breath, and with a paper towel wiped off my damp forehead. Then I brushed my teeth with a spare brush and toothpaste I kept downstairs and as I brushed reflected that the first thing to do would be to find out for sure whether or not I was pregnant. I was still thinking about this when Mother came down, followed shortly by Mushroom.

"You haven't finished your English muffin," Mother said, looking at the plate I'd just carried out to the kitchen.

"I wasn't hungry this morning."

"Are you sure you're all right? First runs and now you aren't hungry."

"Of course I'm all right. I'm just not that hungry. Lots of times I'm not hungry at breakfast."

"That's true, Mom," Mushroom said. "Sam's never been one of your dedicated eaters."

"No," Mother agreed doubtfully.

"Stop hovering," Mushroom said. "You're beginning to sound like a mother."

"I *am* a mother. All these years you haven't noticed?"

Mushroom turned on an electric grill and stuck an open muffin inside. "One of the reasons I've always approved of you is that you've kept your more virulent attacks of motherhood to a minimum."

"Thanks a lot," Mother said.

Mushroom grinned.

"I don't suppose you feel like driving into Leominster for me," Mother said, a few minutes later. "There are some items I'm supposed to pick up, things you can't get in the village here. But what with one thing and another I'm behind on my deadline."

"Sure," Mushroom said. "Why not? Gene is supposed to be doing a little handshaking and pressing the flesh in Leominster today. I might go lick some stamps for his office."

"I should think that Gene with his enlightened views would be anathema in a town like that."

"Oh, there's always the odd vote."

"Can I go with you?" I asked in my casual voice. "There are a couple of books I want to see if they have in the library there."

"If it weren't for my recent reprimand I'd be inclined to inquire what books. However," Mother said with elaborate sarcasm, "I'll keep my more blatant impulses of motherhood in control. I hope you both have a good time."

"That's a good mother," Mushroom said.

I giggled.

"Would you like to see if Charles wants to come?" Mushroom said, as we got into the car.

I was about to refuse when I thought, why not? It might keep Mushroom from asking me leading questions, and since Charles knew the score with me and Steve, I could tell him what I wanted to do.

"Okay. Want me to go and call him?"

"Yes, but hurry. Tell him we can pick him up where the path to Headlands joins the village road."

Half an hour later all three of us were on our way to Leominster. I managed to insist on Charles, with his long legs, sitting in the front seat of Mushroom's open coupe, because the back was so narrow. "It won't bother me," I said heroically. "I can curl up with no trouble at all."

"I've curled up in a few cars myself," Charles said.

I hopped in the back seat. "I really like it back here." Which, of course, was true. Isolated in the back seat in an open car with the wind roaring past I was in no position to answer intimate questions. Driving off towards the main road, I saw Mushroom give me a rather ironic look in the rear-view mirror.

"Do you know where the library is?" Mushroom asked as we entered the outskirts of the town.

"No," I yelled back.

"I do," Charles said. "Is that where you want to go?"

"That's where Sam wants to go."

"I can tell you how to get there."

Well, I thought, a library was as good a place as any to find out where I could get a blood test taken. When we finally got there, it turned out to be a large red gothic-looking building on the town square.

"Okay, kids," Mushroom said. "Why don't we say Gene's headquarters at around four this afternoon. Do you think you can find the place?"

"Sure," I said. "What's it called?"

"The Gene Larabee for Congress office, of course. If you run out of things to do you can always come and lick stamps and stuff envelopes there."

"Thanks a lot." I smiled at her. "Maybe I wouldn't vote for him."

"People who make negative comments about Gene don't get free rides back to the Cove. How do you feel about him, Charles?"

"A great guy, a great guy," Charles said promptly. "What's he for, other than motherhood and apple pie?"

"You're a cynic," Mushroom said amiably. "See you later." She drove off.

"What are we going to do in the library?" Charles asked.

"I don't know what you're going to do, but..." I found myself thinking that perhaps I shouldn't tell Charles. It wasn't that I didn't trust him. It was just that all of a sudden I wondered if it was the right thing to do. Then I looked up into his face and knew that I could always tell him the truth. "Charles, I have to go and have a blood test, and I don't know where to go. I just said the library when Mother asked me what I wanted to do in Leominster, because it was the first thing I thought of."

Charles didn't speak for a minute. He took off his floppy hat and wiped his forehead on his arm, then put it back on. He was only nineteen, but his red hair was already receding. "What kind of blood test?"

"You know—the frog test, or what used to be the frog test."

"Oh—for pregnancy."

"Yes. What did you think it was for?"

"I just wondered. It doesn't matter. Well, one place to look would be the telephone directory, and we can certainly look that up in the library. *Andiamo.*"

"What does that mean?"

"It means let's go."

"There you are," Charles said a few minutes later. "Prenatal clinic. I bet you could get a test there."

"Where is it?"

Charles peered at the address for a minute. "If I have the street number right, then it's fairly near the industrial area. I'll head you in that direction."

"What are you going to do?"

"Strange as it may seem, come back to the library. There are a couple of things I'd like to check on."

We walked across the square. It was a beautiful day, but it was going to be hot. Just as we got to the other side, we noticed a knot of people standing around the steps of a big gray building.

"I wonder what they're all about?" Charles said casually.

It was hotter than I had thought, or I was feeling it more. The sweat was breaking out on my forehead and head. "I don't know. Is it a lot farther to the clinic?"

But Charles had stopped and was staring at the various groups, and at a couple that seemed to be carrying placards of some kind. "My God! I forgot! Today's the day the court is going to hear the conservationists' case for the injunction. I wonder what time they're going to hear it, or whether it's on now."

"I think I'd better get to the clinic," I said. "I don't feel so hot. Or rather, I feel terribly hot and clammy at the same time."

He looked at me. "I'll get a taxi." He glanced around and then held up his arm. A car marked "Taxi" pulled up. Charles gave the clinic's address.

With the breeze on me I felt suddenly a lot better, in fact, rather foolish that I hadn't waited a minute or two before announcing that I didn't feel well. "I feel much better now, Charles. I'm sorry to have made you get a taxi."

"No problem. I think we're here."

We got out and he paid the driver. Then he turned to me. "Look, Sam, I like you a lot. Maybe more than you figure. But if you're going to have a baby, I'm not about to take the flak from your family for being the father. I'm not the father. I didn't have the fun and I'm not going to pay the piper. Beyond that I'll give you any support and friendship you need. *Capish*?"

204

"*Capish*. Thanks, Charles." I stood on tiptoe and kissed him.

"Do you have any idea how long all this—the blood test—will take?"

"No."

"Well..." He glanced at his watch. "It's ten-thirty. I'll be in the library at least until twelve-thirty. At which point I might wander out and have some lunch. If you're through by then and want to join me, fine. If not, I'll be at the Congressman's office at the appointed hour, whatever it is."

"Four."

"Yes. Four. Are you going to be all right?"

"Fine," I said.

"Okay. See ya."

"Name," the woman said. She was dressed in white and looked cross. Above her desk a big wall clock said a quarter to one. The line had moved like glue on a cold day. Charles would long since have left the library, and I was so hungry I could have eaten the woman's ashtray.

"You have a name, don't you?"

"Sarah."

"Sarah what?"

It hadn't occurred to me before not to give my real name. But suddenly Lacey sounded terribly individual, unusual, and easily identifiable. "Lamont," I said.

"Okay, Sarah Lamont. How old are you?"

"Eighteen."

The woman's cold brown eyes looked me up and down. "You don't look it."

"Thank you."

"It wasn't meant as a compliment."

I didn't say anything.

"When was your last period?"

I told her, and answered the other questions she read from a long form.

"Okay," she said, when she was through. "You can call at four this afternoon for the results. Go through that door here. Take this piece of paper. Next."

Once I got into the room where another woman took the blood, the whole thing was over in a few minutes. The nurse who probed around the inside of my elbow to find a vein was much nicer. She was young and had her hair up in a big bun. Somebody addressed her as Miss Slovesky—or what sounded like Slovesky. I wondered if she knew Steve. The moment I thought that, Steve became real to me, so real I thought that if I closed my eyes a minute and then opened them, he'd be there, smiling at me.

"Pay on your way out. Take this, and when you call back this afternoon refer to this number here."

I slid off the stool. "Thanks."

I went back over to the library anyway, in hopes that Charles would still be there, and he was. I walked up to him in the large airy reading room. "Hi," I whispered. "I'm glad you're still here."

He closed the book he was reading. "I had a feeling you might be longer than I had originally allowed for. Hungry?"

"Starved."

"Let's go eat."

While we were sitting at a counter down the square from the library Charles said around his tuna-fish sandwich, "I tried to get into the courtroom, but I couldn't get within yards of it."

"Have they finished the hearing yet?"

"I don't know. I shouldn't think so. We can stroll over there after lunch."

But we didn't have to go after lunch. When we came out there was a newspaper propped in front of a stand. The huge headline read, COURT BLOCKS BUILDER.

"Well," Charles said, buying a paper. "That's one in the eye for Schreiber."

"I'm glad," I said. "I'm glad for the wildlife sanctuary, and I'm glad it's the court that has decided."

"Why?"

"Well—if the court decides, then it's not anybody's fault, really. I mean, won't tempers go down?"

Charles was staring at me. "Are you really that naive Sam? I'm afraid it's just begun. So far from accepting the ruling of the court, the townies will just think it's one more example of the ruling WASPs getting in cahoots together against them."

There were knots of people all over town that day. Charles and I strolled around, killing time before we were due to turn up at Gene's headquarters. When we got to the common in front of the courthouse there were already tables set up with "Save Our Sanctuary" placards around and propped in front.

"There's Peter," I said, seeing my brother conferring with Bruce and Linda and a couple of others in front of the courthouse steps. "What are they trying to do now? They've won, haven't they?"

"They're probably trying to see if they can drum up any town support for the injunction. Because there's no doubt that Schreiber and Co. will try and overturn it."

"But wouldn't that take months?"

"Almost certainly."

"In months Peter will back in Cambridge and it'll be the middle of winter."

"And there'll be no more summer people up here to keep the fight for the injunction going."

I looked at Charles. "You mean the sanctuary could lose out?"

"Not only could, but probably will. One side will have pretty much left the turf. And while judges should—theoretically—be above all that, they're human like everybody else. If the forces that pushed through the injunction seem to have disappeared, then the higher decision might almost go by default to the opposition, Schreiber. Unless, of course, Peter succeeds in doing what it looks like he might be trying to do—fan it up into a national cause, maybe like Seabrook. In which case, with national office and friendly media coverage, they can keep the conservationists' fires burning."

I looked up at Charles's profile, which seemed to consist of hat and nose. "You sound almost like you think Peter's doing this cynically. Do you think he is?" I was pondering what Mother had said about Peter, that he was an "against" person.

"I doubt if anybody knows that—least of all Peter. He would probably swear to his convictions about the sanctuary on a stack of Testaments. That doesn't mean he doesn't recognize a promising political issue when he sees it. And I strongly suspect that after Peter gets his law degree—or even before—he's going to go into politics. That's why he's not about to let this first minor victory get lost in the shuffle."

The moment Charles said this, I knew in my bones he was right. "I wish politics didn't exist. I wish people could just get together and talk."

"And the lion lie down with the lamb? That's a long way off, Sam. People have been wishing that for centuries."

"Well why can't they do it, then?" I was tired and hot and

207

depressed. There was nothing about this situation that boded anything but trouble for Steve and me.

"Because they prefer fighting." Charles glanced down at me. "You feel okay? You look a little white. What did the blood test say? Or do you know yet?"

"I'm supposed to call after four. I'll telephone just before we go to Gene's office. What time is it now? I left my watch at home."

Charles glanced up and I saw we were facing the clock on the courthouse. The hands pointed to three. "Oh, I didn't see the clock."

"We can stroll towards Gene's office now. You look as though you could use a seat in an air-conditioned place. You can always duck out to a phone booth to make your call if you have to."

We walked silently along the side of the small common opposite to Peter and his tables. After we'd left the common we struck right along a street of rather seedy-looking offices and warehouses that, considering it was a weekday, looked strangely deserted.

"Nobody seems to be around," I said after a while.

"I have the feeling they're either inside working or gathered somewhere else."

The "somewhere else" turned out to be another small square, or rather triangle, with a plot of green occupying the junction of about five main roads. We heard the sound—a sort of buzz of voices, with a few rising above—before we actually got there. Then, as we approached the square, the noise suddenly got much louder, and we emerged into the open area.

It looked like a mass meeting. The green was almost invisible under all the people milling around on it. There were placards everywhere. Some were being carried on poles. Others were nailed to trees or hung from branches. One of them read, "Last century the WASPs threw out the Irish to make room for horses. This year they throw out jobs to make room for birds. We're for people all the way." Another said, "People before birds. Another said, "Jobs are better than welfare." At the opposite side of the green there was a small platform. On it were two or three men, including a priest and Steve, and a couple of women, including a nun. People were trickling into the square from the roads feeding it. Charles and I were standing on a corner when suddenly I felt something jostling

208

me. A whole clutch of young people went past, crossing the road into the green. There seemed to be almost no traffic.

"I wonder where the cars are," Charles said in a low voice. "Probably rerouted somewhere else. Let's go up and see what's going on."

"Yes." I was eager to see if Steve was going to say anything.

Charles took my hand and we crossed into the square and started slowly working our way nearer the platform. Finally we got within about twenty yards of it. "Let's stay here," Charles said.

In a few minutes one of the men on the platform stepped up to a microphone that had been placed up there. I noticed then, off to our side, a television camera set up and crew around it. The man on the platform glanced over and spoke to Steve, who nodded. Steve was taller than anyone on the platform, and better built. His stomach was flat, his waist narrow and his arms, under the rolled-up sleeves, tanned and muscular. A sense of pride filled me. This was my guy, the one who'd made love to me, the one who'd said so many times how much he loved me, the one who'd given me the baby I was somehow sure I was going to have, who would become my husband. Mrs. Steve—no, Stefan—Novak. . . .

I realized I wasn't really listening to whatever the man was saying: something about tractors and bulldozers. Then I heard Charles say under his breath, "This could get ugly."

"What do you mean?" I asked, jerked to attention.

"Didn't you hear what he was saying?"

"No. I was thinking about something else."

Charles glanced down at me. "You oughtn't to be here. This is an angry crowd. Let's get over to Gene's headquarters."

"No, I want to hear Steve."

"That's not a good idea, Sam. C'mon, let's go."

"No. I'm not going."

"Okay. It's your funeral."

Then Steve stepped up to the front of the platform and started to talk. "We don't have to put up with this," he said. He didn't yell or rant. He didn't have to. He had a wonderful voice. Without shouting or even raising it, his voice could be heard clearly anywhere in that square. "Those conservationists don't even come from the state. In a month or less they'll go home to their private incomes, their coupon clipping, their university posts and corporate offices and forget their summer hobby. And, thanks to their influence at court, we—and

209

our wives and children—can line up at the local welfare office. Maybe we ought to do that...that's the only group that those elitists seem to care about. The people on welfare must have jobs, must have quotas, must be shoved in front...everything has to be given them: free lunches, free milk, public schools....And what happens to our kids in parochial school? You know the answer, don't you?"

There was a roar from the crowd.

"If one of them gets half a glass of orange juice from the state then our wonderful summer people discover that the separation of church and state is as endangered as their birds. And you'd better believe nobody's pushing to get them in college!"

There was another roar from the crowd.

"You're very good at words, Steve, but what are we going to do about it?"

The speaker was a huge man in jeans and red T-shirt, standing with a group of other men. A couple of them had on bright orange vests such as roadworkers often wear to make them highly visible. Two more had on tin hats.

"We're going to stop them," Steve said, addressing the man in the red T-shirt.

"Yeah? How? And when?"

Queer, I thought. It was as though the rally, which had been solidly behind Steve, had suddenly turned into a personal duel between these two men. And it was a duel between...between a steel blade and a club. The images in my mind were so clear and vivid it was almost funny. Yet there was nothing at all funny about the enmity that crackled between Steve and the heckler.

Steve leaned forward. "By taking our bulldozers out to their so-called sanctuary and getting it torn up before they know what's going on. What can they do to the whole town? Declare war? And if so, we can take them on, can't we? After all, when the country goes to war, we know who really does the fighting, don't we, Fred?"

There was a laugh and then a roar as the crowd moved forward, once again solidly behind Steve.

"I guess Fred must have sat out Vietnam at home," Charles murmured.

"I wonder why he's against Steve?" I said.

"Probably wants to take the leadership away from him. That's the usual reason."

Suddenly I found my eyes on a middle-aged woman and

210

two girls about my age, standing in front of the crowd but a little to one side. They were smiling, and gazing up at Steve. Why my gaze fixed on them I don't know. But there was something about them that looked vaguely familiar.

The crowd behind us seemed to be pressing forward, pushing us a little.

"Come on, Sam," Charles whispered. "Let's go. We have no business here. Any minute somebody's going to discover we're from the Cove—which makes us the Enemy."

But I was watching Steve. His brown curly hair looked clean and shiny in the sunlight. His face was as tanned as anybody's from the beach. He was smiling down at the woman and the two girls, and I then knew why they looked familiar. The family resemblance was strong. The woman, who was also tall, was broader than Steve, and there was gray in her hair, but the wide-boned features were the same, and at least one of the girls beside her shared the likeness.

"I bet that's Steve's mother," I whispered.

Charles had hold of my arm. "We're leaving."

But I pulled my arm away. "Let's wait. The speeches will be over soon. Then maybe... well maybe something will happen."

"It will," Charles said grimly. "That's why there's a meeting. But it's not going to do you and Steve any good. Come on, Sam. This is not the time or the place."

His words had no reality for me. Afterwards I decided that heat and dizziness must have fuddled my brain. It was as though everything else—the rally, the people, the speeches— were a painted backdrop. The only things that were real were Steve, his mother and me. And somehow God or Heaven or Fate had provided this opportunity to bring us all together without apparent effort or design....

"What we have to do," Steve cried from the platform, "is catch them short and hit them hard before they know what's happened. How many of you can bring trucks, tractors, any large equipment out to the sanctuary this afternoon?"

There was a surge of voices. Everybody yelled at once. The crowd started to move. Steve jumped down off the platform and began speaking to one or two of the men.

"Talk, talk, talk," jeered the man in the red T-shirt. "When's there gonna be some action?"

"Now!" Steve said, and started forward.

Smiling slightly, his mother drew near to him. "Stefan—"

"I ran forward. "Steve!" I called out.

Charles tugged at my arm, but I shook him off. "Steve!"

I saw the man in the red shirt turn and look at me and grin, then say something to the group around him, all of whom looked over in my direction. But it had no impact on me. My attention was on Steve.

"Steve!" I yelled, loud this time.

He heard me then, and turned.

"Oh my God!" Charles said.

For a minute we all seemed frozen, or at least Steve and his mother and the girls and Charles and I did. Then, in two strides, Steve came up to us.

"What the hell are you doing here?"

"Steve, is that your mother? I want to meet her."

Steve looked at Charles. "You've got to be out of your mind to have come here and brought her."

"Okay, it was stupid. I'm trying to get her away, but she doesn't seem to have taken in what's happening, and she's bent on meeting your mother."

"Meeting Mom?" He looked at me as though I had stated my determination to take off my clothes. "No."

But it was too late for him to say that. The woman was there beside him, and beside her, the two girls. Her curly brown hair was caught up in a sort of twist at the back. She was handsome in a heavy way, and in a sleeveless dress looked meaty. But standing next to Steve, with her eyes slanted in the same way above her cheekbones, they seemed extraordinarily alike.

"Stefan, who is this?"

I stuck out my hand. "How do you do, Mrs. Novak. I'm tremendously glad to meet you."

She looked at my hand as though it were an obscene object. "I have asked you a question, Stefan. Who is this?"

"Mom, you know I'm working on a studio cottage for a Professor and Mrs. Lacey. This is Sarah Lacey, their daughter." —

"Steve—" I said.

"And what is this daughter to you?"

"Sarah is not well and I'm taking her to meet her sister," Charles said.

"Steve," I said. "Tell your mother—"

Steve raised his voice. "I want you both to get out of here, right now. Things are going to get a lot rougher. Steve's voice rose above mine, as I kept trying to get his attention. "Get her out right now. There's a taxi over there. Take it."

I suddenly saw Charles's nose hovering straight over my head as he stared down at me. He put his hand around my wrist and gripped it so hard it hurt. "So you want to ruin everything for yourself? Because if you don't, you'll just come with me now."

At the same moment I saw Steve put his arm around the older woman. "Mom, come away from here. I don't want you here either. I'll explain everything later."

Even then, probably, I wouldn't have let Charles take me away, but there was the sound of machinery coming and I looked up and saw three tractors and a bulldozer coming down two of the side streets and seeming to close in on us. A strange dizziness hit my head, making everything look as though it had suddenly turned sideways. I felt hot and cold and nauseated, all at the same time. There was an odd, roaring sound. And then everything went out.

Chapter

11

I came to, staring up at a ceiling, with a wet cloth over my forehead and somebody's hand holding it.

"Steve—" I said.

The cloth was withdrawn. I was looking up at Mushroom.

"How do you feel?" she said.

"Queer."

"You look a little queer, too."

I glanced around. I was in Gene's headquarters, lying across two chairs. "How did I get here?"

"Charles brought you in a taxi."

"Yes. I remember now."

I had a vague recollection of heat, voices, of being carried, of air going past my face and of asking Charles where we were. "In a taxi," he had said.

I tried to sit up.

"I wouldn't do that. Just stay still for a few minutes."

I lay back down. Somebody had put something under my head that felt like a pillow. "What happened?"

"You fainted. Which, considering you seem to have invaded a mass meeting of the townies, isn't altogether surprising. I must say." Mushroom said, squeezing the rag out in a pan on the floor, "I was not polite to Charles when he told me that he'd taken you there."

"He didn't take me there," I said. "We went."

"It was a damn fool thing to do. Why on earth did you do it?"

I decided it was time to try and sit up again. This time I made it. Charles and the Congressmen were off at the other end of the small room looking at some literature and talking to a couple of helpers.

"What did you want to go to the townies' meeting for?" Mushroom asked again.

My head was swimming. For a moment I wasn't quite sure whether my insides were going to heave or not. Then they seemed to settle, but I could feel a sweat break out on my forehead. "I don't feel so hot," I muttered.

"I told you not to sit up. Lie back down again. Maybe I can get something from the drugstore to make you feel better. What were you doing all day besides going to that stupid meeting?"

"I was at the library."

"All day?"

"We had lunch." I put my arm over my face. It must be well past four by now, which meant I could call the clinic. But even if I could sit up without getting sick, I couldn't telephone from Gene's office with everyone standing around. I lay there, fighting nausea, which had come back, and an unpleasant clammy feeling. And yet, uncomfortable as the queasiness was, I knew that behind it lay something worse: misery over Steve's obvious fear of his mother's knowing about him and me.

Charles wandered over. "How're you feeling?"

"She's feeling rotten," Mushroom said. "What did you all have for lunch?"

"Tuna-fish sandwiches," Charles said.

"Both of you?"

"There was not a big gourmet selection. Why?"

"Well, you're not sick, unless you've been doing a stoic act. So I guess it can't be bad fish or mayonnaise."

"Oh," Charles said. Then, "No, I don't think it's that." He stopped abruptly.

"Well, what is it, then?" Mushroom snapped.

Charles didn't say anything.

I said, "I think I'll be all right if we can just get back home to the Cove. It's cooler there, and there's a breeze."

216

"I'm sure you will be. But I don't want you to be sick on the way home."

Gene strolled over, soda in hand. "How's the patient?"

"Not so good," Mushroom said. "I don't suppose you know a doctor in this benighted town."

"Sure I do. Joe Belovsky. He's one of my few supporters. Want me to give him a ring?"

"No!" I yelled.

"Yes," Mushroom said. "Pay no attention to Sam. At least he might give her something to tide her over until we get home."

"Will do."

"I don't want to see a doctor," I said. I could just see the scene, as in the old movies on the late show: Aged family doctor: "*I'm happy to report your sister is in excellent condition, considering....*" "*Considering what?*" the anxious sister would ask (in front, of course, of all interested parties). "*Why, that she's pregnant,*" the doctor would say, beaming. "*Who's the happy father?*"

"No," I said again, more firmly. And looked up at Charles. He was looking down at me sardonically.

"Maybe just some cold water," Charles said finally. "It might do the trick. Then we can drive her home."

"No," Mushroom said. "I don't like the way she looks. I don't see why she should have to go for a long drive in this heat without something to make her feel better."

At that point Gene returned. "Joe said to come over to his office right away. He was on the point of leaving, and you won't have to wait. He'll look at you and, if he thinks it a good idea, might give you something to hold you until you get home. I'll drive you."

I felt so miserable going over I couldn't really be sorry that I was going to see the doctor. Perhaps he could give me something to settle my head and stomach.

"Sorry you don't feel well," Gene said. His car was air-conditioned and a lot bigger and more comfortable than Mushroom's coupe, which was the reason I was in it. Mushroom and Charles were behind us in her car.

"The doctor's waiting for you," the nurse said, as I walked in.

"I'll go in with you." Mushroom sounded very much like Mother, I thought.

"No," I said. "I'd rather go in alone."

217

"Come on, Margaret," the Congressman said. "She's a big girl now."

The doctor was a thin, middle-aged man who stood up briskly and shook hands. The interview did not take long. He asked me a few leading questions, to which I gave truthful and obvious answers. "I thought it might be that when you came in the room," he said, "despite your age. Not that it makes much difference nowadays."

"How could you tell?" I asked, relieved that he knew so easily and without fuss. "It couldn't show."

"Well, it's something of an old wives' tale, but there is an element of truth in what's called the pregnant mask, and you have it. Anyway, given the symptoms Gene described, and with a patient who is female and between the ages of twelve and forty-two, it's the first obvious thing you think of. Want me to call the prenatal clinic to get the official report?"

I nodded. "Please."

"It's official," he said a few minutes later, putting the phone down. "You're pregnant."

We looked at each other.

"Do you have a doctor in the Cove there?"

"No."

He got up. "Come on, let's go into the next room and let me examine you."

"Everything seems to be more or less in order," he said a while later. "I'd say about four to six weeks. I take it you didn't use precautions."

I got off the table. "Not all the time."

He looked at me sympathetically. "Are you going to have a lot of flak?"

"I guess so. But we...that is...St—the guy I'm in love with, we'll probably be married pretty soon."

"Fine. But keep in touch with a doctor, whatever you decide."

There was a note in his voice that made me pause. "Is something wrong?"

"No. Not wrong exactly. But you may not have entirely plain sailing every step of the way. What I'd like you to do is see a gynecologist regularly. I'd recommend one here, but you live in New York, don't you?"

"Yes."

"Maybe you ought to establish yourself with somebody here, and then he can give you the name of somebody in New York, unless your family has one."

My family . . . if Steve and I were married. I'd be here. But I didn't want to have to go to another doctor now. It would be horribly complicated. "Can't I just use you?"

"Sure. If that's all right with you. I take it you don't want your family to know for the moment."

"No. I'll tell them, when . . . when it's right."

"Very well. I'll give you a prescription for something that will keep down your nausea and make you less dizzy. You can get it filled at the corner. Take one right away. You'll feel a lot better immediately. And come and see me in two weeks. In the meantime, if you have any problems, call me. Here's one of my cards. The telephone number's on it. And rest!"

I put it in my jeans pocket.

"What's wrong?" Mushroom said when I came out.

"I have a slight stomach upset. He gave me a prescription which we can fill at the corner. He said as soon as I've taken one I'll feel better."

Mushroom took the prescription out of my hand before I knew what she was doing. After she looked at it she said crossly, "I bet they teach them this hen scratch in medical school. Part of the mystique of being a doctor." She handed me back the paper.

The doctor was right. It took only a minute or two to make up the prescription, and I swallowed a tablet immediately, washed down by water supplied from the soda fountain. It was like magic. By the time we were less than an hour out of town I felt much better—physically. Well enough to brood over Steve's attitude towards me in front of his mother.

Charles was driving Mushroom's coupe and I was sitting beside him. Mushroom was driving back with Gene in his car, and they were right behind us.

"Well," Charles said finally. "Are you?"

"Am I what?"

"Pregnant."

"Yes."

Long pause. "What are you going to do?"

"I'm going to tell Steve and we can be married." I believed it. Yet there was a terrible fear underneath that, a fear that was suddenly much worse because I was pregnant. With an effort that was almost visible I pushed the fear down. "He loves me. I know he does."

"I guess he does, at that."

219

"Then he'll see we should be married—especially as his family is very pro-baby and all that."

Charles didn't say anything.

"Don't you think?"

"Sam, I don't know. That's for you and Steve to settle." The way he said it was like his closing a door. He obviously didn't want to talk about it. We didn't say anything else all the way home.

When we got home the house was empty. Peter, of course, was probably still signing up sympathizers outside the courthouse, or protesting somewhere with the other conservationists. Father could be heard typing away in his studio on one side of the house, and Mother's typewriter was clacking upstairs in her temporary study—my room.

"I'm going up to get Mom out of your room so you can lie down," Mushroom said.

"No," I almost shouted. Then I added more quietly, "I feel fine now. I really do. It was the heat and probably something I ate at lunch. I'm okay." I looked at Mushroom. "Please don't tell Mom."

"Why not?" Mushroom was giving me one of her penetrating looks. "What's there about it for her not to know?"

"Nothing," I said quickly, before she could do any more thinking along that line. "It's just that I don't feel like being fussed... or hovered over. What I'd really like to do is take Jill for a walk along the beach. After the heat in the town it'd feel cool and terrific." I was counting on the fact that Mushroom hated being fussed over, too.

"All right. Although I never knew you hated heat that much. You're usually the one who puts on sweaters just about the time everybody else is taking them off." Pause. "Is there anything you're not telling me?"

"No." I hated lying, especially to Mushroom. "I think I'll go get Jill."

Jill, who'd had a boring day, flung herself at me, and when I collected her chewed-up tennis ball from the top of the refrigerator, almost went out of her mind with anticipation.

"You're really a fantastic dog," I said, hugging her.

What I wanted more than anything was to be alone. I wanted to think about Steve and me and being pregnant, and I hadn't been alone since the doctor put down the phone and said, "It's official."

I walked along the beach, throwing the ball for Jill. She

raced after it, picked it up, then brought it back, head up, tail waving, to put at my feet.

"You must have some retriever in you," I said, after about the twentieth throw. We walked far up along the beach, away from the direction of Headlands, until finally the sand beach started narrowing and the rocks came farther and farther down. At the point where the rocks plunged into the water, we were out of sight of the house—of any house—and I sat down on a slab of rock and stared out at the water, which was amethyst, turquoise and gray, depending on where you looked.

I thought about being pregnant. The strange part was, I really didn't feel anything at all. It was a word. It was hard even for me to connect it with the fact that I had fainted. I connected the fainting with feeling sick and hot. But the doctor had said that when he heard about my symptoms he thought I might be pregnant, so obviously there was a link. I closed my eyes and tried to imagine what the pregnant bit of me looked like. I'd never had any courses in physiology. When I finally came back to American schools everyone had had sex education, but I'd missed it. Mother had told me about what the man did and what the woman did and lent me a book. The trouble was, I read in detail all the parts about the act of conception—and studied the diagrams. But I skimmed the bit about what an egg and a beginning baby looked like. And I'd long since lost the book. . . .

Pregnant. Well. A month pregnant probably meant that the embryo was now about half an inch long and looked like a tadpole. Somewhere I'd read that the foetus went through all the evolutionary stages of human development, and after the worm came the tadpole . . . or something.

Pregnant. Pregnant. It was funny, I thought, you said a word to yourself often enough and after a while it had no meaning at all. People talked about a pregnant pause, or a situation pregnant with meaning. But I was pregnant with baby. Pregnant was a thing that happened to other women, older women, women. I was not a woman . . . yet. Except, of course, that I was pregnant. Which meant automatically that I was a woman.

"Today I am a man. . . ." That was what I had heard Jewish boys of thirteen said at a Bar Mitzvah. Well, today I was a woman, although of course technically I'd been one since I'd started menstuating four years before. Almost five years.

I leaned down, picked up a pebble, and threw it as far as

221

I could into the water. Jill tore into the water after it. "Come back, you silly dog," I said.

But Jill was swimming like a water spaniel straight out to where she thought the pebble was. "Come back here, Jill," I yelled. "Now come on back."

For a minute I was afraid that she'd go on looking for the wretched stone, but she turned around, and with her head carving through the water in front of her, she swam back and ran over to me and gave herself a huge shake, transferring a large part of the water from herself to me. "Thanks a lot," I said, and threw the ball again along the beach.

After some more throws to help Jill dry off and keep warm, I dragged my mind back to the subject of my being pregnant, because while I was mooning around about the word "pregnant," I was avoiding thinking about what it meant to and for Steve and me. And for the first time since the town meeting I let myself focus on how he'd reacted to having his mother and me there together.

"Watch out for the boy who doesn't want to introduce you to his family...." The statement leaped into my mind before I knew I was thinking about it. Who had said it? Mother? Mushroom? Had I read it? Somehow I didn't think I'd read it, but I couldn't think who'd spoken the words. It was then that panic went through me like an arrow. But it was gone immediately. Don't be stupid, I told myself. There's nothing to get panicky over. It was brainless of me to expect Steve to do anything as important as introducing me to his mother in the middle of a town meeting where feelings about the sanctuary were running rampant. It was rotten timing and he knew it and didn't want anything to get started on the wrong foot. He was simply protecting us, protecting me...and anyway, we'd talk about it tonight. This was not one of the nights he said he would have to work. He'd be there in the Barretts' drive and I would tell him about my being pregnant....

I got off the rock and started walking back. I had no idea what time it was, because I didn't have on my watch. But it was certainly dinner time, if not later, and if I didn't want to have any flak about slipping away to see (as they would think) Charles, I'd better get back and do my share of cleaning up afterwards. A little anxiously I wondered if everybody would accept that I'd go out to see Charles the night after I'd been in town with him all day and been sick to boot. But after all, people in love were well known never to have enough of one another....

"Come on, Jill," I said. "Let's run."

They were already at the dinner table when I got back.

"Where've you been?" Mother said immediately. She looked worried.

"I just took Jill for a walk."

"Mushroom's told me about your fainting fit. I'm going to have our doctor here look over you tomorrow."

My panic arrow winged through me again. "I'm fine, Mom. Really. And anyway, I've been looked at by a doctor. Didn't Mushroom tell you?"

"Some local Polack," Mother said.

"That's a prejudiced comment," I said angrily. "I thought we didn't say that kind of thing."

"Listen to Liza the Liberal," My father spoke in his dry voice. "I never realized that all my good coaching produced fruit."

"You once nearly threw out somebody who made an anti-Semitic comment at our table in New York. You said you didn't allow that kind of thing in your home."

"That's different," Peter said.

"Why?" I was suddenly very angry.

"Because Jews do not represent the most regressive element in our society today. That's why. Probably per capita they're the most enlightened group we have."

"What's that got to do with it—even if you're right? And what about blacks or Puerto Ricans? I've heard you be very morally superior towards people who make ethnic slurs against them."

"Also different. They've been the target of repressive acts on our part for our entire history—"

"Come off it, Peter," Mushroom said. "I agree with you about the Jews and the blacks, but I don't believe in your kind of selective tolerance. If ethnic slurs are bad for one lot, then they're bad for another."

"True." Father helped himself to salad. "But we'd be more than human if we didn't have our preferences. And I prefer groups that do not try to keep our secular society in the grip of a mediaeval church. Would someone please pass the dressing?"

"I don't believe this," I said. "Here I've been brought up to believe that the kind of thing you're saying is the worst

223

sin there is. But you're talking like all the people you make speeches against."

"Who's being morally superior now? And anyway, what's it to you?"

"Yes," Mother said. She was looking at me hard. "That's what I'd like to know."

"Did you hear that your friend Steve Novak is going to lead some kind of bulldozer parade out to the sanctuary to dig it up? That is, he says he's going to. If the police don't stop him." Peter pushed his plate away and pulled over a dish of strawberries. He put one in his mouth. "Umm, good! Mushroom says you were there at the rally with Charles, who must have been out of his mind to take you there. But then he's always had more brains than sense. Anyway, you heard Steve, you know what he's going to do."

Suddenly, as though I were watching a movie in my head, I saw that line of ducklings, swimming single-file behind their mother.

"He won't," I said quickly.

"Yeah? What makes you think so? The police don't think you're right. They're all set to block the road up there, even though as good ethnics themselves their sympathies are probably with their buddies."

"He wouldn't do that," I said again. "He likes birds. I told you."

Peter put down the strawberry he was about to swallow. He stared at me. "So you did. So you did. Glad you reminded me." He stood up. "Excuse me!"

"Where are you going?" I said.

"Out."

"I want *you* to go to bed," Mother said to me. "Right after washing up. Even though Steve Novak obviously put his politics above his job and didn't show up to work on my studio this afternoon, I can use it tomorrow if the weather's decent, and I want you to have a rest. I don't like to bring up unpleasant subjects, but you are supposed to be preparing for more surgery in the fall, and overworking and running around a hot town in the peak of the day is not my idea of proper relaxation."

I got up. I knew now that things at home were going from bad to worse, and before too long they would get very much worse indeed. But right now the only thing that mattered was seeing Steve. After I was sure that he and I . . . that every-

224

thing was going to be fine with us...after that I could cope with anything. I walked to the door.

"Sarah Lacey," Mother said. "Did you hear what I just said?"

I opened the door and turned. "I'm a grown woman and I can decide for myself what I'm going to do. Right now I'm going out." And I shut the door after me before anyone could give me an argument.

But Steve wasn't there.

At first I couldn't believe that he wasn't coming, and decided I must be early. I still hadn't remembered to put on my watch, so couldn't be sure what time it actually was. It wasn't quite dark, but then it hadn't been completely dark when we met for the past several weeks. Walking up the high grass bank that led into the little wood surrounding the Barretts' house, I sat down with my back to a tree to wait until Steve's van would turn into the drive.

I thought about being pregnant, and the panic that had come and gone so rapidly before came again and showed signs of staying, so I pushed my mind off the word "pregnant" and onto the word "wedding." I had been to two weddings in my life, one when I was ten and was a flower girl at the marriage of an older cousin. It had taken place in one of the more fashionable Episcopal churches in Manhattan. I had worn a deep pink dress with a hair ribbon of the same color and had carried a bouquet of daisies. I'd enjoyed every minute of it: the dress, the wedding rehearsal and the wedding. I'd never before been in a church, and loved the slow, formal words, the loose white garment the priest wore, and the music. I'd decided then and there that that was the way to be married and said so afterwards to my parents.

"Of course the whole thing is anachronistic," my father had commented, "but I'll grant that the Episcopalians do it in style."

The other time was in a garden in Connecticut, when the daughter of one of Father's colleagues was married for the third time. All I remembered about that was being eaten alive by mosquitoes while somebody in a dashiki read aloud from the *Rubaiyat*....

This wedding—mine, Steve's and mine—would be in a church exactly like the one from which my cousin was married. I could easily find out what music was played, and I would wear a long white dress with a white lace veil....

My daydream was interrupted by the stings of mosquitoes that kept attacking my ankles below the bottoms of my jeans.

"Ouch!" I said aloud, and scratched frantically.

As I scratched I realized it had become dark. That reality hit me along with two others: that I was cold and that Steve had still not come. I began to shiver. Getting up, I groped my way down to the drive and then out to the main road. Here, away from the thick wood, it was lighter. The moon was almost full and the stars were brilliant. But the trees had also been a protection, and it was colder. I had forgotten how much the air cooled at night near the water.

Steve hadn't come.... My mind rushed forward with excuses: He might have had to attend some kind of meeting after that huge rally.... he might not have been able to get away.... he might have been trying to calm down the hotter heads (after that speech of his? some voice within me jeered). But the excuses were just words, words, words. The fact, the reality was that he had not come. Of course he didn't know I was pregnant.... The pain jabbed again and brought the old panic with it. If he had known I was pregnant, would it have made any difference? Suddenly I remembered him as he was in the motel, laughing, tender and funny, his finger running gently down my body. If he had known I was pregnant, of course he would have come—of course, of course, of course ... wouldn't he?

As I stumbled towards the house I had a curious flash of memory, something I hadn't thought of in years: myself sitting on the stage of a school in Germany, peering out into the audience to the empty seat beside Mother. Father had promised that this time he would come to the prize-giving, especially as, this time, I was, *mirabile dictu*, going to receive a prize, for writing. He had promised ... but he never came.

I finally made it to the side door, swearing that never again would I leave my watch off. If I could just know what time it now was, I would also know whether or not the kitchen clean-up was over and where most of the family would probably be located. And from that I could decide on the best way to get into the house with the least chance of running into somebody—anybody.

It was weird. While with one part of my mind I was calculating the odds of meeting someone on the way in, and which of the family would offer me the fewest problems, with another part I knew perfectly well there was no way I could avoid a confrontation with Mother. Even if I managed to slip upstairs and into bed without her knowing, she would not go to bed herself without finding out whether or not I was in. And not being dense, she would check on my room from time to time. After all, she had been well trained by two other children.

But even realizing all this, I turned the knob of the side door as quietly as I could, and was sneaking into the dark kitchen when Mother was suddenly in the doorway.

"You might as well save yourself all that elaborate tip-toeing around. We're waiting for you. Come along." She turned and went back into the living room. Because there was really nothing else to do, I followed her. Peter wasn't there. But Father, Mother and Mushroom were. And so was Charles.

"All right, Sarah," Mother said. And the fact that she called me Sarah instead of Sam depressed me even more than I was already. "Where were you?"

I looked across at Charles. Without his funny canvas hat he looked older, perhaps because of his high forehead.

Mother caught my glance. "There's no need to look that way at Charles. He wandered in here quite innocently to see how you were doing after your fainting spell today. It was at that point that a few things came to light: such as the fact that we assumed you were with him as we assumed you had been with him all these nights. So he's had a few questions thrown at him, too. What I want to know is, who were you meeting?"

Again I looked at Charles. He shook his head. "Sorry I spilled the beans. I couldn't keep up the scenario that you and I were making violent love in the moonlight. But I have offered no further information. So don't look at me as though I were a rat. I'm not."

"No," I said. "You're not. You've been a help. Thanks." The whole scene felt to me as though it were being acted underwater. Everything was slow and heavy.

"Well, I'm not sure I'm going to go along with that hand-some endorsement," Mother said, "considering that help was to assist Sam in lying to us."

"Come on, Mom," Mushroom cut in. "that's not fair, and you know it. If Charles is Sam's friend what do you expect him to do? Hold up his hand in horror while he intones piously that he won't be a party to any gross deceptions?"

Father, looking grim, said, "This doesn't concern you, Margaret. I suggest that you leave us."

"While the two of you have a glorious time flagellating Sam? Not on your life!"

I was tremendously touched. Between my being abroad and Mushroom's being in boarding school, we hadn't had much of a chance to know one another. I'd really no idea she could be so terrific.

"I resent that statement and I resent your tone," Mother said to Mushroom. "We happen to be fond of Sam, too."

"Maybe, but you're beginning to sound like the opening ceremonies of the Spanish Inquisition."

Mother opened her mouth, but Charles beat her to the draw. "May I make another suggestion? Why doesn't everybody let Sam speak for herself? She can be pretty snappy with the comeback when she feels like it. She's not an orphan abandoned in the snow."

"Thank you for your help today, Charles," Father started, in what was pretty obviously going to be a suggestion that Charles shut up and/or leave.

"That's all right," Charles said, getting up. "If you need any assistance, Sam, just yell."

I ignored them all and went over to Charles. Just as he was opening the front door I went up on tiptoe and kissed him. "Thanks."

He gave me a hug in return and then left.

"Okay," Father said, when I came back to the center of the room. "Who is it?"

I was so angry at Steve that the temptation to blurt out his name was overwhelming. There was nothing about him that my family would approve of. Furthermore, I was pregnant. Furthermore, I was a minor. But I always seemed to suffer queer thoughts at the wrong time. Just as I saw the ducklings clearly in my mind when I was at the town meeting, so now I suddenly had this vivid picture of Steve with Chico on his head. My family could really ruin him....

"I'm going to bed," I said. "I don't have to answer any questions I don't want to." I made for the stairs.

"Sarah!" That was my father, who had stood up.

I turned to him. "Do you know what I thought about tonight when—well just when. I thought about that time in Germany when I won a prize. Maybe the only time I won a prize. You had promised to come and see the prize-giving. But you didn't. And you didn't phone or anything. Maybe I'm

228

not such a satisfactory daughter. But you haven't been much of a father. Goodnight."

That time I made it upstairs, closed my door, and locked it. Then to make sure nobody broke in, put a chair under the knob. But I needn't have bothered. Everybody left me alone.

Chapter

12

I didn't sleep much, partly because—during the first hour anyway—I was waiting for the voice at the door, the knock and then the rattling of the doorknob, none of which ever came. After I decided that the family was going to leave me alone until morning, I continued to lie awake, because I had to plan what I was going to do, and how I would get out of the house to do it.

Finally, at four, I got up as quietly as I could. It was still dark, of course, and I depended on the fact that if Mother heard me, which she would because mothers seemed to hear everything, she'd assume that someone had to go to the bathroom in the middle of the night. But before I unlocked and opened the door, I slid into my jeans and another T-shirt, got all the money I had from my bureau drawer, pocketed a small flashlight and put on sneakers. Then I opened the door, signed to Jill to go out, went to the bathroom, then closed my bedroom door again, only with me outside it. Hoping that the sound of the water still flushing would cover any other irregular noise, I crept downstairs. I had decided in the course of my planning to take Jill with me, quite why I wasn't sure. But I was still uncertain as to how the family regarded her, and I also felt in strong need of an ally. And Jill was about the best and most uncritical there was.

I would have liked to have taken something to eat from the refrigerator, but I didn't want to risk that much noise or delay. Getting out of the house was the easiest part. I collected the leash I had bought for Jill in the village and simply closed the door softly after me. In this part of the country nobody locked doors. Then I kept to the back of the house, away from the windows of the master bedroom, which faced front. Just before I reached the road I turned back and looked at the house. There still wasn't a light on, so I had apparently gotten away with my escape. But I kept looking anyway, because I had the queerest feeling that I would be in some way different when I saw it again.

I had thought of waking up Charles by throwing stones at his window and asking him to lend me his car. I could drive, even though I did not have a license. But I knew it would be unfair. He'd already been criticized by my parents for helping me as much as he had. I would have to hitchhike. If worse came to worse, I'd have to walk. Leominster was fifteen miles to the west. Before the car smash, I'd have thought nothing of hiking fifteen miles. I'd belonged to a hiking club in Europe and had done more than that many times. But, since I'd come out of the hospital, I hadn't walked more than three. "We'll get a ride," I said to Jill, "you'll see."

Crossing the beach hadn't been too difficult. It was still dark, but a faint pearly glow made it possible to see. The path through the rocks to the main road was more difficult, and here I used my pocket flash. But by the time I hit the main road, the dawn was already streaking the eastern sky.

The first car that stopped had only the driver in it, and I didn't much like the way he looked or talked, so I said I wanted the exercise. He wasn't very nice about that, but he drove on. The second was driven by a woman. I was about to accept a ride from her when she said, "What are you doing out at this hour by yourself?" And I had a horrible feeling that she wouldn't drop me until she had the entire story out of me including my parents' phone number. The third was a truck, and both drivers sounded as though they'd been drinking. The fourth offer I accepted. It, too, was a truck, but the driver looked elderly, he spoke nicely to Jill and when I looked into the cab, there was a Bible on the seat. Besides which, I was hungry and my leg was beginning to ache. A final factor in my accepting the ride was the thought that the woman driver might alert the police that a minor was trying to run away from home and I could have state troopers looking for me before I could even get to the city.

After I climbed into the truck and put Jill between me and the driver, we arrived in Leominster in about half an hour. On the way I discovered the reason for the Bible. The driver belonged to a fiercely evangelistic sect and proselytized me all the way into the city.

"Where do you want me to drop you?" he said. "I could take you to our youth center, if you like. They have a dormitory for girls."

"Thank you, but I'm going to see a friend."

"I'm not sure that I should drop a young girl like you just anywhere."

"I don't want to be dropped just anywhere," I said. "I want to be dropped at the Y." I held my breath, not knowing whether or not there was a Y in Leominster.

"I thought you said you were going to see a friend."

"I am. Tomorrow. In the meantime I'm going to the Y."

He didn't say anything, and I was extremely relieved when he did draw up outside a YM/WCA. "Just remember," he called after me as I ran with Jill up the steps, "all the things I told you."

"I will." I shoved frantically against the door, hoping it would open. It was locked, but as I could see through the glass panel somebody was passing at that moment and opened it. "We don't open until seven," he said.

"Just let me in. I'm getting away from that man." Which was true, if a little unfair.

The Y custodian peered through the door. "Hurry," I said.

Slowly, obviously reluctantly, he turned the bolt and opened the door. "I'm not supposed to do this." He saw Jill behind me then. "And we don't allow animals."

"You'll get a medal, for helping a damsel in distress." I pushed in, dragging Jill behind me. "Honestly."

"Yeah, well, now you're in what do you want me to do?"

"Tell me where the ladies' room is."

"I'm not supposed—well, all right. It's back through that hall there and to the left. But if you're not out in a few minutes, I'm coming to get you."

"I'll be out."

He looked like he meant it, so Jill and I were back in the front hall before he could get suspicious."

"We don't allow no animals," the custodian said again, eyeing Jill.

With all the reason in the world not to, Jill loved the human race. She wagged her whole backside.

The custodian shuffled over and held out his hand. Jill licked it, then jumped up on his front. "Good dog," he said. Then, to my total astonishment, his eyes filled with tears. He hugged Jill. "My dog died last week. Thirteen years old. Had her since she was four weeks."

"I'm sorry." I really didn't know what else to say. I looked down at Jill, who was now sitting at my feet as though she had a postgraduate degree in obedience training. If I had her for thirteen years I'd be . . . thirty, thirty-one. I'd liked her before, and wanted to save her from being destroyed, but she'd been a dog. Suddenly she was a person, with a personality, just like mine or Mushroom's or Steve's. "We'll be together thirteen years, won't we, Jill?"

She thumped her tail. I leaned down and hugged her. Curiously, it was easier to feel optimistic about thirteen years ahead than about the next twenty-four hours. With that thought I remembered everything else: that I was pregnant, that I had to see Steve, that . . . I closed my mind down quickly. But not quite quickly enough. The next thought—marriage—slipped through, and brought with it the hollow feeling I was afraid of.

"Could I see your phone book?"

"All right." He leaned down and stroked Jill's head. "Had breakfast?"

"No."

"Well, I have some coffee in the room back there and some muffins. My dog always liked muffins. You can have some. I bet your dog'd like some, too."

"Thanks. We would."

He straightened, a heavy, middle-aged man, and shambled over to the reception desk, pulled open a drawer and got out a directory. You can look in this. I'll get the coffee and the muffins."

I looked down at Jill. "It's because he's fallen for you. Thanks." She thumped her tail.

I looked up Novak in the directory. There was a column of Novaks. Evidently it was a popular name. But I concentrated on two: "Stefan Novak," and then "Steve Novak, Bus." The second address I recognized as being Steve's loft. I glanced at my watch. Ten to six. If he had spent the night there, which he said he sometimes did, then he'd be there now. What I needed now was a phone. I had no idea at what time Steve got up, but something told me he was a very early riser. There was bound to be a pay phone somewhere. I glanced down the long tiled hall. At that moment the custodian came out of a door marked "Utility." Under his arm he carried a thermos. In one hand he had two mugs and in the other a brown paper bag. "Breakfast, Jill," I said. She must have smelled something enticing, because she got up and waggled her behind again.

I was impatient, but waited until the custodian had poured the two cups of mud-colored liquid and opened the muffins on a piece of wax paper.

"Here," he said lovingly to Jill, and broke up half a muffin in small pieces and put it on the paper bag, which he then placed on the floor. Jill ate the pieces so fast it looked almost as though she had inhaled them. The custodian's face broke into a wide grin. "Atta girl." He broke up the other half and put it down. While Jill was busy inhaling that I asked, "Is there a pay phone here?"

"Down the hall to the left."

What I got was Steve's answering tape. The trouble was, I had no number to give him to call back. By the time I had figured out what I might say, the tape had obviously run out, so I dialed again. This time I said, "Steve, this is Sarah. I came to Leominster early this morning to see you. I'm at the Y now at this number"—and I gave the number on the dial in front of me. "It's a public pay phone and I may not be able to stay. But I'll keep calling."

When I got back all the muffin was gone, and Jill was stretched out, nose on paws, sated and happy.

"I meant to save you one, but your dog...well, she was hungry."

So was I. Ravenous. But I smiled at him. Then I said, "Can't I stay here in the hall, or in a lounge or something?"

"People from the office start coming in around eight. They're not going to let you stay without you takin' a room."

I had enough money for a room, but I'd left the pay-phone number for Steve. "If I got a call on the pay phone, would they know how to get me?"

"I dunno. But I don't think so. Calls for people staying here come through the switchboard. And they still wouldn't be crazy about your hanging around the hall." He looked

235

down at Jill. "They wouldn't let you anyway, with this dog here. Or give you a room. What's her name?"

"Jill."

He leaned down and patted her head. "That's a good girl, Jill."

"You ought to get another dog."

"Yeah. I know. But Spot—I can't forget her." Slowly he unbent. "Miss, you're goin' to have to leave soon, or I'll get in trouble. Some of the people staying here will start getting up pretty soon, and they could report me."

"All right. Anyway, thanks a lot. Can you tell me how to get to 123 Spring Street?" That was the address of Steve's loft.

He looked at me for a minute. "What do ya wanna go down there for, near the river? That's not a good place for you to be."

"A friend has his office there. I have to see him."

He repeated stubbornly, "That's no place for a young girl to be."

"I'll be all right. Truly."

He was still peering intently at me. "Who'd ya wanna see there?"

I hesitated, then said, "Steve Novak."

"You know Steve?"

"Yes. Do you?"

He grinned. "Sure. Everybody in town knows Steve. You one of his girls?"

Jealousy stabbed through me. I couldn't think of what to answer. Then I said, "Does he have that many?"

"Sure. All the girls like Steve. He's a good-lookin' young feller. And," the custodian went on, "men like him, too—most of 'em anyway, when they're not jealous. Specially since he's going to show those high-hat snobs out at the Cove they can't come here and tell us what to do. Like that woman last year, trying to talk about birth control."

I had a sudden mental picture of Mother's blue suit with the tomato smearing down it. I toyed with the idea of saying, "That's my mother you're talking about," but decided not to. It would just make everything more complicated. But I felt a little cowardly.

The custodian was picking up the brown paper bag off the floor, crumpling up the wax paper and collecting the cups. I knew I had to go. Besides, if I didn't get something to eat I might faint again.

236

"Thanks anyway, for helping me out and feeding Jill. She says thank you, too."

He didn't say anything, but when Jill got up patted her on the head again. I went to the front door. Then I turned and said, "I don't think Spot would mind if you took another dog. I think she'd be glad, particularly if the dog was a stray, like Jill here." Then I went out.

I found a coffee shop that didn't object to Jill sitting at my feet as long as I sat at a table and not the counter, and treated myself to scrambled eggs and an English muffin. When I was finished with that, it was still only seven. There was nothing to do but go and sit in the nearby square and walk around.

I spent the next four frustrating hours doing that—sitting in the square or walking around calling every half hour to see if Steve was in his workshop. He wasn't. I bought a newspaper, a lot of which was devoted to the road-block the police set up to stop the parade of bulldozers going to the sanctuary. The blockade had worked, but there had been some ugly fighting between the townies who had accompanied the bulldozers and the conservationists who had stationed themselves in front of the police. The way the news story was written, it was hard to decide who had struck the first blow, but it was fairly clear which side the reporter was on: the townies'. They were the good guys, the conservationists—led by Peter Lacey—were the bad ones.

I turned to the editorial page. The editorial was even more emphatic in its allocation of virtue and evil. Peter got a bad mention in that, too. And the letters were the angriest of all.

I folded the paper and put it down on the bench beside me. At least one thing was clear: where Steve had been the previous evening. He was sitting on top of a bulldozer or earthmover or in a truck or in his van leading the townies' parade. I wondered if he even remembered that we had had a date.... Then I got up and wandered around some more and tried Steve's phone again. When I heard the tape I hung up, wondering if he had even picked up the first message. I knew he could pick up messages with a square electronic key that I saw him use when he called for messages from the van phone. If I went back to the Y would anyone know or tell me if he had called there on the pay phone? Almost certainly not. I could, of course, try the phone number belonging to Stefan Novak. It could be my Steve or no relation whatever. It could be his father's house, or at least be the family house still listed in his father's name....And what if his mother answered the telephone? Did Steve say whether or not she worked? I couldn't remember but I rather thought she did. What would be the reaction of one of his sisters if I said, "This is Sarah Lacey"? especially in view of the day's news. And why, why, why, did this stupid business about the sanctuary have to blow up now? If it hadn't been for that...

I called back Steve's office. The tape again. Then I looked up Stefan Novak's address and asked a passerby how to get there.

I glanced at my watch. It was now eleven-thirty. I had expected to be hungry again. But I wasn't hungry at all. In fact, the idea of food repelled me. What I would like more than anything else in the world would be to swim in cool water, I thought, standing in the middle of the sidewalk, trying to make up my mind. It was going to be even hotter today than it was yesterday, and I hadn't slept.

But none of this was important. Even if the address did not belong to Steve's family, then all would not be lost. That Novak might know the right address. According to the passerby it would take me about half an hour to walk, which I would have to do, because the city buses did not take dogs.

"Come on, Jill. Let's go."

Half an hour later I was standing in another small square, surrounded by row houses, fighting heat, fatigue and a sense of depression that had descended out of nowhere. On the way over I couldn't block out the knowledge that by now Mother had known for hours that I was missing, and my feeling vacillated between guilt and fear that she would have informed the police and that they would be looking for me. I was still a minor, or below the age of consent, or something. Or was I? And anyway, didn't the missing person have to be gone for twenty-four hours? As I was standing there, thinking about this, a police car cruised past, and the cop looked out the window and saw me. Did he slow down? I sat down on a nearby bench. I was still not hungry. If anything I felt a little sick. But most of all I felt tired, wiped out. I put a hand to my head. It was clammy to the touch. What was it the doctor had said? Something about my not having plain sailing....

Funny, I hadn't even thought much about that. All I thought about was telling Steve so we could be married, which, of course, we would be...I was sure of it....But now I couldn't reach him.

I looked around, saw a phone booth, got up and tried

Steve's phone again. I got a tape, but this time a different tape. Obviously he had picked up my message and gone back to his loft to record another, because his recorded voice said, "If this is Sarah, I'm not going to be in my office today. A lot has come up. I'll call you tomorrow."

I stood there until the tape ran out and the dial tone came over the telephone. Then I hung up, put more money in and dialed to hear the message again. I couldn't believe it. I couldn't believe that if I had come into Leominster to see him he'd simply leave a message saying he was too busy. Maybe it was the heat, perhaps it was the shock of the message, but suddenly dizziness hit me as though it were a blow on the side of the head, and I clung to the door of the phone booth.

"Are you all right?" a voice said.

I opened my eyes. A pleasant, square, middle-aged woman was standing there.

"I'm just dizzy. It's so hot."

The woman came up. "There's a bench there. Do you want me to help you to it?"

"If I could just go somewhere cool for a minute, and get something cool to drink."

"There's a coffee shop over there. I'll help you there, if you like."

"Thanks."

She took my arm and guided me across the square and the road and into the coffee shop. Then she sat me down at a table, with Jill at my feet. "I'm not sure how they feel about dogs," she said.

"Then I'll have to leave."

"Well—I'll explain how you feel. Just stay there. I'll get some water. Is there anything you'd like?"

"A soda. Let me give you some money."

"No, that's all right. You can pay me back."

In a minute she came back with the manager.

"Here's a soda," he said. "The lady's right. We don't allow dogs. But you can stay here with him until you feel better. It's just that it's the law."

"Okay, and thanks."

I took a drink or two of the sweet soda and suddenly felt less dizzy. The clammy feeling went. Jill got up and looked hungrily at the glass. "I don't have anything to eat," I told her. "But I'll get us a sandwich to take out." I looked up at the woman, who was still hovering there. "Thanks a lot. I'll be all right now. Did you pay for the soda?"

"No. The manager'll give you a check. Are you all right? Is there anything more I can bring you?"

"No." I held out my hand. "I'm really grateful. It was terrifically kind."

She smiled. "That's all right. Glad to be of help." She started to move away. I asked, "Can you tell me where 385 Cannon Street is?"

"A few blocks down the next street to your right as you leave here."

"Okay. Thanks again."

Before I finished the soda the manager came over with another one.

"Thanks," I said. "Could you give me a chicken sandwich..." I glanced at Jill. "Two chicken sandwiches, and I'll take them out to the park and eat them there."

"Eat 'em here. It's cool." He glanced at Jill. "Just a minute." He went away to the back and returned with a newspaper. "She can eat her sandwich on that."

I was too angry to be really hungry, but I made myself eat my sandwich and put half the bread and all the chicken of Jill's sandwich down on the paper. I knew the last place Steve would want to see me would be his family house. Until I heard that message from him I hadn't really made up my mind whether or not I'd ring the doorbell when I got there, provided that that Stefan Novak turned out to be the right one. But I knew now that I would.

Jill and I were walking on Cannon Street three blocks from the square when I saw the back of Steve's van. I stopped. Then I went on towards it to find that the van was parked in front of number 385. A woman coming towards me looked at me curiously as she passed. A couple of teenagers talked to one another with a bicycle between them. I had the odd feeling that they were watching me, but when I turned and faced them, they seemed absorbed in each other.

Number 385 was an ordinary brick house with a dark wooden door. There were curtains at the windows and the blinds were half drawn. It was Jill, nosing around the door, who made me notice something on the top step against the door, something colored. I looked down, closed my eyes, then opened them again. The ducks, limp and dead, had been tied together by a piece of string. Three of them were ducklings. One had half its head blown off. Another's webbed foot trailed front to back. They'd been shot. Blood was all over them and on the paper on which they rested. I felt the nausea rising again and held onto the little railing leading up to the front door. After a minute I found myself staring at what I thought was the local newspaper. But it was the wrong size and print. After a minute I realized it was a sheet put out by the conservationists—with the same type and lettering as some of the other editions I'd brought home. Scrawled across the top in black crayon were crudely printed letters: "You like birds? Here are some birds. There'll be more when we start building—without you. Rat!"

The words didn't make any sense. Sickened, holding tight to Jill's leash, I drew close enough to read the type on the printed sheet: "A touching story has come to our ears," the conservationist leaflet's reporting started, "concerning one of the more macho leaders of the bulldozer gang pledged to destroy the sanctuary and the wildlife that has so long considered it a refuge. It seems that Steve Novak in his hardhat heart really cherishes birds...." And what followed was some kind of weird parody or takeoff on what I had told Peter, my brother, about Steve and Chico. Only instead of being touching, it was derisive. Steve came out of it looking like a klutz, and a hypocritical one at that.

The door above me suddenly opened. I straightened. Mrs. Novak stood there. She looked at me and I looked at her.

"What are you doing here?" she said.

"I came to see Steve."

"Haven't you done enough to him? Caused him damage?" At that moment her eye was caught by the heap of ducks. "Ach!" She bent down, picked up the ducks and looked at the paper. Then she picked that up and read it. "This," she said to me, holding out the bloody news sheet. "This is your doing. You told them about Chico—right?"

"Yes, but I didn't mean—I was trying to tell P—trying to say that he didn't hate birds and wildlife. That's why I said it."

"Then you must be an innocent—foolish, stupid, to think they wouldn't use it, if you are telling the truth, of course."

I had been feeling guilty, but the word "stupid" was enough to make me furious. "I may be foolish but I am not stupid. I wouldn't hurt Steve for anything in the world. You should know that. You ought..." The dizziness and nausea struck like a blow. I'd been feeling it off and on all day, but it was worse now than ever before. The final horror would be to throw up on Mrs. Novak's clean doorstep. I clutched at the railing, letting the leash slide out of my hand. "Jill," I said, but it came out a gurgle. And then the worst happened. I was very, very sick.

I was dimly aware of the woman beside me, an arm around me, of stumbling up steps and into a cool hall.

"Back here," Mrs. Novak said.

And then I was in a small bathroom being sick again and again. Things were vague after that. When they stopped being vague I was lying on the living-room sofa with something cold and wet on my face. I was also terribly aware that something was wrong, missing. But I couldn't think what it was. "Where—" I started, not knowing what I was going to ask.

"Don't speak!" The cloth was removed and another colder one put on my face. It felt wonderful. My head cleared a little. I opened my eyes and stared up at Mrs. Novak. It was odd, I found myself thinking, Steve wasn't really that much like her. Her face was broader and somehow tougher. She was looking back at me.

"I'm sorry," I said, struggling up. "About being sick on your steps."

She shrugged. "That is easily mended." Her accent was fairly strong, but she spoke fluently.

"Where is Steve?"

"He is not here."

"His van is in front."

She stooped down, picked up the bowl of ice and water that was resting on the floor beside the sofa and stood up. "He walked down the street to speak to some friends —to some men who *were* his friends before your brother made a fool of him and blackened his good name." She had brought me in and bathed my face, but her voice and expression were implacably hostile. I swung my feet to the floor.

"You had better wait until you can be sure you will not be sick again." She walked out, bearing the ice bowl.

I decided to wait, and sat still, looking around the room. It was a small room, with too much furniture and too many ornaments. The dark carpet and heavy upholstery made the room seem hotter than it was. One whole side was covered with bookshelves to the ceiling. There was a piano, with photographs on top. More photographs on the table, the mantelpiece and hanging on the walls. Slowly I pushed myself up on my feet and went over and examined them. I had no trouble finding Steve, represented at all ages, blond as a child, darker as he grew up. The man standing beside him when he was a child looked much like Steve today. There were none of the man in later photographs. So this was what my child might look like, I thought. This would be half his—or her—heritage. The Polish genes would be right there with the Yankee, equal in number. Which would predominate? There was one of Steve that I particularly liked: he must have been about seven, an oddly foreign-looking child, although the photograph was taken standing in front of one of Boston's more famous and historic churches. The word "church" in my mind made me aware that there was something else I had seen and unconsciously noted, but had not registered consciously: my eyes roved around. There it was: a crucifix, the tortured body made from ivory nailed to the wood . . . and hanging from the lock at the center of the window was a round stained-glass icon. I was staring at this when I heard the front door open. There were steps approaching the room. I turned around. Steve stood there.

For a minute neither of us said anything. Then, "Steve!" I said. I wanted desperately not to be angry at him. I wanted so much for things to be all right.

"Were you the one who was sick on the front steps?"

"Yes. I'm sorry."

"Can't say I blame you—given what you found there, at least what was there when I left the house."

"You saw the ducks and didn't take them away?"

"Hustle them out of sight so that people wouldn't see them? No, why should I? They were left there to make a point. I wasn't going to go scurrying around removing it all, afraid of what people might think. Let people think what they want. Besides—I'd already had one calling card of that kind left at the loft. Only that wasn't a bunch of ducks I couldn't care less about—that was Chico, with his neck wrung. Thanks a lot, by the way, for remembering to tell your brother so he'd be sure to print it."

"Chico!" In my mind I saw the little green parakeet. "Oh no! Peter wouldn't do it!"

"Peter? Of course not. He didn't have to. My friends did that for him. I'll say this for your brother. He's a dynamite politician. Don't just kick the opposition. Divide and scatter! It was my side—my ex-buddies—that killed Chico and the ducks. And that touch about my taking kickbacks was pretty neat, too."

"Wha—what kickbacks?" I knew, of course, even though I hadn't seen the article.

243

"Oh—you didn't see? What a shame! Let me remedy that immediately!" Steve reached into his back pocket and brought out a copy of the same sheet that had been under the ducks. Only they'd been on top of the column on the right side. "CONSTRUCTION LEADER STANDS TO MAKE FORTUNE OFF HIS BUDDIES."

"Read it," Steve said, holding the sheet under my face. "Don't miss a single word."

"Don't talk to me that way, Steve. You know I didn't tell Peter that. How could I? It's not true, is it?"

His glanced wavered a little. His hand went down. "If you mean I'm trying to do something illegal, of course it's not true. It's true that Harry said if he could buy the land and get it drained, he'd see I got some kind of a subcontract from the main builders."

"Did everybody know this?"

"Why should they? It's nobody's business but mine."

"But it looks like you've got an extra axe to grind."

"Why the hell not?" He exploded. "You wonderful WASPs! How the hell do you think your families got the fortunes that built your lovely homes and sent you to your private schools and made you the ruling class? Some of the deals those fine old families of Boston and New York made to establish their dynasties would put them in jail today—bootlegging, slave ships and sweat shops are just three I can think of now. But I guess two or three generations of invested theft makes it clean, right? And gives you and your goddam brother the right to be morally superior and take potshots at us—and all in the name of the wildlife and the lovely environment that *your* people claimed four hundred years ago and *your* people chopped down and *your* people drained and *your* people settled and *your* people destroyed a whole other race—the Indians— to get, and enslaved another whole race—the blacks—to cultivate. But now that the money is in and the profits made and the trusts set up and the families firmly established at the top, you are all suddenly terribly, terribly concerned about the impurity of the profit motive...."

"Steve, listen to me. I'm sorry about that. I'm sorry about what Peter did. But that's not what I wanted to see you about. There's something else...something terribly important..."

But I knew already that it was no use, that the time was wrong. Not now. It would be like saying something in a foreign language, or shouting in a totally soundproofed room. But I had to anyway.

"I'm pregnant, Steve. I'm going to have our baby."

He had been walking around the room. But he stopped, his hand with its workman's fingers resting lightly on the back of the armchair. For a minute he looked as though I'd struck him. Then his face tightened.

"Congratulations," he said.

We were still looking at each other, not saying anything, when his mother came back in. Then all three of us stood there.

"I'd like to talk to Steve alone," I said.

She hesitated and glanced at Steve.

"There's no reason why my mother has to leave her own living room in her own house. We don't have anything more to talk about."

"I just told you—"

"It's an old ploy, Sarah. But it won't work."

"You saw I was sick outside."

Again I thought I saw his eyes flicker. But he said, "Heat, humidity and a bad hamburger could do that—especially to people who're used to spending their summers in summer cottages by the beach."

His mother looked at him. I knew she knew what I was talking about and that it was true. "Tell him it's true," I said.

She looked back at me. There was no doubt at all on her face. "I thought you wanted to talk to him alone."

There was another weird silence. I felt as though something, or someone, had been tried and a guilty verdict had not been pronounced. But who had been tried? The baby inside me? And who had decided the guilty verdict? You did, a voice said inside me. Out in the street some children shrieked, and from the open window at the back there was a squawk from a blue jay. A car horn sounded. In a minute I would start to cry.

It was then that I, deep within me, pronounced the verdict. What was it the judge said in the old English courts? *And you shall hang by the neck until you are dead.* But I mustn't cry. Not here. Later, outside, but not here. I walked out the door, into the small hall and out the front door. The kids with the bicycle were now standing in the road outside, along with three smaller children and a couple of elderly adults. I had expected to see my own vomit. I hadn't expected the blood all over the step. I walked down the steps, turned right and walked to the square. It felt like a mile, because I was determined not to turn around, convinced that all those eyes were boring into my back like laser beams. To keep my back straight and my head forward I invented a fantasy: I had a magic ability to create an area of poison right under my skin, so that when hostile laser beams, poking out from people's eyes to bore through me and do me damage, penetrated my skin, they would be turned back to poison the senders. What a pity, I thought, they couldn't go double strength towards Steve and his mother. But I stopped thinking about them immediately. Finally at the square I turned right, walked along the sidewalk and then, well away from Cannon Street, crossed into the park. Then I sat down on a bench.

It was when I saw a white West Highland terrier that I suddenly remembered Jill. That was what had been bothering me while I was lying on the sofa. I had let go of her leash when I was sick, and that monster-woman, Mrs. Novak, had left her outside.

I closed my eyes. Where was Jill now? Running around the streets looking for me? Darting in front of cars? It didn't bear thinking about.

I stood up. At least I could walk around and look for her. How long had I been in that terrible house? How far could Jill have got? I was turning from the bench when the pain hit. It was like a giant monkey wrench, closing its teeth over my lower abdomen. I gasped and bent over and held my breath as it got worse and worse. Then it stopped. Slowly, I straightened, breathing almost timidly in case it returned. But it seemed as vanished as it had been present. I walked out of the park and was about to cross an intersection when it hit again, this time worse. My grunt became a cry. Reaching out, I grasped the side of the pole holding the traffic light. The pain bore down and down. I heard a noise and realized I had made it. Dimly I heard a voice asking me if I were all right. Then I heard other voices, like a buzz, coming through a cushion, an incredibly hot cushion around my head. Then, as before, the pain started to abate, but more slowly this time. I straightened. What made me realize I could not go looking for Jill was not so much the certainty that the pain would return, but the wetness between my legs. I had on jeans, not a skirt. I glanced down. The denim was thick, and underneath I had on a pair of cotton knit pants. Even so, I could see the beginning of the dark stain.

"Taxi," I said. "I have to have a taxi."

Miraculously, someone hailed one. "Here," a male voice said near to me. "Here's one. Do you have enough money?"

Without bothering to think whether or not I did, I nodded. I had to get away from these people, fast. Someone opened the car door and I got in. "Would you like me to come with you?" a woman's voice said.

"No!" I belted the word out. Then, "Thanks." I slammed the door closed.

The driver was looking at me. "Where to?"

"Just drive ahead. I'll find the address in a minute."

He stamped on the accelerator, throwing me back on the seat. I righted myself and glanced in the rear-view mirror. He was watching me. "Okay. Where to?"

The pain was coming back. I could feel it. "Dr. Belovsky's office," I gasped.

"Where's that?"

I hadn't the faintest idea, but just as I was about to say so and give in to the appalling pain I remembered the card in my jeans pocket. Somehow I managed to get it out. "Number 4 Rearden Road," I said, forcing the words out. "Hurry!"

Again he stamped on the accelerator and proceeded to sweep down streets and around corners, driving like a maniac. I didn't care. I was half lying on the back, my knees drawn up. How long it was before I felt the cab jerk to a stop I didn't know. I felt as though a force were driving my legs apart, but I was holding them together with my arms.

The next thing I knew a nurse and the doctors were in the taxi with me.

"Okay now, relax as much as you can," I heard the doctor say.

"I don't want no accident in my taxi," I heard the driver whimper behind the doctor's back.

Slowly, the pain started to go away. Tentatively, shakily, I started to breathe.

"That's fine," the doctor said. "Now relax your body."

I felt their hands go under my arms. "Can you talk?"

"Yes," I said. I looked down. The stain had spread. But there was nothing I could do about it. The pain was now almost gone. I felt sick. And my forehead and head were clammy.

Somehow I got in the doctor's office, and somebody must have paid the taxi. We walked through a room with some people sitting reading.

"I have to go to the bathroom," I said.

"All right." The nurse stopped me in front of a door. "Here.

There's a toilet in there, but don't flush. Do you hear me? Don't flush."

"All right," I gasped. The pain was coming back fast. Fingers undid the buttons at the top of my jeans, slid the zipper down and then pulled jeans and pants down. "Okay now."

I sank onto the toilet. Then I cried out as the pain ground down and something finally discharged itself into the water below.

When I woke up I was lying on a cot in a small room with various pieces of medical equipment around me. Someone had taken my jeans and put a blanket over me. I must have slept. *And you shall be hanged by the neck until you are dead....*

I was tired, unbelievably tired. What I wanted to do more than anything else was sleep. I put my hand up to my face and found my cheeks were wet. The door opened. Mushroom looked in.

"Mushroom," I said.

"Hi, baby." She came over and sat on the edge of the cot.

"Oh Mushroom," I said.

Her arms went around me and pulled me up, and I leaned against her while she held me. There was a vast muddle of things in my head: Steve, the baby, my miscarriage, Steve again, saying "Congratulations," the ducks and the blood on the Novaks' steps, Chico, Steve's hand on the back of the chair, the miscarriage...What I said was, "I've lost Jill and couldn't wait to look for her."

"Does the family know?" I said.

Mushroom and I were in her car driving back to the Cove.

"Yes."

"Do they know it's Steve?" I had blurted it out to Mushroom before the doctor had come back into the room where we were.

"Yes. I had to tell them."

"How did you find out? From Charles?"

"No. He wouldn't tell me. I asked him, of course. As soon as it became obvious you'd run away, I went over to talk to him. But he just looked down that long nose of his and said you were adult and had a right to make your own decisions and that if you'd wanted us to know you would have told us and he had to respect that. It was the twins. I didn't think anything about their overhearing while Charles and I talked in the garden of the house. Jamie suddenly appeared and chirped up, 'Sarah likes Steve, doesn't she, Charles?' And Charles then admitted that the two of you had a big thing going. When he said that, everything fell into place, including your sticking up for the townies."

I thought about that. I was horribly tired and Dr. Belovsky had said I had to stay in bed for several days. And to try and figure out how I felt now seemed more of an effort than I could make. But I said finally, "I don't think being in love with Steve Novak has anything to do with whether or not the townies have a point."

"No. I guess not. It had occurred to me once or twice before that Steve was an attractive man and that you liked him. But we were all so sure it was Charles."

"When did you find out it was Steve?"

"Around eleven o'clock. Mother had tried to call Charles before, but he'd been out for an early swim or something. Anyway, when I got up I said I'd go over. When I brought the glad tidings back I'd forgotten about Peter's project and spilled the beans in front of him. The next thing I knew Peter went off and called your boyfriend's home and got him and proceeded to accuse him of every sin under the sun, interpreting the whole thing, of course, as only Peter would, as a political move on Steve's part for revenge. It was nasty. I finally wrenched the phone out of his hand."

"Peter's as bad as Steve," I said. "Or whoever killed the ducks and Chico." I'd told her about that.

"He's worse. After all, according to Charles, Steve was in love with you. Peter's just in love with the divinity of his own opinion. His own rightness. Even Father told him he was crazy."

"Did you know I was pregnant then?"

"No. Which makes what Peter said worse. But when Gene called in the afternoon saying that Dr. Belovsky had telephoned him and told us why, none of us was surprised. Somewhere Mother and I, at least, must have suspected something like that might be true. Certainly I did, after knowing you hadn't even bothered to take any precautions for so long. You're crazy, you know that, don't you?"

We drove for a while in silence. Then Mushroom put her hand on my knee. "Look, Sam. It could be worse. You would have had to have an abortion."

"Maybe I would have had the baby."

"Having a baby and bringing it up *sans* husband is a hell of a job to take on. Especially when you're seventeen."

I thought a little about the little tadpole I'd expelled. How did I feel about it? Relieved? Yes. But also terrible. "I did have an abortion."

"You had a miscarriage—thank God!"

"Who is God?"

Silence. Then, "This isn't the time for a metaphysical fight. You *did* have a miscarriage."

But I was sure that at some point I had decided the child had to die. "No," I said.

"Yes." Mushroom pulled the car to the side of the highway. "Now listen to me, Sam. Dr. Belovsky said he had warned you that you might not have plain sailing. Didn't he?"

I had forgotten that. But I remembered now. "Yes. But he didn't say why."

"Because your uterus was retroverted, which means, I think, upside down or tilted or something. Sometimes a uterus like that rights itself when pregnancy occurs. But yours didn't. You could *not* have carried that child."

"All right," I said. "Thanks." But even with what Mushroom said, I couldn't be certain. Not immediately, anyway.

I did as the doctor told me and stayed in bed for the next several days. Mother hadn't said anything when I got home. She just hugged me and said we'd talk sometime when I felt better. Father also didn't say anything. He simply looked at me. Peter wasn't there. Mushroom and Mother took turns bringing me meals and books and magazines and mail. Once Mother said, "I'm sorry about Jill. Mushroom told me."

I tried hard not to cry when she said that, but it wasn't any use. The tears poured down. I missed her a lot.

"You didn't eat your lunch," Mother said.

"I wasn't hungry."

"And you weren't very hungry for breakfast or dinner last night, either."

"No." Food, at that moment, struck me as irrelevant.

Mother sat on the bed, stared at the tray, and then at me. "You know," she said, "it's called a postpartum depression, and you have it whether you have a miscarriage or a live birth. It's physiological and has to do with hormone balance, or imbalance, after everything goes back to normal. I had it after all three of you were born."

I didn't say anything.

"I just wanted you to know," Mother went on doggedly,

"that what you're feeling is perfectly normal—under the circumstances."

I still couldn't think of anything to say.

"What are you thinking about most?" Mother asked. "Steve?" Despite her obvious efforts, I could hear the anger in her voice when she spoke his name.

"No. I don't think about him a lot any more. It's over."

The funny part was it was true. It was as though everything I'd ever felt for him had been given a huge shot of novacaine. It was dead. It was as though the man I'd loved had gone away somewhere, and somebody who looked like him—some sneering, hateful stranger—was living in his skin in Leominster.

Two days later I was half reading a book when the knob on the door turned and the door opened. The next thing I knew a body hurled itself onto the bed beside me.

"Jill!" I cried. "Oh, Jill, you're back!" I hugged her while she frantically licked my face and her tail whacked the bed. It was an ecstatic few minutes. She was filthy, some of her long hair was matted and every rib showed. "Who brought you back?" I said. "Who's there?" I called out.

Father's face appeared in the doorway.

I was astonished. "Did *you* get Jill?" My disbelief must have showed in my voice, because he gave a wry smile. "Yes."

"Well—thanks. Where...where did you find her?"

"In the pound. I've been calling every day, describing her. Today the man said he thought she'd been picked up. So I went in and got her. She's a little on the dirty side, and I almost took her to a grooming place. But I thought you might want to give her a bath."

I looked at Father, remembering what he'd said about her being a very democratic dog. "Well, I think I will. Do you think it will make her less democratic?"

He laughed, and then looked embarrassed. "I'm better at philosophic discourse than I am at apology, but I'm sorry about...well, about a lot of things."

"It's okay." I looked down at Jill and then swung my legs out of bed. "I think I *will* give her a bath."

Eventually Mother and I had that talk. It started when the school sent a follow-up letter to the one I'd confiscated, and Mother opened it. Jill and I were sitting on the sand in front of the house.

"It doesn't matter, Mom," I said, when she came up holding

the letter. "I'm not going back." I looked at her. "Whatever you say, I'm not going back."

She sat down on the sand beside me. "What are you going to do?"

"I'm going to art school. If I have to have a high school certificate, I'll take an equivalency test. But I don't think I have to have that simply to take an art course."

"No. But it would be a good idea to have it. You'll probably need it later on. I wish I could talk you into going to college."

"I'll take courses at night. I was going to do that, anyway. Writing and history and lit courses. But I'm not going to school in the usual way, and you know as well as I do that no decent college would take me."

"That's true."

We sat there for a while, watching the water. Gently I rubbed one of Jill's ears. Queer, I thought, I'd expected a huge battle. "But I also want to earn some money," I said. "I'm going to get a part-time job. The only thing at that horrible school that was any good at all was typing. I'm going to take a night shorthand course."

"You'll be pretty busy. Are you sure school wouldn't be easier?"

"It might be easier, but also a lot more boring, and it wouldn't be the way I wanted to do it." I took a breath. "And there's another thing. I'm grown up now. I'm not a child. And I don't want to be treated like I was dumb or unattractive or a baby. I'm not any of those."

"Fair enough," Mother said. "And back in New York you can have either Peter's or Mushroom's room and your own bath."

"Aren't they coming home?"

Mother sighed a little. "I don't expect so. Peter's got his eyes on Washington, and I wouldn't be surprised to see Mushroom there after she graduates."

I smiled. "Her Congressman?"

Mother smiled back. "Her Congressman."

"She always told me muscles not brains turned her on."

"I guess that was a phase. She's now over it."

The next day Charles strolled over. "I thought you'd be interested to know," he said, "that Dad is selling Headlands to Schreiber. He—Schreiber—wants to pull down the house and put up his resort. Dad's also going to buy the sanctuary land and give it to the state as a permanent wildlife refuge."

252

I looked up at Charles, who was still wearing his beat-up canvas hat. "Did you persuade him?"

"Well, yes. But it wasn't hard. I managed to insert the idea that the sanctuary could be called Brewster Park, or some such."

I thought briefly of Matilda Brewster. Would her ghost that loved and protected children disappear forever when the house was pulled down? Then I glanced at Charles.

"That's terrific. And thanks also for not telling anybody about Steve—at least not until Jamie spilled the beans."

Charles squatted down. "I sort of take it you had a miscarriage. Is that right?"

"Yes." I waited for him to say that it was all for the best. But he didn't.

"I told Steve Novak when he was finishing up the garage that I thought that was what had happened."

I still didn't say anything.

"Well," Charles said, getting up again. "I'm leaving tomorrow. Nancy and the twins have already gone."

"I'm surprised the people around here didn't start up protesting again about your father's sale."

"I think they shot their wad over the sanctuary. And I also think they're a little ashamed of their arrogance over the townies. They also know that Steve, finally, got it from both sides."

"How did they know that?"

"Because he told them. They had a meeting here the other day, and Steve showed up, by himself, which took guts, and stood on his feet and told them what he thought of what he called their long-distance virtue."

For the first time in the ten days since the miscarriage pain uncoiled inside me. But there was nothing to say.

"By the way," Charles said, "I'll be going to Columbia Law School this year. So I'll be in New York. Will you be there?"

"Yes. I'm going to art school."

"Good for you. Well, I'll give you a buzz."

"Okay." It would be nice to see Charles, I thought.

Two days later I was in my room working on my fantasy. There was a knock on the door. "Yes?" I said. "Come in."

Mother opened the door. "Steve Novak's downstairs. He wants to talk to you."

I thought about refusing. I thought about sending back a

253

snotty message. Finally I uncoiled my legs and got off the bed. "Thanks."

Steve was waiting on the steps in front of the screen door.

"I thought maybe we could take a walk," he said.

We walked along the sand without saying anything. It was funny, I thought. I didn't care who saw us now. Now that it didn't matter.

"I'm sorry," Steve said.

I nodded.

After a while he said, "Funny thing is, the day before...before that sheet appeared around town, I'd made up my mind to...to suggest we get married."

"It's more than funny," I said. "In view of everything, it's hilarious."

He didn't comment.

I said, "If your mother knew what you just told me she'd feel that that attack on you wasn't all bad."

"She knows. In her way, she's sorry too. But—there's the religion thing..."

"I read a quotation once: 'Somebody pronounces a principle, and somebody else dies.' I guess that's true of religion."

"And politics. Which are the two things people feel strongly about." He looked at me. "Maybe it wouldn't have worked, anyway."

"Probably not." My anger was back, hard-edged like a knife. "Did you get the subcontract, now that Harry Schreiber's going to build his hotel on Headlands?"

"No. He gave it to another guy. He said the feeling in the town ran against me."

"Because you didn't tell them about it?"

"That's the reason they gave."

"But it wasn't because of that, was it? It was because of us."

"Yes."

He stopped and so did I. Without consultation we turned and started walking back to the house.

"I'm going back to college part-time," Steve said. "And I've got a new job. I'll be leaving Leominster."

"Where?"

"In the southwest."

"Well, lotsa luck."

"I'll write to you."

"I don't think I'll answer."

"I'll write anyway."

We walked back to the house. I turned. "I'm going back in. Goodbye."

He didn't reply. Just looked at me out of those long slanted blue eyes. I turned and went towards the house. Jill was on the porch, waiting for me. After Steve had left, I thought, we'd go for a walk.

5 Books for Young Adults from
FAWCETT JUNIPER

A MATTER OF FEELING
by Janine Boissard   70001 $2.25
   In a cozy house on the outskirts of Paris live four sisters on the verge of womanhood.

THE BALLAD OF T. RANTULA
by Kit Reed   70003 $1.95
   Sometimes when you're a kid, you need a special kind of hero—especially when your parents are getting divorced.

WHAT DO YOU DO IN QUICKSAND?
by Lois Ruby   70004 $1.95
   Matt is 17 years old. A high school senior. And an unwed father caring for the daughter he loves.

THE LANGUAGE OF GOLDFISH
by Zibby Oneal   70005 $1.95
   For Carrie Stokes, growing up is harder than for her classmates, and she finds herself breaking down.

THE DAY THE LOVING STOPPED
by Julie Autumn List   70006 $2.25
   A Daughter's View of Her Parents' Divorce. A nonfiction account.